FATED IN STONE

A SEVEN FAMILIES NOVEL: WOLF
BOOK THREE

KAT SIMONS

T&D
PUBLISHING

FATED IN STONE

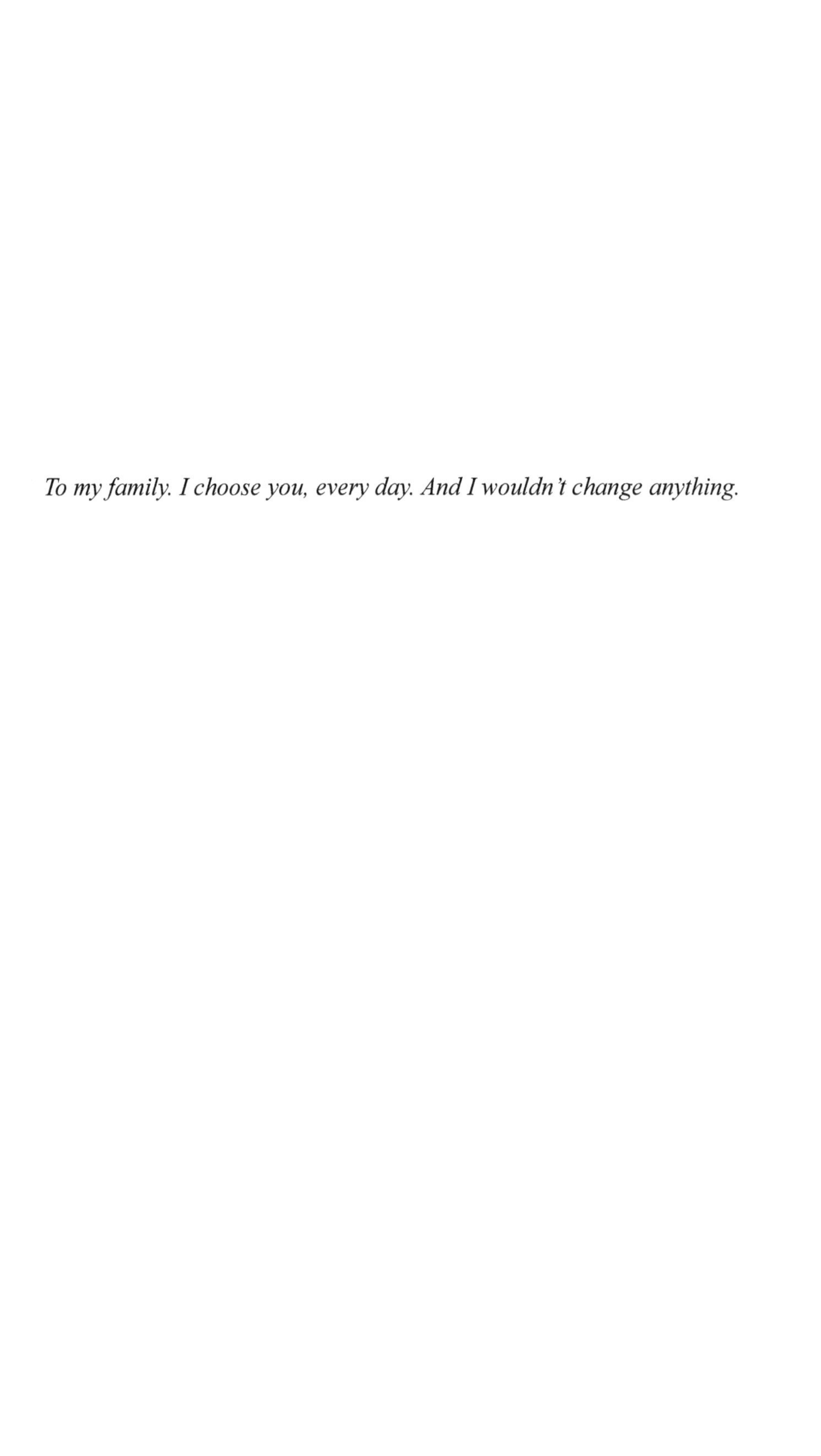

To my family. I choose you, every day. And I wouldn't change anything.

CHAPTER ONE

Benjamin Logan remained deep in the woods as he watched the woman, staying far enough in the shadows to avoid her sensing him in any way as she studied the house. It was just after sunset, but even in the dark, he wouldn't have had trouble seeing her.

She was an average looking woman. Not too tall but not short. Dark blond hair cut into a short, loose style. Pale skin. Cargo pants, hiking boots, and a t-shirt. No jacket, even though it was still early enough in spring to be cold in the woods after dark. She was too far away for him to see details, like eye color, but his general impression was one of efficient movements and watchfulness. He was upwind of her so couldn't catch her scent. Unfortunate. That would have made it easier to figure out what side of all this she was on.

The way she scanned the area, slowly, taking in the house, the surrounding woods. She didn't approach the place like she belonged here. She stuck close to the tree line as she studied things, not moving out into the narrow clearing circling the house. She hadn't come in a car. He'd have heard that. So she must have walked in from somewhere. Which hinted that she didn't want anyone to know she was approaching.

There were two black SUVs parked against one side of the house.

If the woman had belonged here, wouldn't she have just driven up and parked with the other cars?

When she finally moved toward the house, she did so carefully, slowly, furtively. Her gaze continually scanning the surroundings as she headed for the side of the building instead of the front door.

The others went in through the front.

She wasn't with the others, then. Not one of the Elemental's humans.

So what was she doing here?

He started toward the house, only to stop in place again when something else caught his attention. A movement through the trees. A flickering of…something. Something gray.

A scent reached him.

Monster.

Without pausing to think, Ben raced toward the house. The woman was still on the side of the building, approaching carefully. He moved too fast for her to see and reached the back door before she rounded the corner. With a hard twist, he turned the handle, breaking the lock. A lock designed to slow humans down, not someone like him. An oversight by the Elemental's people.

He edged inside, keeping his senses alert. Stacks of crates made the interior of the building more like a storage unit than a house. Using those crates as cover, he headed in the direction of the single light source at the center of the building. Toward the smells of reagents and cleaners and human sweat.

He heard the woman ease inside the building moments later. But his focus was on the people ahead. The geneticist.

A monster was approaching the house.

Ben had to get the geneticist out before the monster got him.

* * *

ELLE BARKER STARED AT THE HOUSE FROM JUST INSIDE THE TREE LINE. It wasn't what she'd been expecting. Especially since it wasn't a real house.

From the outside, the building—roughly the size of a three-bedroom, single story ranch—looked a little rundown, maybe not used for a few years. The surrounding north Michigan woods moved in close, encroaching on any yard space. There was some room at the front of the house, with two black SUVs parked along the side, and a little clearing between the back of the house and the woods. A boxy building with a slate roof and worn walls in desperate need of a paint.

But that was where the resemblance to a home ended. No windows. No light leaking out of the wooden slate sides, though it was dark now and if there were people inside, there should be some light. But, most telling, was the steel front door that looked more solid than the walls. No way to confuse this for a slightly rundown family home.

The door being more solid than the walls was interesting, and it nearly threw her off the scent. The look of the place from the outside made her distrust her information. How could *this* be the place?

She'd seen places like this in her years of tracking people. Especially in the early days, when she'd specialized in finding men that were like her father. Back then she'd been working with various law enforcement agencies. Now she worked for herself, and she went looking for who she wanted, when she wanted. No more hunting down budding domestic terrorists. Now she found people whose families actually wanted them back.

She liked this work better. Much better.

But being up north again and seeing this particular building brought her back to those early years and made her doubt her instincts, her information, and her skills. This couldn't possibly be where the professor was being kept.

Circling the outside of the house, she took note of the generator, humming quietly, that kept the building in electricity but off the grid. And there was a small hole in the wall, high, near the roof, that leaked some faint light. That hole was interesting. An anomaly, like walls that weren't as strong as the steel door in the front of the building. Or the steel door in the back of the house.

That was open.

Her tracking sense started to tingle. This was the place. This had to be the place.

Finding lost things, specifically lost people—even if they were "lost" because they wanted to be unfindable—was a skill she'd had for as long as she could remember. She'd been ten years old before she realized not everyone had that particular sense of *where* things and people were.

But Elle didn't rely on her unique talent for finding things when she worked. She did her research. She used more conventional methods. Especially when she'd worked with law enforcement, because she had to ensure she could *explain* how she'd tracked someone, could provide information that went onto official records and sometimes got introduced into court cases. She rarely had to go to court these days. That was for the lawyers and cops and federal agents. But she did sometimes have to give testimony or be deposed, sometimes file a police report, and she needed an understandable and legitimate record of the things she'd done and used to track her targets.

Telling a skeptical judge or lawyer that she'd "just known" didn't go over well. Telling *anyone* she had a psychic sense that helped her track people was not going to happen.

Those conventional methods reassured *her* as well, most of the time. She trusted that other sense…to a degree. Because it had always worked for her. But she worried that one day, it wouldn't, and she'd be unable to find someone who was the light and life of the people looking for them. Failure wasn't an option in those cases. So she ensured she used every skill at her disposal to find the people she was hired to find.

In this case, a beloved husband and father. Kidnapped from his university office more than a year ago. His family were desperate. They knew he was still alive. He was allowed to call once a month to speak to his wife and kids. No one ever asked his family for money— which they didn't have enough of to pay a huge ransom, but they would have found it among friends and associates if they had to—and there was no sign of the professor being returned. The police had put the case onto a backburner because nothing had changed and the man was still alive.

After talking to the officer in charge of the case, Elle realized why they'd backburnered things. They were convinced the man had left his family, of his own volition, and just wasn't ready to admit it to them yet. The police assumed Professor Gabe Arron was living with a mistress or second family or something and faking the whole "kidnapped" thing for shits and giggles.

Elle knew better. The minute Sherry Arron had walked into her Detroit office, Elle had known the truth. But with no help from the police, Sherry was desperate. She'd come to Elle. And Elle had promised to find her husband.

A search which had led Elle to this seemingly old and abandoned house in the middle of the northern Michigan woods.

With an open back door.

The open door had alarm klaxons screaming in her head. It wasn't wide open. Just enough to look like someone had either forgotten to close it fully or had purposefully left it ajar. Just enough to get back out without making noise, but not so open as to be obvious.

Whatever the reason, that open door gave Elle her way inside.

After a last check of the surroundings, ensuring no one spotted her entering the building, she slid quietly past the heavy steel door. Just inside, she paused. The building felt very large. A lot larger than it had looked from the outside. Even the roof felt higher, peaked and with no attic or anything to lower the ceiling. The building was one big open space, as far as she could tell. Turned into a maze by stacks and stacks of wooden crates that piled almost to, but not quite as high as, the roof. Like a warehouse.

There wasn't much light either. Without windows, the shadows beneath the crates were deep enough she could have used a flashlight. She wasn't going to turn one on, but it would have helped. There seemed to be a single light source coming from somewhere in the middle of the maze, which gave just enough illumination throughout the building she could see to navigate. That light source also gave her a direction to head.

She made her way silently through the maze of crates, pausing often to listen. The soft whirring sounds of a machine of some kind echoed through the building. And a faint hint of something dripping. The smells caught her attention, too. A medicinal smell like strong bleach softened by lemons. She also picked up a hint of something burning? Not like a campfire, or fire in a fireplace, or even a gas stove. Something a little more… She wasn't sure. She wanted to say metallic, like metal was burning. She squinted at a few of the wood crates as she passed, looking for hints as to what they held. But they were either plain with no writing on them, or the marks were things she didn't understand and the language used one she didn't know.

As she neared the source of light, she saw a single bulb hanging from an unadorned wire dropping down from the roof. Except for that slow drip of some liquid and soft whirring of a machine, the house was silent. A silence that made her nerves jangle. Once again, she might have doubted her information and her instincts. If that back door hadn't been open. That opened door set off all her tracking instincts. She was in the right place.

But she was a little worried she was going to find a body instead of a living man.

Her heart hammered hard, way beyond the effort it had taken her to hike up to this house from where she'd parked her car. She steadied her breathing, carefully controlled the rush of adrenaline that whispered she had to hurry. Eased through the boxes, her hiking boots quiet on the scuffed wooden floor.

A sound. A creak of wood and a whoosh. Behind her.

She spun, prepared to dive for cover. But nothing appeared in the shadows. No movement. She stared into the dimness back the way she'd come. No one rushed her. No strange glints, like the light hitting metal on a gun. No shadows changed sizes.

She scanned the tops of the stacked crates. Nothing up there either.

Releasing a slow, calming breath, she faced the lightbulb and the machine noise again. The hairs on the back of her neck prickled.

She was almost to the part of the maze where she could see what the lightbulb illuminated when she finally heard voices.

"Hurry." A man, his voice deep and urgent.

"I'm doing the best I can. You didn't give me any warning. If I leave this…everything will be lost." Another man. A nice tenor rumble to his voice. A crisp clip of vowels. The second man sounded only a little less panicked than the first.

"We don't have time to worry about that," the first man said. "You'll just have to redo everything."

"I have been working on this for eight months. I can't just *redo everything*. Not in the timeline I've been given."

"You don't, professor, you die. So I suggest you figure it out. But not now. Once we get to the next location."

"I can't work like this," the second man muttered. The "professor."

That was her target. Sherry Arron's husband. Professor Gabe Arron.

Elle eased forward, careful of her steps so she didn't make the wooden floor creak, careful of her breathing so she didn't give herself away in the mostly quiet building. The high ceiling ensured sound carried, echoed. Like the voices ahead of her.

"Stop that," the second man snapped. Professor Arron. "You'll destroy it. That won't make your boss happy."

"The boss wants you in a new location immediately. That'll make the boss happy. Move it."

The sound of footsteps. Heavy and thudding. From the direction of the front door. "We gotta move," a third voice. Yet another man. "Someone's here."

Shit. She must have left a footprint or something that a scout had found. She'd tried to be careful. But it had rained two days ago and there were still muddy spots in places under the trees.

A rush of fear froze her in place. What did she do now? If they ran, she was too far away from her car to follow immediately. She'd have to hurry back to her car and pick up the trail from there. More time. More chance the ones holding Professor Arron would panic and kill him. Not a chance she wanted to take.

But there were at least two men guarding the professor, and there could be more in here who just hadn't spoken yet. She was one unarmed person. If the guards had guns…

She shook her head. She'd worry about that when she spotted the guns. For the moment, she needed to get closer, see what she was working with. See exactly how much danger the professor was in.

And how much trouble she was in.

CHAPTER TWO

Elle slid as close to the voices as she could get while still keeping behind the cover of all the stacked crates. The scent of cleaning products and that strange metallic burning scent got stronger as she neared the area illuminated by the single, hanging lightbulb.

Where she finally got her first clear look at the man she was here to rescue.

Professor Gabe Arron was a medium build, medium height Black man in his late fifties, dressed in a pair of gray sweatpants with a white lab coat over his gray t-shirt. His black, tightly curled hair was a little longer than it had been in the picture his wife had shown Elle. In the picture, Gabe Arron had been smiling, wearing his formal robe and sash at a graduation ceremony, the sun shining, giving his dark skin a healthy glow. In the bright overhead light from the single bulb, his skin had an ashy cast to it now. He still looked about the same weight, so he'd been fed properly while captive, but there was a sort of gaunt, haggardness to him. Like he hadn't been sleeping much. The skin around his eyes looked darker, almost purple, though some of that might have been the light reflecting off his glasses. He was clean shaven, but there were lines bracketing his mouth that hadn't been visible in the smiling sunshine picture.

But he was alive. And well, if tired looking. Now she just had to keep him alive and get him back to his wife and kids.

There were four men with the professor, two more than she'd heard speaking. Damn it. She nearly cursed aloud. That didn't help her odds. Especially since they knew someone was here.

"Hurry, professor," one of the men, the one she'd heard speaking earlier, said. "We're out of time." He was a few inches taller than Professor Arron, a white man with a tan that made his age hard to judge. Maybe forties? A little younger than the professor anyway, but not by much. His brown hair was buzzed close to his head and he was dressed in forest green cargo pants and a dark green sweater that fit tight to his body. He wasn't particularly large and muscled, but he looked fit enough. And he had a gun in a holster at his hip. He didn't have the gun drawn, but it was enough knowing there was at least one gun here.

The fatigues gave Elle a moment's pause. In this location, already a place that reminded her too much of that particularly strange and dark few years of her childhood, a white man in that kind of outfit, with the near military cut of him, really brought her back to those days. Filling her with dread.

She shook off the overwhelming sensation to focus on her job. Getting Professor Arron out of here.

"If I lose any of these notes," the professor said to the man without looking at him, "all this work has been wasted. You want me to move faster, help me pack everything up."

He shoved papers and marble notebooks by the dozens into a large, hard-sided, wheeled suitcase as all four of his guards stood around watching the crates. None of them were looking in her particular direction, but they were scanning the entire area, their backs to the professor.

The careful attention to his notes caught Elle's interest, but she'd ask later. The area illuminated by the single bulb reminded her of a chemistry lab. The table with all the notebooks and papers was to one side of the otherwise open space. In the middle were a series of tables set up in a square with various tubes and beakers, a still-burning

Bunsen burner—the source of the metallic burning smell—and things percolating and moving through some of the tubes. There was something she thought might be a centrifuge on one table—the source of the whirring sound. And at the opposite side of the space from Elle, three huge, free-standing freezers with glass front doors.

The racks inside two of the freezers were filled with glass vials, though Elle couldn't see what was in the vials from this distance. The third had larger glass containers, only about eight, or ten of them, on shelves. Those contained what looked like… Well, it was hard to tell without getting closer. Maybe preserved animal parts?

Since Professor Arron was a geneticist, the animal parts were a possibility. His captors had obviously had him working here. But working on what?

"The boss is coming," a man who hadn't spoken before commented. "You don't want him to think you're stalling, do you, doc?" This man was an inch or two shorter than the professor, an Asian man, his hair dyed a nearly white blond and cut loosely but short. He was wearing a similar style of fatigues to the first guard, but he had two guns in his belt holster and had a long sword strapped across his back. The sword was…not something Elle had been expecting.

His shoulders were more relaxed than the first man's and he was smiling, really more of a smirk, but he was no less vigilantly searching the shadows around the crates. And he didn't seem inclined to help the professor pack either.

A third man, another white man, stood close enough for Elle to see his eye color—brown. He was paler than the first man, no tan, and he hadn't buzzed his brown hair, but it was still cut short and tight to his head. He was the tallest of the group, maybe six four, and built like a linebacker. Not someone Elle wanted to tangle with, if she could avoid it. He had a gun in a hip holster too, wore similar fatigues to his comrades, though he had on a t-shirt instead of the green sweater, and he stood with his arms crossed as he scanned the area entirely too close to where Elle hid. He didn't say anything, but she saw him wince when the "boss" was mentioned.

Interesting.

The fourth guard was across the large lab space, with his back to Elle, and there were tables and equipment in the way, so she couldn't get a good look at him. But based on his location, she assumed he was the third voice she'd heard before seeing the group. The one who'd announced someone was here. Who'd somehow found evidence of her. She'd berate herself for that later. The fact that none of them were hunting through the crates looking for her yet at least gave her time.

But the fact that their boss was on the way did not help the situation.

A situation that was already impossible. Four armed guards surrounding Professor Arron meant she couldn't just sneak in and get him out. She didn't have any weapons of her own—she'd left those behind in her car since she hadn't been planning on a gun fight—and she didn't want bullets to start flying anyway because Professor Arron could get injured. She could move out and call the cops, but this place was so far out in the woods, by the time anyone got here—if anyone came—the group would be long gone. Whatever had triggered the exodus, they were on the move.

She wondered about the contents of the freezers. Everyone seemed to be ignoring those. Even Professor Arron. But that meant they'd be leaving evidence behind. Evidence of what, she wasn't sure yet. Still. She'd have thought *someone* would be doing something about the freezer contents.

Maybe they would just cut the power. Let what was in the freezers rot. Possible.

And peripheral to her main problem.

She couldn't dive in and just drag Professor Arron out. They'd both get killed. She couldn't contact the nearest sheriff's department as they'd never get here in time. It didn't look like the guards wanted to kill the professor—they could have done that by now. Hell, they could have done that any time in the last year. It seemed like his captors wanted him alive. So that at least bought her some time.

With a silent, resigned sigh, she knew she was going to have to just follow them, continue tracking until they were in a position that she could call in the authorities and get some help getting the professor out.

Or maybe she'd get an opportunity to sneak him away from his guards on her own. That would be the best option. Getting law enforcement involved was always chancy. More possibilities that the wrong person got shot.

Yeah, it would be better if she could get the professor out without having to call in anyone else. But she wasn't getting him out of here, with all four guards on alert and the "boss" on his way.

She was debating returning to her car so she could follow the group when they left—she hated to leave the professor now that she'd found him, but she didn't have a lot of choices here—when she heard a sound from the direction opposite her position. Closer to the guard she still couldn't see.

Another guard? Or the boss?

Everyone in the room looked toward that sound. Even Professor Arron stopped frantically packing notebooks to look toward the front of the house.

A scraping noise cut through the quiet, almost like nails on a chalkboard but maybe a little less grating. Definitely deliberate, though. A slow approach, giving everyone in the room time to wait, time to anticipate, time to worry.

The man closest to Elle hunched his shoulders, very slightly. He was the only one who turned his back on the approaching sound, refocusing on the crates toward the back of the house. But he dropped his arms to hang loose at his sides. One hand resting close to the guns in his hip holster.

For some reason, Elle couldn't decide if him turning his back to the boss was brave or foolhardy. Whoever was coming, the sound of their approach set her teeth on edge and filled her with a kind of dread that seemed far more intense than the situation actually called for. There wasn't enough money in the world to get her to turn her back on that sound.

She found herself holding her breath as the scraping neared, and the fine hairs on the back of her neck rose.

And then, from the maze of crates opposite her…

It took Elle's brain several shocked moments to translate what her eyes were seeing into *something*. But even when they did, she couldn't believe what her brain was telling her.

Huge. Gray, scaled tentacles. Skeletal face. Rags like clothing covering a body that rose up nearly to the ceiling. Standing on thicker tentacles. Surrounded by more tentacles. And two arms. And two legs hovering above the ground. Because tentacles. Everything gray. Except its eyes. Which were black.

The thing smiled revealing rows of pointed teeth. Turned some of its tentacles toward the group. On the tips of those tentacles…

More black eyes blinked open.

Elle's brain screeched and screamed toward the void. That last was too much. Her muscles all tightened, adrenaline surged into her blood, the urge to run overwhelmed her common sense, and she opened her mouth to scream.

A hand clamped down across her mouth so fast she didn't even get a wheeze out.

Her response to the hand was instantaneous and instinctive. She swung backward, surged forward, struggled with everything in her like she was about to be killed. Swinging fists and elbows in a desperate bid to free herself.

"Please calm down," a deep voice said against her ear. "I'm not going to hurt you. If you'd screamed, you would have drawn its attention."

The words took a moment to slide in past her panic. She threw one last backward elbow that connected with soft tissue. A grunt muffled against the side of her face. And then she forced herself to still.

He was right. Whoever *he* was. The struggle, the noise, would draw that *thing's* attention. Nothing could be worse than that. Even a strange man holding her captive. She could escape from an ordinary man. She'd done that before. But from that… That…

She wasn't even sure what to call it.

"Monster," the man murmured against her ear again, as if she'd spoken aloud.

Monster. Yeah. That was the word.

The man's voice was very low, so low even the guard nearest them didn't react as if he'd heard anything. She only realized in that moment that her struggles could have, should have, drawn the attention of the nearest guard. The fact that it hadn't was a damned miracle. Though, since she still didn't know who the man holding her was, maybe it wasn't such a miracle. The man with his hand firmly clamped over her mouth might just be another guard.

But given he was taking such pains to be quiet—even taking her blows without making more than that quiet grunt—she suspected he didn't want anyone to see him either.

She remembered that fourth guard, approaching from the front door, saying someone was here… She'd assumed he meant her. But maybe he hadn't. Maybe the man with his hand over her mouth was that someone.

Or had the guard been referring to the monster?

Except…

Slowly, slowly the actions of the others in the room sank in. None of them were running, screaming. No one had scattered or dove behind crates. The guard nearest her was still staring into the maze, his back to the creature. Fucking ballsy and insane! She could barely drag her gaze away from the monster because she was afraid if she looked away, it would suddenly materialize in front of her. The guard's shoulders were tense, and by the slight tilt of his head, he was listening closely to what the monster was doing, but he kept his back to the creature.

Professor Arron dropped a few notebooks. He was the only one who showed much physical reaction. His hands trembled as he bent forward to pick the marble notebooks up again. And he didn't take his gaze off the creature.

Maybe he was worried about what it would do if he looked away, too.

The man behind Elle leaned in even closer, bringing her tight up against his much larger frame. That part only slowly sank in, too. He was a lot bigger than her. Almost folding over her as he kept his hand on her mouth, his mouth near her ear. He didn't wrap his other arm around her, which meant she had room to move, to fight and get away.

But the sheer physical size of him behind her was a little intimidating once she finally recognized it.

"Technically," he whispered, "that's a grinluk. But monster will do."

That thing had a name? She'd be fascinated when—*if*—she survived this.

"If I remove my hand," the man murmured, "will you be able to keep from screaming? It will be better not to draw the monster's attention."

She couldn't agree more with that last statement. As to his question… Would she scream if he took his hand off her mouth? Close call. She might. Her brain was screaming. Her adrenaline was screaming. Her nerves were screaming. Everything in her demanded she run screaming out of this house-turned-warehouse as fast as her legs could carry her.

But she'd felt all of that before, when facing human monsters, so… Yeah, she could probably keep it together. Hopefully.

She gave a single, tense nod.

The man slowly eased his hand off her mouth, as if he might clamp down again if she'd lied.

She appreciated the care because, to be honest, the minute his hand lifted off her lips, she felt the scream bubble up her throat, felt the terror try to rip out of her physically. She pressed her lips together in a hard line, an effort to hold the scream in herself, lock it down behind her clenched teeth.

When it seemed clear her scream wouldn't escape, the man finally dropped his hand from in front of her face, but he remained folded over her, his mouth near her ear, his breath hot against her cheek.

She gave herself another beat before she was certain she'd contained the scream as a thick lump in her throat. She couldn't speak yet—if she opened her mouth, the scream would escape—but she let her muscles relax a little so he'd know she was aware and in control. And not going to lash out at him again. Yet.

She still didn't even know who he was or what he looked like or anything else because she couldn't look away from the monster. All she knew of the man behind her was that he was large, wide as well as tall based on the sense she had of him at her back, and his palm had had calluses that roughened his fingertips.

For some reason, both the size of him and those calluses were… reassuring? That was strange. She shouldn't be reassured. Not by a stranger. A stranger who had a *name* for a monster.

That last really should have been a bigger red flag for her self-preservation instincts.

Instead, she found herself leaning back into him, turning her face up so she could say something to him. She still didn't take her attention off the monster, just waited for the man to put his ear close to her mouth so she could speak. The fact that she trusted he'd know to do that, and would absolutely do that, should probably have been the next red flag.

"It isn't attacking anyone," she whispered, her voice barely coming out. She wondered if he'd even hear her. But the fact that the monster wasn't attacking anyone had finally sunk in and that was…strange.

Not that any of this wasn't strange.

"It's working with the humans," the man said against her ear, his voice as quiet as hers had been. "With the geneticist. Well…the geneticist is being coerced. But the grinluk is here to ensure the geneticist continues to work. It isn't here to kill him. Yet."

Everything the man had just said sounded perfectly reasonable and didn't make any sense at all. A monster working with humans? Why? To what end?

Before she could get the questions out, the monster slid another few inches forward, under the single bright overhead lightbulb. Bringing all its gray horror more clearly into view.

"Time to leave," it said.

And Elle found the man's hand clamped over her mouth again before she even realized she was about to scream.

The sound of the monster's voice was literally the stuff of nightmares. It whispered and hissed and insinuated and danced over every fear center her lizard brain had. She had no idea who the man at her back was, but he was human, and to her lizard brain in that moment, him being human mattered a lot. She pressed into him, taking in the heat of him, the solid muscle, the awareness of him being something she understood, and held onto that tightly so she didn't lose her fucking mind.

It was a close thing, though. She was very very close to losing her fucking mind.

Why was there a monster here? What was it? And how had poor Professor Arron ended up kidnapped for a *year* by people working with a literal monster?

She pressed her lips together as her heartbeat continued to hammer hard against her chest, but she felt the scream clawing at her throat subside finally, even as her entire body rebelled at what she was seeing, what she'd just heard. When she was pretty sure the scream wasn't going to come out, she gave another brief nod, and the man, without a word, released his hand from her mouth.

He also dropped his arm from around her waist, which was the first moment she realized he'd also been holding her. Not restraining her. His hold had been gentle, firm, and…comforting.

The comforting part was something she'd need to analyze later.

"What do we do?" she whispered, turning her head only slightly to reach his ear. He was still leaning over her.

Another realization crept in past her terror. He smelled nice. Nothing she could pinpoint precisely. Just…nice. Musky. Earthy. Not cologne. Maybe soap. But… She wasn't able to think enough to pick out what it was about the way he smelled that she liked, just that it was good, and she was comforted by that scent. And that was strange enough to distract her brain. Just enough to allow for some sort of rational thought.

"Why are you here?" he whispered.

A reasonable question she supposed. Since they didn't know each other or each other's motives. The "what do we do?" part would be entirely dependent on those motives.

If he was working with the others, he wasn't giving her up to them. In fact, he was actively working to keep her from giving herself away. For the moment, she was going to slot him into the not-the-bad-guys category. Which wasn't the good-guys category yet, but did mean he might be an ally in this terrifying moment.

"I'm here to find Professor Arron." And get him back to his wife. But the details could wait.

"You've found him. What was your plan after that?"

"To follow them until there was an opening to get the professor out."

She felt his nod, his hair brushing against her cheek. The requirements of whispering right into his ear, and he into hers, meant they had to remain touching. Surprisingly, she didn't mind the touching.

Except he was a stranger. Possibly an enemy. She really had lost her mind.

"You would have had trouble tracking them. They're good at hiding their trail."

She didn't comment.

"We've been tracking them for months, and they keep getting away."

We? she wanted to ask. She didn't. But if the chance arose later, she really wanted to know who "we" was. Instead, she said, "You have a plan?"

"You're going to stay hidden. The monster will use you, kill you, if it sees you. I'll get the professor out. Then we can all run away."

She pressed her lips together so the sudden, and wholly unexpected, laugh didn't burst out of her, giving them away as surely as her scream would have. The thought of just...running away was absurd. And yet, what else would they do? Running away with the professor safely in tow was, actually, her plan, too. She'd just intended on doing it subtly, before his kidnappers knew he was missing. And if she couldn't do that, she'd intended on calling law enforcement in to extricate him.

She got a feeling law enforcement wasn't an option anymore. Not if she didn't want to watch a bunch of them get killed by a literal monster.

A *literal* monster.

She was still staring at the tentacles. Tentacles with eyes on them. Looking at everyone. A mouth full of pointy teeth. And a smile that made her want to curl up in a corner as her brain melted under the fear.

The temporary burst of absurd humor sunk under the reality of what they were facing. And it occurred to her that the man behind her had a *terrible* plan. What the hell was he going to do against a monster that didn't get him killed?

The fact that he'd had a name for the monster came back to her, through all the terror of the last few minutes—only a few minutes?— and that reminder, that tidbit of information had her narrowing her eyes.

"You've dealt with this monster before?" She was only half asking. He had a name for the thing. He knew what it was. How? And more importantly, why?

"I have," he whispered. "At least its kind. Killed them, too. You don't need to worry that I don't know what I'm doing."

"I'm more worried that you do," she said without filtering the thought. The fact that he knew how to kill this monster, that there were *more* of them than just this one… So much terror filled her she felt like she'd moved beyond even being able to experience fear. She was overwhelmed and going numb fast.

His breath brushed her cheek. "Stay hidden. Stay safe. I'll get the professor out. Alive."

She turned to whisper something back, not entirely sure what she'd say.

Only to discover he was gone.

CHAPTER THREE

Ben moved back into the stacks of crates, away from the woman, even though everything in him protested. And protested so loudly he nearly hadn't done it. He'd nearly picked her up and carried her away from the danger so he could tuck her gently away somewhere safe and sheltered where she'd never be hurt or injured or even inconvenienced ever again.

His Nam-tar.

Fucking hell.

Of all the places to meet her. All the places to encounter her. Here? When there were men with guns, and the geneticist's life in the balance, and there was a fucking grinluk right there?

He couldn't have just met her at a bar or during one of the many charity events his family attended to pretend they were a normal human family—a super wealthy one, but normal nonetheless. That would have made sense. Meeting her in a calm, non-deadly setting where he could actually introduce himself and set about earning her.

Instead, he found her in the middle of a situation that could get her killed, and he had to concentrate on saving someone *else*.

His every instinct argued against that.

No one would blame him if he snatched her up and raced away

with her. Even his Family. Maybe especially his Family. Since they all understood at a bone-deep level what it meant to find his Nam-tar.

But if he left now, they'd lose this chance to extricate one of the scientists. The one being coerced into the work.

There were others, others not averse to doing what the sided-Elementals and monsters wanted them to do. Those weren't likely to provide much information. But finding *any* of the scientists had proven difficult. Every time the Families got close the entire lab moved. By the time the Families tracked a new location and arrived, the place was cleared out. Abandoned. And only vague clues left behind for what the scientists were doing.

It had taken them months of searching to get even a hint of what was happening. And even more frustrating months of arriving too late to stop any one of the labs. He'd finally arrived at one *before* the monsters shut it down. He had to take this chance to rescue the geneticist and uncover the details of the plot.

But not running away with his Nam-tar to ensure her safety took an act of will.

He crept through the stacks, his steps silent, working his way around to one of the gunmen. One not too close to the woman.

Shit. He hadn't even gotten her name yet. Calling his Nam-tar, the one person in the entire world who could change his life and break his curse, "the woman" felt wrong on so many levels. But he'd rectify that soon. First, he had to ensure she was safe and they got the geneticist out alive.

That meant taking out the human guards and the grinluk.

Unfortunately, he didn't have any weapons but his hands to do that. And killing a grinluk required a weapon. He'd come in expecting to find only humans. He could take out humans with his bare hands. It was safer and quieter to do things that way.

But he needed a sword for the grinluk, something that would take off its head.

The fact that *he* of all people wasn't armed was a horrible bit of irony.

One of the guards actually had a sword on him, which struck Ben as strange but useful. Maybe that one knew a gun was useless against a grinluk and had the sword as a sort of backup in case the monster turned against all the humans. Smart if that was true. Even if it wasn't, the sword would help Ben.

So that was the guard he approached first.

Human guards. But humans used to working with monsters and Elementals. Enough so only one of them had flinched visibly at the grinluk's voice. Ben didn't take that for granted.

When he took out the first guard, he did it fast, moving at his top speed. Hand over the man's mouth. Jerked him back into the stacks. Pressure at a nerve point in his neck. Wait until he was definitely unconscious before moving.

He relieved the man of his sword and both guns after stretching him out quietly on the wooden floor. He should probably kill him. He was an enemy, and if he woke up before Ben was finished, he'd be a problem. But Ben killed monsters and rescued humans. It was his divine duty, ordained by the god En millennia ago. Killing a human for expedience went against the grain.

Not that he hadn't done it before. He just didn't like to.

He secured one of the guns before tucking it beneath the waistband of his cargo pants. It wasn't useful against the grinluk, but better to have a few options just in case. The second gun he emptied, then broke in half, masking the sound of metal crunching with his hands, and left the pieces on top of a nearby crate. He ensured the unconscious man didn't have any other weapons on him that might be a problem later, then eased back into the maze, working his way fast but silently around to another guard.

He reached the guard closest to his Nam-tar just as the grinluk noticed one of the men was missing.

"What is happening?" it hissed. Then, "He's here. Stop him!"

Fuck. Ben dropped subtly and raced to the second guard, pulling him into the stacks before the man knew what had hit him. But the others noticed his sudden disappearance. Bullets thumped into the crates around Ben's head height even though he was too far into the cover of the maze for the bullets to endanger him.

They might get his Nam-tar, though.

He resisted the call to race to her and get her out of there. He had to hope she had enough sense to stay out of the line of fire. Maybe she'd left already, given the monster. He wouldn't have blamed her. Though, he had a feeling he wasn't that lucky.

Giving himself a shake as he disarmed the second guard and left him unconscious in the maze, he circled back toward the center of the lab. Focus on the dangers now. Only way to ensure his Nam-tar was safe.

And if he could kill a grinluk in the process, he wouldn't be upset about that.

Except the grinluk had disappeared. Dammit. His entire body rebelled at not knowing where the monster was when he wasn't guarding his Nam-tar.

The geneticist was ducking low, near a table, with one human guard standing over him, gun out, firing randomly into the crates. The last of the four guards was approaching the area where the second guard had disappeared, gun raised, scanning for danger. That guard was the one who'd been closest to the grinluk, the least bothered by its presence. So…a dangerous human.

Ben scanned the layout of the open area. Tables and lab equipment were in his way. He could leap over most of it, reach the geneticist, and race away before the humans saw more than a blur of him. But he'd likely break things in the process, giving his movements and direction away.

Worse, though, the grinluk would see him. It could move almost as fast as he could, and its myriad eyes could track his movements in a way humans couldn't.

And he didn't know where the fucker was.

He swung the sword around, holding it in front of him one-handed. He'd do better moving around the edge and looking for the grinluk. The humans were less of an issue. They weren't going to kill the geneticist. And now that there were only two, he could deal with them. But the monster wasn't so easy.

Thoughts of his vulnerable human Nam-tar somewhere in the maze distracted him again. He had to get his head out of his ass. To save her, he needed to take care of the monster and the men with guns. He wouldn't be able to do that if he lost focus.

He eased through the crates. Some of which had been riddled with a lot of bullets in that first volley, splintering open the wood. Something thick, viscous, and black oozed out of one. He picked up a putrid scent that made him regret his heightened sense of smell. What the hell was in all these crates?

The presence of the woman had distracted him from reading any of the labels. He'd assumed lab equipment of some kind. He was a smith, an engineer, not a scientist. Especially not a geneticist. That was his sister's domain. So he had no idea how much or what kind of equipment the geneticist might need for his work.

Black, oozing stuff that stank. That didn't strike Ben as lab equipment.

Before he could look closer, though, he caught a brief flash of gray from the corner of his eye.

Grinluk. Heading in the direction of the woman.

Fuck. He flew after it. Chasing the grinluk as much as racing to save her. But when he reached the spot where he'd left her, she was gone. And no sign of the monster either.

He scented the air. Away from the stench of the ooze, he picked up her lingering scent. And the moldy smell of the monster. He followed the woman's scent. Something he wanted to pause and analyze more. Something that called to him and woke the wolf spirit that lived in him. Later, he wanted to spend time absorbing the woman's scent. The reality of her.

Now, he just wanted to find her again.

The human man guarding the geneticist had pulled him back to his feet and was easing him in the direction of the front door, while the geneticist lugged the suitcase he'd been filling with notebooks. The guard who'd been heading toward the crates had disappeared into the maze.

Ben caught another flash of gray tentacle. He raced that direction, following the faint trail of the grinluk's scent. Crates fell in his path.

He cursed and dodged them, jumping onto others, spinning away from the flying wooden boulders.

Behind him a few crates shattered but he didn't have time to study the contents. He knocked a crate coming at his head to the side and charged forward.

Only to come up short when he saw the woman, her back to him, edging toward the front door. He wasn't sure if she was trying to escape or to cut off the geneticist and his guard. What he could tell at a glance, though, was that she didn't see the man coming up behind her. With his gun raised. A guard Ben hadn't detected before now.

With a gun aimed right at his Nam-tar.

In an almost slow-motion dawning of horror, Ben watched the man ease close to the woman. Watched the woman's complete unawareness of the danger. Watched the man's finger settled against the trigger on his gun.

The woman just starting to turn, to glance behind her.

The man's finger pressing the trigger.

Ben didn't make a conscious decision to move. He didn't think at all in that moment. His body reacted on pure instinct.

He flashed forward, put himself between the woman and the gunman.

Took the bullet meant for her.

Right in the chest.

CHAPTER FOUR

Elle gasped a scream she tried to hold in but couldn't completely. A huge man—the one who'd held his hand over her mouth?—was suddenly in front of her, falling back into her just as the sound of a gun firing reached her.

It took her precious, shocked seconds to realize what had just happened. Seconds of scrambling to hold his big body as he collapsed. Seconds to realize he'd been shot. That the guard who'd shot him was still aiming a gun in their direction.

She acted before the terror of it all immobilized her. Desperation and fear sent adrenaline through her so hard and fast her vision blurred.

But that didn't stop her moving. She dragged the man back behind cover just as another bullet thumped past her, landing hard into the crate where she'd just been. She continued to drag the man—fuck, he was heavy—as fast as she could, deeper into the maze. It took her a moment to realize he wasn't unconscious. Another moment to realize he was trying to help her get deeper into cover by pushing off the ground with his legs even as she had to drag him by his shoulders.

When she was sure she wasn't in immediate danger of being shot, she looked down.

Blood seeped out of a wound in his chest, bubbling out of the bullet hole and dripping down his t-shirt. She lifted him enough to check his back. Bullet hadn't come out that side. Too small a caliber. Still inside him. But what damage? The location of the dripping wound was center of his chest. Too near lungs. Important arteries. His heart.

So much blood.

Even during those harrowing years with her father, she'd only seen one human being shot. Mostly just deer. And once a dog—which she still wasn't over. The men had talked big about killing, but they'd only ever shot game when she'd been around. Except that one time. And her father had mostly shielded her from that view. She wasn't sure it counted.

She'd had to go to work for law enforcement before she'd really *seen* another human being riddled with bullet holes.

It never got easier, or less terrifying.

Instinct to keep the man from bleeding out kicked in, even though the possibility of internal damage was the real danger. She tucked them both into a nook behind a corner of crates, where they had cover on three sides. No escape route, but she could more easily guard him this way.

She propped him against the crates so she could get a better look at his wound. And realized he was clutching a sword in one hand. Had he had that the whole time or was that the sword the one guard had had? She took hold of the hilt, trying to ease it from his grip. He clenched it tighter, made a sort of gurgling noise that shot terror through her.

"Don't argue with me," she whispered. "I need to get your shirt off. See how bad this is. Get some pressure on it." He didn't release his tight hold on the sword. She cursed. "Fine. But I'm going to have to rip your shirt."

From another part of the house, she heard shouts. The voice of Professor Arron. She could hear noise in the maze too, close to her hiding spot.

Her shoulders tense, the back of her neck prickling with the fear of being discovered, she took the man's shirt in both hands and ripped around where the hole was, tearing until she could get a good look at the wound.

Swallowing hard at the sight of the bullet hole, the bubbling blood. The smell of slightly burnt skin. She ignored the gorge rising in her throat and tore at the shirt more until she had it freed from one of his arms and pulled around enough, she could use it to put pressure on the wound. There was less blood oozing out now. Maybe it wasn't as bad as she'd feared?

She didn't think she was that lucky.

"You took a bullet meant for me," she whispered, keeping her voice barely audible. "Stupid." She wasn't sure he'd even hear her. His eyes were closed, his breathing sharp and ragged. When she pressed the remains of his t-shirt against the hole in his chest, he winced visibly, but didn't open his eyes. Sweat coated his skin, turning his pale complexion ashy. He almost looked gray.

So much had happened, in such a short period of time, she realized she hadn't even taken in what the man looked like. She knew who he was, though, without having seen him earlier. Knew this was the man who'd kept her from screaming and drawing the attention of a monster. Knew he'd just saved her life by taking a bullet meant for her.

Knew he wasn't going to last long like this, and she had no way to get him to help quickly.

Her car was more than a mile away. Over uneven ground through the woods. The nearest emergency service, hospital, or doctor, was thirty miles away. And while a backwoods clinic might be used to bullet wounds from hunting accidents, she wasn't sure they were set up to operate on a chest wound like this.

Panic and fear clouded her thinking. Shit, Elle. Think. Think. She had to get him out of here. He'd saved her life. She had to get him to help. How? How?

As she pressed the bunched material of his t-shirt against his wound, she swore she felt something move under her hand. Not his breathing, which was shallow and raspy. Not just the lift of his chest. Something seemed to press against her hand from *under* his skin.

She was afraid to lift the t-shirt and take pressure off the wound, but the sensation of something moving under his skin was so startling, so disturbing, she lifted the shirt. Saw something distort his skin, moving beneath it.

What the hell?

And then she heard footsteps. Close by. Too close.

She snatched the gun from the waistband of his pants, which she'd only barely noticed as she'd torn his shirt, and spun around to face the threat, stepping just far enough out of the nook formed by the crates that she could keep the man covered and protected.

Gun held at the ready, she used the edge of a crate to give her some protection and watched the section of the maze where she'd heard the footsteps.

"Drop the gun," a deep voice said.

Not one she'd heard before. The man who'd shot her savior hadn't been a guard she'd seen before either. How many were in here that she didn't know about?

She didn't bother responding to the stupid order. Just took a moment to ensure the safety was off. Knew from the weight the gun was loaded. Memories flooded back, but she pressed them down. No time for that now.

"I said, drop the gun. Or I will shoot you."

She still didn't comment. But really? Like he wasn't going to shoot her no matter what?

From behind her, she heard the man's breath wheezing, that scary rattle that made her own heart stop. She couldn't risk looking back at him and taking her attention off the area where the gunman was, but panic sent another flush of adrenaline through her and her pulse pounded so hard in her ears she could barely hear around it.

Some movement behind her. She wanted to tell him not to move. To stay still.

"Come out and drop the gun," the guard shouted this time.

"No," she said simply.

"We don't want to kill you."

A snort escaped before she could stop it. Did anyone ever believe that sort of thing when people said it in these circumstances? Did the guard honestly believe what he was saying? She doubted that last very much.

The sounds behind her settled. Too much. She wasn't hearing anything now. She wasn't even sure she could hear the man breathing.

Fuck. Tears sprang into her eyes. She wasn't sure why or where they'd come from. She hadn't cried in years. She'd been a little worried she'd cried herself out and didn't have any left. But there they were. For a stranger who may well be dying behind her. Tears gathering in her eyes, threatening her vision.

She blinked hard, forcing the dampness away so she could see clearly.

The guard poked his head around a crate.

She very carefully and precisely pulled the trigger on the gun. Little kickback sent the bullet into the crate beside his head. She'd been aiming a little lower. She adjusted her aim for the next shot, hitting the crate two inches below the last shot, exactly where she wanted the bullet to go. Both shots splintered open large holes in the wooden box.

The man cursed and ducked back behind cover.

The lack of noise from behind her had her chest and throat tight. She blinked hard again when more tears sprang into her eyes. He was a stranger. She didn't even know his name. She didn't know why he was here. But having him die practically in her arms…

She waited for the guard carefully hiding behind the crates to say something else. She didn't have to wait long.

"You have no idea what you're involved in," he said. "What you're messing with. It's nothing you've ever dealt with before."

"The monster you mean," she finally responded. "The grinluk."

A pause. Then, "You know what it's called."

Not a question precisely. A sort of half question, half surprised realization. What did it mean to him that she would know a monster's…name? Species? What did she even call it? Didn't matter, she supposed. The guard reacted to her knowledge of the name. And that was interesting.

She didn't have a chance to respond to his not-question, though.

What happened next…

It took her a couple of moments to process afterward because several things happened at the exact same time.

She heard something behind her, a movement, a scrape, something that sparked hope in her. He wasn't dead! She needed to help him.

The monster itself slithered out from behind one of the crates, not fifty yards away, its tentacles flicking the air as it rose high up over her head, the eyes on its tentacles all pointing toward her.

The guard with the gun started to step out from behind the crates.

She raised her gun to shoot the monster, knowing the guard would shoot her at the same time, but panic had her aiming for the biggest threat.

And then something hit her in the back.

But not hard. Not enough to knock her down. Just enough to shover her forward a step.

And then…

Then she watched a…a shadow? A spirit maybe? Something insubstantial, ephemeral, move out from her chest. A wolf. Leaping from her chest.

Which was strange enough she stopped breathing. But even stranger…the wolf became solid as it leapt forward.

As it emerged from her chest, it turned into an actual, solid wolf.

The whole thing happened so fast, it took a long moment to register that the wolf had leapt *through* her. Not past her. Not over her. Not around her.

Through her.

A spirt wolf. That became a corporeal wolf.

A real, honest to god, wolf.

A wolf. That leapt. *Through*. Her.

CHAPTER FIVE

The animal landed a few yards in front of Elle, between her and the monster. It growled at the monster.

But that was the only sound. Or movement.

Both humans and monster froze, held perfectly still. Not even the shadows cast from the stacks of crates surrounding them seemed to move. As if the appearance of the wolf had pressed a pause button on reality.

The monster stared at the animal, its black eyes narrowed. The guard stared at her, his mouth open. She stared at the wolf, her heartbeat hammering.

What the hell had just happened?

"How?" the monster hissed, its voice the first thing to break the silence.

Wincing at the sound of that horrible, nightmare voice, Elle looked up at the grinluk, back at the wolf, then back up at the monster.

"How can your wolf leave you and you are still there?" it said.

"Just a knack?" she said and asked. She had no idea what the grinluk was talking about. Where the wolf had come from. How it had leapt *through* her. Any of it. She was just as confused as the monster.

But what was worse was that it seemed to know at least some of what was happening. She couldn't begin to guess what was going on.

"Impossible!" the monster snarled. "No one in the Families can release their animal this way. You cannot be separated."

Families? "If you say so," she murmured. She glanced down at the wolf again.

The wolf snarled at the monster.

Elle raised her gun and fired at the monster just as the wolf lunged toward it. The bullet hit the monster in the face. It screamed and red blood sprayed from the wound. The wolf grabbed a tentacle with its mouth.

The human guard fired at the wolf. Elle fired at him, purposely hitting him in the shoulder. He cursed and dove back behind the crates.

The monster waved its tentacles hard, sending the wolf crashing into a stack of crates. The crates shifted and started to fall…

Elle looked up in time to see them falling toward her.

The next instant a solid body hit her mid-stomach and she and the solid thing went flying backward.

She hit the ground hard enough to loosen her grip on the gun, though she didn't release it, but it did fire, the noise of the shot lost in the cacophony of crashing wooden boxes a few feet away.

She looked up to see the wolf sprawled on her chest.

And she froze. A wolf was on her chest. Looking down at her. Its eyes were dark and luminous in the dim interior, under the shadows of more crates. It whined softly and nosed her shoulder, gently. For all the world like it was asking if she was okay.

The wolf had knocked her away from the falling crates.

After leaping *through* her.

A few moments passed with her just staring up at the wolf in wonder. Not sure what to make of all this. A little afraid her mind had decided to step out for some fresh air and left her living in a dream.

How was any of this real? A monster with eyes on its tentacles. Guards with guns and a sword. A kidnapped geneticist in the middle of a house turned lab and storage facility in the Michigan woods. A wolf that could leap through solid objects and rescued women in danger.

Random enough to be a dream. Even the location could be part of a dream as it spoke to her past, reminded her vaguely of her childhood. Of other monsters. Seemed like creating a tentacled real monster would fit in exactly to that kind of a nightmare.

But the wolf. And the man. Where would she have come up with those images?

The man!

She started to sit up, only to realize the wolf's weight kept her pinned to the wooden floor. It was heavy! Were wolves heavy? She had no idea. She'd never had one sitting on her chest before.

Not attacking her. Just laying on her as it gently nudged her shoulder and whined quietly.

That was strange. But since it wasn't attacking her and had actively saved her from the collapsing crates, she had to assume it wasn't out to kill her, so she said, "I need to get up. They'll be here soon. And there's a man back there. I have to check on him."

The wolf eased slowly off her, like he understood exactly what she'd just said, but he didn't look away from her.

She climbed to her feet, biting back a curse as her right elbow and wrist twinged with a short sharp pain. She stayed behind more crates as she took a quick assessment. She'd have some bruising, but nothing felt broken. She moved the gun she still held to her left hand, tested her right by flexing her fingers. Her wrist wasn't happy with her, but she didn't feel any weakness or numbness in her hand so she'd count that as good. She could fire the gun with her left hand— her father had ensured she could—but her aim wasn't as good left-handed.

The wolf settled at her side, close to her leg but not quite touching her. The animal was huge. Larger than she'd expect of an average wolf. Or maybe he just seemed huge because of everything that had happened.

Because he had leapt *through* her.

How the hell had a wolf done that?

If this was a dream, she'd be able to write it all off as a strange manifestation of her mind when she woke up. But for now, she felt too sore for this to be a dream, which meant she needed to deal with the situation like it was real life.

That meant finding the wounded man. If he'd somehow managed to survive a gunshot wound to the chest only to get crushed by falling crates, she was going to scream.

There was also a monster around here still to worry about.

Except, even as she thought that, she heard some shouts from another part of the house. The front door slamming. More shouts. And then the sound of several engines firing up.

She cursed, realizing the guards were getting away—and probably had the professor with them. She hoped he was okay. Still alive. She'd have to check the house in a minute.

She eased back toward the spot where she'd tucked the injured man. No sign of the monster. No sign of the guard who'd been shooting at her, who'd shot the man.

To the wolf, she whispered, "The monster?"

It huffed and to her surprised, shook its head, like it was saying "no."

"It's gone?" she asked, just to see what the wolf would do.

It nodded yes.

"You understand what I'm saying?"

Another yes nod.

"That's pretty fucking freaky, you know that, right?"

Another head nod.

"At least we're in agreement."

She scrambled over some broken crates, ignoring the contents that had spilled out, as she hurried to the man's side. The place she'd left him was fortunately still mostly intact. Only one side of the nook had toppled and it had collapsed forward and out, away from him instead of on top of him. She climbed over a small pile of broken wood to get inside what was left of the three-sided nook.

Only to rear back.

This… This really did have to be a dream. There was no way this was reality. But how on earth had her mind manufactured this? Where had her imagination even gotten these images?

Where the man had been, now reclined a solid stone statue. That looked exactly like the man. Right down to a ripped shirt bunched up on his chest, and the way he was half propped against the boxes behind him. But he was solid stone. A gray-white colored, smoothly polished marble. Like a statue in a museum.

A statue that looked exactly like the man.

She blinked a few times. As she stared, she wondered if it really *did* look like him, or was she just imposing what she vaguely remembered of the man onto the statue. Things had been happening so fast. Her memory of what he looked like was fuzzy. Maybe this was just a coincidence. There'd been a statue in one of the crates, it had fallen here, into this position, and she was imagining that it looked like the man who'd saved her life.

Except…

The way there was a shirt bunched up and positioned over his chest seemed unrealistically coincidental.

More slamming from outside. And the screech of tires in gravel as they churned up the dirt road leading away from the house.

And then silence. A deep, deep silence.

Filled with a lot of questions.

Elle wasn't precisely sure how much time passed as she stared down at the stone statue and contemplated the silence filling the house-turned-warehouse-and-lab with the wolf standing just beside her. She was vaguely aware of the wolf at her right hip, opposite side from the gun she still held in her uninjured hand. Smart wolf.

A faint dripping noise sank into her muddled thinking. She assumed some of the professor's beakers had broken. Didn't sound like a water main break. Just the *drip drip drip* of liquid falling off a table onto the wooden floor.

Around her, the chaos of broken boxes and strange dim lighting went mostly unnoticed. She was too focused on the statue that looked so much like the man who'd saved her life and who she thought was dying of a gunshot wound.

Thought he was dead, actually. She'd been certain he'd died while she was exchanging gunfire with the guard.

Was he dead? Was she seeing things in the strangely shadowed light? Imagining she was looking at stone, when she was actually just looking at a man with no life left in him?

She knelt beside the body, pressed her fingers gently against his shoulder. Jerked her hand away quickly. Nope. That was definitely stone.

"What the hell is going on?" she asked aloud.

The wolf beside her whined softly.

She glanced at him. He had moved up beside the statue too and stared at her across the body.

"If you're expecting me to explain all this, you'll be waiting a while," she said. "I am beyond baffled." She glanced between the statue and the wolf. "Speaking of baffling, how the hell did you leap *through* me? Or did I imagine that?"

Had she? Everything had happened so fast. Maybe the wolf really had leapt around her and she'd…thought she saw it jumping through her? Another trick of shadows?

But… But the monster had reacted strangely to the appearance of the wolf, hadn't it? Saying something about how it wasn't possible?

She couldn't remember its exact words. Shock was already making her memory of those moments jumbled and unclear. Shock was a fucker for that, and it's what made eye-witness stories so unreliable. She felt like her brain was doing that to her now, mixing up things that had happened too fast for her to full register, altering what had happened to fit into a neater story.

Except why would *neater* involve an animal that was clearly solid right now leaping *through* her instead of around her?

Was the wolf solid? Yes, of course he was. He had knocked her away from the falling stack. She'd felt his weight on her chest. He was definitely a solid, living thing.

She rubbed her free hand over her head, tunneling her fingers through her short hair and tugging slightly, hoping it would ease some of the pressure on her skull. The movement strained her tweaked wrist but not enough to clear her muddled thinking. All it did was remind her she was sore from hitting the ground hard a few minutes ago.

"So now what?" she asked the room at large. The wolf couldn't exactly answer that question. Still, she felt the need to ask aloud.

She glanced around. The house felt empty now. Just her, the wolf, and the crates. And the stone statue of course. But she should still check. There'd been more guards than she'd been aware of, hiding in the stacks. She needed to make sure there were no more enemies lurking in the shadows.

Elle looked between the statue and the wolf again, hesitating to leave the statue for reasons she couldn't quite name. Then she contemplated the nook the statue was in. And something she hadn't considered occurred to her. The wolf had come from in here. From a boxed off area where she'd purposefully stashed the man so there was only one way to get into the nook, a way she could block to guard him. But the wolf had still come from this direction.

The wolf could have come up over the top of the crates, technically, she guessed. Glancing up she confirmed the crates of the two remaining sections of the nook were stacked high, but not all the way to the open, peaked roof. Which, now she thought about it, made her "safe nook" not so safe. The monster could have just come over the top, too. The thought that she'd underestimated the danger, or more to the point, didn't see all the permutations of danger in that moment, left her light-headed as a surge of fear for what could have happened hit her. She wobbled, nearly dropping back onto her ass.

No. No, she didn't have time to think about the what-ifs now. She'd let those join her nightmares. She had so many already, what were a few more? Right now, she needed to ensure the house was truly empty and she was safe for the moment. Then she'd contemplate…the rest.

She glanced at the wolf again. "I need to make sure the house is secure. I'm hesitating to leave…" She gestured at the statue. "I'm not sure why. Stone statue. Should be safe enough, right? But…" She was explaining all this to a wolf? Shaking her head, she said, "I'll be back. Don't run away."

The wolf whined softly and made a move to go with her.

"Please. I'd rather someone stayed with…him. I don't know what this is. If he's dead or… But I don't want to leave him, and I still need to check the house." She lifted the gun, the muzzle carefully pointed out between the crates and not at either the wolf or the statue. "There are still bullets in here. If something happens, there will be gunfire. You'll know I've found someone." Or something. Like a monster.

The wolf nudged the sword on the ground. The man had had that clenched in his hand. It wasn't clenched in the statue's hand, though. The weapon clanked against the wooden floor when the wolf pushed it toward her with his nose.

"It'll be useless to me," she said. "I know how to use the gun. Don't have the first clue how to use a sword. I'll just get hurt. Gun will have to do."

Another whine, but the wolf stopped shoving the sword at her.

"Stay here. I'll be fine. Quiet and careful. Promise." She had no idea why she was trying to reassure a *wolf.*

She eased out of the nook, once against easing up over some of the fallen, broken crates. Secure the house first. Contemplate impossibilities later. One step at a time until they were safe.

Just as she'd learned in her childhood.

CHAPTER SIX

Not following the woman took a great deal of willpower. Ben had to talk his wolf out of disregarding her request because the wolf wanted to stick by her side. Both he and the wolf knew full well the human body was fine as it was. Especially since the house was empty now. He could hear it. And he could sense it. There was a stillness. Even the monster was gone.

But the woman didn't know that, and she was worried about him. Also very confused.

She wasn't the only one.

He had *not* meant for his wolf to leap out and *through* her. That was… That was for later. After she knew what she was to him. After he knew her fucking name! After they'd established trust and she'd *agreed* to stay with him. The curse wouldn't break if she didn't agree. She had to stay of her own free will. He couldn't coerce her. The choice to stay was entirely hers.

Except… He'd done something now that linked them. Solidly. Maybe irrevocably. And he had no idea how that affected all this. Had he accidentally taken away her choice? Had he doomed himself to forever live under Ne's curse?

When the ancient god En had created the Seven Families to hunt and kill Ne's monsters, Ne had cursed the Families to a horrible death. A death with their animal spirits corporealizing inside their bodies and literally trying to rip out of the human forms as they turn to stone. A curse En couldn't just wave a hand and end. But he could mitigate it. Could give the Families a way to end it. He'd promised them a destined love. Their Nam-tar. And if the Nam-tar agreed to stay with their destined hunter, the hunter's curse was broken.

All very romantic. Except the hunters of the Seven Families didn't live human lifetimes. They lived significantly longer. He was over three hundred years old. And most Nam-tar were human. Not all—his sister Rebecca had found hers a year and a half ago, and he was a werewolf—but most were ordinary humans, even if they had some additional attribute, something a little *more*. Like his oldest brother Eric's Nam-tar being psychic. The problem with humans, though, was that they had quite short lives. Nothing that would match a hunter's life span. A cruel joke to find one's destined mate, only to lose them after a few short decades. *If* the hunter could keep their Nam-tar alive even that long.

So En provided one more gift. One more reward for doing their duty and destroying the monsters. A Nam-tar could agree to a ritual that involved the hunter's animal—in his Family's case, the wolf— leaping *through* the Nam-tar. Once on the way out of the human host body. Once on the way back into the human host body. This left just enough of the wolf behind to extend a Nam-tar's life to match their mate's. It didn't give the Nam-tar their own animal spirit. Didn't make them into what Ben and his Family were, what all the Seven Families were—though it did add to their strength and healing ability—but it did enough to ensure the couple could live together for much longer than they would otherwise.

But all of that happened *after* the Nam-tar agreed to stay. After trust. After love. After…all of it. It was a final step. A step that involved a lot of trust. And not every Nam-tar agreed to it. It wasn't a requirement for breaking the curse. It was a sort of bonus. A non-required bonus.

He'd quite literally jumped all those steps. On accident. In the moments of realizing he'd die without letting his wolf leap from his body, riding the wolf's form while his injured human form turned to stone and healed, he'd been too focused on surviving. On the fact that after all this time, he'd found his Nam-tar and he wasn't going to die yet. He wasn't going to let her be killed either. There was a grinluk threatening her. The man who'd shot him still had a gun.

All those worries rolled through him fast and relentlessly. And he knew he had to leave his body, let the wolf out, rejoin the fight. But in all that fear and worry…he'd forgotten when his wolf leapt free, he wouldn't just knock the woman to the side. That had been his intent. To knock her away from the man aiming a gun at her. Except she wasn't an ordinary woman to him. And he hadn't knocked her aside.

He'd gone *through* her instead.

The confusion this caused everyone had been pretty impressive. He hadn't minded that part at all.

But it meant they had another problem now. Not only had he potentially ruined any chance of ending his own curse, not only had he started his introduction to his Nam-tar by violating her choice—even if done on accident—but he'd inadvertently given the grinluk the idea that she was a Family member. That the wolf had been hers and she'd somehow managed to do something no Family member could do— have their animal leap and leave the human spirit behind in the human host body.

The animal and human spirits were never meant to exist separately. They were in a symbiotic relationship that meant one couldn't exist without the other. No matter what body they were in, human or animal, they remained together in that body. One in spirit, the other corporeal. But always together.

By leaping through the woman in front of the monster, Ben had accidentally given the monster the impression she didn't have to do this. That she could let her symbiotic animal leap free without her human spirit having to go with it.

This was…not a good turn of events.

The monster would come for her now. It would have anyway, for interfering. And if it got even a hint that she was important to Ben, that she was a Nam-tar, it would absolutely try to kill her as soon as it could. But this…

This could bring more than just the grinluk. Maybe even more than the Elemental or Elementals working with the grinluk and other monsters. This could bring all the monsters and threats to the Families down on her.

A human woman with no idea any of these things even exist.

This was very very bad.

His wolf agreed. So much so, he couldn't stand still. He paced restlessly around his stone body, resenting the gunshot wound that forced him into this form. A form he couldn't talk to her from. The wolf had a lot of advantages, but the ability to use human language wasn't one of them. And Ben needed desperately to talk to the woman. To explain…as much as he dared.

Damn it all, what was he going to do? Had he screwed up his chance to end his curse? Had he destroyed any hope of earning his Nam-tar? And what had he done to her? If he didn't jump back through her, would that leave her able to return to normal? If he didn't complete the ritual, would she be okay?

None of this was a scenario he'd thought to ask about growing up. Someone had to know, though. This couldn't be the first time in sixteen thousand years this had happened. Someone had to know what to do.

He needed answers. Answers he wasn't going to get like this.

There was still the problem of the geneticist, too. Once again, they'd lost the chance to extract one of the scientists and find out *exactly* what the monsters were having them do.

Fuck. What a mess.

He was still pacing restlessly when the woman finally returned. Having her back, having her near, filled him with so much relief and joy, his wolf actually danced over to her before the logic that was his human spirit thought to calm the wolf's enthusiasm.

She doesn't know us. She doesn't know she should be welcoming a strange wolf who's excited to see her.

The wolf stopped short of jumping up to put his paws on her shoulders and lick her face. But it was a close thing.

She gave him a funny look, then said, "The house is clear. Nothing living. But…" She shivered. "There are things in jars in a storage fridge that I'm not sure I want to know more about. Especially after that tentacled monster thing *spoke*. How the hell does a monster speak?"

Did she realize she was talking to him, to the wolf, as if he would understand her? He'd tried to let her know he did when she'd asked yes-no questions. But she'd fallen into talking to him as if he could definitely understand all she was saying. He liked that. Loved that. But…did she even realize she was doing it?

She gave the stone body of his human form a little frown. Then looked back at the wolf. "I'm talking to you like you understand," she said.

He shouldn't have been surprised they were thinking along the same lines. She was his Nam-tar. He just fucking wished he knew her name.

"I'm not sure why I'm doing that except that I need to say all this out loud so I know I'm not crazy. Even though, frankly, I'm pretty sure I'm crazy right now. Still not able to talk myself out of knowing you managed to jump through me and not over or around me. Not through me as in pushing me down and jumping over the top of me. You went *through me*. And I know that's not possible." She frowned. "Although the monster seemed to think it meant something." She shook her head. "So where did you come from? Are you related to him?" She nodded to his statue body. "Is he dead?"

This was something Ben could answer. He shook his head hard in a no.

"Okay." She let out a long, slow breath. "Okay. Well, that's good."

He was very happy she thought so.

"But the fact that there's a stone statue here where he should be means I can't ask him about why he's a stone statue now. And then there's you to consider…"

He whined softly.

"A wolf. There are wolves in these woods. A long time ago… Well, that's not important now. Anyway, I know there are wolves in these woods. But you don't act like a normal wolf. And since you managed to turn yourself insubstantial enough to go through me, even though that should be impossible, I'm going to assume you're not a normal wolf. Anymore than the things in the jars are normal. Or that the monster was normal." She shivered again. "And since I'm already talking to you like you understand, I also feel impolite not introducing myself. Is that weird?" She sort of half laughed, but there didn't seem to be a lot of humor in it.

He waited on his haunches, trying not to leap up and down in his impatience to have her name.

She glanced at the broken crates nearest them. "Not sure if you've noticed, but… There are *things* in the crates, too. After the jars in the storage fridge, I haven't looked too closely, but…" She swallowed hard. "But I think we need to get out of this house, even if there aren't any men with guns anymore." She glanced at the statue. "But I'm not sure how to move him."

Your name! What's your name? He wanted to shout but all that came out of his wolf was a whine. She was his future, and it felt so wrong that he didn't know what her name was.

She misinterpreted his wolf's whine. "Is moving him bad? Will we…hurt him or something if we try?"

He shook his head no, but… But his statue would be too hard for her to move, too heavy.

He really needed to talk to her. He had to get back into his body, even if only for a few minutes. The wound would have healed enough by now for him to survive it. Not enough to be healed. He'd have to stay out of that body for a few more hours to fully heal. But he could leap back in, tell her what she needed to know, make introductions, and then leap out again. Or maybe get them both out of here first, then leap out again.

Would his body be capable of that yet? He hadn't been out of it long. Long enough to save himself. Long enough he was pretty sure he wouldn't die going back in yet.

There was also the issue of *not* jumping back through her to get into his body again, of not finishing the ritual. But…

Well, he'd just have to hope he hadn't fucked that up completely. They had more immediate issues to worry about. Like getting her out of here.

He gave her a gentle nudge with his nose, careful so as not to scare her, and urged her back from the body.

She complied, but the furrow in her brow deepened. "You don't want us to move him?"

Rather than try to communicate like this, in nods and headshakes, he trotted a few feet from the statue, and then took the run and dive back into his body.

He knew what the process looked like from the outside. He'd seen his family do this over and over again, all his life. But it was the first time he'd wondered what a stranger saw. What someone who hadn't grown up with this process might see. When they were in a safer place, and he was fully healed, he'd ask her.

Right now, he just needed his human body's ability to speak.

The transition for him was…well, as natural as breathing. The wolf returning to the human host, turning incorporeal as it melted back into the human body, the stone retreating and returning to living flesh. The cold that swept through him before he felt warm again. The transition to breathing, smelling, seeing, feeling with his human body again.

And, this particular time, the burning pain of a gunshot wound still ripping through his chest.

CHAPTER SEVEN

The man gasped, dragging in a ragged, rough breath. And all Elle could do for a long long moment was stare.

The wolf had leapt *into* the stone statue. Turning into a ghost as it went. Entering the stone body. As it did, the stone had seemed to flow away, flow outward toward the limbs, replaced by actual human flesh. The process was fast enough she really only processed the change after it had happened, separating out the different impressions of the change once it was finished. But once it was finished, the living, breathing man she'd dragged into this nook blinked up at her.

Flesh and blood again.

Oh! Blood.

The wound in his chest seeped blood more slowly now. And there was less of a hole than there'd been just twenty minutes ago—or was it less time? She'd lost complete sense of how much time had actually passed. Still, she knew that wound should be worse. That not enough time had passed for that much healing to have occurred.

And yet, she'd just watched a stone statue become a living man right before her eyes, after a wolf that had been solid jumped *into* the statue and became not solid. So…

What she was certain of and not certain of was pretty much out the window.

Along with her sanity. She was certain now that had flown the coop. Probably the instant she'd seen a monster and heard it speak.

"I can't stay like this long. I need to transition out of this body again for the wound to heal fully." The man spoke as if what had just happened wasn't impossible.

The fact that he was speaking at all was just…

"Okay," she said, because he paused like she was supposed to contribute to the conversation now.

"I know I have a lot to explain to you."

She snorted out a laugh that might have been a little too close to hysterics and definitely didn't have any humor in it.

"We don't have much time. We need to get somewhere safe. I'll explain as soon as I can. You can move the stone statue of my body, that won't hurt me, but I'm heavy that way. So I'll stay this way long enough for us to get out of here."

"Will that kill you?" She gestured at the still seeping wound. She wanted to put pressure on that bleed. To reapply the shirt that had slipped off the injury when he'd gone from stone back to flesh. But she was also afraid to get too close. To touch him.

Afraid of what, Elle? He'll turn you to stone with a touch? She scoffed at her own reactions. Even though a part of her was worried about just that.

"I'll manage. If it gets too bad, though, I'll have to leap. When this body is stone, it heals faster."

"So…doing that will keep you from dying?"

He nodded. "I never got your name."

That felt like a non sequitur from the conversation about him dying, but she answered automatically. And with her real name. "Elle."

"Benjamin. I go by Ben."

"Alright, Ben. Let's get you out of here."

She hesitated a brief moment, watching him leverage himself on one side and push up. Then she moved in and took his arm gently over her shoulders, so she could help him stand. This time around, she noticed that she was touching his bare skin, his bare chest. She tried hard to ignore that fact. Because he still had a pretty significant gunshot wound, and it seemed rude to notice he had nice muscles and his arms were magnificent.

He leaned to one side and scooped up the fallen sword. She wasn't sure whether to be pleased he thought to keep hold of a weapon or annoyed he was likely doing more damage to his injury. She caught his torn t-shirt just as it was about to fall and shoved it back against his wound, using it to keep pressure there, even though the blood dripped more slowly.

"You still have a bullet inside you," she pointed out. "It didn't go through."

"My body will push it out as it heals. Don't worry. I'll be fine." He was sweating as they started limping toward the back door. His voice was already pretty deep, but the strain deepened the sound into a rough rumble. She could practically hear his gritted teeth and from the corner of her eye, she saw his jaw muscles bunch tight.

"You sound like shit and you're sweating a lot. Not sure this counts as fine."

He chuckled faintly. An actual chuckle. "Had worse."

Which wasn't necessarily reassuring news. What did he do that he'd been injured *worse* than this before?

Well, Elle, he has a wolf that leaps in and out of him so, you know, maybe it's not something you want to know more about?

"You like…a…a werewolf or something." She had this vague idea that werewolf shifts were different, but having thought they were fictional up to this point, she hadn't actually given werewolf shifts much thought. In the movies they were different, though.

"Not a werewolf."

"Okay." Was that good or bad? "If you explain all this to me, is that knowledge going to get me killed?"

He paused for a beat, and while she couldn't be certain the pause wasn't caused by him trying to walk while sporting a gunshot wound to the chest, she wasn't certain that pause meant good things for her.

"Not the knowledge itself, no. This isn't a 'I could tell you but then I'd have to kill you' kind of situation."

"Well that's something I guess." But he was hedging and being careful with his wording. "I'm curious enough to want answers anyway. But I'm leery."

"Good instincts," he muttered. "The crates… Could you identify anything in them? You said you didn't look closely after the storage fridge, but…is there anything you did see?"

The realization that he'd heard all that while she was saying it to the wolf and he was a stone statue was surprising for some reason. She wasn't sure why. Obviously, he and the wolf were somehow one and the same, even if he wasn't a werewolf. Still, the fact that he'd heard her and remembered what she'd been saying—or at least knew what the wolf had heard her say was… Well, she should probably be disturbed by it.

Instead, she was just relieved. She didn't have to reexplain everything.

"Nothing good," she said, suppressing a shudder. "You probably don't want to know."

"Tell me anyway."

"Body parts. Animal mostly. That I could see while trying not to look. But…there were a few human body parts. Or at least, they seemed to be human. Hard to tell."

Another pointed pause, then, "Why hard to tell?"

"The various parts are all…attached to other parts. I didn't look close enough to see how. I don't really want to know. When I spotted the first eye buried inside something that looked furry with something like a budding mouth over the top of the eye, I decided I didn't want the details."

None of the hunting she'd done with her father had really prepared her for the things she'd seen spilling out of the broken crates, and she didn't want to think about those things too long. Her nightmares were vivid enough already.

And maybe that's what this was. Maybe she was actually asleep in her car, and this was her having a nightmare. Vivid and detailed. But not real.

Except… The man—Ben, his name was Ben—Ben didn't feel like part of a dream. Not when she was tucked up under his shoulder this way. Not with the heat of him lining her side and the weight of him solidly against her. He felt very real. And she realized she'd be weirdly disappointed to wake up and have him turn out to be just a figment of her imagination.

How strange. She'd actually miss him.

They clambered around more broken crates, some of which seemed to have been toppled purposefully in the way, like someone—or something—had dumped over some of the maze to make getting to the back door more difficult. She hadn't noticed that seemingly deliberate wreckage when checking the house for monsters and gunmen, but then, she hadn't been trying to get to the back door. And maybe it only felt deliberate now because she needed to get this large, heavy man through the destruction.

She probably should have thought more about all the broken and tumbled crates when she'd been searching the house. There shouldn't be this much of a mess.

A scraping sound behind her nearly sent her jumping out of her skin. Her spin to face the sound was truncated, because Ben was still leaning heavily on her, but she still twisted to see if the noise was just a rat or if she'd missed a guard. Or a monster.

She regretted looking.

She should have just run.

From the broken crates, *something* oozed forward. A collection of pieces that seemed connected by a gelatinous black goo. As the goo rolled forward, things like eyes appeared and disappeared, and…parts —tentacles, a human looking arm, a clawed foot like something from a huge eagle—all stuck out of the goo, sometimes more than at other times. The mess of…stuff rolled toward them, scraping over the wooden floor as it pushed broken wooden bits aside. As it moved, it seemed to scoop up some of the other things that had fallen out of the crates as well as some of the broken wood.

"That is one disgusting sponge," she murmured.

"Fuck," Ben muttered. "We have to go. Fast."

"Yeah. Yeah." But he was still sporting a gunshot wound. He wasn't in a position to run.

Or so she'd thought.

The next thing she knew, they were racing toward the back door. She was still tucked under one of his arms, and the run was more like a lurch, awkward and disjointed. But also a hell of a lot faster than she'd expected. They rushed past more crates just as more…things started to ooze out of the broken wood.

"Fuck." Her turn to curse. She screamed when a crate nearby crashed to the ground and unleashed something with wings that screeched from a beak implanted in the black goo.

She'd never even had nightmares about things like this. If this was one of her super vivid nightmares, she was plumbing new depths of horror. And she was not happy about it. She didn't even read horror. Where had her imagination come up with these *things*?

"Get back," Ben ordered suddenly, coming to an abrupt halt.

Elle found herself pushed behind him—even though he was the one with the bleeding wound! He swung the large sword he held one-handed and sliced through something made of the goo. The stench that unleashed nearly had her doubling over. Nothing had ever smelled that bad before in the history of bad smells. It was like rotting meat mixed with sewage mixed with festering puss and while she'd smelled each of those things individually, the combination made her eyes water and her gorge rise.

She was still gaging and trying not to throw up when Ben grabbed her hand and pulled her past the hissing steam coming out of the goo.

"There are no fucking heads to cut off," he muttered. "We have to get out of here."

"Heads?" Oh, she did not want to see heads.

"They'll have them," he said, almost grudgingly. "But I don't have time to find them."

She screamed against when something just beside her crashed through some still-standing crates.

Ben swung his sword across whatever the thing was before she'd even had time to register what she was seeing. So fast she barely saw Ben move.

A tentacle and some talons dropped to the ground and then Ben was pulling her rapidly toward the back door again.

They shoved outside just as something like human fingers on the end of a lion's leg reached for them from the depth of more black goo.

Heart hammering, panic and fear tight in her chest, Elle never thought to object when Ben ran straight for the woods. She wanted to get as far from that house as possible, as fast as possible. Before the goo got out!

But the thought of those horrors escaping the house left her breathless.

She was about to pull Ben to a stop when he came to an abrupt halt on his own.

"I can't leave the place like that," he said. "I have to destroy the things inside."

"Yeah. We do." She looked back at the now creaking wooden walls of the building. "Wood burns. There's a lot of wood there."

"Got a handy match?"

She pulled a small, wax wrapped bundle of stick matches from the thigh pocket of her cargo pants. "Always." She studied the house, then pointed. "The generator. I can rig that to blow."

There were a lot of things she regretted and hated about the years she'd spent with her father. But some of the skills he'd insisted she learn had turned out to be unexpectedly useful.

Ben gave her a look, but she ignored him as she continued to study the house. None of the goo had escaped. Yet. There were no windows for it to leak out of—fortunately—and they'd slammed the metal back door closed on the way out. Or Ben must have. She'd been too panicked to think about it.

But with some distance from the immediate danger, she was able to think again. Frantic and desperate, but still thinking. Thinking about how to destroy those monstrosities inside that house.

"Will the explosion spread?" Ben asked.

"Might. So might a fire. But the area is pretty damp from the rain two days ago." She winced. Probably not damp enough. If sparks flew or something that was on fire tried to crawl out of the house…a fire could easily spread.

Ben leaned against a tree, his sword lowered and held at his side, reminding her he was still very seriously injured. And he'd just been swinging that sword around like he wasn't.

"We need to get you to my car—or yours?—soon so you can…do that thing you do and heal."

"House first," he said, ignoring the drip of sweat trickling down his cheek. "Fire. No explosions if we can avoid it. Draw too much attention. Last thing we need is humans investigating."

"Gonna need a fire crew eventually to put out the fire, though. Can't leave it burning to ash."

"Why not?"

She blinked at him. "It'll spread. There's no way it won't spread."

"It's gotta burn to the ground to ensure what's in there doesn't get out. And we have to work fast, because what's in there is starting to get out. I'll stay here until it's done. You can go back to your car—I assume you have a cellphone?" When she nodded, he said, "Get to somewhere there's cell service and you'll be able to call for help. By the time anyone gets here, the fire will be burnt low enough, we won't have to worry."

She was shaking her head before he'd finished talking. "I'm not leaving you. You've been shot. You're in pain. You need to…do that thing you do." She raised a hand when he opened his mouth. "I'm not leaving. Shut up and deal with it. We don't have time to argue." She looked back at the house. Then said, "Ordinary fire's going to take too long to spread. Something will get out."

She started back toward the house, even though every single part of her rebelled at the thought. She did *not* want to be anywhere near that goo. Those…whatever they were. Monsters. Though monsters seemed pretty fucking basic a word for what was inside that house. They'd spent too much time talking already, though. And they could only see one side of the house. Something might have already gotten out the front.

An explosion would bring attention. Which meant emergency services would come quicker. There wasn't anyone in the area for miles and miles. But a generator blowing up was still bound to draw attention.

She hoped. They really were pretty isolated out here. This wasn't someplace with good roads leading back to it. A single dirt track left the paved roads far behind to get here. Might even be impossible for a fire truck to reach the house. Might need one of those planes that put out forest fires. Which would take more time. The fire could spread. Lots could go wrong.

But there were monsters in there that needed to be thoroughly destroyed and an explosion was the fast way to do it.

She couldn't afford to get her or Ben caught in the explosion, though. They had to have time to get away. But not so much time a lot of monsters got out of the house first.

She dropped the magazine out of the gun she still carried and removed one of the rounds, testing its weight in her palm. It would do. Maybe two rounds.

Ben was at her side before she'd gotten the second cartridge out.

"You should have stayed where you were. You're in no shape—" she started, but he cut her off.

"I'll manage. What will you do?"

"Gonna rig the powder in the cartridges with a match, drop it into the generator's gas tank, then run." She looked at him, at the sweat on his face and the way his chest wound still seeped blood. He wasn't gushing blood. But he was pale even in the dark. And he was still bleeding.

"You should have stayed where you were," she said again. "You won't be able to run fast enough."

He raised his brows at her, a funny little smile on his face.

"Why are you smiling?"

"I'll explain later. Rig the generator. I'll check the front of the house. Shout if…anything approaches."

She shivered, but didn't ask what might approach. She concentrated on her part of the job.

The gas-powered generator was still humming gently as she approached. Inside the house, beyond the wooden walls, Elle swore she heard things scraping and moving. Other sounds too. Like moaning. She didn't want to think about that even a little bit.

After wrapping the two cartridges together with a rubber band she also had in one pocket, she tucked a few of the matches inside the band. She then very carefully pried the bullets from the casings, gently, using the plyers in her multi-purpose knife, which she carried in the thigh pocket opposite the matches. She winced, knowing plyers were not a safe tool for this, but she didn't have a lot of choices. And her father had taught her a number of ways to do things like this in a pinch.

The fact that all the things her paranoid, survivalist, prepper, militia father taught her managed to come in handy so she could destroy some monsters that shouldn't exist in the real world was an irony not lost on her.

She opened the gas tank on the generator and dropped in a rock, listening for the splash. Didn't take long. Tank was three-quarters full. Pulling in a deep breath, she struck one of the matches not banded to the open casings against a rough patch of wood on the house. The flare of the little flame lit the shadowed area and made tiny dark spots swim in her vision. She took a deep breath, then lit the matches banded to the open cartridges and set the bundle on the very edge of the generator near the gas tank opening.

Taking a moment to ensure everything was balanced right and would work as she hoped, she edged back from the generator. A small trickle of gun powered flowed from the open casing, into the gas. As the weight balance in the cartridges shifted, the whole bundle tipped toward the tank.

"Ben," she shouted and started backing toward the woods, fast.

An instant later, strong arms wrapped around her, lifting her off her feet. She blinked. A whoosh of air movement. A queasy sensation in her gut.

She blinked again and she was deep in the woods, the house a faint silhouette in the distance.

What the…?

She hadn't even had time to think, to react. Strange arms coming around her triggered a knee jerk response in most situations. She went immediately into fight mode. A survival instinct forged in her childhood that she didn't have much control over, even now. But…she hadn't had even a chance to *start* to struggle before she was already hundreds of yards from the house, cradled in a stranger's arms.

And she knew without looking whose arms enveloped her.

"Sometime soon, I'm going to need an explanation for…you," she murmured.

"Soon," Ben agreed.

Which sort of surprised her. She might want an explanation. But he didn't have any obligation to indulge her curiosity. In fact, she'd have assumed he'd disappear and leave her with all her questions. He obviously had secrets. He wasn't an ordinary man—an understatement that almost made her laugh. Why would he reveal anything to a perfect stranger just because they'd survived monsters together?

The moment he'd jumped in front of her, taken the bullet meant for her, played out in her mind.

She shook away the thought and, reluctantly, eased away from him. He'd lifted her, one arm under her thighs, the other behind her back, cradling her to his chest. Which, she knew was still injured and bleeding. But he still held her securely, and he wasn't shaking, despite her weight. Like she didn't weigh that much at all.

Well, he was the size of a grizzly bear and could become a stone statue. Maybe she didn't feel heavy to him.

The instant she gave his shoulders a slight push, he let her slide back to her feet, holding her only long enough to ensure she got her balance and then letting her go and taking a step away.

"Sorry I didn't warn you about that," he murmured. "But a monster had gotten out and was heading your way."

Shit. "Did you…"

"I… Well, I don't know if killed is the right word since I'm pretty sure I didn't find its 'head.' But I sliced through enough of it to slow it down."

She let out a slow breath through her mouth. And finally remembered he'd had a sword on him. He'd held it in the hand that had been around her back. He'd run at that speed, holding her, with a sword in one hand that hadn't cut either one of them in the escape, all with a chest wound.

Who *was* he?

"And I wasn't sure how long it would take for the generator to blow," he added with an almost embarrassed shrug.

She glanced back, wondering that too…

Just as the generator exploded in an ear-shattering, blinding flash of fire.

CHAPTER EIGHT

They were deep enough in the woods, far enough away from the house, that when the generator blew, they were in no danger. Still, Elle ducked her head and crouched low, an instinctive reaction to watching the explosion flare and spread, breaking through the house, throwing wood and metal into the air in a fireball of heat she felt even this far away.

Secondary explosions happened within the house. Smaller but cumulative. Sending more debris flying through the clearing around the house and into the woods.

She winced at that, really hoping they didn't start a forest fire.

It took her several seconds of watching the explosions before two things occurred to her. One, that there must have been more explosive material in the lab part of the house, or else the monsters themselves, that black goo whatever it was, were flammable.

And two, that Ben was standing in front of her, blocking her physically from the explosion. Even though it was too far away for any of the debris to reach them.

His chest was still bleeding from a gunshot wound. A wound he'd gotten by jumping between her and a bullet. And now he stood between her and an explosion. As if he'd take that for her, too.

She wasn't sure whether to be appalled or enamored. The soft, melty feeling in her chest seemed to indicate she was feeling more enamored.

Of a man who had a wolf living inside him that jumped out of his human body and left the human body stone.

Okay, good reminder. Well timed bucket of cold water. No getting romantic notions about heroes and that sort of bullshit. He wasn't her hero. He was a stranger.

Who'd taken a bullet for her and stood between her and an explosion.

"You okay?" he murmured.

"Fine. Looks like my impromptu bomb worked."

"Very well," he said dryly. "But that should take care of…whatever was in there." He sighed as he stared at the fire now burning bright in the distance, a huge bonfire of destruction. "Unfortunately, probably destroyed any evidence, too."

He said this quietly, almost to himself.

"Evidence?"

He shook his head. With his back still to her, she couldn't read his expression. "Doesn't matter. Had to be done."

"Evidence of hinky genetics experiments? Because…there was definitely some of that going on in there."

"There was. More than anywhere else we've seen so far."

We? He'd said "we" before. "Anywhere else?"

He finally turned to face her. "Long story."

She flicked a look down to his chest. The seeping blood had mostly clotted. Barely anything came from the wound anymore. But there was still blood across his chest and that made her painfully aware he'd nearly died and could still yet die. And she was also very aware that there was still a bullet in him. That he'd been doing all this while a bullet was lodged somewhere in his chest—near his lungs? His heart? That bullet could be doing all kinds of damage, even if they couldn't see it on the outside yet.

But he'd said his body would push the bullet out or something when he did the thing where he turned to a statue. He needed to do that again. Soon.

"You need to…do that turning to stone thing," she said, gesturing to his chest.

"I will. I want to make sure none of the monsters escape the fire first." A furrow formed between his brows as he stared at her.

For some reason, that look made her heart pound. She wasn't sure why.

But after a moment of that look, he turned his attention back to the burning house.

The debris that had scattered had started small fires, but so far none of it seemed to be spreading very far. The recent rain and damp ground were actually helping. But Elle still nervously watched those small fires, her gaze jumping between them and the house.

If this was a horror movie, something would come lurching out of the building any moment. Either when they had their backs turned, so they'd miss it, or as they watched and they'd know the monsters were still after them. She hadn't watched horror movies growing up. She'd lived through real-life human monsters and found the fake monsters in a horror too…well, boring. She couldn't enjoy the movies because they seemed ridiculous to her and not in a fun, good way. Some people she knew who'd faced horrible things loved watching horror movies *because* they were so obviously fictional. She wasn't one of those people.

But as she stood there waiting for real-life monsters that weren't humans but were actual monsters that might appear in those horror movies, she started to regret not watching more. Be helpful to have a playbook for this kind of thing. What was it called…? Jump-scares? She was waiting for the jump-scare. And that waiting had her anxiety high and her nerves pulled tight.

She hadn't thought she'd made a sound, a move, a gesture, but just as her anxiety was climbing so high it was clogging her throat, she felt a large hand wrap around hers, squeeze gently. She squeezed back, comforted much more by that gesture from a virtual stranger than she should have been.

When nothing lurched from the house after a few minutes, she took a deep breath and reluctantly released Ben's hand. But neither of them moved. They just stood there, watching the house burn, watching the small fires that had started.

And as they watched, the realization that she'd lost Professor Arron sank in once more. She'd have to start tracking him again as soon as she could. First get Ben taken care of. Then she'd have to leave to follow the professor.

Although. She glanced at Ben from the corner of her eye. He was going after the people holding the professor, wasn't he? That's why he was here. Maybe they could…work together?

She didn't usually work closely with other people because she didn't want them to realize her tracking skills weren't entirely normal. But this man occasionally turned to stone. A little thing like psychic hunting skills probably wouldn't faze him. Right?

But she didn't actually know him or what he'd intended here. Not really. He knew all about monsters, and he'd been trying to find out what was happening inside. She presumed he'd intended to stop it. He wouldn't have burned the place to the ground if he wanted to…use the monsters or study them or anything.

And he'd gotten shot saving her life. He'd risked his life to get her past the monsters. And he'd trusted her to blow the generator.

She wouldn't call this feeling trust. She trusted no one—a lesson from her father she'd never shaken, even when she'd tried—but maybe acceptance of a possible ally?

Lot of hedging in that thought.

She considered how to bring up their mutual goal of finding the professor and the monster again, when his barely audible curse made her look back at the house.

Some of the smaller fires were growing. And the conflagration of the house was throwing huge plumes of black smoke into the night sky. The stench had finally reached them. Not a nice campfire smell. The smell of things already grotesquely stomach-churning without heat applied got infinitely worse when set on fire. Enough to make her gag. She put a hand over her nose in a vain attempt to block the stench. But still. Gross. Whichever poor first responder got here to put that out was going to throw up if they took their masks off.

But the smell wasn't the scary part. The scary part was the fact that the fire seemed to be spreading now. A tree behind the house had caught and was burning fast. That was going to spread to the other trees soon.

Shit. Exactly what they didn't want to happen.

"Now what?" she asked around her hand since she wasn't prepared to move it from pinching her nose closed.

Ben scowled.

But before he could answer, the sound of thunder rolled through the woods. And the next thing she knew, a torrential downpouring of rain soaked them. Sheets of rain so thick she couldn't see more than a blur of orange and yellow where the house was. She was so suddenly and completely wet, she might as well have stepped into a shower. Only this was worse. She'd have had time to adjust to a shower. And it would be warm. And she wouldn't—probably—be fully dressed. Soaking wet cargo pants were not very comfortable. Though they were better than jeans. That was something, she supposed. But since she wasn't wearing a jacket, the cold rain left her shivering.

The downpour seemed to contain the fire, though. The orange and yellow blur looked to be shrinking. Their surroundings got progressively darker, until the size of remaining glow looked like little more than a campfire in the distance.

Ben glared up at the sky as Elle said, "That was…fortuitous. Weird. But lucky."

"Maybe," Ben said.

"Didn't think we were due rain today," she both said and asked as she shaded her eyes and glanced up toward the sky. There hadn't been any clouds earlier. And she hadn't noticed any rolling in since they left the house. But she'd had bigger things on her mind since then—like monsters that shouldn't really exist. Clouds could have crept in while she wasn't paying attention.

The rain was freezing, though, so while it might have been a handy way to put the fire out, she had to wrap her arms around herself in an attempt to stop her shivering. No handy raincoat in her pockets either. She had one in the trunk of her car, along with all sorts of backup and emergency gear. But her car was a few miles away.

Walking through this icy rain back to the car was going to be miserable.

"We need to go," Ben said, still looking up at the rain suspiciously.

"My car is a couple miles away. Where's yours?"

"We'll go to yours. Mine's…farther."

Farther? He must have come in on foot from a long way away.

Well, given how fast he moved, maybe he just ran here from the closest town. Did he need cars and things like that?

"You still have a bullet in you," she pointed out.

"Let's get out of the rain first, worry about that then."

The wound on his chest was fully clotted and closed now. The blood on his chest washing off in the rain. His bare chest. In freezing rain. After he'd nearly died less than an hour ago.

She took his hand. "This way."

Taking him to her car had to rank up there with one of her least paranoid actions. And the paranoia instilled by her father rose to warn her this was a bad idea. She didn't know him. He could be the enemy.

Blah blah blah.

He'd gotten shot saving her, and so far, he hadn't done anything but help her. From things she didn't even have a name for. The paranoia had a place in this world—which was an irony she hated—but in this case, she ignored it. Ben, whatever he might be, wasn't her immediate enemy. He was an ally. And he was an ally that was injured and caught out without even a t-shirt in the soaking, freezing rain.

An instinct to take care of him, to ensure he was okay, overrode the distrust and fears she carried through most other interactions with strangers, especially strange men. And wasn't that something she'd have to analyze soon. Once she was out of the rain.

Ben turned away from the banked fire reluctantly, but another glance at the sky had him picking up speed as they hiked through the trees. The way he kept glancing back in the direction of the house, then up at the sky, had Elle's instincts humming. She held her questions, though. Her fingers were so cold she could barely feel them, and she was going to start trembling uncontrollably soon. Everything but getting out of this icy rain and to the pseudo safety of her car took a backseat.

They weren't very far away from the house before the darkness got so thorough, Elle could no longer see where she was going. Shit. She stopped long enough to take a penlight out of her boot. The light didn't illuminate much at all, a tiny circle of visibility a foot in front of her, but it was enough to keep her from panicking or twisting an ankle.

"I can see," Ben said, as if he'd sensed her panic. "What direction are we going? I'll make sure we get to your car."

Why was that such a relief and not scary? "West and a little north. I pulled off a dirt road without a name, but it was only about a couple of miles from the closest paved road."

She moved in the direction unerringly. She could *feel* the car with that ability to track things that mostly she used to track people. She hadn't consciously tried to use that skill to find her car, but when she was looking for something, anything at all, the skill kicked in. She needed to find the car in the middle of the woods, her tracking skills turned on, and she could sense where she had to go.

So she pointed that direction, using her little penlight in its waterproofed casing to keep from tripping, and relied on Ben's eyes to ensure she didn't walk off a cliff or into a tree.

The hike back to the car felt a lot longer, and a lot more precarious, than the hike to the house had felt. By the time they reached her used Corolla, the rain had stopped, leaving muddy puddles to squish up around her boots. This far from the fire, the stink of burning *things* no longer filled her nose or coated her tongue, and the soft scent of rain-soaked pines and earth would have been a pleasant reprieve if she wasn't nearly numb from being so cold.

Her hands shook as she took her keys out to open the door, and she dropped the fob into the mud despite her best efforts. She cursed and swept the keys up, her fingers clumsy and awkward as she pressed the button to open the doors and then opened the trunk.

"You're probably freezing," she said to Ben, because if she was cold, he had to be. "Get in. I'm just getting out some blankets." She had a few thick wool blankets in the trunk and a sleeping bag that would help warm him up.

He didn't get into the car, though. He stayed at her side, scanning the surroundings, his shoulders stiff, the sword still in hand. He wasn't shivering, which she took as a good sign. He also didn't drop his vigilance.

She handed him a wool blanket, which he took without looking and absently wrapped around his shoulders one-handed, which was a neat trick.

He glanced at her briefly and said, "Wrap up too. You're shivering."

Who was taking care of who here?

She hid an irrational smile as she pulled out the sleeping bag and one more wool blanket. She had some emergency mylar blankets she added to the pile, but she found those less useful than they were supposed to be. Especially when she was wet.

When she'd gotten everything she needed to keep them warm, she walked around the car and dumped everything into the passenger seat. Then she pulled out some bottles of water from the trunk and put those into the car's cupholders. Satisfied, she closed the trunk and motioned Ben into the backseat.

"If you're going to do that stone thing, you'll need to lay down in the back. I presume you don't want casual observers on the highway to see you."

He grunted. She took that as a yes.

They were both inside the car, the doors closed and locked, when she heard Ben take a long, slow breath, letting it out in a whoosh that sounded like relief.

"Worried about more monsters coming for us?" she asked.

"Something like that." He shoved the sleeping bag she pushed at him back to her. "You use that. I won't be cold in a minute. My wolf won't be wet."

"Okay." That was going to take some getting used to. And sparked a lot of questions. Which, very soon, he wouldn't be able to answer.

And also, why did she think she'd have to get used to this since they were separating soon? "Where am I taking you? Back to your car or…?"

He frowned, but the expression didn't look so much worried as… awkward. Charmingly awkward. How strange. She wouldn't have thought of him as awkward about anything.

It was too dark inside her car to see him clearly. She realized she hadn't *really* looked at him closely since this all started. A little, while he'd been wounded. Enough to know generally what he looked like. But…at the same time she didn't. She wanted to study him closer, to really *see* him. In the light. When they weren't bedraggled from rain, or nursing a chest wound, or racing from monsters.

The desire to get a really good look at him in good light without scary stuff happening was pretty overpowering. And yet, she was about to say goodbye to him.

Maybe.

She remembered her earlier thought, that they had a mutual goal and could maybe work together. How did she bring that up?

And why was she so reluctant to say goodbye?

CHAPTER NINE

Ben stared at the back of her passenger seat wondering how exactly to say he didn't want to go anywhere but with her. He couldn't say it *that* way. Elle had dealt with enough for one night. She didn't need a stranger announcing he intended to stay with her wherever she went from now on.

Even he was having some trouble with that idea.

Not that he didn't want to spend more time with his Nam-tar, earn her trust, earn her acceptance. Convince her to stay with him. But… There was so much, and everything had happened so suddenly, and he was still adjusting to the fact that she was here. Right in front of him.

And he may well have fucked everything up already.

By leaping through her. By not leaping *back* through her. They were linked now. He had no idea what that had done to either of them. Or how it would affect them going forward. And he wasn't going to get answers to those questions right away because she was right. He had to let his wolf out so he could finish healing. The bullet had been pushed forward enough to be wedged in muscle and not too near his heart or lungs, but still there. And it hurt like hell. Plus, the injury was slowing him down. He couldn't afford that right now.

He had to go after the geneticist and the grinluk. After losing the lab, and any records that could have made clear what was happening, he couldn't let the geneticist get away this time. This was the only one they'd identified that didn't want to be working with the monsters. Or at least hadn't started out wanting to work with the monsters. Ben was pretty sure Gabe Arron would tell them everything. So long as they could get him away from his captors.

Which was something Elle wanted to do, too. She'd come to find Arron. To extricate him from his kidnappers. They had a similar goal.

So...so they could work together. That would give him time. Time to broach...everything else. Time to get to know her, and more importantly, for her to get to know him. Time to earn her trust.

And time to find out if that leap through her had fucked up any hope of breaking his curse.

She was frowning at him, her gaze unfocused. It was probably too dark inside the car for her to see him clearly, but his night vision was excellent so he saw her every expression. And right now, she looked hesitant. Maybe a little awkward. Was it strange he found the awkward comforting and also adorable?

Since she was his Nam-tar, he supposed it wasn't strange.

"Before I leap," he said, trying to get the suggestion out without sounding too desperate to stay with her, "before I can't discuss this for a while... You were here tonight to rescue the geneticist, to get Professor Arron away from his captors."

"I was." Her eyes narrowed. "And you were here to stop... whatever it is they were doing."

"As well as extricate the professor. He can explain exactly what was happening, and I need that information. Especially since we had to burn down the house."

A fire that had been put out by a sudden downpour of rain. Given the participation of at least one sided-Water Elemental in all this, he didn't trust that rain for a minute. But no Elemental had leapt from the puddles to kill them, so he couldn't be sure if the rain was the work of an Elemental purposefully getting involved or just a coincidence. Another something he had to look into but couldn't now when he still had to finish healing the gunshot wound. And a Nam-tar to convince to work with him.

"I was thinking," she said, hesitating. "I was thinking we might... might work together. We have the same goal—get Professor Arron away from his captors. Working together would... Well, it would keep us from getting in each other's way." She tried to smile, even though the expression looked more uncomfortable than natural.

"I was thinking the same thing," he said. "That working together would be more efficient and we should do that." Did that sound too eager? He was trying *not* to sound too eager. But the fact that they'd both been on the same page left him more relieved than he would have expected. So relieved he lifted his hand to reach for her before he checked the motion.

She considered him a stranger, and really, outside of being his Nam-tar, he didn't know her either. Reaching out to take her hand or brush his fingers along her shoulder was not the sort of gesture that would earn her trust right now.

But her smile, her little release of breath, the way her shoulders relaxed, and the way she said, "Yeah. Exactly. Good. That would be good." left him feeling weirdly light and excited.

"I need to heal first," he said, "but I should be fine by the morning. We can pick up the trail then." Easier said than done, but he'd worry about that tomorrow.

"Are you...do you have a hotel room somewhere nearby, or do you live near here or...?"

Her pale cheeks darkened with a blush that made him want to smile. He didn't. But he wanted to. "I've been camping while I hunted for the professor, so I don't have a hotel room or anything." And he really didn't want to camp out with so many puddles nearby which could bring out dangerous Water Elementals. But if he had to, they could camp and his wolf could keep watch overnight. The wolf wouldn't need to sleep while his body healed.

"I have a motel room," she said, slowly, again hesitating over her words. She wasn't looking at him as she spoke, her gaze on the divider between the front seats. "It's about an hour away. Obviously, since everything is about an hour away from here. But it's a private place for you to heal. Clean and dry at least."

She forced another smile but all he saw was the darkening color in her cheeks again. Not brushing his fingers across her blush took a concerted effort.

"I don't want to make you uncomfortable, having a stranger in your room," he said, which was true. They didn't know each other and she had no idea that they were destined for each other. To her, he was just a man she'd encountered in a strange situation who could do strange things. She had every reason to run screaming away from him. The fact that she wasn't, that she wanted to work with him, was offering her motel room as a place for them to rest was…

Amazing. Filled him with hope. And filled him with worry all at once.

"You'll be a stone statue, right?" she said with a little shrug. "So long as the wolf isn't going to attack me, I think we'll be safe enough."

"The wolf would never hurt you," he said with deep sincerity. The wolf knew what she meant to them. What she was to them. The wolf would be more likely to crawl into her lap looking for attention than attack.

"Okay. Good to know." She nodded, her gaze dancing around the car's interior. "I'd… I know I'm a stranger and in no position to ask, but I'd really love an explanation for…all of this. For you. For the wolf."

"I'll tell you everything," he said, again with full sincerity. She needed to know everything anyway. She had to choose to stay in his world with him. And to make that choice, she had to know everything. Eventually.

"Thank you." She smiled again, but this one was more natural. "Not really used to people trusting me with information."

And that was something he wanted to know more about. "We'll be working together. It's important you understand what I am and what I can do."

She sat quietly with that for a moment, then pulled in a deep breath. "Okay. If you want to do the stone thing while we're driving, that'd probably be good. But I'm not going to be able to carry a stone statue into my motel room. The room is on the second floor. How often can you do the stone thing?"

"As often as I need to," he said. "We can return to this body long enough to get up the stairs."

"Does all this moving back and forth make the healing more difficult?"

"I heal fast anyway. Faster than…you would. But not as fast as when the wolf and I are out of this body."

Her eyes narrowed. "I have so many questions."

"I know. We'll get to them soon."

She faced forward and started the car, turning the heating on and up, sighing as the hot air hit her. He'd forgotten how cold she must be after the soaking. Damn, he should have had her running the heater this whole time.

"Would you be able to… I don't know, belt your body in place or something? I don't want to worry about the statue falling back there and breaking. Can you break like that?"

"I'll wrap the lap belt around me," he said to reassure her more than for his own safety. The stone statue could absolutely be broken, and if it shattered, that would kill him, but he wasn't worried about tumbling off the seat onto the car floor. Still, to make her happy, he'd do whatever it took.

He considered just sitting up and shaping himself so casual passersby on the highway wouldn't notice the person in the backseat was a statue and not a person. It was dark enough they could get away with it. And he could leap back into the body before they got to the motel parking lot.

"Tell me when we're almost there," he said as she pulled the car forward, putting it gently back onto the dirt road. She'd parked with the car pointing the direction she'd want to drive, instead of leaving it in a way that would require her turning it around on the narrow road. Had she done that on purpose? Thought about that ahead of time?

Given her multi-tool knife, the penlight, and her wax-wrapped matches, he was pretty certain she'd positioned the car purposefully.

She seemed to be ready for most contingencies. Even down to the gear in her trunk, the blankets and water, the rolled-up tent, a bag he suspected had emergency rations in it. Was she always like this or was this just something she'd done while trying to rescue Arron?

He had a lot of things to explain to her, a lot about his world she needed to know, but what surprised him—and it probably shouldn't have—was just how fascinated he was, how much he wanted to know, how many questions he had for *her*.

Those questions had to remain unasked for the moment, though. He settled himself into the seat, belted in, leaving the chest strap off, and positioned himself so his back was half to the side window.

Then he made the leap.

CHAPTER TEN

The drive back to her motel wasn't quite as nerve-wracking as she'd anticipated, but still wasn't a comfortable hour-long ride. The wolf remained curled up on the backseat just behind her. Which probably should have made her edgy and nervous. She had a *wolf* in her fucking car! But this particular wolf didn't trigger her fight or flight instincts. He was comforting. Like having a dog in the back. A rather large dog. With some impressively sharp teeth. But that was the weirdly comforting part.

She could see the statue that was Ben's body in her rearview mirror, if she glanced back just right. That was scarier than the wolf. She wasn't sure why. He'd huddled against the window in a way that probably made him look like a sleeping passenger to any casual observers. But for reasons surpassing logic, he seemed vulnerable to her like that. Stone and marble could break, shatter. Would that kill him? If they got into a car accident, would he have escaped a gunshot wound and monsters, only to have his physical human body destroyed? And if that happened, did that mean he just stayed a wolf?

So so many questions.

The highway was busy, and the road was slick after the downpour, but they still made good time. As she pulled off the highway, she said, "We'll be coming into the parking lot in five minutes. I don't know if you want to get back into your body now or not, but it might be a good idea. There'll be more light once we get to the motel."

The tree lined slip road they were on wasn't lit. Only her headlights provided any illumination. There weren't even any other cars around. The motel was a beacon of light up ahead, but for the next few minutes they had complete darkness to work with.

She didn't watch to see him leap back into his body. For some reason, even though she'd seen him do it already, the process felt… intimate. Private. Like getting dressed or something. She wasn't entirely sure why she felt that way. He didn't seem to care. But she still felt like she should afford him some privacy as the wolf went back into his body.

Or maybe she was just uncomfortable with the process. It wasn't like anything she'd ever even heard of before.

By the time they reached the motel parking lot, Ben was back in his body, back to flesh and bone. She let out her breath slowly, keeping her eyes on the half full lot, the two-story building with only a handful of lights behind closed curtains. The swimming pool area was empty— too cold for swimming anyway this time of night—and there weren't any people moving around the lot. The small office on the first floor under the stairs was lit, but no one was currently at the desk that she could see. There was a gas station and a chain diner on the other side of the motel, neither of which looked busy. The trees surrounding the lot blocked the slip road, but didn't do much to cushion against the noise from the highway.

Not that she minded. She actually found noise soothing. The years living in the deep woods with her father had been full of silence, nature sounds, the occasional sound of gunfire. But lots and lots of silence. So…yeah, she didn't mind noise now.

What she didn't want at the moment was witnesses. She didn't think anyone would pay much attention to a woman walking a shirtless man up to her room at a highway motel, but she didn't want people to see them even in passing. Just in case. More of the paranoia she'd spent years learning and couldn't quite shake. The less people knew about her business, the better off she'd be.

"You ready?" she asked when she was sure there was no one to casually spot them heading into the motel.

"Ready," he said.

His voice was quiet and a little rough, the sound in the dark tickling along her nerves, raising the hair on the back of her neck. She couldn't decide if that reaction was fear or…something else. So she decided not to think about it too closely.

"How's your wound?" She glanced at him in the rearview mirror, briefly, long enough to catch his eyes, but not long enough to study him.

"Healing. I'll need to leap one more time, probably overnight." He said the last almost like a question.

"Not planning on going anywhere tonight anyway," she said.

She could pick up the direction Professor Arron had been taken in the morning. She didn't think his captors would kill him in the next few days. They'd gone through too much trouble to get him out. If they'd intended on killing him, they could have left his body as they made their own escape. She'd seen no sign of the professor or his suitcase of marble notebooks when she'd searched the house. Whatever experiments they'd been doing, they wanted to keep the professor working on them. They'd take him to another lab, another safehouse. She just had to find the new one. And she could pick that trail up in the morning. When she and Ben were both rested. And he was no longer sporting a gunshot wound to the chest.

The fact that he'd not only survived that, but had fought off monsters and helped her blow up a house afterward was…

She wasn't sure what it was. That was another of those many questions she had for him.

"Let's go. The coast is clear for the moment."

She popped open the trunk and stuffed the blankets back with the rest of her gear. She'd refold and organize everything in the morning.

She took the sleeping bag, though, and another couple of bottles of water plus her first aid case.

When she closed the trunk, Ben was standing next to the car, just out of sight, staying carefully in the shadows thrown by one of the large pines lining the edge of the lot. "That's a big first aid kit," he commented, though his gaze was scanning his surroundings.

"Never know when you might need something," she said. Her standard answer.

"My family keeps kits like that everywhere," he said. "Same reason."

Her curiosity raised its head, but she pushed it down again. Later. Later, Elle. "Do you need help getting up the stairs?" He hadn't needed much help walking or moving or, hell, fighting up to now. But she didn't want to make assumptions. Adrenaline could do amazing things, and push people well past their normal capabilities. But that usually came with a price when the adrenaline faded.

"I'll be good."

They made it up the concrete stairs to the second floor and to her room halfway down the open walkway without encountering anyone. Without anyone seeing them she hoped. She let Ben into the small, serviceable room. Then she set up her portable travel lock on the door, flipped the bolt, set the chain, and shoved a chair under the door handle. Finally, she peaked out the window to ensure no one had followed them or was hanging around just outside or by their car in the parking lot. Once she was certain no one had paid any attention to them, she pulled the curtain fully closed over the front window, blocking the bright light from the walkway.

When she faced the room again, Ben had his brows raised in question. She shrugged. "Can't be too careful."

He didn't comment and she didn't justify her actions any further. There were some instilled paranoias that actually did serve her well as an adult.

The reality of the small room hit, though, when she looked around for a place for Ben to sit. She had been focused on getting here, getting them somewhere safe where he could heal and they could regroup. But she'd gotten a small room—she made decent money finding people for other people, but she kept to a tight budget, mostly out of habit—and it only had a single, queen-sized bed. There was a chair, but it was yellow plastic, and currently blocking her door. The narrow, wooden desk with open-sided cabinets that doubled as storage was not wide enough to pretend it could be a bed. And the floor was a linoleum faux wood with no cushioning or rugs, which made for easy cleaning but wasn't going to suit anyone for sleeping.

Since Ben was going to be a stone statue soon, she supposed that single bed didn't matter much. It was large enough for her to sleep next to a stone statue. And the wolf probably didn't care about sleeping on a hard floor. Although, if he did, she could toss him the pillow that a stone statue wasn't going to need.

The entire idea of that was just wild.

Her room was dim—she'd left the bathroom light on, and the TV on with the volume low as an added safety measure, giving the illusion someone was in here, but otherwise she'd turned off the rest of the room's lights before going out—which left only the flickering of the flatscreen to see Ben by. The changing colors painted his skin, casting the still healing injury on his chest in swirling blues and yellows. Where there'd been a bleeding hole, there was now a lot of lumpy, healing scar tissue. Not fully healed, but getting there. Which was both a relief and a bit terrifying. He'd been shot in the chest a couple of hours ago. And he was nearly recovered now.

When she stopped to think about tonight, really think about it, her brain was going to rebel. And she wasn't sure this was a situation she could discuss with her therapist. In fact, she was pretty certain this was a situation she couldn't discuss with anyone. Mainly because no one would believe her.

She sighed and gestured to the bed. "Sit. Let me wash my hands, and I'll put a bandage on that chest wound."

"That's not necessary. I'll be fine."

"I can see it's almost healed, but…" She shrugged. "I'm not familiar with…what you are and how fast you heal, so, I don't know. Old habits. I guess you don't really need a bandage, do you?"

He shook his head, then glanced at the bed, before giving her a narrow-eyed look. "I'll sit in the chair to leap." With a small smile, he said, "Add to the security. Stone statue weighing the chair down'll make it hard to move."

She snorted a near laugh. She was too tired for a full laugh, but he was right and that was so strange it was funny. "Do you think any monsters will try to track us here?" she asked so she didn't forget the reality of all this.

"It would be hard for them to. Driving over a highway…confuses their senses and even if the grinluk could move fast enough, it had left the area by the time we drove away. It'd have to try tracking us from where your car was. That'll be difficult. So, we should be careful, but I think we're safe enough here to sleep and rest."

She nodded, her shoulders sagging with her relief. "Let me get cleaned up, then you can have the bathroom to wash." He still had some blood matted in his chest hair, despite the rain. If she were him, she'd want that off as soon as possible.

A little unsteady as her own adrenaline waned, she grabbed a fresh t-shirt and her flannel pajama bottoms and disappeared into the bathroom. The narrow space, with a standing shower and no bathtub, felt comfortingly small and enclosed just then. Giving her some quiet isolation and privacy she hadn't realized she needed. So much had happened, so much was still happening, she hadn't processed any of it. Wasn't even sure she'd be able to process it all.

And she still had a job to do.

She leaned against the black sink counter and looked up into the mirror. Winced. The bright overhead light didn't leave much room for pretending. She was a wreck, her short hair in wild disarray, her skin pale and pasty looking, like she was in shock. There were smudges of dirt and other things on her face and hands and clothing—she tried not to think about what the other things were—and she had deep purple circles under her eyes, eyes which looked too wide, her pupils blown in the bathroom brightness.

She looked like she'd been through some shit tonight. Which wasn't an attractive look. With a quiet groan, she pealed off her dirty shirt and tossed it under the sink. She'd consider whether to salvage it or burn it in the morning. She realized how badly she smelled when she removed the shirt, though, and frowned at the glass enclosed, circular shower stall. Yeah, she wasn't going to sleep if she didn't shower. But she didn't want to leave Ben waiting outside for long. He probably felt even more worn and dirty than she did.

The shower water scalded her chilled skin and felt glorious for the five minutes she took to wash her hair and scrub her body clean. Luxuries like letting the conditioner soak into her scalp for more than thirty seconds and letting the hot water sloosh over her long enough to soften her tense muscles would have to wait.

She hadn't brought fresh underwear into the bathroom with her, so she just pulled up the pajama bottoms and dragged the t-shirt over her head. She was going to sleep soon anyway. Exhaustion was dragging her limbs down. Niceties like bras and underwear seemed silly things to worry about given the night they'd lived through.

Still, Ben was a stranger. And walking back out into the main room to face him took a surprising effort. Not because she didn't want to see him. Weirdly, because she wanted to get back to him a little more desperately than she should.

She shoved her dirty clothes into a pile under the floating sink counter and forced herself out the door. Ben was sitting in the plastic chair, his head lowered but his gaze raised to her as she walked out. He had dark eyes, she realized. Brown but they looked nearly black in the reflected TV light. And the expression on his face was strangely hungry. He blinked and his expression cleared. Maybe she'd imagined the look.

"All yours," she said. "There are clean towels. Use what you need."

He nodded, rising slowly from the chair. Not like he was sore, though, as she would have expected. More like he was moving slowly so he didn't startle her. The shear size of him in the small room really sank in then. He really was huge. Six and a half feet tall at a guess, maybe more. And wide, his shoulders thick, the muscles on his arms corded, his chest broad. The blood matting his chest hair and the angry welt of red skin where he'd been shot brought her back to earth fast. But the size of him…

No wonder he'd stood slowly. He probably scared people regularly and was used to moving carefully if he wanted to appear less intimidating. The fact that he was taking that care with her was sweet.

She stepped out of his way as he disappeared wordlessly into the bathroom, then she frowned. He needed something clean to wear, too. But given how big he was, she didn't have anything that would fit him. She wasn't even sure he'd be able to squeeze those huge shoulders into one of her baggy sleep t-shirts. Cotton could only stretch so far.

She was still contemplating the conundrum of what he might wear when the bathroom door clicked open.

He'd showered, too, his hair wet and messy, his skin glistening with dampness. He'd put his cargo pants back on and they hung low on his hips, revealing that deep muscle over his hip joints that some men got. She couldn't remember the name of that muscle in that moment, she could barely remember her own name, but it was a sign of a very fit, strong frame. Without the injury to keep her distracted, awareness of just how very male he was, how large he was, made something flutter in her stomach.

With the uneven light, she still felt like she wasn't getting a great look at his face, but without the blood and adrenaline, she could at least take in more of him now. He had a strong jaw line, currently covered in day old beard scruff, hooded dark eyes, his light brown hair short but loose, no buzz cut for him. She thought he might be handsome but that impression could have just been a side effect of the night. After what they'd been through, she'd have been surprised if she hadn't found him at least a little attractive.

Sucking in a quiet breath, she said, "I'm sorry I don't have anything that will fit you. Even my t-shirts." She gestured vaguely at his shoulders.

"I'm fine. I'll be hanging out inside a fur coat soon."

"Oh. Right." She blinked hard a few times. Then glanced at the wound on his chest. "You really don't need a bandage?"

He shook his head. "Another hour or two and I should be good."

"Do you need… I don't know. Painkillers or anything?"

"I drank some of your water." He waved at an empty bottle. "I'm good now."

They stood awkwardly staring at each other for a few moments. Without the monsters, the danger, the guns, the explosions, the torrential rain… Without the fear and adrenaline pushing her, she no longer knew exactly what to say to him.

And was saved from having to think of anything by a huge and unexpected yawn exploding from her.

She closed her eyes and shook her head, laughing at herself. "Guess I'm tired."

"Been a busy night."

"Understatement. Do you need anything else before you…what do you call it? Leap?"

"No. And for the record, the wolf can sleep on the floor, and he'll be perfectly comfortable. He also won't hurt you. You can sleep with him in the room."

She actually knew that, which felt like a strange bit of knowledge to have about a stranger and a wolf. "When we've slept and you're fully healed, will you explain…you to me, then?"

"I promised I would. I'd explain tonight but, no offense, you look like you're going to fall down."

She chuckled, running a hand up through her hair and mussing the damp strands. She'd regret not blowing her hair dry in the morning but didn't have the energy tonight. "I am about to fall down," she admitted.

"Sleep." He nodded to the bed. "We're safe for the night. We can talk in the morning."

They had a lot to talk about. "You?"

"I'll sit in the chair. The wolf will sleep on the floor. We'll be fine."

"If you're sure." Her energy was waning fast. She grabbed a bottle of water, downed its contents, then crawled under the bedspread. By the time she'd settled, the wolf was in the room. She glanced at the chair in front of the door. A statue of Ben sat there, leaning back a little, hands on his thighs, gaze focused ahead.

The wolf whined softly, then curled up at the foot of her bed, out of sight when she laid down.

Having him there, the statue in front of the door, the living wolf at the foot of her bed, was an awful lot more comforting than it should have been. She drifted off to sleep surprisingly quickly, feeling safer than she had in a long long time.

Something she'd recognize as very odd in the morning.

CHAPTER ELEVEN

Elle let herself reach consciousness slowly, taking in the sounds of her surroundings first, letting her brain adapt to the strange room without washing her with panic. She'd learned a long time ago that when she wasn't in her own home, she had to come back to her waking world slowly or she got hit by an instant panic attack—*where am I? what's going on? why am I here?* Now, when she was in a hotel for a job, her brain automatically went into the slow, careful return to wakefulness.

The sounds of heavy traffic outside the motel. The very faint smell of cigarette smoke that even a full redo of the room couldn't quite erase from the walls. The quiet electrical hum of a TV that was still on but muted. That flickering of TV light against her eyelids.

The sound of someone else in the room breathing.

The night before came rushing in, the strangeness and panic and fear and…

And the man who wasn't a human man. The man who became a wolf. Who'd stepped into a bullet to save her. Who'd risked his own life to help her get out of a house full of nightmare monsters, and then helped her ensure those monsters didn't escape the house.

She slowly blinked her eyes open. In her sleep, she'd rolled to her side to face the door. Facing the door was another, almost unconscious, habit when she was staying by herself in a motel or hotel room. She couldn't get comfortable enough to sleep if her back was to the door. But this position meant the first thing she saw was the statue of Ben sitting in the chair, physically blocking anyone from entering the room.

A sense of security, of peace she didn't normally experience when she was out on a job, washed through her. Which was so strange, so unusual to the circumstances, that it took her a few minutes to realize she wasn't looking at a stone statue anymore. The man sitting in that hard plastic chair was flesh now, his skin a healthy pale color in the faint light leaking past the side of the blackout curtains. At least, she thought he looked healthy enough. Certainly not stone anymore.

His eyes were closed but the rise and fall of his chest proved he was breathing. A peaceful sort of rhythm, too, not anything erratic or showing signs of fever or pain. So sleeping. And because he was sleeping—sitting up in a hard plastic chair! Poor man—she took a moment to study him. His chest looked fully healed now. No rough, red, lumpy skin around the place he'd been shot. Healthy skin stretched over impressive muscles beneath a mat of chest hair that made her fingers flex against the bedsheets.

The room was still quite dark, except for the bright light leaking just around the edge of the curtain near him, but what light there was put specks of blond through his brown hair. The dim lighting cut shadows across his strong jaw and under his cheekbones. But that all gave him the look of a sleeping mythic hero rather than some sinister villain. And his presence was reassuringly comforting even when he shouldn't have been.

She shouldn't feel safe around Ben. He was very large, making the chair he sat in look comically inadequate and almost like a child's seat, and his jaw was strong enough to look like he could break rocks with it. His expression in sleep was softened. But she remembered the anger when he'd talked about the monsters last night. The coldness when he'd stared at the house deciding how to destroy all those monsters. He hadn't looked soft last night, even after they'd returned to the motel room. And yet, none of that had scared her. She'd felt awkward as hell, and uncertain. But never once had she felt afraid of him.

Hell, even when he'd clamped a hand over her mouth to keep her from screaming at the grinluk, she'd felt more comfortable with him than she should have. A strange man who'd come up behind her and clamped a hand over her mouth? That should have triggered all her most primitive fears, all the childhood nightmares. Instead, she'd leaned into him and found safety with him.

And made excuses to keep him close.

So *strange*.

With the daylight just outside the pale blackout curtains, she considered their mutual decision to work together. They had the same goal. Find the professor and get him away from his captors. Ben had more he wanted from the kidnappers, more information he needed. But getting that also meant rescuing Gabe Arron.

So they'd continue to work together. The relief at that thought felt out of proportion to their current relationship.

Which was…what exactly? How would she describe what they were to each other in that moment?

Associates? Compatriots? Strangers working toward a similar goal?

That last made the most sense and yet seemed the least true. Which was as bizarre as her comfort with a strange man his size sleeping in her motel room.

A handsome man, she thought. That hadn't just been a trick of the adrenaline last night. He was objectively handsome. Quite good looking actually. Especially like this, when he was asleep, when he was relaxed and his expression softened. He was the sort of handsome that made people look twice. But not because the attractiveness was overtly obvious on the first look. That took a minute to sink in. When it did… Well, yeah, he was very attractive.

That thought was fresh in her mind when he blinked his eyes open, looking right at her, catching her in mid-stare.

Thinking about how good looking he was.

She might have blushed. Her cheeks definitely felt too warm for the temperature in the room—which was cool to the point of being cold. Fortunately, the room was dark. He couldn't possibly see a blush in this light, with the TV still casting weird flickering shadows around the place. Still, he'd caught her staring. Which was embarrassing.

Not enough for her to look away. But embarrassing still.

"Good morning," she murmured.

"Morning."

"You're all better, all healed." A silly comment since he would still be the wolf if he wasn't, wouldn't he? "When did you…?" She gestured vaguely in his direction, hoping he understood. She wasn't sure what to call what he did, the whole turning to stone thing. He'd said something about his wolf "leaping," but was that the same for when it went…back in?

"A few hours ago. I didn't want to wake you."

"That chair couldn't be comfortable."

"It was fine."

His voice was a little deeper and huskier this early in the morning. She felt the sound along her spine in a way that wasn't entirely unpleasant but also probably very inappropriate.

Her gaze flicked to his chest, to his healed skin, before she met his stare again. A stare that made her fidgety. But an odd sort of fidgety. Not like she was intimidated and uncomfortable. The stare made her feel like there was too much distance between them and maybe he should be next to her in this bed.

That thought was so *not* like her, she nearly gasped aloud. Was it just that they'd survived something weird and scary last night? Was that why she felt all these out-of-character feelings? This draw to him? Intense circumstances making her feel more attached to him than they actually were?

Probably. At least that was the excuse she was going to use. Because she definitely needed an excuse for the direction of her thoughts.

"We should…" She swallowed and reached for the bottle of water beside the bed, a move that forced her to stop staring at him. "We should make a plan. You need clothes. And we need to find the professor."

"I have to get my gear. I left it in the woods not too far from the house," he said, and his mouth ticked up at one corner. "I have a change of clothes there, if you don't mind me going shirtless a little longer."

"Whatever works." Was she blushing again? She felt like she might be blushing again. She hid that by taking a gulp of water.

"And I'll need to contact my Family. They might have some information to help put us on the grinluk's trail."

She shivered at the reminder of the giant gray monster with eyes on its tentacles. That thing's voice was a sound that turned her brain to a screaming ball of mush. Not something she wanted to confront again. If she could get the professor out without ever seeing a *grinluk* again, she'd count herself lucky. Though she didn't think she was that lucky.

"You have names for monsters," she said, knowing that was part of his still-untold story. A part that really should have made her more nervous.

"We do."

"Your family?"

He nodded.

There was so much more there. But when he didn't comment further, she decided to move on. He'd said he'd explain everything eventually. She just hoped he'd give her that explanation sooner rather than later. "I need to see the house again. Will that be safe? I can start tracking the professor from there."

He raised his brows. "How?"

Rubber, meet road, she thought. "So, you know how you turn into a statue and there's this wolf that jumps out of you?"

He flashed another faint smile that made her heart beat harder.

She gripped the water bottle tighter and sat up in the bed, putting her back to the hard, wooden headboard. "Well…" She let out a long breath. "I don't know what that all is or what you are, but since you have a name for a monster and you do that statue thing, I'm assuming you're not unfamiliar with unique talents and phenomenon?"

"I'm quite familiar with unusual things, yes," he said.

"And, I assume, not in the habit of talking about those unusual things to, say, the authorities?"

"There are things, a lot of things, that it's better the human authorities don't know about. Like monsters. And people like me."

"And people like me," she said, while filing away the way he'd called them "human" authorities. Not the first time he'd referred to humans as if they were *other*.

"You're human." Not a question.

"Well, yes," she answered his non-question anyway. "You aren't, I take it?"

"It's complicated. But I'm human enough if that makes you more comfortable. I'm not one of the monsters."

"I didn't think you were." Had he been worried she did? "I'm a human—" so weird to say that out loud like that, "—but I have this… talent I guess you'd call it."

"You're psychic."

Again, he didn't ask a question. He just made a statement. Like it was a perfectly ordinary thing, being psychic. And maybe it was in his world full of monsters and people with wolves leaping out of them as they turned to stone.

"I have a very specific kind of ability," she said, "which you could call psychic. I don't have a better word for it. I'm a tracker. I find things. I'm very good at it, and I don't always know the hows and whys of my ability to find things. So psychic is as good a word as any."

"You used this skill to find the geneticist?"

She nodded. "I turned finding people into a job. I'm very good at that job." She tried to keep any defensiveness from her voice, but she'd dealt with enough disbelief in her career the defensive bite was still there in her tone, like she had to defend her skills. Because the disbelief hadn't even been from people knowing she was psychic, since she kept that to herself. A lot of people didn't buy that *she* could track so well.

"Why are you telling me?" he asked, his voice quiet.

"It'll make working together easier." Honestly, she wasn't sure beyond that, why she trusted him with the information. Maybe since she knew something personal about him, even if she didn't understand it, maybe she felt the need to share something about herself?

And really, she just didn't want to play games and pretend with him, not if they were going to find the professor before the monsters holding him killed him. She wasn't sure Professor Arron had that kind of time.

"Thank you," he said, again quietly.

The sincerity of his comment caught her off guard. She hid her sudden discomfort by taking another swig of water. "We should get ready. We have a lot of ground to cover today."

"I'll call my Family while you're getting dressed." He glanced at the window. "Do you mind if I step outside?"

Why would she? Now that he didn't have an obvious bullet hole in his chest, no one would look at him twice. Or well, they might because he was shirtless and looked magnificent shirtless. But this was a roadside motel in the middle of northern Michigan. No one was going to get into other people's business if that business didn't look suspicious. And while anyone passing might remember him because how could anyone look at him and *not* remember him, there was no reason for suspicion. Suspicion in other people's minds was what she liked to avoid. Suspicion stuck in the memory.

"I don't mind." She climbed out of bed, grabbed a fresh t-shirt, cargo pants, and clean underclothes from her duffle bag, and disappeared into the bathroom, making an effort not to think about him putting that big body into motion. For some reason, the idea was entirely too interesting.

Yeah. Interesting was the word.

And she was a little afraid of being *interested* in a man whose last name she didn't even know, who knew all about monsters.

CHAPTER TWELVE

Ben stepped out onto the walkway, the cool morning air helping to chill some of the heat building under his skin, the itchy restless feeling he'd had since returning to his human form. The restlessness had him pacing the breezeway near the stairwell, cellphone to his ear as he waited for his brother to pick up.

He knew the restlessness was because of Elle, but he wasn't sure what to do with all this energy. His wolf had ideas about claiming her, ensuring she stayed by seducing her. But... He was still edgy over having leapt through her, over what that might have done to her, to them. And he was very aware of the message his mother had drilled into him over the years.

You can't force her or push her. She has to make the choice.

He couldn't *make* her stay. He had to do this right. If not, he wouldn't break his curse, and he'd remain doomed to a horrible death. And since he'd had a moment, after getting shot, when he would have died if he hadn't leapt at that exact moment, to feel what that death might be like, he didn't want to spend the rest of his life facing that end.

Especially now that he'd actually met his Nam-tar.

Eric Logan, Ben's oldest brother and now the head of the Logan Family—the wolf branch of the Seven Families—answered after two rings. "What happened? Did you find the geneticist?"

"Good to hear from you, too. I'm fine. Thanks for asking."

"Why do my siblings insist on that kind of response to perfectly justified questions?"

Ben smiled despite himself. Eric might be the head of the Family, but giving him shit was still the responsibility of all their brothers and sisters. "I don't have the geneticist. Yet."

"What happened? What went wrong?"

"There was a grinluk there. And a woman…" He hesitated. Did he tell Eric the woman was his Nam-tar? Was he ready to say that out loud yet? He needed to know if he'd fucked things up with Elle already, but… But he couldn't seem to get the words out. "The woman is also trying to rescue Professor Arron from his captors. She was hired by his family."

"Is she going to be a problem?"

"No." Not that kind of problem at least. "We're working together to get Professor Arron back."

"Working with a human woman could complicate things."

Little did Eric know. But since Ben wasn't ready to talk about Elle's significance yet, he instead explained the rest of the night to his brother. As head of the Family, Eric needed to know most of the details anyway. After he'd told Eric about everything they'd seen, he finished with the rain that had put out the house fire.

"An Elemental?" Eric asked quietly.

"If so, it was a helpful one."

"Maybe. Or maybe it was just trying to end the destruction of… whatever the hell it is they're doing."

"I think what they're doing is exactly what we've been worried about. They're making new monsters."

"Or just using old monsters and improving on them."

Their sister Becca had come across a new and improved species of monster a year and a half ago, around the same time Eric had discovered that a sided-Elemental, a Water, was up to some nefarious plan, and that plan had involved the murder of the Logan patriarch, their father.

Two and a half years later, nearly three years, and he still couldn't quite believe his father was gone.

"From what I saw at this house," Ben said, "it looks like they're trying to create new ones, too. The things coming out of the storage crates weren't any variation on currently documented monsters. Those were collections of things combined with a black substance I've never seen before. Maybe those were just…intermediate steps in an experiment. Not supposed to be sentient and turned loose. But even if they weren't meant to be used, they were potentially deadly things. Things that could be used against humans all on their own."

"We need to know exactly what's happening. From one of the people doing the work."

"The woman I'm working with is good at tracking humans. It's what she does for a living. We'll find Professor Aaron."

"He's still a reluctant participant? Not been converted to a willing one like most of the others?"

"Without talking to him, I can't be sure. There wasn't time to hear much of his conversation with his guards before they ran."

"You're healed?" Eric asked. "No residual damage from the bullet?"

"Oh, now you're all brotherly concern." Ben lightened his sardonic comment with a chuckle.

Ben knew Eric's question related to his ability to do the job, too. But he also knew his brother—despite everything—cared what happened to the rest of them. None of them had taken the murder of their father well. But it had been up to Eric to dole out the justice for that murder. And he took his other responsibilities to the Family very seriously. Maybe too seriously sometimes.

Ben was the closest in age to Eric, born only about ten years apart, which for their long-lived Families was really close. They'd been tight growing up. And they'd been close with one cousin too, who'd been about their same age. But that cousin had sided with the monsters and was responsible for their father's murder. Jason had been their friend as well as Family. Ben felt his betrayal deeply, maybe as deeply as Eric did.

But he hadn't been the one who'd had to dole out justice, who'd had to kill Jason. That responsibility, along with everything else, had fallen to Eric. Sometimes, Ben worried about how that affected his brother, how he was dealing with it all. That was why he continued to give Eric grief and treat him like he'd always treated him. With everything Eric was going through, he needed his brothers and sisters to still be his brothers and sisters, not just Family members to coordinate in their divine quest to rid the world of monsters.

"I'm fine," Ben said, with as much reassurance as he could. "I had enough time in the wolf to fully heal."

"The woman…" Eric's hesitance spoke volumes.

"She saw what I did, knows about the wolf. Some of it. Not everything." Yet. But she would know everything. Sooner rather than later.

The silence stretched, long enough Ben narrowed his eyes at the phone, making sure it hadn't disconnected. "What are you thinking so hard about that you've actually shut up?"

"That there's something you're not telling me," Eric said.

"I'm not telling you everything, because I'm not ready to yet."

And that was as much a confession as if he'd just said he'd found his Nam-tar out loud. He was certain Eric would guess. Especially since he'd just found his own Nam-tar only a year and a half ago. So had Becca, in a werewolf of all people. Eric would be very much aware of the…complicated feelings involved in finding one's Nam-tar. Hopefully, that would keep him from pushing for more.

Eric didn't disappoint him. "When you're ready, then. Or you can always call mom. She's good for helpful advice."

"I'll consider that. How's she doing?" He hadn't had time to talk to his mother recently, but they'd all been checking in on her more since their father's death.

"Fine. Tanny's with her. Apparently, there's been a lot of opera involved in their visit."

His mother lived in Vienna and loved opera. Fortunately, their sister Tanya did too, because not all of the siblings did. "Good." He glanced back down the breezeway toward Elle's room. No one was walking around this time of morning, but the highway was busy enough to drown out most casual sounds, even for his sensitive hearing. Being away from Elle, and not being able to hear her moving around, was starting to bother him. The edgy energy turning more… insistent that he return to her.

"I'd better get going," he said.

"Call when you have more information. Or…if you need to…talk."

"Don't choke on that offer," Ben said with a snort. "Call if you hear anything I need to know."

"You have the right weapons if a Water shows up?"

"I make those weapons. Of course I have some on hand." Or well, with his gear still in the woods. But close enough.

Since the first Water had shown up, all the Family had kept Ben's specially made Fire weapons on hand. He'd spent two months after that first appearance making as many of the Fire daggers and Fire arrows as he could manage. The original sided-Water wasn't currently a threat, but there was no telling how many sided-Waters there were, which meant they couldn't be too careful.

The rainstorm last night seemed to confirm that caution. Though he still wasn't sure if that storm had been to help or hinder.

"Don't get killed," Eric said by way of goodbye. "We'll talk soon."

Ben stuffed his cellphone into the pocket of his cargo pants as he stalked back to Elle's room. Don't get killed… Easier said than done.

And now, Ben had a lot more to lose.

He knocked to get back into the room. He didn't have a key, and he hadn't felt safe leaving the door latched open, even though he could have reached Elle's side in an instant if something went wrong and she needed help. Still, she'd been in the bathroom and unprepared for something unexpected. So he'd closed the door and locked himself out.

As he waited for her, he had a brief moment of panicky worry. What if she didn't let him back in? What if she'd already left?

Even though he knew better—he would have noticed since he'd been watching her door—he glanced out over the parking lot, seeing her car just where they'd parked it last night. The relief was enough to make him sag.

When she opened the door, relief turned into something…more restless. And full of anticipation.

He took a moment to study her as she stepped aside to let him in. She'd taken another shower because her hair was still a little damp, and she'd finger-combed the short blond locks into a spiky style that highlighted her high cheekbones and sharp chin. Her blue eyes were surrounded by thick dark lashes, and were almost a little too big for her face. So was her mouth, just a little big for her angular features. And yet everything all worked to create a really striking face.

His Nam-tar was beautiful, yes, but a unique sort of beauty. The kind of beauty he knew he'd want to keep studying for a very long time.

She shifted from one foot to the other, and he realized he'd been staring too long. He gave himself an internal shake, nodded at the bathroom, and said, "I'll be quick. Then we can get on the road. I'll explain some things while we're driving. More private."

Her mouth quirked up. "I would appreciate some explanations, if you're okay with giving them. If not, it's fine, too. Whatever makes you most comfortable."

The way she was careful about his privacy was an intriguing insight into her character. She was very curious. The smell of her curiosity filtered through her scent, a sort of sweet spice flavor, like nutmeg, to her natural flavors. Without the stench of monster and burning house and his own blood in his nose, he was able to pick up her scent better. A subtle, delicious, remarkably complex mix with almonds and vanilla at the base. Last night, he'd thought that slight almond scent might have been the motel's shampoo, but no. It was all her. And like her expressive face, her scent was something he could spend a very long time studying.

He'd known that scent instinctively in the house, one of the ways he'd known she was his Nam-tar. Though he would have known without the scent. Her voice, her breath against his palm, her presence…anything really. It was impossible to mistake that feeling of recognition as anything but what it was. The Families always knew the instant they met their Nam-tar—part of the promise from En. But he would have been able to find her in the dark using only her scent even without having had time to analyze it last night.

The bond, the instantaneous worry for her, the pressure in his chest, the…edginess. Was that because she was his Nam-tar? Or because he'd accidentally leapt through her? Had he already left a little piece of his wolf with her? He'd do that willingly once he earned her, once she decided to stay with him. But she didn't even know that was an option yet.

She shuffled from one foot to the other again, and without looking at him, said, "I…I left one of my flannel shirts in the bathroom. I doubt it's big enough for you, but…in case. Since…" She winced. "I didn't want you to be cold."

He bit back his smile, but only barely and only because she looked so uncomfortable. "I'm not cold, but thank you for the offer."

He'd never fit in anything she could wear, even if she bought her flannels several sizes too big for her. She wasn't exactly tiny. She was maybe five seven, five eight. A good foot shorter than him. And she was curvy, deliciously curvy. Lush was the word that kept coming to mind. The sort of lush that made him regret she'd put a bra back on this morning, though the well fitted t-shirt helped mollify him. But there was just no way anything that fit her even remotely was going to stretch across his shoulders.

This was the second time she'd brought up putting him back in a shirt, though, and each time her scent filled with her reluctant… interest. A hint of sweetened smokey spicy against his tongue. Which only fired his own interest more. And made that restless energy coursing through his blood worse.

Also made him want to stay shirtless, just to see what she'd do about it.

Right now, she was studiously *not* looking directly at him. Her gaze kept jumping around the room, lighting on him only briefly before dancing away again. But when she did glance at him, her pupils dilated a little and that smokey spice flavor threaded through her scent again, and a hint of a pink flush crept across her neck and chest. Keeping his distance took an act of will.

"I'll be back out in a minute," he said, clearing his throat. "You must be hungry. Do you want to go to the diner?"

On cue, her stomach grumbled. And again, he had to bite back a grin. Especially when her cheeks pinkened.

"Hungry, yes, but I don't want to waste time in the diner. Drive thru breakfast somewhere on route is fine." She blinked up at him and her eyes widened. "Oh. Sorry. Unless you need something." Her gaze darted down to his chest again, where the wound had been. "You must need food after…everything yesterday. We can go to the diner."

"Drive thru is fine." He was in a hurry to get back to the house, too. To make sure nothing had escaped. Eric's suspicion that the rain stopped the fire to prevent the destruction of the monsters rather than to prevent a forest fire hovered in the back of Ben's mind. He also worried about the trail to find Professor Arron going cold.

Though, if what Elle had told him was accurate, she had a unique skill for tracking the professor, which was going to be really helpful.

"Okay. That'll work then." She blinked a few times. "My treat. I assume you don't have any cash on you?"

He patted his pockets. "Sorry. No. But I'll pay you—"

She waved away his offer before he'd gotten it out. "You saved my life. Breakfast is the least I can do."

Since she was destined to save *his* life, or at least save him from Ne's curse, he opened his mouth to argue her point. Then snapped it shut. They could have this discussion after she knew more.

He hurried through his morning routine, cleaning up as best he could. There was still blood on his pants, which would draw human attention if they went in anywhere. And his beard scruff gave him a pretty rough look. Maybe that's why Elle didn't want to go into the diner. Between his shirtless state—which meant he probably wouldn't be allowed in the diner anyway—blood on his pants, and his rough appearance, he wasn't really fit company for the public. He rubbed his jaw, wishing for a razor, and a little surprised he cared.

He'd been walking this earth for more than three hundred years. He'd been in wars, fought monsters on every continent, and spent a good part of his time with this form confined in stone while he walked around inside his wolf symbiote. And when he wasn't fighting monsters, he was in his smithy and his workshop, building weapons to help fight monsters, pouring out some of his unique skill, a kind of magic that was rare in the Families, to forge those weapons. Outside of the occasional, required, charity event hosted by his Family, he rarely considered his appearance these days. Hadn't thought much about it since his first fifty years, maybe. Suddenly now, though, he was concerned with a little beard scruff and blood on his clothes.

For Elle.

His mother had warned him. Warned them all. Still, finding his Nam-tar was a jolt in more ways than one.

When he came out of the bathroom, Elle was sitting on the bed, her well-worn, green duffle bag packed and sitting by the door. But she was staring at the television, frowning, even though the volume was muted. He glanced at the screen. Without even reading the closed captioning, he knew what had caught Elle's attention.

"Fuck." He snarled at the TV screen.

"Something got out," Elle murmured. "Didn't it?"

The news was reporting sightings of a strange "animal" that witnesses couldn't quite identify because each story was a little different. They all agreed the thing looked sort of black and slimy, that there may or may not have been tentacles, and some reported a mewing noise, almost like a wounded animal. A few pets had disappeared, witnesses saying this "animal" took them overnight. But there was a lot of confusion around what the creature was. Animal control had been called in and were investigating.

The disappearances were happening in a small town about twenty miles from the house Ben and Elle had blown up last night.

"Either we missed something, something got out, or something was already out when we burned down the house," Ben said. He opened his mouth to say more when his cellphone rang again. He didn't even have to look at the screen. "I'm seeing it," he said to Eric when he answered.

"You got this or you want someone to join you?"

"I've got this," he said. "But I'll let you know if it's bigger than just this one monster."

"Good." A short silence, then, "We're stretched. The appearances have gotten more frequent the last two months. All the Families are stretched."

Ben's frown deepened. He hadn't heard. He knew his immediate family, his brothers and sisters, had been really busy lately chasing down the scientists working with the monsters, trying to stop whatever plot the Water Elemental had put into motion. But he hadn't really considered the bigger picture, or what was happening outside his Family, because that wasn't his job. That was Eric's. Ben's job was to follow his brother's instructions, kill monsters, and make weapons that helped facilitate that divine duty.

He'd had no idea the other Families were stretched. That the monster sightings had increased that much.

"Fuck," he muttered again.

"Yeah," Eric said. "Stay sharp. Let me know if you need backup."

"I will." But if things were that bad, he'd try handling this on his own if he could.

He glanced at Elle as he hung up. "I have a lot to explain."

She nodded, staring at him now instead of the screen.

"I don't have a lot of time for it. I have to go track down that monster and kill it before it starts eating humans instead of just their pets."

She shivered. "Bad enough it's pets." She stood and swept up her bag. "Where to first? The house or the town?"

A strange mix of emotions moved through him so suddenly and unexpectedly he froze in place.

The first closed his throat. Fear. The sort of fear he hadn't experienced in several centuries—until last night. Fear for her. He wanted her nowhere near the monsters. He wanted to put her into a safe, cozy house somewhere with all the comforts she desired, as far away from monsters and death as possible, so she could be safe and alive and not hurt and never have to go through what they'd gone through last night ever again.

The reaction was so instantaneous and complete it took his breath away.

The other reaction was just as sudden, just as instinctive, and just as weirdly complex. He was overjoyed, elated, amazed, awed, and thankful. All at once. Joyous. That his Nam-tar was so strong, so willing to fight to rescue people. So brave. No hesitation at all. Just… let's get to saving the people and killing the monster. It was glorious. And he felt like his heart might explode from just how amazing she was.

All that in an instant. All that mixing together into a push and pull of desires and needs he couldn't even explain. That dual need to whisk her away and protect her, and charge into battle with her at his side… Neither stronger than the other, either. Both reactions were equally strong, demanding he follow through with the same level of urgency. An imperative to do both at the exact same time.

And the combination was so disorienting that he just stood there, blinking at her, not sure what to do next.

Elle broke him out of his stupor. She moved close and put a hand on his arm, her palm warm and soft against his bicep. "It's okay. We'll stop the monster before it gets to any humans. It's okay."

He looked down into her soft eyes, her attempt to reassure him, and finally understood everything his mother had ever said about having a Nam-tar. At least, he was starting to understand. All the things he'd been too arrogant and young to really *get*. He got them now.

How the hell had his father survived this after finding his mother? How had his sister Judith managed? How were Eric and Becca dealing with all this…emotion? Ben felt like he was going to lose his mind and do so happily because it was for Elle.

He still didn't even know her last name.

He gave his head a hard shake, pulling out of thoughts he didn't have time to sort through yet. "We'll go to the town first. I have to take care of the monster that's out there. Then the house. Then we go after Professor Arron."

"Right." She hitched her bag over her shoulder. "Let's get going, then."

He followed her out the door, those dual emotions of fear and elation pumping hard in his chest.

CHAPTER THIRTEEN

lle turned off the highway, taking the exit to the town where the monster had been sighted. Though the news reports hadn't called it a monster. They couldn't, could they? Even if the witnesses might have described it that way. But monsters like the things she'd seen last night weren't supposed to exist outside of horror novels and movies. So of course the thing was labeled an unidentified "animal" and left at that.

She knew better. The minute she'd seen the report, she'd known better.

And she knew people would get killed going after that thing thinking it was just a strange animal. Even if they were careful—assuming the thing was rabid or whatever—animal control was in no way prepared for what they'd find.

She wasn't even prepared to face it, and she had a good idea what she was getting into.

She glanced at Ben. He'd been quiet for most of the drive. She'd hoped for some explanations of what he was, why he had to be the one to kill the monster, how he knew what monsters were. But she was okay with the quiet because her own thoughts were churning and she needed some time to work through them.

Not least because she'd so readily volunteered to go hunt a monster with him.

The response had been instant. No question, no thought. Just…they both had to go stop that monster. Not *he* had to go. *They* had to go.

When the shock of her own instantaneous reaction wore off, she considered offering to split up, divide the tasks ahead. He could go after the monster while she did her thing and tracked Professor Arron. Then Ben could catch up with her after the monster was dead.

But her throat had closed up and her chest tightened and every cell in her body rebelled at the thought of splitting up and not being with him. The reaction was almost like an imperative. Like she *had* to be with him. The idea of her letting him go hunt that monster on his own without knowing what happened, without being there to have his back… She couldn't tolerate the *thought* nonetheless offer to actually do that. The words just refused to leave her mouth.

And that strange reaction kept her quiet as they drove down the highway.

They'd gone through a drive thru for breakfast and coffee, and she'd bolted down her breakfast burrito fast in the parking lot so she could focus on driving. The food had settled like a lump in her belly, but she knew she needed the sustenance so she ignored the sensation. Now that they were on the road to the town with the monster, though, she was feeling that too-hurriedly eaten burrito again as her gut tightened and fear started to send little jolts of adrenaline into her blood stream.

She was really out of her depth here. Until last night, she'd had no idea that monsters like this existed. She didn't know how to fight them. She didn't know how to kill them. And she'd purposefully avoided anything that involved killing for most of her life. Never even considered joining the military or law enforcement. She didn't even go hunting or even fishing as an adult.

Her father had ensured she could kill. Ensured she knew exactly what to do if "the government came for them." And she'd buried that knowledge deep and ensured she wasn't in a position to have to use it.

Yet hadn't she destroyed a lot of the monsters last night with the explosion? Hadn't she just killed last night?

Somehow that felt less…immediate. Less something she'd done and more something she'd witnessed, even though she'd started the explosion. And she wasn't opposed to killing monsters. These were *real* monsters. They couldn't be allowed out in the world. The escaped one was already killing poor innocent pets. It would move on to people. It had to be destroyed.

That wasn't what bothered her.

What bothered her was that she wasn't more bothered about killing the monster. And that she wasn't more afraid even though she was out of her depth. She was scared. But more scared that she was so focused on getting to the creature fast. She was terrified of her own response to the situation.

All of which got mixed up with how she was feeling about Ben, which was equally strange and scary. She didn't even know his last name, and yet the idea of being separated from him caused her actual, physical pain. That wasn't normal.

She glanced at him again, from the corner of her eye. He still didn't have a shirt on. He hadn't even tried to stretch her flannel across those big shoulders, which was probably best. He would have ripped the material. Her hands flexed around the steering wheel as she remembered the feel of his bicep under her palm, the way his muscles had flexed when she'd touched him and he'd leaned in a little closer to her.

Had he even noticed doing that? She'd noticed. Noticed his warmth pumping from his body into hers. The way his skin felt against her palm, smooth and hard and hot. And that got her thinking too much about other parts of him, and what they might feel like. He'd had his arms around her last night. He'd carried her away from the house explosion. She knew what it felt like to be surrounded by him, engulfed by him, and the feeling was…something she wanted more of.

Almost as frightening a thought as this imperative to stay with him.

They were a mile outside the town when Ben finally spoke. "I assume you've guessed I'm familiar with monsters."

She snorted. "That's a Captain Obvious statement, right?"

He narrowed his eyes at her, a gesture she caught from the corner of her eye.

She glanced at him. "Pop culture reference?"

"I get it." He was quiet a moment, then said, "I'm not one of them. The monsters."

"I know. And we've covered that."

"Just verifying. Because…with the wolf thing, some people might assume… But my Family was created specifically to fight monsters. To hunt them down and destroy them before they kill too many humans."

There was a lot in that little speech. She went for the first question that came to her. "Created? Like the way the professor and those others created the things in the crates? Like… Frankenstein's Monster or something?"

"No. By a god. Millenia ago."

"Millenia?" A god? "Which god?"

"Sixteen thousand years. The god En. And no, you won't have heard of him. He and his brother Ne, very very old gods, were renamed and integrated into other gods in early human mythology. The names my Family know them by disappeared to time. En created us to fight the monsters his brother Ne created to destroy humans. Ne's second attempt to destroy humans. En stopped his first attempt, too."

"What'd Ne have against humans?"

"Jealous that his brother and his uncle-mentor loved them. Thought they were a plague on the Earth."

"We kind of are," she said with a pragmatic shrug. "In a lot of ways."

"You want to get eaten by a monster?"

She shuddered and flashed him a scowl. "That's not what I'm saying."

"Sorry. Sensitive subject. Mainly because…the ones behind the professor's kidnapping are working to destroy humanity again for the same reasons Ne created the monsters."

"Cause humans are a plague?"

"Because they're damaging the Earth, yes."

"Very environmentally minded of the bad guys." Her turn to scowl. "Not sure how to feel about that statement since I'd like the Earth to remain habitable, so saving the environment sounds like a good idea. But I also want humanity to survive, since I am a human."

And he wasn't. Not entirely. She was talking about this all like it was normal conversation. Like she was taking in something that she already knew about or suspected. Except all of this was new and weird and sounded like something out of a book or TV show. Gods named Ne and En? Sure. For fiction. But for real life?

Not that she was a god expert. Her father's fucked up version of Christianity got dumped the minute she returned to her mother, and she'd been mostly agnostic about the whole religion thing since. So she had a hard time thinking about all this god talk as anything but mythology and not actually real. Especially when the gods—multiple —were sixteen thousand years old.

"You're not sixteen thousand years old, are you?" she asked, suddenly appalled. She'd made a pop culture reference to a man that old?

"No," he said.

She let out a relieved breath.

"The Families were created that long ago. None of us are that old. But I am over three hundred years old."

"Fuck me," she muttered. Three *hundred* years. As a teenager, she'd assumed if she lived to forty, she'd have won the lottery. Now, in her early thirties, she still had a vague desire just to outlive her father's fifty-five years. If she got there, she'd count that as a win. She couldn't even conceive of three *hundred* years.

"That bothers you?"

"That stuns me. You don't look your age." Though, what would someone who could live that long look like? Did they even show age?

"I can't decide if that was a compliment or not," he said.

She could feel his gaze on the side of her face and her cheeks heated. "You fishing for compliments?" she muttered.

"Maybe."

That response startled a laugh from her. This wasn't a laughing moment. Why was she charmed by his response?

"You look good for you age," she said. "Very good." Too good. Especially without a shirt on. Definitely too good. Her cheeks got hotter. Blushing because she found a three hundred year old man sexy. What had her life become?

No wonder he hadn't blinked at her admission to psychic skills. He had a wolf leap out of his chest occasionally, and he was three hundred years old.

And his family had been *created* by a god named En to fight monsters.

"There's more to the mythology about those old gods, isn't there?" she asked.

"There is. I'll tell you the whole story when we have more time. But you needed to know this is a…a duty for my Family. It's what we do. We hunt and destroy monsters, hopefully before they get to humans. It's my divine duty."

"Divine duty, huh? Sounds pretty serious."

"It is."

"Why are you telling me this?"

There was a beat of silence that carried a lot more weight than Elle thought he meant to convey. Then he said, "You're curious. After last night, you deserve some explanation. And I want you to know. To know what you're getting into. And to know that I *know* what I'm doing and what I'm dealing with."

He was being honest, to a point. But she got the feeling there was more, things he wasn't telling her. "You said families. En created families, not just family."

"There are seven Families."

"Big families?"

She caught his smile from the corner of her eye again. "Mine is big. The Families are large and extended now. But we live a long time, obviously, so there's been time to expand."

"Obviously," she said dryly.

They pulled onto the main road of the small town where reports of missing pets had hit the morning news. A few stores, an open coffee shop, a gas station, some houses. There were a lot of roads branching off, one leading to a giant hardware store, another to a larger grocery store. Some more houses. A nice small town that looked neat and clean and taken care of. Not run down and abandoned. There weren't any closed-up stores or wood-covered windows. Some people climbing out of cars they'd parked along the road or in small parking lots. A couple of people obviously heading out to fish walking out of a bait shop. Not a busy morning, but not so early it was empty.

And somewhere around here, there was a monster lurking.

"Will the monster only come out at night or will it not have that kind of sense?" She had this impression that monsters were a nighttime thing. A thing that only came out after the sun set and that's why the night scared humans so much that they'd invented fire.

Although, if there were old gods who'd created seven whole families to fight the monsters, maybe the gods gave humans fire for the same reason?

Now she was sounding like one of the mystics her mother had loved before becoming an atheist.

She shook off all the deep thoughts. That way lay madness when she had a client's husband to rescue and a monster to stop. She could contemplate old gods when everyone was safe.

Was anyone ever really safe? a small voice that sounded suspiciously like her as a child whispered. She ignored that voice.

"What was at the house was an amalgamation of experiments and different monsters," Ben said, his gaze scanning the streets. "I can't be sure what one of those blobs will do. Most monsters are more active at night. Not all, but most. So chances are good it's in hiding now."

"That helpful or not helpful?" She pulled into a parking lot next to the bait store, hoping they'd have some flannels or something that Ben could use as a shirt. Walking around town with him half-dressed was going to draw too much attention. And it was very distracting for her, too. Being distracted by her three-hundred-year-old associate's impressive chest while hunting a monster seemed like a good way to get eaten by the monster.

She shut off the engine and turned to face him. He was studying the surroundings, a frown tugging down his mouth. The scruff on his cheeks was thicker now, nearly a beard this morning. He looked good with a beard. But she felt an overwhelming desire to see him without one, too. Just to know what he'd look like all cleaned up and clean shaven.

"Helpful in that the monster won't be hunting humans," he said, distracted. "But harder to find."

She used her skills specifically for tracking people most of the time. People were the easiest for her. But they weren't the only things she could find. She'd been able to track down missing pets, animals when her father forced her to go hunting, occasionally objects, though objects were the hardest for her. She knew there were psychics who could find objects really easily, but she wasn't one of those. Her skills leaned toward people. Which was funny, maybe even ironic, given her father's distain for people in general and her mother's overall indifference toward people not related to or loved by her.

But Elle could find things that weren't people. So she might be able to do that with a monster.

"I could attempt to track it," she said, then felt strangely awkward. She didn't talk about this kind of thing with people. Out loud. Like it was normal.

Then again, they were talking about monsters and the fact that Ben was three hundred years old and his family had been specially created by some old gods to fight monsters, so… Really, what was normal now anyway?

Ben gave her a speculative look. "That could be helpful if you're able. But…"

"You want to keep me as far away from the monster as possible?"

His shoulders relaxed with his resigned sigh. "How'd you guess?"

He seemed like that kind of man, but she wasn't sure how to say that without sounding weird. "Your job is to keep monsters from killing humans. I'd assume you wouldn't want to purposefully get more humans around those monsters."

"Good assumption," he muttered, looking out the window again.

His slight frown changed. "Why did you park at the bait shop and not at a grocery store or on the street?"

"Thought they might have a shirt for you," she said with a shrug, trying not to be embarrassed. "Probably draw a lot of attention if you walk around this town without one."

She ignored the little tick at one corner of his mouth that looked suspiciously like a smile.

"Fair enough. Except I don't have any money on me."

She waved that away. "You'll owe me." Not that she'd mention collecting that money ever. Buying him a flannel so *she* was more comfortable didn't seem like something *he* should be paying her back for.

Plus, he'd saved her life last night. She was still reeling from that, processing it. Still considering what it meant to her, beyond being alive. Because it did mean something, that he'd taken a bullet for her, almost died for her. She just…wasn't sure what yet.

The minute they climbed out of the car, Elle was glad they'd decided to dress Ben. He might look scruffy and unshaven, but that did nothing to disguise that he was also magnificent in the full light of day. Like some kind of Viking warrior or something. All he needed was longer hair and braids and the town would start thinking they needed to lock their doors and hide their valuables.

She swallowed when he rounded the car to stand next to her. Gosh, he was big. So big, really he should have been intimidating. Hadn't she just been thinking of him as a Viking warrior? But she wasn't feeling scared or intimidated standing next to him. She was feeling…soft, and antsy, and her stomach fluttered like a teenager. And she really wanted to wrap herself around that big body and see where that took them.

He stared down at her, silent, but his gaze intent, and her heartbeat hammered so hard he could probably hear it. This close, she could feel the warmth of his skin radiating toward her through the cool early spring air. And he smelled…well better than he should given everything. She wasn't sure what it was, just a sort of heady male scent —a ridiculous description but she didn't know how else to describe it. A bit earthy and musky in a good way. There was a hint of the soap from the hotel. And if warmth could have a smell, his warmth did. The kind of smell that wound around her, made her want to lean close, bury her face against his neck, breathe him in, lick his throat, taste his skin…

Still don't even know his last name, Elle, she reminded herself with an internal shake. Rein in the hormones.

She knew he was either divinely destined to hunt monsters or he was delusional, and since she'd seen the monsters last night, she was okay with accepting divine destiny. She knew he had a big family, and she knew he was gentle around her. And he'd saved her life, probably more than once, last night. And he was pretty fucking sexy when she stopped to think about it.

But she *still* didn't know his last name. Feeling like she knew him, or at the very least she could trust him, went against every ounce of training pounded into her from a young age.

That was as terrifying as the monsters.

CHAPTER FOURTEEN

The bait shop felt like one of those familiar places from her childhood, before her father had gone full-blown prepper and disappeared into the woods, taking her with him. When things had still felt safe and normal. The smell of earth, salt, and fish. The scuffed hardwood floors and pictures of huge catches on the walls. The shelves of fishing gear, spools of fishing line, racks of poles and nets, boxes of various lures, and hooks in all sizes.

And to Elle's great relief, a couple of circular racks with flannel shirts and t-shirts near the back of the store, by the wader pants and rubber boots.

She made a beeline for the shirts, because she needed to get Ben dressed for her own sanity.

He'd followed her into the store, prowling behind her like a protective bodyguard, like he was the wolf now instead of in his human body. And again, that knowledge that she should be more intimidated and less turned on by this didn't stop her from being turned on. Really, the way he kept his attention, his full focus, completely on her should have made her uncomfortable. Why was she comforted instead?

She plucked a few extra-large flannels off the rack and handed them to him without looking. "Anything you like? We should get a few backup t-shirts, too." She thumbed through the shirts and picked a few that were as plain as possible. She wasn't sure if he liked giant fish and pithy sayings on his shirts, but since they were going to find and destroy a monster, she felt plain might be more appropriate.

Then again, what did she know?

He took what she handed him without a word. When she finally looked at him with raised brows, he said, "Anything is good." He wasn't even holding the clothes up to see if they'd fit.

She sighed. "Is any of that going to fit you? Which ones do you want?"

He glanced at the flannels she'd handed him, at the inner tag with the size on it, and shrugged. "They'll fit." Then he looked at her patiently.

That was it. That was the extent of his opinion on the pile of clothing? She shook her head. There was a phrase for this, right? Low maintenance or something? Except the low and high maintenance labels had always sounded judgy to her. But he definitely didn't seem very fussy about his clothes.

Since there weren't a lot of choices available, probably a good thing he didn't care. "Which one do you want?"

He glanced at the pile of material in his arms again. There was a beat when she had no idea what he was thinking. And then he gently hung everything but one blue flannel shirt and a relatively plain black t-shirt back on the rack. "Perfect," he said.

Okay. "One more t-shirt. Just in case." She murmured this as she held his gaze. Killing a monster was going to be messy. And yes, they'd go get his gear afterward, but in the meantime… Just in case.

He reluctantly picked up a second black t-shirt.

She wondered at his reluctance, though. Glancing at his stained pants, she sighed. Not a lot to be done about that. The only "pants" in the store were hip waders for river fishing and she figured those would be too awkward for running after monsters. His pants were stained, and the light tan color didn't hide the dark brown spots, but she could almost pretend they didn't look like blood. Hopefully, other people would think paint first and not look any closer.

At the register, the man ringing up their purchases kept giving Ben wary glances. The store clerk wasn't exactly a small man himself, probably six foot and broad enough he didn't seem like the type of person easily intimidated. His thick beard and mustache hid some of his expression, but the wariness in his quick, fleeting glances at Ben were hard to miss. He wore a ball cap with the name of the bait shop embossed on the front, and he tipped the rim back when he gave her the cost of their purchases.

It occurred to her that the fact that Ben didn't have a shirt on was probably the thing making the clerk leery. That and Ben's size. But there weren't any questions, or comments, and the clerk didn't impose the "no shirt, no shoes, no service" sign that hung just behind the register.

She paid with cash, as she did with most things even though she had a credit card for emergencies, and waved off a bag. Ben slipped on one of the black t-shirts as they walked out the door, the little bell overhead ringing as they left.

When they were back in the parking lot, she let out a long breath.

"Was something wrong in there?" Ben asked.

She blinked, surprised he'd noticed her tension. "Beyond the clerk paying too much attention to you when we're here to hunt for a monster and that might draw the attention of the authorities?"

"Besides that," he said, his mouth ticking up at one corner.

"No, nothing wrong." She shook her head, then shrugged. "Place just…invoked some childhood memories, I suppose. But mostly, I was hoping we could do that without making an impression on anyone. The clerk will remember us, though. He'll remember what we looked like, what time we were here."

"It won't be a problem," Ben said, quietly. "I promise. My Family is used to handling these kinds of things."

She let out a little huff. She supposed they would be, wouldn't they? Given how old he was, and the fact that she'd gone her whole life never hearing even a whiff of stories about people who had animals leap from them while they turned to stone, she was going to assume his family was pretty adept at keeping secrets.

Elle had mixed feelings about secrets. She liked them—she had many of her own she intended to keep—but secrecy as a verb reminded her too much of those paranoid years with her father. That created a complicated set of emotions around something she generally found useful.

"It's fine," she said. "So long as we get to the monster before it gets away."

Ben stepped closer, and her heart started that pounding thing again. The urge to lean into him a lot stronger than the urge to step away. He'd shrugged on the flannel over his t-shirt on the way to the car. Having his magnificent chest and shoulders covered should have helped. It didn't. He still looked way too impressive. Comfortable in the ordinary clothes and still somehow magnificent, as if he was wearing more than just a t-shirt and blue flannel.

Yeah, he just wasn't the sort of man to blend into his surroundings.

For some reason, that left her as edgy and restless as the need to see how flannel felt covering his thick biceps.

When he leaned down, just a little, she caught her breath. Time to step away from him, time to break whatever the hell spell this was.

She couldn't seem to find the will to move.

But instead of getting even closer, he lowered his voice to say, "I don't suppose I could talk you into staying here in town. Going into that coffee shop and waiting for me?" He gestured across the street to a little mom-and-pop place with a big neon "coffee" sign over the door.

"You want to go hunting monsters on your own and leave me behind in the town?"

"I…" His frown deepened, creating ridges between his brows. "It'll be safer here. This isn't your job. It's mine."

"And what if the monster comes wandering through town while you're somewhere else?" Not likely, she knew, but still. The safest place in this town was right next to the person who actually knew what they were facing and how to kill it. Besides, letting him go off into danger without anyone having his back felt absolutely gut-wrenching. She couldn't do it, even if she'd wanted to. Which she didn't. "I'll go with you."

A complex play of emotions crossed his expression. Most of them she couldn't read. But the way his shoulders relaxed a little, the way he let out a quiet breath that brushed her temple, he almost seemed… relieved. Huh. She wasn't sure what to make of that.

"Okay," he said. "We need to find a quiet place to leave the car, somewhere no one will think about it but where I can pull the sword out without anyone noticing."

She'd nearly forgotten about the sword he'd taken from the guard last night, and then shoved under the backseat so no one casually looking into the car would see it.

"There's probably a quiet street at the outskirts of town. We'll find something." There might even be a place by a lake or river, where people would assume the car belonged to someone fishing. She didn't know this immediate area, so she'd have to check on her phone's map app. "Anything else?"

"Just…you're sure you want to come with me? It won't be pretty. It'll be dangerous."

"You're not going alone," she said firmly. "Besides, I can find the thing easier, with less obvious poking around." At least she hoped she could do her thing with the monster. She'd only tracked human monsters in the past.

"Do you need anything to help you?" he asked. "A…way to link to the monster?" He whispered the words, careful of the occasional person passing on the sidewalk only a few yards away.

She forced herself to look away from him, only realizing she'd been staring this whole time when she finally dragged her attention to their surroundings. "I need to get quiet and focus on it," she said. "Sometimes that's all it takes, if I'm in the right vicinity. It helps, having something of the person's I'm trying to track, but not absolutely necessary."

That was how she'd originally started tracking Professor Arron, though. His wife had given Elle one of his favorite ties, not because Sherry knew it would help Elle find her husband, but because she wanted Elle to give it to him when she found him.

Elle thought of the news report, the neighborhood where the pets had gone missing, where the strange sightings had been. Location helped a lot. She was going to use location to pick up the professor's trail again. Without something of the monster's to use, and without a clear image of the creature itself to draw on, location might be her best option.

"The other thing that helps is going to the last location someone was seen. Let's find the monster's last known location, and I can track it from there."

Without a word, he nodded and rounded the car to get in. Being able to talk about all this, without have to prevaricate or come up with a realistic explanation was incredibly freeing. But also felt very strange and maybe even a little too intimate.

They found a quiet street near the part of town where the monster has been sighted, a street next to a small playground and not too far from a river. It was a weekday, a school day, so there weren't any kids in the playground, and they were far enough away the car didn't look suspicious. Hopefully, with the river so close, people who didn't recognize the car would assume it belonged to someone fishing or a tourist. It was a strange time of year for tourists, but still possible this early in the spring.

Ben carefully scanned the area, a frown making a crease between his brows. "Daylight is tricky," he muttered. "Someone's going to see me walking around with the sword."

"And no handy scabbard to try and disguise it," she said, also scanning their surroundings. There was no one here to see Ben pull out the sword, but they would be walking around where people might see them. Unless the trail for the monster led into the woods encircling the town and away from the populated areas.

"Let me see if I can find a direction to go," she said. "Before we start trying to figure out a way to hide the sword."

He nodded, continuing to scan the area in between glancing her direction.

She let her gaze soften and stepped a few feet away from the car, studying the houses she could see through patches of pine trees. The river that led deeper into the woods. The empty playground. There were a few houses beyond the playground visible through some more pines, along a curved street on the opposite side of the river. The closest house to their parking spot was one of the places that had a pet disappear.

It had turned into a truly beautiful day. Clear blue skies, chill in the air that wasn't too cold, green pines all around, and flowers popping up in a handful of yards. The generous number of trees throughout the town, and patches of thick woods rolling up close to the edges of town, gave the monster a lot of good hiding places, though. Plus, there'd be deer in the woods to eat.

Unfortunately, there might also be fishermen.

She tried to picture the goo things she and Ben had escaped last night, all that creeping black gunk filled with weird and random body parts. The strange sightings reported in the news were just hints of shadows and something that looked like maybe tentacles, though most assumed that was a trick of the darkness, and an assumption of bear or wolf seemed to have been the closest natural explanation anyone could come up with. Which made Elle think of teeth and claws. Had anyone seen teeth and claws, or were they just scared and *thought* of teeth and claws?

Another slow circle, her eyes half-closed, as she swept the surroundings, thinking about finding the monster. And then, a tingling down her spine, an unexplainable *push* in a specific direction. When she took a single step that way, her body hummed, like a tuning fork, vibrating with the correctness of going that way. She could *feel* she was on the right trail.

And the right trail led, she was relieved to see, into the woods.

Without looking at Ben, without looking away from the direction her instincts pushed her, she said, "If you were doing this on your own, which way would you go?"

"Toward the woods, the area behind the house where the last pet disappeared. I'd look for evidence of the monster, broken branches, scraped ground, scat, evidence of blood. My senses are better than a human's so I can see and smell things more like my wolf. I'd use smell and an awareness of small disturbances to attempt to track the creature.

Once I get the scent, tracking is easier. I can follow that. But I'd have to hunt around for it first, until I picked up the monster's trail."

She nodded, smiling. He'd given her such a thorough answer, more than she thought he might. Like they were partners. Like she had a right to ask the question and a right to more than a cursory answer.

"If I was working with someone who didn't know about my psychic skill," she said quietly, "that's how I'd pretend to find the monster's path. Not that I have the sense of smell to work with, but the other things… I'd make it look like I'd picked a few directions based on a logical guess—location where the last animal was taken—and then I'd pretend to hunt around for signs of disturbance. Sometimes, I'd even see that disturbance and be able to point to it. But the entire time, I'd know which way to go."

"You know where to go now."

There was no question in his sentence. Her smile grew, turned crooked. And she wasn't entirely sure why his assurance made her happy.

"This way," she said, walking him toward the woods.

CHAPTER FIFTEEN

Ben used his newly purchased flannel shirt and wrapped it around the sword, holding the entire thing against his thigh and hoping any casual observers would just see a man carrying a flannel shirt in a strange way.

He was feeling a little strange, but not because of the hunt or the possibility of being observed by nosy humans. Strange because he was hunting with his Nam-tar.

And she was good at it.

For some reason, when he'd thought about his Nam-tar more in his youth, it hadn't occurred to him that she'd be able to track monsters. That was his job. His Nam-tar could be anything, could have any sort of passion or job. The idea that she might have skills that made hunting and tracking monsters easier hadn't crossed his mind. In hindsight, he wasn't sure why. Except that most of the Nam-tar in his Family, and those he'd met from other Families, had stayed out of the monster hunting side of things. None of them had had Elle's specific skill set.

After more than three centuries, he'd assumed he'd seen it all. He'd been wrong.

And watching Elle work was a revelation.

She walked into a section of pines and sugar maple behind a row of three houses set relatively close together. This section of trees bracketed the river that ran through town and led into the deeper woods beyond town. They followed along the river, keeping to one bank as Elle continually glanced between their side of the water and the opposite bank.

The river was high, the water moving rapidly, bubbling over rocks. The setting might have been idyllic with sunshine filtering through the trees, the noisy roll of the river, and the scent of fresh water and pine sap melded with rich soil. But the knowledge that a monster lurked in these woods somewhere robbed the scenery of its perfection.

The section of river they followed wasn't particularly wide. Too wide for a human to jump across, though. There were some road bridges through town, but where he and Elle were walking, there weren't any handy bridges or logs crossing from one bank to the other. The water was too high and moving too fast for Elle to ford it. But so far, her tracking instincts had kept them on this side of the river.

He studied her almost as much as he studied their surroundings. On a hunt, being distracted could get them both killed, but he couldn't seem to look away from her for long. Every cell in his body was drawn to her. He was amazed by his own relief that she'd come on this hunt with him even though she was a distraction and she was in danger here. But at least if she stayed with him, he could protect her. He'd know what she was doing, where she was, and he'd be able to keep her safe. If she'd remained in town, he wouldn't be able to ensure her safety. And ensuring she was safe was as important to him as his next breath. Maybe even more so.

She'd bought him clothes.

The thought kept springing up, out of the blue, the memory of her plucking things off the rack and handing them to him without looking at him. The way he'd just stood there holding everything she gave him, prepared to take it all if that made her happy. Only realizing when she asked what he wanted that he wasn't paying for all this. At least not immediately. He had no idea what her finances were like, and he'd felt like an ass that it hadn't occurred to him before that moment. He didn't often think about money, unless he needed a large amount for a weapon he was making, but since that was for the Family, the money was readily made available. All his other needs were seen to by Family money—and the Logan's had a lot of it—so he just didn't pause to think about it much.

But most humans did. Most humans had to worry about where their money came from, how they'd pay for things, where their meals and housing came from… She'd been paying for everything so far because he didn't have access to his money. If she hadn't been, he'd have just managed. Returned to his gear, where he had food and clothes and cards and cash to handle anything he might need next on the hunt. But she'd been generously ensuring he had food and clothes. Taking care of him. Someone she viewed as mostly a stranger.

He was humbled by her kindness. And he desperately hoped she'd let him repay that care.

The moments by her car outside the bait shop, when he'd leaned close and she'd reacted to his nearness, when he'd scented her desire rising, had tested his patience. He was, in general, a very patient man. He had to be to create weapons that often took days, weeks, sometimes months of work. Stalking monsters could take time, too.

But when it came to Elle, when he really needed to be patient, to ensure he didn't chase her away, his patience seemed to be in short supply. Because in those moments, with the heady scent of her desire between them, he'd been very close to sweeping her against him and tasting that lush mouth, tasting all those flavors of her scent on his tongue. He very much wanted to see if her skin felt as silky as it looked, to tunnel his fingers through her short hair, to devour her mouth until she moaned. *Not* doing those things pushed his patience to the breaking point.

Only the sound of his mother's voice telling him he couldn't rush or force his Nam-tar into staying ensured he kept his hands to himself.

Well, that and the fact that they had a monster to catch.

Within a mile of the nearest house, Ben started to see evidence of that monster. Subtle at first. Some broken branches, a smoothed path through a patch of detritus. A possible print in the wet soil along the river bank. Nothing too obvious, things easily missed if he hadn't been watching for them. But the little signs confirmed they were on the right path.

Quickly, thanks to Elle.

A slight snuffling sound ahead, too faint for human ears, stopped him in his tracks. To his amazement, Elle stopped too, before he could warn her. She shouldn't be able to hear that noise. He barely heard it. Was she that attuned to him? The idea thrilled him, but they hadn't even known each other for twenty-four hours yet. That would be…fast.

The faint noise distracted him and he turned his full attention to the potential threat ahead. With a gentle hand around her bicep, he eased Elle behind him. She didn't argue. Didn't even comment when he handed her the flannel shirt that had been covering the sword.

The sword was a good one. Well balanced and weighted. He'd barely had time to notice that last night, but as he silently stalked closer to that very faint noise, passing the sword to his dominant left hand, he could appreciate the weapon better. He was still curious why a human guard with a gun felt the need for the sword, but given what the man had been guarding, what had been in those crates, he was inclined to think that guard knew what he was doing more than the others.

A patch of fern ahead, not far from the river bank, shimmied. Again, very faintly. The sort of movement someone not paying attention might think was just the breeze blowing through the undergrowth. Might walk past that patch of undergrowth without any idea what was waiting inside.

Even as close as he was, Ben couldn't see anything directly. Either the monster was quite small, or it was able to make itself small. He picked up the stench now, but it wasn't as strong as what had been in the crates. Not pleasant, but almost entirely hidden beneath the stronger smells of earth and pine and river. Another passing animal would give the ferns a wide berth, but might also not pick up the danger until too late. He had to get pretty close before the faint sewage and rot smell crept out to him.

He was expecting a sort of goo animal amalgam, like the things in the crates. Something that had gotten away from the house as it burned and escaped his notice. And what was in the ferns could still be that.

But there had been other things in that house. There'd been freezers with things in them. Things that were still there before he and Elle had had to flee. The grinluk and humans hadn't emptied the freezers. One of those experiments could have gotten out.

The patch of fern shivered again. Barely. A brush of breeze. Another faint scuffing sound. The creeping stench of rot. The sounds of the river as it raced over stones and rocks covered his own movements, but also made it harder to detect more than those faint sounds from the monster.

He was within a foot of the ferns, his sword stretched in front of him, ready to part the long leaves, when a sharp sound pierced the quiet and a tentacle snapped out.

Ben sliced through the limb and jumped back a few feet in an instant, instinctive reaction. The creature rolled out of cover moving as fast as Ben, it's lost limb barely seeming to register and certainly not slowing it down.

Ben had a chance to take in the rounded gray body—not black goo—and brown feathers along its spine. Spikes circling a head that looked sort of pig-like, but also long and horsy. Tentacles as well as clawed bird legs pulled it across the damp ground. No wings. No tail. And only four large remaining tentacles. But each was as thick as his thigh, and the creature used them to move like a spider. It's clawed bird legs were tucked up under the gray blob of its body.

That was as much as he could catalogue before the creature attacked, strange horse mouth opened under the pig-like snout to reveal a circular hole of teeth. Layers of teeth moving down its throat.

A tentacle snapped out at him again. He sliced through it, leaping away, closer to the river and away from Elle. The creature followed him, skittering around to face him. He got a second chance at the injured tentacle and severed it cleanly from the body this time. The creature didn't screech or react to the limb's removal at all beyond a slight stumble in its forward movement.

Over the creature, he spotted Elle, hanging back and using the cover of a pine tree to stay out of the way. The relief nearly distracted him. Washed through him so hard he had to blink back spots. But then the creature skittered close and he had to focus.

An incongruous mewing sound came from the creature's mouth snout, a noise that didn't seem to go with either a pig or a horse. The mewing noise crawled along his skin, making the hairs on the back of his neck prickle.

This wasn't a familiar monster, not something they had a name for and a biological history of, a catalogue of vulnerabilities and weapons. But unlike the goo monsters in the house last night, the "head" on this one was obvious.

Which meant he knew exactly what he had to remove to kill the beast.

The neck spikes, however, complicated matters.

One of the remaining three tentacles swatted at him as the creature lowered closer to the ground and stood on the clawed bird legs finally. This left all three tentacles free to swat at him, but also left the creature awkwardly balanced and it fell onto its face once without any help from his sword.

Ben drew the creature back farther, getting it safely away from Elle before he killed it. He had no idea what sort of fluids would flow from this thing when he cut its head off—the big problem with not knowing the monster's basic biological makeup—and he didn't want to risk her getting sprayed with something deadly to vulnerable human skin.

His skin… Well, it would heal in his statue form. He could jump to the wolf if he needed to. Elle didn't have that luxury.

The monster lunged toward him again, a new, higher pitched sound leaving its teeth-lined mouth. It used two tentacles and its bird legs to move while it whipped the remaining tentacle at him. He made note of the tiny pin-sized spines sticking out of the end of the tentacles, something he'd have analyzed if he could get any of the monster to his sister.

He slashed through the flailing tentacle, severing it completely, then took another as the monster tried to get around him. With only one tentacle and two bird legs left to move around on, the monster's attacks slowed.

Ben pressed his advantage, pushing the monster into the knot of roots beneath a maple. He swung for the creature's head, cut through spikes instead, and cursed when the monster lunged for him.

Damned spikes around its neck. He swung a few more times, once again impressed with the weight and balance of his acquired sword, and pleased the guard had kept it in good shape, sharp and clean. He hated when people didn't care properly for their weapons.

Two more hacks broke off enough spikes to expose the neck.

He took the head with a final swing.

The monster's strange horsy-pig head rolled like a barrel toward the river, stopping in thick brush and mud on the bank. The body collapsed like a deflated balloon as goo like the black stuff from last night ran out of it and pooled on the dark soil. The faint stench he'd picked up from the monster earlier now filled the area with rot and sewage. Strong enough to make him wince and regret his excellent sense of smell.

The hissing noise the goo made when it came into contact with the damp dirt made him glad he'd led the beast away from Elle.

When she came out from behind the tree and started walking toward him, he pointed at the goo with his sword. "Stay back. I'm pretty sure this stuff is not safe."

She froze in her tracks, staring at the flattened monster body and the goo bubbling out of it. "I'm not sure I've ever smelled anything that bad before in my entire life," she said, backing closer to the pine tree again. "Except for maybe last night."

"Are you going to throw up?" He made a move toward her but she waved him away.

"No. But only because I'm over here. I'm not going to be able to get closer."

"I don't want you closer. I'll take care of cleaning this up."

He glanced around at all the wet wood. Actually, burning the creature was going to take some effort. But he had to ensure the body burned thoroughly so no unsuspecting human or other animal came across the remains and hurt themselves.

"You still have those matches?" he asked.

"Of course." She pulled them out of her thigh pocket. "I'm not this good a shot, though. If I throw them to you, they're going to end up in the mud." She looked around. "I can help gather good wood for a fire." She faced him again. "I assume that's what you're going to do? Burn the remains."

He had to force himself not to smile because this wasn't a smiling moment, but the fact that she understood all this without explanation and was so willing to help was… He wasn't sure.

Amazing was the closest word he had. And it made him feel more hopeful for the future than he could ever remember feeling.

So long as he could keep her.

Ben carefully skirted the flattened carcass and the bubbling goo as he headed toward Elle, eager to put a little distance between him and the monster's stench. "Stay where you are, I'll come to you for the matches. I do need to burn everything. Can't have random animals finding this since I don't know what this black stuff does."

He frowned, considering the monster's death. There hadn't been any internal organs inside it. Just the goo. The goo seemed to be the stuff that animated it.

Most of Ne's monsters, the ones he'd originally created and the ones that evolved from those first creatures, had some internal biology similar to other animals. Not the same. But there was usually a heart and blood and a digestive system of some kind. Nothing was necessarily in a place one might expect, but all the various bits were there. Depending on the species there could be lungs or gills, but still something that allowed for the exchange of oxygen and carbon dioxide. There were even a few species that made that exchange like a plant, through stomata-like pores, and had chlorophyl bodies inside their cells for turning sunlight into energy—energy the monster used to hunt and kill humans. While all of it was strange and unique to the monsters, it all followed a sort of biological sense.

Ben had never encountered a monster whose entire body was filled with nothing but a gelatinous mass. No blood or digestive track or anything. Just the goo. Like the monsters at the house yesterday, only more…put together.

Was this what the scientists were doing? Not just creating new monsters, not just forcing the evolution of older monsters, but making an entirely new *kind* of monster?

If so, that had serious repercussions. Not least was that the Families wouldn't have any idea what they were up against going forward.

That was how the hunters ended up dead.

"You okay?"

The sound of Elle's voice so close made him look up. He hadn't realized he'd reached her already, and that was a sure sign of how distracted he'd been. Because now that he noticed she was right in front of him, her scent wrapped around him and drew him even closer. He resisted the pull, because he hadn't cleaned up after the fight, hadn't ensured he didn't have any of that goo anywhere, and he didn't want to risk getting any on her.

But the desire to wrap her up in his arms and see if that scent flavored her kiss kept all his muscles tight when he reached for the matches she offered.

"I was thinking of the fact that the monster doesn't have any internal organs," he said, "just that goo."

"Not normal?"

"Not typical, no. Never encountered a monster like this before."

"That sounds bad. Since it's your…your job, right?"

"My job." He nodded. "My duty. My Family's duty. And we've catalogued all the monsters that exist or have existed for the last sixteen thousand years. This kind of change is…"

"Scary and dangerous."

He nodded. "Very."

She swallowed and glanced past him. "It is dead, right? I mean, since it's new…"

He followed her gaze to the flattened carcass, then toward the head where it remained lodged in the mud near the fast-moving river. "It's dead. Removing the head kills all monsters. It's the only way to kill them."

She was frowning at the carcass when he faced her again. "But, if this is new, if you don't know how these monsters work, doesn't that mean killing them might be different, too?" She blinked at him. "There are other monsters involved. That thing with the tentacles. And a geneticist was kidnapped to work on all this. Isn't it possible, if they created a whole new kind of monster, they'd also changed the way they're killed?"

Ben hadn't thought the knot in his gut could get any tighter. He glanced back at the flattened creature again. Nothing around the body moved except the still bubbling goo. The head remained where it was. The tentacles he'd severed didn't spontaneously start flailing.

But she was right. If the scientists were creating monsters the Families couldn't predict, creating brand new things, there was no reason they couldn't also be changing the way the things died.

Or what happened after they died.

Suddenly that bubbling goo felt like a threat.

"We need dry wood. Now."

Elle didn't hesitate. She hurried back into the trees behind them while he stared at the monster's remains, at the head, hoping this new fear clutching his chest was unfounded. Most things died when you removed their heads. Even vampires and faeries and other beings considered immortal. Removing the head and burning the body to ash ensured death in…everything. Nothing survived that.

But the burning to ash part of the process had never felt more important. And not just because some unsuspecting animal might come across dangerous remains. He couldn't even risk saving some of the monster for his sister Judith to analyze. Everything had to burn.

He heard Elle's returning footsteps before she spoke. The quiet sounds of her breathing more settling than he would have expected.

"I got enough to get a fire started." She nudged him with her shoulder then handed him an armful of sticks when he looked down at her. "I'll get more while you get things going. We need to burn it completely, don't we?"

"Yes."

By the time she returned with more sticks, he had a fire burning over the top of the carcass. The black goo crackled and popped as the fire caught it, ratcheting up the stench so much it made his stomach turn. And he'd smelled some truly horrific things over the years.

"I might throw up," Elle said, from a good twenty yards away.

"Wouldn't blame you," he muttered, flexing his nostrils in an attempt to keep them closed. The wolf spirit that lived inside him shifted restlessly at the stench. That sign of discomfort with the smell just confirmed how horrendous it was. "It's burning," he said. "That's good at least."

"I'm leaving the wood here. I'll go get more. Thoroughly burned, right?" she repeated, as if assuring herself that was the goal.

"Down to ash."

She dropped the kindling and hurried back into the trees, no doubt trying to escape the smell. He wouldn't have minded going with her. But he had to make sure the body burned.

Once he was certain the fire wouldn't go out, he skewered the head with the sword and carefully carried it to the fire. More of the goo dripped down the sword from the head so he held it away from him. Then he skewered each of the severed tentacles and added those to the fire. After he'd tossed everything in, he used the flames to clean the sword. He didn't dare just wipe the goo off. He didn't want to get his skin that close to it.

He collected the second pile of sticks Elle had left—once again all dry wood that would burn rather than smoke—and fed them into the fire. Then he searched the area around where the head had been, where the tentacles had fallen, and the paths he'd walked bringing everything back to the fire, hunting for drips of the goo. Anything he found with the substance on it, any leaf or stick or rock, went into the flames, too.

By the time Elle returned with a third, larger haul of kindling, Ben was confident he'd cleaned the entire area. The only goo he'd missed was anything that had sunk into the soil and was no longer visible. That possibility nagged at him, worried him, but he wasn't sure what to do about it. He couldn't burn the entire area—damp as it was, he could start a forest fire and this area was entirely too close to the town. They'd risked that danger last night because they'd had to. And the downpour, whether that was luck or had a more supernatural explanation, had stopped the fire spreading. He couldn't count on that kind of luck—or intervention—today.

When he joined Elle to get the last of the wood, she was studying the small fire he had going, one hand covering her nose and mouth to block the smell. Around that, she said, "This is working?"

"Seems to be."

"You can clean the sword in the fire."

He couldn't help his quick, brief smile. "Yes. Already done, but I'll give it another few minutes in the flames to make sure I got everything."

She gave him a sideways glance. "Sorry. I should have assumed you'd know that."

"It's fine. You don't know me very well." Yet. "But for the record, I know my way around weapons."

"Since you fight monsters, that makes sense."

"I also make a lot of our weapons. I'm a blacksmith."

And he had just a little magic tied in with that skill. Most of the Families didn't have traditional magic. There were some individual members with some magical skills, though, in almost every generation. At least one member of every Family with a skill like his turned up. The ability to make certain weapons was imperative to fighting the monsters. In his Family, that ability, and responsibility, fell to him.

She faced him, her eyes wide. "You make the weapons? Like swords and stuff?"

"And stuff," he said. "I have a collection of weaponry in my gear. I'll show it to you when I get it."

"I'd love that."

Why did he want to preen at her pleasure?

But her pleasure banked a moment later and something clouded her eyes. She glanced away before he could analyze those clouds. When she spoke, she still sounded happy. "That's a really cool skill. You don't meet a lot of blacksmiths nowadays." She shrugged. "At least I haven't."

"Met a few, though?" he asked, half-joking.

"One or two." She spoke quietly, and the lightness in her tone dimmed.

There was a story there. One he wanted to dig into that very moment. But they didn't have the time. Would she even trust him with her stories yet? Maybe not. He'd have to earn those.

And he intended on doing just that. Soon.

CHAPTER SIXTEEN

en fed the rest of the wood Elle had collected into the flames, watching the remains of the monster burn. The river bubbled loudly over rocks a few feet away, but even the circling pines and clean water couldn't hide the stench of the creature. He was glad Elle was keeping well away. His eyes were watering from the smell.

As the creature burned, he hunted the surrounding area again, looking for any of the goo that might have escaped his attention. A nagging sense of unease had settled in his chest, about that stuff making up the monster's insides, animating it. He knew some of it could have sunk into the earth beyond reach, but he didn't want to risk any on the surface.

He also needed to call Eric soon and tell him about all this so he could pass the word to the others.

"Find anything else?" Elle called from her place near a pine tree twenty yards away. She still had a hand covering her mouth and nose, so her voice was muffled. But he'd have been able to hear her even if she hadn't been shouting.

"Nothing on the surface anymore," he said.

"And nothing to be done about any that might have soaked into the ground," she said.

Confirming once again that she picked up on all this without him having to explain. She had only learned the Seven Families existed that morning. She had only learned monsters existed last night. Her ability to adapt to his world was nothing short of a miracle. She was a miracle.

"Ben," she called again, her voice sounding strained. "Look at the fire. What's happening? I'm too far away to see it clearly."

He scowled, walking slowly back, his gut tightening. He held his newly cleaned sword out in front of himself, angled down, at the ready. Why he felt the need, he wasn't sure. Instincts.

Even before he got close to the fire, he spotted what Elle had seen. Near the base in the wood, something dark seemed to be popping up into the white-orange flames. The closer he got, the clearer those shadows became.

"Fucking hell." One curse wasn't enough, so he cursed a few more times.

"What's wrong? What is it?"

Inside the flames, little…things—monsters, miniature versions of the thing he'd just killed—were jumping out of the black goo as it burned, then catching fire and burning up themselves. A bubble in the boiling goo burst while he watched and another one of the little monsters popped out. It caught fire instantly, but still tried to make a run for the edge of the flames. It burned to ash before it made the side of the pit, sinking back into the wood and growing pile of ash inside the fire. But even as it did, another bubble burst and another monster popped out.

Ben frantically hunted the surroundings, looking for any of those miniature monsters that might have actually escaped the fire, any little running sparks of flame.

"What is it?" Elle called again, her voice growing more frantic.

Her panic forced his own back under control so he could reassure her. "The fire is destroying them," he said, then winced when he heard her squeak.

"Them? Them what?"

The little monsters looked a bit like misshapen spiders as they rose out of the goo bubbles and caught fire. There wasn't much goo left, thankfully. It burned to ash as he watched, but he didn't dare move away again until all of it burned. He kept one eye on the fire and continued to scan the area for any escaped flames, any new fires starting where they shouldn't.

Things just kept getting fucking worse. How was all this happening *right* when he met his Nam-tar? No time to even get her last name. No time to do any of the normal courtship rituals like ask her on a date and ask all those questions he had about her and her life. Just right into the deep end of his deadly world with no pause.

"I'm going to start nagging you if you don't tell me what's happening. Soon."

She sounded annoyed as hell, but he wanted to chuckle at her threat—who considered nagging as a worse threat than any other possible retribution? "What's happening is that little monsters, miniatures of the original, are popping out of the goo bubbles. They're burning up instantly. None seemed to have escaped. But the fact that monsters are spontaneously arising from the goo is bad."

"Ya think?"

He could practically hear her snarl, even without looking up at her. The remaining goo turned gray as it burned. Some of the bubbles hardened. Little monsters stopped bursting free. He poked at the hardened bubbles with the tip of his sword, ensuring no monsters survived inside. He didn't turn away from the fire until he was sure that everything inside was ash.

He blinked when he heard a crunch of pine needles and the squelch of damp soil close, raising his sword as well as his gaze. To find Elle standing there with more dry kindling. She got close enough to the fire to lean forward, stretching to feed the wood into the flames while still staying as far from the fire pit as she could manage. She didn't toss the wood in from a distance, which might have risked sparks and sending things inside the fire scattering. She just feed in each stick with one hand from as far away as she could manage the task.

She had her face all screwed up as she tried not to breathe in the stench, though that was finally easing as most of the remains finished immolating. But she wasn't running in the opposite direction. She was helping ensure everything burned.

Ben felt that strange, disorienting tightening in his chest again. How had he only known her for less than twenty-four hours? It felt like they'd always worked together, like she'd always been beside him on hunts, helping him destroy the monsters. His memory even wanted to insert her into places she obviously hadn't been. Was this what having a Nam-tar was? This feeling that they had always been together, just hadn't met yet? It must be. There was no other reason he should feel so in sync with her.

This was what destiny felt like.

Swallowing down all the things he wanted to say for fear he'd scare her away, he acknowledged her help instead. "Thanks."

She waved a hand with a stick in it before gently feeding the stick into the fire. "They need to burn, they're going to burn. No escapees on my watch."

His lips twitched. How could she keep making him want to smile in the middle of this mess?

The flames rose hotter and higher for a little longer, churning through the added fuel Elle had added. They watched the fire until it ate through all the new wood, until it started to bank again. They watched the ashes of monster remains closely, the dried flakes of glowing gray at the bottom of the pit shifting in the air currents inside the ebbing flames. Ben didn't rush to put the fire out. Elle didn't rush him to put it out. They both waited, watching, until the fire died and flickered out all on its own.

The remaining red coals in the base of the firepit glowed through the surrounding ash. The stench still lingered in the smoke, but wasn't quite as horrific anymore. They remained silently staring as the coals slowly dimmed. By the time Ben was satisfied the goo was thoroughly destroyed and no more of those mini-monsters would be popping out, no heat came off the ash anymore.

Without discussing it, he hunted up a thicker branch that would serve as a makeshift shovel and dug a hole in the damp soil next to the firepit. Then he pushed the ash into the hole. Elle quickly found another branch and helped him until they'd shifted every bit of the ash into the hole and covered it with more soil.

The burial of ash served to ensure the fire was completely out, no lingering spark to start and spread a dangerous fire, and it ensured all the monster remains were buried away from curious humans and most animals.

The process was more time consuming than killing the creature had been. But years of hunting and destroying monsters had only confirmed the full process was necessary. Any missed step, any attempt to rush the process, could result in a less than dead monster coming back to cause more havoc. And after those miniature versions popping out of the goo, Ben didn't dare try to skip any of the steps.

"It's past lunch time now and I'm not even a little hungry," Elle said. "I normally have a good appetite, but that smell…" She wrinkled her nose.

"Let's get back to the car. Maybe after we've collected my stuff and seen the house again, you'll get your appetite back."

He could eat or not at that moment. His body would need fuel soon, so he'd have to find something. But, unlike his youngest sister and her impossible-to-disrupt appetite, he wasn't feeling particularly hungry right now either. He wouldn't mind clearing the stench of the morning's work out of his nose first.

Elle stared at the place where they'd buried the ash. "Those… I don't know what to call them. The little monsters. That normal?"

"The goo isn't normal, so no, the miniature monsters weren't normal. Monsters have a host of ways to reproduce, some of them extremely unpleasant—"

"No need to elaborate."

"Fair enough." He wasn't going to go into detail with her anyway. He wanted to keep her in his life, not chase her away with some of those horror stories. "But this way of creating new monsters is new. Not something we've seen before."

"The things that were in the crates at the house…" Her brow furrowed as she looked between him and the disturbed ground over the buried remains. "They were made up of that goo. Do you suppose they could do—" She gestured at the ground. "And if so, was all that goo burned up enough in the explosion and fire to stop it?" She winced and looked at him. "Or are we going to find the burnt remains of the house covered in miniature monsters?"

Fuck. The idea was so horrible he cursed out loud. Then he gave her as honest an answer as he could.

"I have no idea."

CHAPTER SEVENTEEN

They went straight to the house instead of going to retrieve Ben's gear first. The drive was quiet. Again. And Elle was grateful. She was so overwhelmed by what she'd just seen, and had to smell, she didn't want to talk about it. She was a little horrified that what they'd find at the house from last night would send what was left of her mental fortitude running screaming into the void, leaving her a husk of gibbering terror.

And the knowledge that the monster hunter with her, the person whose apparent god-assigned duty it was to find and destroy monsters like this, had no idea what was happening with these particular creatures was almost enough to push her over that last fingernail-grip hold on sanity.

She'd been naive. She'd been so certain she'd seen the worst things life had to offer. The worst of humanity. And in that, she was probably right. But definitely not the worst things *life* had to offer.

She drove all the way to the house this time. No point in leaving the car hidden and hiking in. She wasn't trying to sneak up on anyone. And frankly, she wanted the car close in case they had to make a fast escape. If there were dozens or hundreds of miniature monsters running around the place, she was going to run away so far so fast she'd make Ben's head spin.

When they reached the patch of dirt that made up the house's front yard, and Elle got her first view of the place since last night, she let out a low whistle.

The explosion had scattered wood all around the clearing where the house sat. Almost all of the building was black and shattered except for a few strangely intact sections of wall that looked essentially untouched by the fire. In the daylight, those sections of wall were a faded green color. A color that would have allowed the house to blend in with its surroundings if someone happened past. Since the building hadn't had windows, there wasn't a lot of shattered glass outside the building remains. One less thing to worry about. And the entire clearing smelled of wet, burnt wood, with only a faint undercurrent of that smelly goo.

She didn't open the car door right away. She wasn't entirely sure she'd be able to make herself open the door. She stared at the house, gripping the steering wheel, waiting for mini-monsters to swarm them.

Ben didn't say anything, and he didn't rush to get out of the car either. He watched the wrecked building in the mid-afternoon light, his expression closed and serious.

Ten minutes passed like that. With neither of them moving or speaking, just staring at the wreckage. Elle was the first to break the silence, and when she did, her voice sounded overloud in the quiet car.

"We should check the surroundings," she said. "Shouldn't we?"

"We will. Or…I will. It's my job. You can stay in the car. I'll let you know if it's clear." He finally glanced at her. "Will you be able to pick up the professor's trail still? Has all this—" he gestured at the debris, "—complicated your abilities?"

"No idea yet," she said, her gaze wandering back to the building. "But I doubt it. I wasn't planning on using anything left in the house to get started."

What she'd intended on doing was standing near where the cars had been, the ones that had driven off with Professor Arron last night, and letting herself orient to the direction they'd gone. Then following her psychic tracking sense from there. But the cars had been parked at the side of the house, and that meant getting close to the house, and that meant potentially being overrun by tiny monsters like a swarm of deadly bugs. And she wasn't sure she could force herself out of her car with that possibility hanging in the air.

"I'll make sure everything is clear," Ben said.

His quiet tone brought her attention back to him.

"Stay here. I'll be right back," he said. "You'll be safe inside the car. Okay."

She swallowed hard and nodded. She wanted to be braver and get out and walk up to that house and not let all this immobilize her. She'd seen so much. She should be able to handle this.

But these weren't the monsters she'd known her whole life. And she'd still have had a tough time facing those human monsters, even after all the therapy and the passage of so many years. Facing this new, deadly, unknown was maybe a step too far for her ability to bounce back and be brave.

Ben touched a gentle finger to her cheek. His hand still smelled faintly of pine resin but not the monster goo and for some reason that was as reassuring as the gesture. The stench could be washed off. The monster could be destroyed. And he knew what he was doing.

"I'll make sure you're safe," he said quietly. "I promise."

His finger brushed her cheekbone, and the simple gesture had Elle's heartbeat pounding harder. Nice not to feel the fear for just a moment and instead feel...something else. "Thanks." Her voice sounded breathless. She cleared her throat. "Thanks."

He cupped her cheek with his whole hand then. His gaze dipped briefly to her mouth but most of his attention focused on her eyes, an intense sort of eye contact that didn't help her breathing. With one last brush of his thumb, he pulled his hand away and turned to face the house. She noticed he fisted his hand in his lap and wondered at that. Then realized her own hands were fisted on the steering wheel, and not because of the fear.

She faced the house again, too, blinking.

"I'll be right back," Ben said. The car door opened and he was out before she could say anything.

Still, after he'd closed the door and started toward the house, she whispered, "Be safe."

Watching him walk toward the burnt wreckage had her adrenaline climbing again, and her pulse hammered in her throat with fear. She was so tense, waiting for something horrible to jump out at him, she could barely breathe.

And then she blinked and he was gone. Just… He'd been standing in front of the house, seemed to move a little too the right, her brain registered a slight blur, and then he was gone.

Had he… Had he moved that fast? Or had something horrible just snatched him up?

Without thought, she reached for the door handle, but before she could unlock it and get out of the car, she spotted Ben again, standing at one side of the house, scowling at it. And then the slight blur and he was gone.

Whoa.

That was him moving. He was moving so fast she couldn't see him. So fast, her brain wasn't even registering it. She'd had some vague idea that he could move that fast of course. He'd whisked her away from the exploding house so fast, she'd blinked and they'd been far enough into the woods to avoid any debris. But honestly, she'd thought she was so shaken up by the night's events, she'd blurred the travel time in her memory. Not that he'd really moved that fast, just that she'd blacked out or something.

And, yes, he'd leapt in front of a bullet to protect her, but human people did that and got shot. He hadn't moved so fast then that she hadn't seen the movement. Had he? She couldn't remember the moment that clearly. Oh, she remembered the instant she realized he'd been shot, remembered him just appearing in front of her to take the bullet. But again, she'd assumed she'd blurred those memories.

Watching him suddenly appear and then disappear around the house… Now she was questioning her own memories. Again. This time, afraid they were more accurate than she'd assumed.

Well, Elle, what did you think? She shook her head at herself. He had a wolf spirit that leapt out of his body and his body turned to stone. He fought monsters because some sixteen-thousand-year-old god wanted him to, and there were seven whole families that did this monster hunting thing. And there were actual monsters in the world that weren't just horrible humans. Him being able to move so fast she couldn't track those movements didn't seem all that far-fetched in the context of all the other stuff.

She remembered the feel of his hand on her face, cupping her cheek, reassuring and gentle. His fingertips rough from calluses. His palm so large he'd covered half her face with his hand. And yet, his touch had been tender and felt weirdly…familiar. Like he'd cupped her face that way before. She brushed her own fingers over her cheekbone, thinking of the brush of his thumb there.

Her pulse slowed the frantic rhythm of fear and dropped into something deeper, something that had her breath deepening. She could still smell him in the car. It was a very good smell.

When he flashed back to the front of the house, he stood there for a long moment, looking at the blackened shell of the building. Then he turned and walked back to the car at a speed she could see. Not flashing close and startling her by just appearing next to her.

The thoughtfulness made her smile as she unlocked and opened her door finally. "All clear?"

"All clear," he called. "Looks like everything that could move inside burned cleanly. "The stuff inside the fridges seems to have died, too. We should be safe enough."

He was beside her as he finished this retelling. And having him close, so big and capable and gentle at the same time, made it a lot easier to step out of the car and stand beside him. She might have felt weak, that his presence comforted her—she didn't like showing weakness and she hated *feeling* weak even more—but for some reason, none of that seemed to matter around Ben. He made her feel safe to be weak around him.

"Is it too much to ask for you to stick with me while I get close to the house?" she asked, quietly, glad at least her voice wasn't shaking.

The sun was starting to go down on the early spring evening. She didn't want to stand in fading light, the tree shadows stretching long across the burnt building, with her attention distracted. She'd have a hard time concentrating enough to pick up Professor Arron's trail if she was constantly pulling her focus to her surroundings to make sure nothing was sneaking up on her.

"That was always my plan," he said. "You'll need to concentrate, right? I'll have your back while you do."

Oh.

Something moved through her, a feeling that left her throat tight and her insides soft. She felt all melty, and warm, and tingly. All things she hadn't felt around a man in a long time. Maybe never.

How had it only been twenty-four hours since they met? How was that possible when it felt like he'd been in her life forever? Like she must have known him all along.

She shook off the weird sense of time collapsing on itself again, messing with her memories, and headed toward the house, toward the side of the building where the cars had been parked. Ben kept pace just beside and behind her.

Giving her room but, as he'd promised, guarding her back.

CHAPTER EIGHTEEN

Ben scanned the surrounding woods, the long shadows growing as the sun got lower in the sky. The earlier hunt and thorough destruction of the monster and miniature monsters had taken up a lot of the shorter spring daylight. The sun was already dropping behind the trees, giving the late afternoon an orange glow. He could feel the sunset in his bones, the approaching night.

He wanted Elle as far away from this house as they could get by the time the darkness settled around them. She was scared. He could smell her fear. And it was driving him mad. Driving his instincts hard. Get her to somewhere safe, keep her there, feed her, make sure she was warm and protected. And then test the softness of her skin again.

Flexing his hand against his thigh, he kept his attention on trees so he wouldn't get lost studying her. She needed him to protect her right now, not get sidetracked thinking about her soft soft skin and her lush lush mouth.

She didn't do much once she'd reached the spot on the side of the building where the cars had been parked last night. She stood very still, and closed her eyes, and settled her breathing to a slow rhythm he found himself following, tracking, to ensure it remained normal. A lot of his awareness of her seemed to be instinct and not under his conscious control. He didn't think, *I need to keep listening to her breathe in case something changes and she needs my help.* He just did it.

And was surprised by how reassuring the sound was. How much that settled his anxious wolf and his own nerves.

He glanced back at the house, letting his gaze skim over Elle, but not lingering. There were still sections of untouched wall here, showing the faint green paint and undamaged wood siding. The fire and explosion had destroyed and blackened almost everything but still left these occasional pieces unscorched. Those isolated, untouched-by-the-fire areas were the first places he'd searched. Looking for spots where the monsters could have found shelter, escaped the destruction, managed to wiggle out of the flames and get away.

When he'd found no evidence of anything possibly surviving, he'd checked the more damaged parts of the house. Most of it was a black shell, the crates and remaining monster goo just so much charred ash and wet soggy black wood. He'd poked around, moved things he dared moved. Nothing.

He still wanted a few of the Logans to get here and clear the house completely. Ensure everything inside was thoroughly burned and buried after collecting any possible clues and evidence that might still be in there. He hadn't given himself time to hunt for clues. And he didn't have time now to thoroughly destroy this lab. If they could reach Professor Arron soon, there was a chance they could get him out before the monsters decided he was more liability than asset. The worry that the monsters would simply kill the professor sooner rather than later had a clock ticking in his head, making him very aware of all the time passing, time they couldn't afford to lose.

But like with the monster earlier, they couldn't afford to leave things lying around for animals and humans to discover. That could be deadly. Or worse. Because it wouldn't be the first time that monster remains had gotten inside a host and created something even more horrible.

The desire to ensure all this was thoroughly destroyed, and the push to reach the geneticist as quick as possible, all while keeping his

Nam-tar safe, were competing priorities tearing Ben's attention into pieces. Something he couldn't afford.

He was going to need help, backup. He needed his Family.

But first he and Elle needed to find Professor Arron's trail.

He glanced at her briefly. She was turning in a slow circle, her eyes half closed, her head tilted down. Her short blond hair caught some of the late afternoon light, adding little strings of gold and pink so that her hair seemed to glow like the sunset itself. He flexed his hand again, refusing to reach out and brush his fingers through those short locks. Despite a near overwhelming desire to do so.

Forcing his attention back on the surroundings, he waited patiently for her to finish doing whatever it was she needed to do. He knew she was done when her breathing changed, when she pulled in a deep gulp of air and let it out on a sigh. He was so attuned to her, he could practically feel her shoulders relaxing. He faced her, waiting for her to open her eyes.

She blinked and looked up at him, smiling. "Got him. Northwest. I need to look at a map. I should be able to get us a route."

"Location or just direction?"

"So far, just direction. But now that I'm on his trail again, I'll be able to get a more exact location the closer we get to him." Her eyes drifted down just a little. "Yes. I've got him now. I'll be able to track him."

"I'm impressed."

She opened her eyes and gave him a narrow, disbelieving look.

"No. I'm serious. I am impressed. That's a very handy talent you have. And it'll save us a lot of time. Might even save the professor's life."

She attempted a casual shrug, but the way her mouth turned up in a small smile and her scent filled with pleasure had him feeling ten feet tall.

"Let's get out of here," she said. "I'll study the map and find us the best route. We'll swing around to get your gear and then we can get on the road."

He wanted to ask her about rest, and food, and all the things a human needed. But he'd do that when they were away from the house. Her gaze kept jumping to the section of wall behind her, the part that hadn't been fully destroyed. The stench of the fire and the dead things inside wasn't as unpleasant as it had been last night, but still wasn't great.

Yeah, the farther he could get her away from this house, the better they'd both feel.

In the car, she pulled out her cellphone and studied her map app. "Okay. Got the highway we need to take. They seem to be heading up toward the Canadian border, though. Dammit."

"What's wrong?"

"You have your passport on you?" she asked with a faint scowl, her attention still on her phone. "If they cross the border, I won't have any backup from the local authorities to bring Arron back to this country. Especially since I doubt he has a passport with him. It just complicates getting him home to his family." She sighed. "Nothing for it, though, if they do cross into Canada."

"I can take care of it," he said, watching her belt in before he pulled across his own seatbelt.

"I don't have my passport on me, either, though," she said as she started the car. "I really don't want to detour to get it. That'll take up too much time."

"Don't worry," he said. "I can take care of it."

She cast him a brief scowl. "How?"

"My Family has all kinds of connections and influence. We'll be able to get over the border and back."

Her gaze narrowed but she didn't ask more until they were back on the dirt road leading away from the house.

"Suppose monsters don't pay any attention to human borders, huh?" she said, her attention on her driving and not him. "Probably have to cross borders all the time."

"We do. Monsters are an international issue."

"I'm not sure if that's reassuring or horrifying."

"Both," he suggested.

They drove in a direction opposite the main highway to get closer to where he'd left his gear. He directed her to park in a scenic turnoff that put him close enough to reach his stuff in a few minutes, ten at the most, moving at top speed.

Unfortunately, moving at top speed and getting back quick, with his backpack and weapon's bag, meant not bringing Elle with him. He could carry her, of course—and the idea was very tempting—but that would slow him down. It would also make it awkward carrying the gear back and that would slow him down even more. He didn't want to cost them that extra time. And with the sun setting, he didn't want to risk having her in the middle of the woods when it got dark. The house might have been clear, but he was very conscious that something might still be in these woods.

But the idea of leaving her, even for fifteen minutes, felt like a wrenching in his gut, like he'd physically have to tear himself away. What if something happened in that time? What if there was still a grinluk around here, or some of the goo monsters had escaped, or just some of the monster's thugs? What if ordinary human monsters found her?

He'd be too far away to help, too far away to hear her. The thought left him physically ill.

He turned to face her and then wasn't sure what to say. Really, he wouldn't be gone long. He needed to move fast. And this was a quiet, empty part of the woods. She'd be fine. He'd be quick. And he'd be by her side again soon. No reason to complicate this. It was just fifteen minutes.

"You want me to come with you?" she asked.

His shoulders slumped with his exhale. The fact that she could read his thoughts probably should have bothered him more. Might have if she wasn't his Nam-tar. "Actually, it's probably better if you stay here locked in the car. I can get there and back faster if I don't have to carry you. But I don't want to leave you here alone." She opened her mouth and he raised a hand. "I know that's not rational. I won't be more than fifteen minutes. You'll be safe. I've told myself all this already."

"But given what we've seen in the last day, you're worried there are other monsters out here and you'll be too far away to help." She nodded. "I'm worried about you for the same reason. And I don't have the speed to reach you in minutes if you're in trouble."

Ben felt a weird sort of tightening and fluttering in his chest. A sensation he hadn't felt before. Soft and fragile. And he was afraid to poke at it, investigate it, because he didn't want it to break.

"I'll be fine, too," he said, but he had to clear his throat. "Do you have a weapon of some kind? Can you use the sword?"

"Yes, and no. You take the sword. I'd just hurt myself with it. But I have a weapon." She winced, very subtly, but he still saw the gesture. "I have a gun. It's my 'Break Glass in Case of Emergency' gun. I'll pull it out."

"Guns aren't much use against monsters. But if one shows up and you have to use the gun, aim for the head. Are you a decent shot?"

She snorted. "Yeah. I'm a good shot." Again, that subtle wince.

"Okay. You hit the monster anywhere but its head, you'll just piss it off. Aim for the head, as much as possible, that'll at least slow it down. Do not hesitate to drive away if a monster shows up. I'll find you. Just get somewhere safe."

"I'll find you," she said, raising her brows. "It's what I do."

His mouth twitched with a faint smile. "We'll find each other again, how about that? But don't let that stop you from running away. I'm used to monsters. I know how to kill them. You don't need to stick around just because you're worried about me. Get safe."

"The only way to kill a monster is to remove its head, right?"

"Right."

"Okay. Got it. But I doubt it'll be an issue."

Hopefully not. "I will be back in fifteen minutes. No more." He gestured at her phone. "My phone is powered down now, but I'll turn it own when I get to my gear. Would you feel comfortable taking my number?"

"I want to make a joke about this being a pretty extreme way to get my phone number, but I'm nervous and will mess up the joke."

He smiled. He couldn't help it. "You can crack the joke when you're less nervous."

"It'll lose its impact," she said with a dramatic sigh. Then flashed him a small smile and swiped opened her phone. "Go."

He rattled off his number as she entered it into her contacts. He was curious what name she gave him. Just Ben, since she didn't know his last name yet, or some string of descriptions so she'd know which Ben he was? The thought that she'd need descriptors to know who he was left a weird pain in his gut.

When she was done, she gave him a look he couldn't read. "Better get going. You'll be running in the dark on the way back. Is that going to be a problem? You have a flashlight?"

"I have excellent night vision. The wolf helps with that."

Her eyebrows bounced up. "I should have thought of that. Will you tell me more about the…the wolf?"

"Everything you want to know," he said.

"We should probably talk about how it jumped through me, too, huh?"

He nodded, but he couldn't quite get words out. He should ask Eric, or maybe even his mother, if he'd fucked things up doing that. Probably his mother. He didn't want to hear crap from his brother. Eric was a great leader of the Logan Family now that he'd settled in. But he was still Ben's older brother and sometimes forgot there were things he wasn't in charge of. He'd probably know if this had happened before. But so would their mother, and talking to his mother would be a lot easier.

Maybe. She'd been deep in grief since their father's murder. Three years wasn't long enough after centuries of a lifetime together. She might not want to discuss her son's Nam-tar while still mourning the loss of her own.

Still, he had to ask someone, find out how this worked now. He had to have something he could tell Elle.

"I'll be back soon," he said, still hesitating to leave but knowing he had to get this done. "I'll turn my phone on as soon as I reach my stuff, so you can text if you need me." Texts sent better up here where cell service was patchy, so were easier than trying to make a phone call. "A simple Help will have me hear in minutes."

She entered the text on her phone and showed it to him. "Can send with a quick tap."

He didn't precisely relax at her preparedness, but opening the car door did get easier. "Fifteen minutes. I'll be back in fifteen."

"Go. I'll be fine. Locking the doors behind you."

He heard the locks click as soon as he closed the door, which made him smile. The expression didn't last, though. Leaving her still felt like a wrenching. Like he'd be leaving some of himself behind and he didn't want those parts separated.

In a way, that was true.

He waved to her through the front windshield, mostly so he could get one last look at her. Then he scanned the trees, oriented to his location, and took off at his fastest run.

He couldn't get back to Elle fast enough.

CHAPTER NINETEEN

lle stayed where she was long enough to see Ben blur and disappear into the trees. The speed he could move. She was never going to get used to that. She glanced down at the number in her phone, at the little message she'd typed out just to make him feel better, and brushed her thumb against the edge of her phone.

She was almost instantly edgy and uncomfortable being separated from him, and that was not a good thing. She'd known him a day and she physically hated the idea of being away from him. Felt a sort of strain that went well beyond the time they'd known each other, even if that time had been filled with A Lot. A lot of danger and stress and…monsters.

Intense. Everything had been so intense since they met. Maybe that's why she didn't want to be separated from him. Or maybe it was just the monsters.

She sighed and leaned over the passenger's seat to pull out the locked gun box she kept underneath. She had spent most of her youth around guns. Knew makes, models, how to take them apart and reassemble them, how to clean and properly care for them. Hell, she even knew how to reload cartridges and make her own ammunition. Her father had trained her to guns from the start. He'd claimed it was for safety reasons, teaching her all about guns. She knew now, as an adult, it had been because he wanted her prepared for the end of the world. But at the time, she'd just thought her father was giving them something they could do together.

As an adult though, knowing what she knew about her father and his associates, seeing the world around her, she wasn't crazy about guns anymore. At least unregulated access to them. There were too many people like her father, like some of the men he'd known, some of the men she'd helped the FBI find years later. Too many angry people who didn't appreciate the power and deadliness of the weapons—or maybe appreciated the deadliness too much, to the point of fetishizing them. She believed in regulation. Well-regulated access.

So the fact that she had a 3D printed plastic gun she could sneak through in pieces on airplanes when she needed to, and kept in a lockbox under her front car seat when she was driving, was something she wasn't entirely proud of. Old habits and paranoias instilled by her dad. She didn't feel safe without some form of protection. And she didn't have the sort of job that justified the hoops for allowing travel with guns. She wasn't unhappy about those hoops. She actually believed in them. Which was why she felt guilty for skirting them when she did. Knowing she probably wasn't the only one was unnerving.

She shook off the guilt and always-present paranoia and assembled the plastic gun pieces without having to think about what she was doing. She'd practiced until she could do this in under a minute without looking. As she loaded the magazine and slipped it into the gun, she scanned the surroundings. Would her little plastic gun with its ammunition designed for humans have any effect at all on a monster? She really didn't want to find out.

Since she'd driven up here from Detroit in her own car, she also had a shotgun in the trunk, under the padding where the spare tire was stored. She considered getting that out now. Her shotgun might work better against a monster, scattered shot pellets potentially causing more damage. But getting to that gun involved unlocking the car doors and stepping outside, and for some reason, that felt as scary as it had at the house.

The time on her phone said five minutes had passed. Only five minutes. Was Ben at his gear yet? Was his phone on? She swiped on her screen and stared at the *Help* text. She backtracked over it and typed in: *text when you turn your phone on please.*

The please was her attempt to soften the demand but her need to know he was okay superseded her need to be polite, so she'd nearly forgotten that last word.

Because she was feeling edgy and jumpy, she reentered the *Help* text, just in case, but turned her screen off so she didn't accidentally send it. Last thing she needed to do was give Ben a heart attack for no reason.

The seconds ticked by as she held her phone in one hand, her gun in the other, and kept her gaze scanning the surrounding trees while still flicking occasional glances down at her phone. Tension tightened in her gut as she waited, every moment without seeing a message pop up from him made the anxiety climb.

When a message finally dinged, she nearly dropped her gun in her haste to check the phone. Good thing she'd left the gun's safety on. Letting out a slow breath and shaking her head at herself, she flicked on her phone to read his full message. Although there wasn't much to read.

Phone's on if you need me. Be there soon.

She sent back a: *thanks.* Then reentered the *Help* message for a third time and started a kind of countdown in her head, even though she couldn't be sure exactly how long it would take him to get back. It had taken him a good eight minutes to turn the phone on. Probably take at least that long to make the return journey. Depending on how much gear he had. That might slow him down, so could be as long as another ten or fifteen minutes.

Longer than the fifteen minutes he'd promised, but not by much. She tried to tell herself she wouldn't need to panic until the twenty-minute mark, a deadline that allowed her to stay in the car and not head into the woods to meet him halfway. He'd hate her wandering around in the dark alone anyway. She hated the thought of wandering these woods alone, too.

She tapped her foot against the baseboard and tried to focus on the trees instead of incessantly glancing at her phone. Her grip on her gun was loose and stable, but the rest of her was jumpy as hell. Beyond the car, the woods had gotten very dark, and without the headlights, she couldn't see far into the shadowed depths under the trees. There was a half moon up tonight, or nearly half moon, which wasn't enough light to see by. For her at least. Having the darkness close in around her added to the anxiety clawing at her insides.

Why the hell was she so nervous? Why did she hate being away from him this much? Had to be the monsters. Everything she'd seen and learned in the last day. But this actual, physical wrenching in her gut… She'd never experienced anything like it. Never felt like a part of herself had gone wandering off and she wouldn't be able to settle until those parts were reunited. She didn't like the feeling. Didn't like it at all. Made her feel needy and dependent. On a virtual stranger of all things!

Except… Well, would she call Ben a stranger now? There was a *lot* she still didn't know about him. Including his last-fucking-name. But *stranger* seemed entirely wrong to describe how she viewed him now. He wasn't a stranger, even if there was a lot about him she still didn't know. He was…something else.

That something else made her stomach flutter when she looked at him. Made her tingly whenever he smiled. Got her heartbeat pounding when he was close enough she could feel the heat on his skin, or smell that delicious scent that was him, a scent she couldn't really describe but would know in the dark without having to see him.

And that was it, the rub, the reason she couldn't think of him as a stranger. She knew in the depths of her soul that she'd recognize him, in the dark, without seeing him, without hearing him, she'd *know* he was close. She'd know it was *him* and no one else.

A bond born of circumstance. Had to be. The side effect of living through an intense situation with someone. Only thing it could be.

She kept repeating those justifications for her feelings as she scanned the dark woods, as she tried not to stare at the time on her phone, willing him to get here soon.

When he appeared at the edge of the tree line, just appeared there as if he'd materialized out of thin air—or she'd conjured him from her will alone—she let out a long, shaky breath, gently set her gun on the console by the drive shaft, unlocked the car, and went right into his arms.

She didn't even think about what she was doing. Just walked to him and threw her arms around him like she hadn't seen him in months and needed that contact more than she needed her next breath.

That his arms came around her without hesitation and he wrapped his big body around her, burying his face against her neck, wasn't lost on her. No pause or hesitance or moment of surprise. Like he'd needed the physical contact as much as she did.

And it did make her feel better, having him close again, having his heat and solid body pressed up against hers. Reassuring herself he was whole and breathing and well.

"You're trembling," he murmured into her hair. "Are you okay? Did something happen? Why didn't you text?"

She smiled and shook her head, her eyes closed. "Nothing happened. I haven't a fucking clue why I'm trembling. I'm okay." She squeezed him tighter and sighed happily when his arms tightened around her as well, lifting her up onto her toes. "Just…don't know. Needed this."

"Me, too." He sounded as confused about that as she felt.

She let out a long, slow breath, and then eased away enough to look into his face. His eyes glittered in the darkness, so close she felt like she could see deep into his soul. And for a moment, she got lost in his eyes. She had to blink herself back to the here and now.

"Okay." She let out another slow breath. "Okay, so, this…this isn't entirely normal. For me at least. I think we need to talk about this. Cause I have never had such a hard time being separated from someone I barely know."

Being taken from her mother and not seeing her for years had been difficult, wrenching, terrifying, horrible, painful, and had left a lot of scars. Some of it she didn't even remember because she'd been so young, and some of it she'd blocked because she didn't want to remember. But she remembered the terror of not being able to see her mother. Maybe that's why she'd reacted this way with Ben. But for someone she barely knew, feeling so lost without him was not a normal reaction.

He nodded, a frown creasing his brow and bracketing his mouth. "Yeah. Yeah. We have a lot we need to talk about. Some things I need to explain." He shook his head. "This isn't the way I wanted to have this conversation, though." He looked around. "And maybe we should get somewhere more comfortable. With food for you. It's been a busy day. You haven't eaten since this morning."

"Neither have you. And you got shot yesterday and nearly died."

His mouth ticked at the corner, not quite a smile, but like he wanted to. "I can go for a while without food if I need to, but, yeah, I wouldn't mind something to eat."

"So we'll start heading in the direction they've taken Professor Arron, and we'll stop for a meal and you can tell me everything."

"You're going to need to sleep, too."

"Can you drive?"

He nodded, his brows raised. "I was around when cars were invented."

"That's wild and I want to hear all about it. Eventually. First, this… weird thing happening between us. And getting to Professor Arron as quickly as we can. So we can take turns driving and sleeping. We'll have privacy in the car to talk, too. Sound like a plan?"

"I'd rather we weren't driving when we discuss…the things I need to tell you."

"That bad, huh?" She sucked in a breath, and his hold on her tightened. She melted against him because it felt natural to do so. Which should have been more disturbing. "Okay, so, let's get on the road, and we'll find somewhere to stop along the way."

She really couldn't think that far out at the moment, with Ben so close and strong and her body reacting in ways that were not entirely in her control. There was a logical part of her brain trying to think, trying to deal with the situation. Then there was the larger part of her brain and body that didn't want to think at all. And the only talking that part of her wanted to do involved dirty talk and some suggestions on where she wanted his mouth.

And *those* thoughts shocked her enough to give her the strength to put some space between them. Reluctantly. With a lot of whining from the part of her that was still hyper focused on his mouth.

It wasn't that she hadn't had instant lust with someone. Or one-night stands. It was that with Ben this didn't feel either instant or like a one-night thing and that was *terrifying*.

She rubbed her palms over her cargo pants and took another step away from him so she wouldn't reach for him again. Touching him shorted out her ability to think. They needed to think.

"We'd better get on the road." Her voice sounded breathy and rough in the darkness.

So did his. "Let's go."

He stowed the large hiking backpack and the long canvas duffle bag that he'd retrieved in the trunk, next to the carefully cleaned sword and her duffle bag. In the car, she disassembled the gun and locked it back in its box, stowing it under the backseat this time. Ben didn't comment on the plastic gun, but he did watch her as she took the thing apart and put it away.

More things they probably had to discuss. So much that she almost wanted to ignore it all. Just get the professor back and then she didn't have to see Ben again and none of this would matter.

Except the idea of never seeing him again hurt so much she wanted to cry.

What the hell was happening to her?

CHAPTER TWENTY

Ben took over the driving a half hour after they hit the highway because he was worried about Elle. The fact that she didn't argue with him, and just let him drive, proved how shellshocked she was. He wasn't feeling much better.

Leaving her, even for those fifteen minutes had felt miserable. But the farther he got from her, the harder it had been to be away from her. To the point his wolf was crawling in his brain pushing him to get back to her instantly. He'd thought it was him, the fear for his Nam-tar, the worry that was probably natural. He hadn't had this experience before and hadn't been around to watch either of his sisters or his brother go through this. Maybe the jumpy, edgy, panicky feelings were normal?

But seeing the panic mixed with relief in Elle's eyes when he'd returned had floored him. Feeling her tremble as she held him had been horrifying. He didn't *want* her feeling like this. It wasn't *right* that she felt like this.

And not just because *he* objected to her being unhappy or uncomfortable.

He was afraid when his wolf leapt through her, it had left something of itself in her. That was what happened when Nam-tar performed that ritual. But he hadn't completed it, hadn't jumped back through her. So he'd hoped he hadn't left any of the wolf behind.

Now he was afraid he had. And because he hadn't finished the ritual, they were both left in a kind of limbo. Without finishing, they were linked in a way that wasn't normal for Nam-tar.

She hadn't made her choice to stay yet, though. She didn't even know what they were to each other yet. But if he didn't finish the trust ritual, they stayed in this weird bond that made being apart physically painful. And if he did finish it, that bonded them permanently. She would carry a piece of his wolf with her. Forever.

They couldn't live like this, being unable to be separated. *She* couldn't be forced to live like this. But no matter what happened now, she would always be linked to him. Could she still make the choice to leave? And if not…

Maybe he was wrong. Maybe she still had the choice. Once the ritual was done, she could still leave. She could still decide she didn't want him. They'd be linked but not in a way that she couldn't mostly ignore. She'd live a much longer life than the humans she knew. And she'd heal faster and be stronger than any human around her. But maybe she wouldn't mind that.

So long as she was still free to make the choice to stay or go, then they'd both be fine.

Well, if she chose to go, he'd be in the same position he was in now. Had always been in really. Meeting his Nam-tar wouldn't have changed anything for him. Except for having had the pleasure and honor to have met her.

He glanced at her from the corner of his eye. She was staring out the window as the trees went past. This section of highway was mostly dark, with just other car lights to give much illumination. That didn't prevent him from seeing her clearly. Her expression was pensive, the area around her eyes and mouth pinched, creases marring her brow. Her fingers picked idly at the edge of her t-shirt. She was deep in thought, and hadn't spoken since he'd taken over the driving. And he really wanted to hear her voice. Even if just to reassure himself she was okay.

She wasn't okay. He wasn't either. But still, he wanted the sound of her voice in that dark car.

He pulled in a deep breath because he at least had her scent, filling her car and helping settle his fears. Somewhat. At least the delicious scent of her settled his pulse and his panic. No more panic meant he could think.

Unfortunately, the answer to their predicament was both clear and complicated.

"You ready to talk yet," he asked, "or do you need quiet for longer?"

Her mouth tilted up in a faint smile. He caught the gesture from the corner of his eye. Her response allowed him to relax his hands on the steering wheel.

"I think we need to talk. What happened to me back there…" She shook her head. "That wasn't good."

"No. It wasn't." He let out a rough exhale. "This is a story."

"We have time."

He took another minute to decide how to start. In the end, he decided to just jump to the point. "The god En, who created the Seven Families, created them because his brother Ne loosed monsters on humans. Ne hated humans, considered them a plague, and wanted them wiped out. At first, he tried to do it himself. When En fought against his army and beat him, Ne angrily created the monsters with the help of the Fallen Heroes—that's just a name. They were more like monsters themselves."

She nodded. "Got the gist of this last night."

"Just making sure because it's important to what happened next. Because En continued to side with the humans, Ne's rage knew no bounds. After En created the Seven Families, Ne cursed them. God curses are…"

"Bad?"

"Bad." He snorted. "And impossible to just remove, even by other gods. En couldn't remove the curse. So he gave the Seven Families a way to break it." Ben swallowed hard and plunged on. She had to know all this. She had to understand what was happening to them both.

"En promised us a partner, a mate, a true love. We call that person our Nam-tar. If we can earn our Nam-tar, if our Nam-tar chooses to stay with us, accepts the destiny of loving us, then our curse is broken."

"How do you 'earn' your Nam-tar?"

"In the larger sense, we continue to do our duty and destroy the monsters, protect humans, ensure the monsters don't overrun the planet."

"Good plan."

Despite himself, he let out a huff of a laugh. "In the smaller sense, on a personal level, we have to allow our Nam-tar the freedom and room to make their choice to stay or go. We have to be worthy mates to them and earn their love and trust. No coercion or force. That won't break the curse. Our Nam-tar have to *want* to stay with us to break the curse."

She nodded. "Okay. Destined love. Sounds a bit romantic for a god curse, but whatever. Old gods were weird."

"Yeah, they were," he muttered. And then hoped En hadn't heard that. Neither brother had interfered in the world of humans for millennia, so Ben was pretty sure they were both sleeping now, as old gods had done through the centuries. But never hurt to stay on En's good side. Just in case.

"So are the destined loves from other families or… How does that work?"

"They're usually humans. Though one of my younger sister's Nam-tar is a werewolf. So it's possible for Nam-tar to come from non-humans."

"So. Werewolf? They are real?"

"They're real."

"What else is real?"

"Lot of things you've probably thought were fiction." He glanced at her briefly. She was staring at him, her brow creased. In the shadowed darkness inside the car, her skin looked a little too pale. Damn. He needed to feed her. He started hunting road signs for the nearest off ramp to restaurants.

"Monsters are real," she said quietly.

"They are."

"Werewolves aren't monsters?"

"Not in this sense. My sister's mate is a nice man. A lot of shifters are just ordinary people going about their business."

She blew out a stream of air through her pursed lips. "Probably good thing my dad didn't know about all this," she muttered under her breath, so quietly Ben assumed he wasn't meant to hear the comment. "Back to the god curse and the destined mates… So a Nam-tar stays, curse is broken, everyone lives happily ever after?"

"Essentially."

"Still fighting monsters?"

"The hunters still fight, yes. The Nam-tar aren't charged with that duty. They can do whatever they've done before or, really anything they want. Some get involved in the monster hunting. Others don't."

"Lot of emphasis on the Nam-tar's choices here."

"It's important."

"What about the members of the Seven Families? Do they get a choice whether to fight monsters or not?"

"Of course. If they don't, though, they don't find their Nam-tar, and their death will be…unpleasant. Some are willing to face that to avoid the duty of monster hunting." He shrugged. "It's not a choice I'd make."

He believed in the cause of protecting humans from the monsters. His cousin Jason hadn't, and that had resulted in his father's murder. Not because Jason just quietly retired and accepted his fate, but because he'd sided *with* the monsters against humans. That, in their world, was a choice that carried real consequences. Murdering the head of the Logan family meant the consequences were death. Jason had died under his curse, and his remains were still in the Logan family statuary garden in their upstate New York home. A message to all other Wolf Family for how betrayal would be treated.

But Jason had had a choice. He'd made the decision to betray the Family. Everyone had a choice, even if the choices weren't always great.

"I think I understand most of this," Elle said. "And I appreciate you telling me. But… What does it have to do with what happened to us in the woods?"

He spotted a road sign for food ahead at the next exit. "This part is difficult for me to tell you. Because… I fucked up. And…" He shook his head. "We're getting off at the next exit for food."

"Fine. What did you fuck up? With your Nam-tar or with the monsters?"

"My Nam-tar," he said, his voice laced with a twist of irony.

"You've met them?"

"I've met her. Last night as a matter of fact."

The silence that followed that blunt statement was so complete, Ben's ears actually rang with it. He wasn't even sure Elle was still breathing. He flicked a glance at her just as they drove under a highway light at the off ramp. Her expression was unreadable, as neutral as a human could get.

Her scent, on the other hand, was a chaotic riot of emotions. Disbelief, fear, confusion. A hint of anger. That peppery spike of anger made his gut clench. Because she hadn't even heard the actual bad part of all this yet.

He turned onto a side road that presented him with four different fast-food restaurants and a diner to choose from. "What do you want to eat?" he asked, nodding toward the choices.

"Don't mind. Whatever you want."

Her voice sounded strained and hollow. Not good signs. He picked one of the burger joints, going for the drive thru. He'd park, and they could talk in the car. He didn't think either of them was up for actually going in anywhere at the moment.

He ordered enough food to feed her for days, which she raised her brows at, and paid in cash now that he had some. Once they had their food, he parked the car at the far end of the restaurant's parking lot, just outside a pool of light from a street lamp, and waited patiently for her to start asking questions. He could smell her disbelief like smoke under the stronger smell of burgers and fries. And still that peppery anger.

She took the burger he handed her and set it on her lap without opening the wrapper. She did turn in her seat to stare at him, though.

But rather than a question, the first thing she said to him after the long silence was, "I don't believe in destined love."

"You don't have to." His hands flexed on the steering wheel. He slowly relaxed his grip and faced her more fully. "This isn't how I wanted this to happen. None of it. From the very beginning. This isn't how I'd have chosen to tell you, or how I'd have approached things if circumstances had been different."

"When did you think you knew?"

"I knew the instant I was close enough to you. Your scent, but also just…a feeling. We know. My oldest brother knew when he heard his Nam-tar's voice on the phone. A call he wouldn't have even normally taken, but he felt compelled to answer. He knew the moment she spoke."

"You were covering my mouth when we met."

He wasn't sure if she was trying to make a joke or not because her tone was still painfully neutral. "Voice. Scent. Doesn't really matter. We know in an instant. It's divine destiny."

"I don't believe in divine destiny, either," she said.

"Most people don't. Not really. Or they don't understand what that phrase means."

"I don't believe in God."

"Okay."

"You're talking about gods."

"Old gods, yes."

"How can I be…chosen for someone by a god I don't believe in?"

"Belief or not really isn't necessary. Not in the gods or the myths. Not for any of this. I have seen the results of the curse with my own eyes. And I've seen Nam-tar meet, get together, break the curse. I fight the monsters regularly. I live this, and know it's true. No *belief* required."

"Monsters are real," she allowed with a shrug. "I didn't believe in them before last night either. At least not that kind." She finally unwrapped her burger and took a big bite.

Watching her eat relaxed something in his gut, allowing his shoulders to loosen.

She nodded at the bags of food stacked on the center console between their seats. "You'd better eat, too."

She was right even if he didn't have an appetite. He devoured two burgers without really tasting them as he waited for her to say more.

"Why me?" she asked after another long silence.

"I don't know."

"Can you have more than one Nam-tar? Will another one come along if this doesn't work out?"

"No. Only one. That's the only chance we get."

She swallowed hard and looked out the front windshield. "What does the curse do?"

He winced, hesitated.

She finally looked at him again. "What does the curse do?"

"We die badly," he said but when she opened her mouth, he stopped her. "I'm hesitant to tell you the details because…" He blew out a sharp breath. "I said we can't force our Nam-tar to choose this destiny. To choose this potential for love. Fated doesn't mean forgone. A Nam-tar has to choose to stay to break the curse. And we can't manipulate that decision. If we do, the curse won't be broken. Free will and free choice are fundamental to this."

"No manipulation is allowed? At all?"

He shrugged. "Well, seduction and…courting aren't considered manipulation for the purposes of the curse, so I suppose there's some flexibility in that rule. But we're not allowed to guilt you into staying, or make you feel obligated to stay. Which is why I don't want to tell you what the curse does. That might be too…manipulatory." He winced at the word.

She nodded, her lips pursed, but she didn't turn away from him. "Seduction, huh?"

"It's allowed."

The moment stretched after that comment as he held her gaze. Color rose into her cheeks, but he wasn't sure if that was the food or a blush. He did note the new flavor in her scent, a hint of desire. That same thread of deliciousness that had been in her scent at the bait shop that morning. And in the hotel room before that.

The desire, the lust had him hopeful he hadn't fucked things up beyond repair. And, yeah, he wasn't opposed to a little seduction to convince Elle they'd be good together.

They would be, too. Very good. His gaze traveled her face, settled on her mouth. Her lips glistened in the dim car interior from a quick flick of her tongue. Tempting him to taste her. Just a taste.

He let his gaze drop to her throat, where he could see the flutter of her pulse, then lower, taking in her lush body, allowing himself the luxury of really studying her. And letting her know he was studying her. Taking in the swell of her breasts, the curve of her waist. Mentally raking his gaze over all the places he wanted to touch.

Her breathing stuttered, and he flexed his hands in his lap to keep from reaching for her.

She swallowed audibly, cleared her throat. Let out a long stream of air through her pursed lips. He drank in every sign, ever flavor of her longing. And it took an act of will not to pull her across the console and onto his lap. He wanted her mouth on his so much that not having her in his arms physically hurt.

She swallowed hard again, and her nostrils flared. Then she nodded and said, "I'm not sure I'd call monster hunting courting."

The humor was enough to cut the building heat and startle a chuckle from him. "I did say I'd have gone about this all differently given a choice."

Her lips twitched with a small smile. "More seduction, less monsters?"

"Definitely. Definitely more seduction."

She blinked hard a few times and gave herself a shake. "This conversation might be getting off topic."

Not really. Seducing her was definitely something he'd have preferred to discuss in that moment. But that wouldn't solve the fundamental problem of him fucking up last night.

"Is this…this Nam-tar stuff why I had such a hard time being separated from you earlier?"

He shook his head. Then winced. Back on topic. "Not exactly. But it's related."

"Nam-tar have to be together? They can't be apart?"

"They can be apart. They often have to be. What happened to us isn't...typical of the Nam-tar relationship."

"Why are we different?"

He liked that she'd said "we" and that she wasn't trying to deny being his Nam-tar anymore. He wasn't even sure if she realized she'd made that switch. He certainly wasn't going to point it out just yet. More hope, though.

Hope he was afraid would be short lived after he revealed this next part.

CHAPTER TWENTY-ONE

Ben studied the remains of the third burger in his lap. He couldn't remember eating it. His body did need fuel after everything that had happened in the last day and a half, but his appetite was off. Worse because of what he had to tell Elle now.

She was still a little pale in the faint yellow glow from the parking lot light at her back. The interior of the car was dark enough their conversation felt hushed and intimate. And how he wished he could go back to talking about seduction instead of the fact that he'd done something that would have a permanent impact on them both. But not in a good way.

He reminded himself it could still be okay. This could still work out. All was not, necessarily, doomed. But that third burger churned in his gut, and his wolf moved around restlessly in his head, and he had serious doubts about his own reassurances.

"Under ordinary circumstance," he started, having to swallow to wet his dry throat. She handed him a soda wordlessly, her gaze locked unflinchingly on his. He took a sip of the drink and started again. "Because the Families live for so long, centuries, and because their mates are usually human, En worked in a rite, a ritual, that would allow us to pass some of our long lives, strength, and healing to our Nam-tar."

"How?"

She already suspected. He was certain of it. The way her jaw flexed. The way she didn't react to the distant sound of a passing big rig's horn suddenly blaring. Her eyes were narrowed, and there was a crease between her brows. The chaos of emotion in her scent was worse now, though, so he was having a harder time reading that. The fear was climbing to wash out the anger. He hated the smell of her fear.

"Normally, there's time for Nam-tar to build trust, love, all the things that make a long-term commitment work, before they go through the ritual. It requires a great deal of trust so it isn't something couples usually do at the start of the relationship, even after a Nam-tar has agreed to stay. The ritual usually happens a few months, as long as a few years into the bond."

"How?" she repeated, slowly and carefully.

"The Nam-tar stands in front of their mate and allows their mate's animal to leap through them. The animal spirit delays becoming corporeal as it moves through the Nam-tar, until its on the other side. Then the animal leaps back through the Nam-tar and into its host human body. The process doesn't take long. As long as it takes for the leap and return. Once done, a bit of the animal spirit is left behind in the Nam-tar and that's enough to extend their lives. They won't have an animal symbiote of their own. They can't leap from their body to ride inside that animal and leave their human form encased in stone. They don't become like us. But the ritual allows them to live in our world safer and longer."

Nothing in Elle's expression changed as he recited all this. She stared at him, without blinking, and not even her scent changed. The same mix of chaos with a high level of fear. Was it good or bad that the fear hadn't actually gotten worse? She looked frozen, a statue herself in the dark car, so he was hesitant to call any of this "good."

After a long, ringing silence broken only by the sounds of traffic on the highway, Elle finally said, "Does this ever happen on accident? With someone who's not a Nam-tar?"

"If the animal leaps and there's someone in the way, and that someone is not that particular hunter's Nam-tar, then the person just gets pushed out of the way by the solid animal. The delay, the passing through another being, that only happens with Nam-tar."

"So. No doubts with us then."

"No doubts."

"Did you… Your wolf leapt through me. Once. But not back. What did that do?"

"I hoped by not jumping back and finishing the ritual, it wouldn't do anything to us. It was a mistake. I didn't mean for that to happen."

"I know. You were dying. Shot. Saving me. I can't imagine you were thinking much at all in that moment."

"Only of surviving to help you. I leapt to survive and to push you aside so you wouldn't get shot. It didn't cross my mind until it was too late that because you were my Nam-tar, that leap would mimic the ritual instead of an ordinary leap."

"You called your wolf a symbiote," she said, skipping over the other stuff in such a subject change, he blinked a few times.

"It is. Like I said last night, I'm not a werewolf. We're not shapeshifters. The wolf and I aren't one and the same but with two different forms. We're two entirely different entities that share a single form at any given point. My consciousness leaps with the wolf when it leaves this body. It's not left behind in the statue. When the wolf comes back into this form, it's a separate consciousness living inside the human body."

"Can it leap without you?"

"No. And I can't be like this—" he gestured at his living flesh, "—without the wolf. We are true symbiotes in that we require each other to exist. But we're not the same entity."

"What happened with the ritual only half completed?"

"I'm not entirely sure. I hoped nothing would happen, but obviously something of the wolf was left behind. And because the ritual wasn't completed, it seems that piece and my wolf can't be separated easily, without the panic and fear and pain."

"That's why we had such a hard time in the woods." Her

expression was still so blank and neutral it was hard for him to witness. Her voice wasn't much better.

"I think that's why we had such a hard time being apart, yes. There's no other explanation. No other reason for that sort of reaction —to that extreme anyway. I would have always had a hard time leaving you because, well, monsters and danger and you being a vulnerable human. But barely being able to be separate from you like that... No, that was my fuck up. My starting and not finishing the ritual."

"Not a fuck up. An accident. Those are different."

"Semantics. I should have known better than to leap with you in the way. I should have realized."

She reached out and squeezed his hand. The sudden contact, any contact at all in that moment, was such a shock he froze. He was afraid to move. Afraid if he did, he'd lose that warm, reassuring touch.

"Accident," she said, firmly. "You were shot. Seriously injured." She swallowed visibly. "Dying. You had to leap and you did the right thing. The rest..." She shrugged. "An accident."

"An accident that has pretty severe consequences for both of us, though."

"Maybe," she allowed, letting her hand slip away from his.

He missed the contact immediately, but didn't dare reach for her. He was afraid if he did, she'd flinch away and that would gut him.

"What happens if we finish it, finish the ritual?" she asked, leaning back against the car door.

"Your life, strength, ability to heal from injuries and illness, all of that will be increased to match mine."

"Do Nam-tar ever outlive their mates?"

"They do. They can. My mother did." He hadn't meant to say that last sentence. His mother and father, his father's murder... That would sidetrack the conversation. He quickly moved past it, because Elle was curious enough to ask more. "But before that they've usually had many years together, even centuries."

"What happens if we don't finish the ritual?"

"That's the part I don't know. I've never encountered this situation before. And I haven't had a chance to talk to anyone who might know what to do."

"If we finish the ritual, does that mean I've…I've made my choice to stay, or…?" She shook her head hard. "How does this affect a Nam-tar's choice to stay or leave?"

"I don't know that either," he said quietly. "I think you'd still have the ability to leave. To choose not to take up this destiny. We'd still be linked but…"

"But your curse wouldn't be broken."

"Right." He shrugged. "I might have ruined any chance of that anyway, though. Last night."

She fell silent and dropped her gaze to the console between their seats, and all the packaging rubbish from their meal.

Finally, quietly, she said, "If I can still leave, if I have that choice still, your curse can still be broken if I choose to stay, though. Right? That's the only thing that makes sense."

"But if you stay because of the ritual, or because you feel obligated to stay, or because the ritual linked us and you're uncomfortable leaving, that's manipulation. That's forcing your hand. And the curse remains."

"Fuck," she muttered.

"Exactly."

She shook her head. "It's been less than two days. Barely over twenty-four hours. I can't make that kind of choice in so short a period of time."

"I don't expect you to. I don't want you to. No one would. There's usual time. For the…seduction part."

"The fun stuff."

Despite himself, he wanted to smile at that. "The fun stuff. The stuff that hopefully convinces a Nam-tar this life and their destined mate are worth the dangers."

"The problem is… I'm not sure how long I can stand to have this half-bond or whatever it is, this half-finished thing hanging out there between us, making being separated impossible. What happens if you die? Or I die? Before we finish. Where would that leave the other person?"

He hadn't considered that. The limbo would probably drive the other person insane if one of them died. The thought of Elle going through that, without him around to help, stabbed him with so much fear and horror there might as well have been a monster outside her window. Actually, he'd have been less afraid of the monster.

"We have to finish the ritual," she said. "One way or the other. And then, after, we can deal with the choice that's before me. Before us. With the other stuff."

"With the seduction?" he asked, not even a little embarrassed by the hope in his voice.

Her mouth softened, only a tiny bit, but it was progress, and while it wasn't precisely a smile, there was a hint of humor in that softening. "With all of it," she said. "But neither of us can remain in this limbo. Not with what we're going into. It's too dangerous."

She was right. He hated that he'd put them in this position. But she was right. They had to finish the process. He had to let his wolf leap back through her.

"It'll work, right?" she asked quietly. "Your wolf leaping back through me. That'll work at finishing the ritual. Won't it?"

Since he had no way of knowing for sure, and since he'd already breached her trust on accident, he gave her the truth. "I don't know. I think it will. But like I said, I've never encountered this before. I'm not certain."

She straightened her shoulders, her gaze steady on him. "We'll find a hotel. Tonight. We do this tonight. We need to know if it'll work or not. Before we reach the professor. Not knowing will make that extraction harder. We need to know."

"If you're sure." He tamped down on his own emotions. His fear and hope equally pushed to the back of his mind. She was the one that mattered here. He'd do whatever she wanted, whatever she asked. And hope it made things right between them.

"I'm sure." She pulled out her phone. "If you're done eating, let's get back on the road. The sooner we find an available room, the sooner we can get this over with."

As she searched for a motel, he cleaned up their dinner and got them back on the highway, his stomach tight with worry. And fear.

And that damned hoped.

CHAPTER TWENTY-TWO

The roadside motel was another serviceable but not magnificent affair. Elle was used to those basic rooms when she was on a job, so she barely considered it. What struck her as interesting was that Ben got them two rooms. Adjoining. Within easy reach should something go wrong or a monster appear. But he made sure she had her own room.

She wasn't entirely sure why this surprised her. Maybe because they had so much to talk about still, so they'd both be in one room for a while. Maybe because being separated was physically so difficult on them both thanks to their accident the night before.

But they'd only known each other such a short amount of time. She really should have her own room. And that he'd thought of that and she hadn't was something she'd have to consider closer.

Nam-tar.

It was a strange word that felt funny in her mouth. More because it seemed to roll around her tongue more naturally than it should. She'd been honest with him. She didn't believe in fate and destiny. She certainly didn't believe in fated love. She only barely believed in love. And even that had taken quite a lot of therapy to work out. Her perspective on love and relationships was a bit skewed. A generous description.

She didn't believe in his gods either. Same as she didn't believe that Zeus and Hera were real gods. And she'd at least heard of them. How on earth could a myth from someone else's family determine her future? That couldn't possibly be real.

But monsters. There were monsters. Real monsters. She'd seen them with her own eyes. Heard one speak with words. Had to fight through them. Watched Ben destroy them. More than just one.

If there were monsters—and, as it turned out, werewolves—there were probably a lot of things in this world she'd considered fiction. Like old gods.

Did that mean destined love might be more than fiction, too?

Once they'd checked in, Ben grabbed their luggage from the trunk, including the sword, which he slid into his longer canvas bag, and carried everything to their rooms. She might have argued with him carrying everything but she was tired and not inclined to be obstinate for the sake of appearances. Plus, he was really strong. It wasn't like her bag would strain his muscles.

She did question the sword with a nod, though.

He said, "Better to be prepared." He lifted the longer bag he'd slid the sword into. "This has all my weaponry. When we have a chance, I'll show you everything. Like I promised. In case we need to use any of it."

She didn't think they'd have trouble with monsters tonight. They were a full day behind the professor and his kidnappers, and well away from the house in the woods now. Still, knowing he was prepared did make her feel better. So did the second, though smaller, gun in her duffle.

Their rooms were as basic as hers last night had been. Neat and clean, but bare. The small desk-dresser unit was inexpensive pressboard, the bed covers on the single queen were serviceable but not luxurious, and the towels in the bathroom a little stiff from bleach. The cleaning solution left a faint lemon scent in the air. The laminate wood floors were free of dust. The soap in the bathroom smelled nice and herby. The flatscreen TV on the wall was a decent size. And the windows looked out on the woods at the back of the motel instead of overlooking the parking lot.

After handing her her bag at the door of her room, Ben warned her he had to make a phone call before coming over, so Elle had a few minutes to assess her room and settle in. But she was too restless to settle. She tried turning on the TV, to check the news, watching for signs of monster activity—would she always do that now?—but after a few minutes of politics and local farm news, she turned the TV back off.

She paced to the door that joined her room with Ben's and flipped open the lock. She hovered her fingers over the lock for a long moment as she considered flipping it back again. Then fisted her hand and walked away. The danger wasn't that Ben could walk into her room. It was that he wouldn't be able to get here easily of something happened.

This need for someone else, for any reason, left her itchy and uncomfortable. She'd spent a lot of years relying on herself, making sure no matter what, she could take care of herself. She didn't trust other people to do that for her. And she didn't trust this feeling now either. Any more than she trusted the idea of destined mates.

And yet…

She couldn't stop instinctively trusting Ben. At least when it came to fighting the monsters. She'd watched his thoroughness and care today. His determination that nothing escape and cause harm. The way he'd hunted the house in the woods, determined to ensure no monsters had gotten out. Whatever else she might think about his story, she had seen with her own eyes how seriously he took this duty to destroy monsters and protect people. She respected that. And trusted he wouldn't let a random monster eat her if he could stop it.

Was that the kind of trust that could lead to other kinds of trust? If she could trust someone with her physical safety, could she maybe one day trust that someone with the safety of her heart?

The thought was shocking enough she sat down hard on the bed, her gaze on the white wall behind the TV.

She gave herself a full body shake when she heard the door

adjoining their rooms click. Instead of just opening the unlocked door and coming in, though, he knocked and didn't enter until she'd given him permission to.

She hid her smile at his consideration by the time he came through.

"Call go okay?" she asked.

"My brother," he explained without hesitance. "We need a team to sweep that house, the woods, thoroughly make sure nothing got out. I can't do that and follow the professor." He shrugged. "Eric will get it sorted out."

"Eric is your brother?"

Ben nodded.

He'd mentioned sisters and brother. "How many siblings?" she asked.

"Twelve. Seven brothers, five sisters."

She raised her brows. "Your parents had thirteen kids? That's…a lot. I'm an only child. I can't even imagine all those siblings."

"There're quite a few years between Eric and our youngest sister. Centuries. So we were pretty spread out. I'm relatively close to Eric in age, so we spent our childhood together. But I was an adult by the time some of my siblings were born, so it wasn't like we were living on top of each other."

"So not really close to them, then?"

He shrugged. "Depends on your definition of close. I wouldn't hesitate to call on one of them now. There's a lot of trust there. We all talk and see each other regularly. Or, well, as regularly as our work allows. From my perspective, I'd say we're close."

"Sounds…nice." She realized she'd left him standing awkwardly in the doorway and motioned to the room's single plastic chair, which she'd wedged against the main door along with her travel lock. "Might as well get comfortable."

He gave the seat a dubious look. "Not sure comfortable is the word I'd use."

The comment startled a laugh from her. She slapped a hand over her mouth. "This doesn't feel like a laughing moment."

"Why not? Laughing helps relieve the stress. And you have a nice laugh." His voice deepened on the last sentence and his gaze dropped to her mouth. "Very nice."

The room suddenly felt a lot smaller. And she became acutely aware that she was sitting on a bed. Ignoring the rest of the world and the consequences and everything else to explore more of that "seduction" idea would definitely relieve her stress. The thought of it had her heart beating harder and her skin heating. She watched his jaw muscle flex when she licked her lips. Watched the way his shoulders tightened and he flexed a hand against his thigh.

For a solid minute, all she could think about was that hand flexing on her, on her waist, her thigh, her breast. She allowed her gaze to travel up his torso, across muscles made strong by a job that involved hammering out weapons and fighting monsters. To shoulders almost as broad as the doorway. He was just so damned big. And instead of scaring her, all that made her want to do was climb up that big body, wrap her legs around his waist, and see if he was large everywhere.

The way his nostrils flared, the way he held so perfectly still, with that one hand still fisted and tight against his leg, she knew it wouldn't take much. A nod. A faint sound. If she stood and took a step toward him, they'd be on each other. And there'd be no talking. At least not the kind of talk they needed to have right now. She could easily forget everything in the world for a few hours, drown herself in Ben's flavors and heat and the feel of his rough hands on her. Fucking and sucking their way through the night while ignoring everything else.

The thought was delicious. Tempting. So tempting she clenched her fingers in the bedspread.

But sex wouldn't solve their current problem. Might in fact make it worse. They still had a conversation they needed to have. And a scary experiment to run. The fear of what they were here to do should have dampened her growing lust. She was pretty surprised it didn't help at all.

She cleared her throat. When she started to speak, her voice sounded rough and breathy, though, so she cleared her throat again. "We need to talk. And then we need to try…recreating what happened…" She couldn't quite bring herself to say they needed to have his wolf jump *through* her.

"We do," he said. The deep, gravely tone of his voice danced along her nerves and made her want to moan.

"Sit. Before I forget we need to do other things."

He hesitated for just a moment, just long enough she thought he might ignore necessity. Giving her just long enough to accept she would welcome his loss of control. She wouldn't argue with him if he broke this tension with a kiss rather than a conversation.

Then he sucked in a deep breath and slowly settled himself into the plastic chair, the flimsy piece groaning under his weight.

That chair wasn't going to be comfortable for him for long. But giving him permission to sit with her on the bed would definitely end any thought that they could have a conversation tonight. And they needed to finish what they'd started. They needed to try and end this inability to be apart. A bond like that couldn't be good for either of them. It might even be a detriment when they finally found the professor. So they had to finish this.

She focused on the thought of a wolf spirit jumping through her, of that weird sensation she'd had last night in the house in the woods, of watching something move *through* her like a ghost and then turn solid as it went. Tried to recall the shock and fear. Those emotions helped dampen her lust. A little. But not nearly as much as she'd hoped.

Because there was something intimate about having a part of Ben pass through her. She fully understood why this was a matter of trust between couples. The thought of going through this without that trust was scary. What if it didn't work? What if the wolf started to turn solid before it got all the way through her? What if the process killed her on accident?

Those thoughts stopped her lust cold. She really hadn't considered the implications of what she was asking him to do. Not the dangers. There'd been no issue the first time, except that it had happened and bonded them when they shouldn't have been yet. But what if this time, things didn't work the way they were supposed to?

"What are you worrying about?" Ben asked softly.

"How could you tell?"

"Your scent changed." He tapped his nose once. "I share my logic and language with the wolf. The wolf shares his heightened senses with me."

"Nice."

"Why are you suddenly scared?"

"What if this doesn't work?"

"It will work."

"But what if it doesn't?"

"And we stay bonded and can't be apart? We'll deal with that until we can find someone who knows how to fix things. I won't stop trying to fix this. I promise."

She waved that away. "I wasn't worried about the weird bond. Well, I mean, I am. But I know we'll figure that out eventually. It's… What if your wolf doesn't… What if it can't jump through me again? Or goes solid before it gets through me, or…?" She started breathing hard at the thought and had to press her lips together and breath through her nose in deep drags to try and calm the panic.

Ben leaned forward in his seat, almost like he'd reach for her, but stopped himself. "You don't have to worry about that. The wolf will not only go halfway through. That can't happen. Either he will corporealize after he's passed through you, or he'll knock you down on the way past because he's corporealized coming out of me. There's no scenario where he can get halfway through you and then not finish the process. Okay. You don't have to worry about that part."

He reached toward her again, just his hand, and she scooted along the bed so she could be close enough to take his hand. She didn't actually think about the fact that his touch was comforting. That she'd needed that comfort from him specifically. But she noticed that the instant his big, callused fingers curled around hers, her pulse rate slowed and her breathing returned to normal and the panic that was starting to overwhelm her subsided.

She took another couple of deep breaths, staring at their joined hands, the way he held her tight but gently. Comforting. But careful of his strength.

"This helps a lot." She squeezed his hand. "More than I would expect."

"Helps me, too."

"Is that the Nam-tar thing, or the we-fucked-up-the-ritual thing?"

"Probably a little of both. But you didn't fuck up anything. That's all on me."

"You didn't do it on purpose. So I don't want you carrying all the blame." She squeezed his hand again.

He slid a little farther forward, which tipped the chair forward, too. The only thing keeping it from falling out from under him was the way it caught on the door handle. "We can wait to do this," he said. "We don't have to try this very minute. We can talk until you're more comfortable."

Would that help or did she just want to get this over with now?

She wanted to try now. Talking more wouldn't calm her worries. Might only make them worse since the things they still had to talk about included how this Nam-tar thing was supposed to break his curse and what the curse did to him. She understood why he didn't want to tell her. If it was bad, and the only thing that would prevent him from going through that was her agreeing to stay, she could see that guilting someone into staying. Or maybe guilt wasn't the right word. Compassion. It could play on someone's compassion and urge them to stay. It might well do that for her. But only because she *liked* Ben. She didn't want him to suffer, in any way.

As she stared at their hands woven together in the space between the bed and his seat, she wondered if what she felt might be more than like. Or at least could be more than like with a little more time.

Yeah. She could see that. With a little more time. Time to get to know him better. She could see this becoming more. The fact that she found him sexy as hell probably helped that assessment. But it was more than that. If he'd been an asshole, all the external sexiness wouldn't have helped him. She'd have still found him an asshole and not wanted to be around him. But he wasn't an asshole. He was kind. Strong. Brave. Gentle. He took duty seriously. And willingly protected humans from monsters.

And he was kind. That kindness really did it for her.

"Okay," she said, letting out a long breath. "Let's try. The ritual stuff. Let's try. We'll know soon enough if it will work or not. And then we'll know what we're dealing with. But I want to get this done, or I'll just lose my nerve."

He held her gaze, his hand on hers squeezing gently. After a beat, he nodded and stood, taking her with him. When she was on her feet, he tugged her close with their still linked hands. The minute she was near enough to feel the warmth of his skin, her heartbeat started pounding harder again. Not from panic. This wasn't panic.

This was distraction.

His gaze darkened as he looked down at her, so she knew she wasn't the only one in this room having this reaction. Then, very carefully, he released her hand and put his on her shoulders. For a split second, she thought he'd pull her into his arms, maybe even kiss her since most of his focus was on her mouth. She'd be a happy and willing partner in that kiss. She'd dive without any hesitation into that kiss.

But instead of pulling her against him, he gently turned her so her back was to his front. They were close, but not quite touching. There was about an inch between her back and his chest and abdomen. Not touching probably had something to do with the ritual, but she desperately wanted to lean into him and feel the length of that big body pressing against her spine.

He bent over her, his breath brushing the side of her face. "We'll stay this close so you have less to worry about. Without much space between us, the process will be fast. You might feel cold as the wolf moves through you. And this body will be stone behind you. Which means if I keep my hands on you—" he flexed his fingers against her upper arms where he was still holding her, "—they'll turn to stone on you. That might be…unsettling. So I'm not going to hold you as this happens. You need to remain right here, though. If you move, that will make the process impossible. Okay?"

She nodded. Cleared her throat. "Okay," she said, but she still sounded hoarse and breathless. She felt pretty breathless having his face so close to the side of her head. She faced him, and the angle meant kissing him would be so so easy.

He brought one hand up to cup her cheek, his thumb rubbing over her cheekbone. "So soft," he murmured, so quietly she wasn't sure she was supposed to hear. Louder, so she was certain he was talking to her, "This will work. You'll be fine. The wolf has to jump through you twice. Because the first time will feel…odd, you might be tempted to move or delay the second jump. Don't. We'll only know if this works if the second leap is completed."

"So just stand here and don't move," she confirmed.

"Please."

The please broke something apart in her, some dam on her emotions she'd been holding onto too tightly. She took advantage of their closeness and brushed her lips against his. Gently, as delicately as his thumb on her cheek. A press and release. A testing and a tasting. But only a quick one. Enough to know she wanted more. Enough to know deepening that kiss would take no effort on her part. He tasted like a heated promise, and she very much wanted to explore that promise more.

When she pulled back, she met his gaze, checking to see if she'd crossed a line.

His nostrils flared and his gaze skimmed over her face like he was trying to memorize her. His voice was very deep when he said, "When this is done, when we've finished the ritual, I'd like to revisit that kiss."

"Should I not have?"

"You should have."

She smiled. "Good. Because I'd like to revisit the kiss, too."

He skimmed his hand over her cheek and down her throat, his thumb brushing against her rapidly pounding pulse. His hand on her upper arm slid downward, brushing his rough palm over her skin. Her nerves tingled and a moan hovered just behind her closed lips. She desperately wanted to lean into him and forget about the ritual. But they couldn't do that. At least not yet.

When he dropped his hands back to his sides, she mourned the loss of contact that left an itching in her skin to get his hands on her again.

"Are you ready?" he asked, his voice rough and quiet.

"As I'll ever be." She straightened her shoulders and faced the wall opposite, near the bathroom at the back of the room. She could do this. They could do this.

And then they could return to that kiss.

CHAPTER TWENTY-THREE

Elle felt Ben take a deep breath behind her as much as she heard him, his huge chest almost brushing her back, close, not quite touching her. For a long moment, it seemed like nothing was happening. She stared at the white motel room wall and listened intently. She heard the faint sound of traffic in the distance from the highway, muted because they were on the opposite side of the building. She heard the wind picking up outside, gusting down the walkway outside the room. She heard Ben breathing and her own stuttering breaths. She could nearly smell her own panic and wondered if that was affecting him, making him hesitate.

And then she felt something cold, suddenly and shockingly, even though she'd been expecting it. A sense of cold swept into her from the back. Through her spine and out her chest. Flowing from her chest in the ghostly form of the wolf.

As the wolf moved through her in a leaping pose, front legs forward, head down, moving fast but not as fast as a real leap would have happened, the nebulous, translucent form turned more solid. The head, the forepaws, the neck, the back. She watched the animal go from transparent to solid as it passed through her and only realized she wasn't breathing when the wolf landed on the floor a few feet away, solid and real.

She blinked at it. Same wolf. Large, gray, dark eyes staring up at her with more intelligence than she'd ever seen in a wolf. He tucked his tail and sat, staring up at her with a curious patience. She stared back, for a long moment, wondering what was happening.

"Aren't you supposed to jump back through now?" she asked.

The wolf gave a slight whine and waved his paw at her.

She frowned. That meant something obviously. But damned if she knew what. She glanced back at Ben, or well now the statue of Ben. Standing so close to a stone statue of a man she'd just been lusting after was very odd. But not nearly as freaky as it should be. She should be more upset and disturbed and weirded out by all this. Her own acceptance and calm surprised the hell out of her.

She was tempted to run a hand over Ben's stone face, to test the texture. The stone looked very smooth, like polished marble, a gray-white color, and capture the man's stunning face in such perfect detail she could practically see the statue breathing. And well, of course that made sense since he was an actual breathing, living person once the wolf reentered him. She pressed her fingers into her thighs so she wouldn't touch the statue. She hadn't asked permission to do that and wasn't sure if it was acceptable or not. Last night, when he'd been injured and she'd seen this for the first time, that had been different.

But now, with the feel of his hands on her skin and the brush of his lips against hers still tingling over her nerves, she thought she might be crossing a line. Swallowing, she faced the wolf again. He was watching her closely. His nostrils flared, and she remembered Ben mentioning his good sense of smell.

That would make hiding her emotions from him pretty difficult, wouldn't it? She wasn't sure how she felt about that.

"You're in there, right?" she said. "Ben?"

The wolf nodded.

"Okay, so…" She looked around. "You still have to leap back through me, right? Why are you still waiting?"

Another whine and another gesture like the wolf was petting the air.

She still wasn't sure what that meant. The wolf whined a little more and settled onto his forepaws before standing up fully again. Then he sat.

The series of gestures showed her a lot of hesitance on the wolf's part. And it slowly sank in that he was waiting for her to be ready. To reassure him he should finish the process.

Not having the ability to smell emotions was a real drawback in this situation. "You're waiting to make sure I'm okay? Okay to finish?"

The wolf nodded.

"I am. You can finish." She braced herself, standing in front of Ben's statue, sucking in a deep breath as she prepared for the cold again. Steeling herself against watching the process from this angle.

She only realized how easy it would be to balk when the wolf took a few steps back, closer to the wall, and then started toward her fast. Watching from this direction was scarier for some reason. Even though not seeing, not knowing what would happen, or when the jump might happen, left a lot of room for fear, actually watching a wolf run toward her, leap into the air at her chest, grabbed her directly in her lizard brain. The instinct to duck and run away was so strong she flinched.

The wolf changed direction mid-leap and landed on the ground next to her, still solid and whole.

"What?" She stared at him, her heartbeat pounding harder as panic started to creep in. "It's not working? You can't go back through?"

The wolf whined and covered his nose with his paw.

"I'm not sure what that gesture means. And this scares me. It's not going to work? Is that the problem?"

The wolf shook his head.

"It will work?"

A nod. Then another whine.

"So why did you stop?" That wasn't a yes-no question, though, so she knew he couldn't answer. Fuck. What was a yes-no question? "Did you stop because I was scared?"

A nod.

Ah. Well shit. "Listen, this is strange and I'm going to be scared, but you need to finish. You have my permission to jump back through even if I flinch. We need to finish the whole process this time, not only do halfway."

The wolf whined quietly.

"It's fine. I promise. Maybe I should close my eyes. That'll be more like when you leap at my back. Waiting is a little nerve-wracking but without watching you jump at me I'll be less likely to flinch. But seriously, even if I do, don't stop again. Just do it. We have to finish this."

The wolf's shoulders hunched and his tail twitched, but he spun and walked back across the room, standing near the bathroom door.

She made a show of closing her eyes. "See, this way I won't flinch."

With her eyes closed, not seeing the wolf run toward her did prevent her from flinching, but the sensation of something hitting her in the chest made her gasp. It wasn't like something solid hitting her, though. More like getting shoved by a very strong wind. She had to brace herself so she didn't fall back into Ben's statue. The thought of knocking it over and breaking it sent a wave of terror through her. She took a single step backward, then held still. And realized the pressure that had knocked her back a step was moving through her now.

And it was warm.

Both previous times, the sensation had been cold, chilling, like an actual ghost moving through her. But this time, the sensation was warm and lovely, like a tropical breeze. Like sinking into a hot bath and all that heat suffused her skin in a delicious, satisfying way that made her sigh.

She did sigh, out loud, and smiled as she felt the warmth move through her chest, out her back, felt the tingles left in its wake, her skin vibrating. She blinked her eyes open to see if she could catch any of the wolf's movement through her but she knew she was too late. She could feel the last of his heat passing out her spine and back into Ben.

For a beat, a breath, she stood perfectly still, savoring the tingly sensations running across her skin and the warmth that filled her, letting the contentment sink deep into her soul.

That was it. Contentment. She felt settled and content with the world.

She smiled and slowly turned to face Ben. He was back to the living man, no more smooth, lifeless marble staring at her.

"Well?" he asked.

"That last part…that was really nice. Warm. Not cold like the other two times. Is that supposed to happen?"

"I have no idea. I've never done this before."

"You never thought to ask anyone you know who has what it felt like?"

He shrugged.

She wanted to roll her eyes. How did you live for multiple centuries and not have any curiosity about this one thing that you were actually hoping to do one day. "What did it feel like to you? Just… normal? Like every other time you do this."

"No. Not exactly normal. I usually feel a sweep of cold in my human body when I leap. And there's a moment of disorientation in the wolf when I have to rearrange my perception to that different form. I still had to reorient as the wolf, but not much. That happened fast. And the cold…wasn't there when the wolf moved back into me. Almost like it brought some of your warmth with it, the passage of the spirit, the way the stone receded, all of that felt hot this time. A good hot. Then a sort of tingling…like when a body part falls asleep and is waking up."

"Pins and needles feeling?"

"That's it. That was all over my skin afterward. Not for long. And not uncomfortable. Well, maybe a little uncomfortable, but not bad. Just strange. That's not what usually happens for me."

"Strange is a good word for what just happened." She looked around. "Should I feel different? How will we know if it worked?"

And what sort of outcome was she hoping for? She didn't want them to be incapable of being apart. That felt horrible and unsustainable. She wanted them to at least be able to separate for fifteen minutes without losing their minds.

But did she want more? He'd said this would extend her life, make her stronger, and help her heal faster. She didn't want to purposely hurt herself to see if she healed fast—she wasn't sure Ben would go along with that either—and she had no way to test if her life would be longer.

Stronger. She could test stronger.

"How much stronger?" she asked.

And despite the fact that the comment came out of nowhere, he seemed to follow her thought process well enough because he didn't miss a beat. "Not quite as strong as me but strong enough to, say pick up the bed."

"Could I pick up a car? Or is that pushing it?"

"For a human, pushing it, but possible now. You could probably flip a car easier than lifting it up."

She could flip a car now? Holy shit. Really good thing her father hadn't known about all this. "I don't want to go flipping cars just yet, but I could try the bed." She gave the furniture a speculative look.

Queen-sized and on an inexpensive metal frame, it wasn't exactly a super heavy-looking bit of furniture. She could easily move it before. But pick up the whole thing…probably not. A side at a time. But not the whole thing.

"Okay. We need to know if this worked and I can't test the other stuff yet. And I don't want to test if we can be apart until we have a better idea if this worked." Because that was such an icky feeling she wasn't in a hurry to relive it. "If I can't pick up the bed, what will that mean?"

"That your body needs more time to adapt to the effects of the ritual," he said. But he didn't sound as certain as she'd have liked.

"What happens if it didn't work?"

"We were able to do it. It worked. We finished it. It worked."

"But the warmth and your pins-and-needles sensation that wasn't normal…"

"I've never done the ritual before because I've never met my Nam-tar before. I have no idea what I should have felt afterward or during. For all I know, that's exactly what was supposed to happen."

"You didn't even ask your brother when you called him?"

"He hasn't gone through the ritual with his Nam-tar yet. They've only been together a little over a year. She's building up to it."

Elle couldn't really blame her. She wouldn't have done this yet—or maybe ever—if they hadn't needed to. Well, maybe she would have eventually. But she'd have taken more time to mull over the consequences. Consequences she was now stuck with and without any time to really come to terms with what this all meant. But better this than be stuck with the unintended side-effects of a half-finished ritual.

"And we had other things to talk about," Ben finished.

"You don't want to tell him, do you?" She didn't have any siblings. She didn't know how brother relationships worked. But she suspected if she had an older sister, she wouldn't want to admit mistakes to her.

"I don't. I don't want a lecture when we have other things to worry about. Eric is better at lectures than—" He cut himself off so abruptly, Elle could practically hear his brain screeching to a stop. "Anyway, let's test your strength. If you can't lift the bed, it won't be a definitive sign this didn't work, but it'll let us know things aren't…settled yet."

She wanted to ask about that abrupt stop, about what he'd left unsaid. But she also didn't want to force confidences from him. If and when he wanted to tell her, he would.

And the fact that she was thinking of them in future terms, in terms of having time to discuss these things and give each other parts of their past, their secrets, was not lost on her.

She wanted to know him better. Spend more time with him. Learn all his secrets.

She wanted to revisit that kiss.

Pulling in a deep breath, she stepped up to the side of the bed and hooked her hands under the metal frame. Then she braced herself and attempted to lift the entire bed off the ground.

The side she was lifting came up so easily and suddenly she accidentally tossed the whole thing into the wall next to the bathroom. The metal frame clattered against the floor as the mattress slid down the wall. She stood blinking at the heap, her hands out in front of her for a long moment before she let them fall back to her sides.

"Uhm."

"Not sure how to judge that," he said.

"Right? Pretty wimpy bed. I might have been able to do that even before the ritual."

"Want to go try and lift your car? It's dark enough, no one should see you. We'll be subtle."

She raised her brows at him. Lifting a car with her bare hands was definitely outside her normal range of strength. "You just said I might only be able to flip it. I don't want to flip the car."

"I don't mean lift the whole thing. Just lift the front bumper a little. Gently." He glanced at the bedframe. "And then set it back down. It'll be a better test."

She also glanced at the bedframe. The metal was a little twisted now. She couldn't tell if that was from her picking it up or from it hitting the ground. "Okay. Gently try to lift a car."

They were parked in the front lot, in the darker shadows a few spots away from the lot light. Hopefully, no one would see them.

She headed for the door, determined to see if this had all worked, but Ben stopped her with a gentle hand on her arm. She turned toward him, realized the move pressed her right up against his chest, and thoughts of anything else besides him left her head entirely. She could feel the rise and fall of his chest rubbing against her breasts, the warm brush of his breath against her mouth as he bent over her.

"Before we go, I just need…" He leaned even closer, his mouth hovering over hers. "If you want me to stop—"

She silenced the rest of his sentence with her mouth.

No soft brush of lips this time, though. The instant she pressed her mouth to his, the kiss exploded. Desperate. Searching. She wrapped her arms around his waist and tried to crawl into him, needed to be as close as they could get. He cupped her face between his big hands and angled his head to deepen the kiss, his tongue sweeping into her mouth. The flavor of him hit her like a shot of whiskey, going right to her head. Making her dizzy.

She clung tighter to him, her hands running up his back, across muscles she'd been trying not to think about for two days. One of his hands slid up through her hair, around to cup the back of her head. His other hand skimmed across her shoulders and around her back. She was engulfed in his embrace and the heat of him seeped into her like desert sun. So warm and delicious she wanted to just soak him up.

His mouth moved over her, a desperate tasting, and she took all that desperation, answered it with all her building want and need. His scent filled her head. Everything about him surrounded her and filled her world. Until there was only him and the places their bodies pressed tight together, his big hand in her hair, gently cradling the back of her head even has the arm around her back flexed and the hand on her waist tightened.

Someone moaned. Might have been her. She was too lost in his kiss to notice. She did feel the press of his erection against her stomach, though. And that only fed her hunger. Knowing he wanted her as much as she wanted him made her head spin and she wasn't sure she'd still be standing on her own feet if he wasn't holding her up.

Elle had no idea how long the kiss lasted, only knew she was breathless and panting when they came up for air. She could have easily ignored the rest of the world and just taken him to bed right then and there.

But that part… This couldn't be just a casual night of sex for them. There were larger implications, consequences they needed to consider. Things she needed to think about first. And being with Ben made thinking impossible.

Still, a very large part of her that was all libido and lust wanted to chuck consequences and focus on getting Ben out of his clothes. There were delectable muscles to explore. And that intriguing hard length of his cock pressed solidly against her stomach to investigate. And an awful lot of things she wanted to do to him.

But not yet. She couldn't chuck consequences and thinking time. Yet.

When she dragged in a shaky breath, her nipples rubbed against his chest, and that didn't help matters at all. She swallowed hard. They probably needed to step away from each other. She made no move to do so.

"I'm going to want to revisit this, too," Ben said, his voice so rough and gravely it made her nerves sing.

"Yeah. Yeah. But…not yet."

"Not yet," he agreed with a nod. "But soon."

There was a lot of promise in that "soon." And maybe just a little threat. The kind of threat that made her tingle everywhere and forget her own name. Made her wet and weak with wanting. She wanted to ask exactly what sort of delights he was threatening her with. But that would lead them down a path she wasn't quite ready for. Yet.

But soon.

CHAPTER TWENTY-FOUR

Ben kept his hands in his pockets and forced himself to focus on Elle's car instead of her. The effort was harder than fighting a hoard of aghrises. He'd rather have to fight the monsters than put in this effort to keep his hands off his Nam-tar.

The kiss still sung in his veins. The feel of her soft and willing was branded on his body. The desire in her scent filled his head. That smokey spice flavored her scent even now and it made thinking about anything beyond getting her naked nearly impossible.

The scent spiked when she looked at him, too, and that didn't help matters.

Even the cold breeze blowing through the parking lot, the lights on the motel breezeway behind him, the knowledge that she was about to try lifting a car and the shadows concealing them weren't deep enough to hide her success if this worked…none of that cooled his need.

He fisted his hands, digging his fingers into his palms, and tried to think about something that wasn't the feel of Elle's breasts rubbing against his chest. A near impossible task.

Clearing his throat, he said, "Try from the front bumper. You'll have a better purchase and the lift will be less obvious from the motel if anyone is watching. They might even think you have a jack under the car." He cleared his throat again. Damn his voice sounded funny. Too deep and almost rusty.

Elle shivered when he spoke, and he might have worried about her if that spike of smokey spice didn't jump into her scent again. He took a step toward her before he could stop himself. Her pulse was pounding in her throat, drawing his attention. He wanted to kiss that delicate sign of her desire so much it hurt. Her skin was so soft and warm. And she was so lush. And he was going to go out of his mind if he didn't get to touch her again soon.

Elle sucked in a sudden breath and scurried around to the front of the car. Smart woman. Smarter than him.

With most of car between them, she finally met his gaze fully. "What happens if this works and I accidentally toss the car?"

"I'll right it, and we'll pretend it was the wind and adrenaline if anyone notices. But maybe don't toss the car." He had to force himself to say that without smiling. "Just lift gently. Pretend you're super strong and can flip the car. That'll help."

"Pretend? I won't be able to, even if things…worked? You said I could."

"You'll lift more gently if you assume you *can* throw the car rather than assuming you won't be able to."

"Makes sense." She wet her lips as she stared down at the hood.

Ben carefully didn't react to that quick flick of her tongue over her lips. Or at least, he kept his reaction carefully to himself. "It'll be okay, Elle," he murmured. "Either way."

At least he hoped it would. His nerves weren't exactly settled. If this hadn't worked, they had a problem they were going to have to deal with. A problem that might even require going to Vienna to talk to his mother in person. But with his and Elle's kiss still sending his nerve centers into overdrive, his worry kept getting pushed to the back of his mind. He only had so much mental space and most of it was occupied by imagining Elle naked.

Elle rubbed her palms together, then squatted low and hooked her hands under the front bumper.

"Remember," he said. "Gentle. Just lift gently."

"And if I can't lift a car?"

"We'll deal with that if it happens." Although he wasn't entirely sure how they'd do that yet.

She huffed out a loud breath, closed her eyes, and lifted.

The front of the car rose off the ground as she stood to her full height. She held the car up, blinking hard at him, her mouth hanging slightly open. "I'm lifting a car. I'm lifting a car!" The last word came out a squeak.

He let out a breath of his own. "Well. Looks like at least that part of the ritual worked."

Relief was almost enough to overwhelm his still simmering lust. The ritual had worked. At least to give her added strength and probably an increased ability to heal. Which meant she'd be safer when they went in to extract the professor. And that was a bonus he hadn't counted on.

Whether or not she could still choose to leave, whether they could break his curse or not, all that was still up in the air. But at least, one way or the other, she'd be safer now. That was worth everything to him. He realized he'd happily remain cursed if it meant Elle was safe. Not something he would have considered before meeting her.

Some of the things Eric had done with his Nam-tar Katie last year, that Ben and his other siblings had thought illogical, were starting to make more sense.

"Better set it down now," he said when Elle continued to stand there staring at the car she held up. "But gently. Remember your strength." He rolled his lips into his mouth so he wouldn't laugh at the glare she sent him.

"This is really freaky," she said. "A *car* feels as light as a blanket. Or maybe more like a bag of groceries. But not a bag full of cans. A few cans and some bread on top maybe."

"That's the most specific description I've ever heard. Are you hungry that you're thinking about groceries?" They'd eaten before reaching the motel, but she'd also had a pretty busy day. He should go hunt her up some food.

"Actually, I am hungry," she said. Then squatted and set the car back down, so gently it barely bounced when the rubber tires hit tarmac. She straightened away from the bumper, blinking hard. "I can't believe I just did that."

"Very impressive," he said and had to contain another grin when she glared at him again. "If you're hungry, we can test the reason we did this. I'll go get some food. You stay here. If we can be apart for the amount of time it takes me to find an open restaurant and get food back here, we should be okay."

Actually, the idea of being away from her still made him feel itchy and restless. He didn't want to be away from her. He wanted to ensure she was safe by bringing her with him. But was that just his protective instincts, or was that the physical sign they were still stuck needing to be in each other's presence?

He wasn't sure he'd ever really *want* to be away from her. But they *needed* to be able to be apart. For so many reasons. Even if she chose to stay and accepted him as her mate, he'd have to go out hunting on his own. She wouldn't always be beside him as he went after monsters. In fact, he'd preferred to keep her as far from the monsters as possible.

She'd want to do things away from him, too. She had work. Work that was as important as his own. Tracking lost people, with an actual psychic skill, bringing them back to their loved ones was vital. But he wouldn't always be able to go with her when she did her work. If nothing else, he could rely on the monsters to have the absolute worst timing. He'd have to go one way while she went another. They *had* to be able to do that. Yet he was reluctant to try the experiment. As reluctant as she'd been to try lifting the car.

Because what if it didn't work?

She rounded the car to join him, a crease between her brows, her luscious mouth turned down in a frown that distracted him because he couldn't stop looking at her lips.

"Since we did all this to try and fix that problem," she said, "I suppose we should test it. Before we face any more monsters."

"We should." She was so close he forgot what they'd been talking about. His arms actually ached to pull her in tight, and all his thoughts turned to exploring her beautiful mouth some more.

Her visible swallow proved she wasn't entirely focused on the conversation either. Her gaze kept dropping to his mouth before jumping back up. And that rapid little bump of her pulse in her throat matched the smokey spice of her lust.

She gave herself a little shake and abruptly handed him the car keys. "Let's test this. You get food. I'll stay here. If we don't lose our minds, we know it worked. Good plan. Good plan. And if it doesn't work…" She shrugged. "We'll figure something out. But we have to know."

At least one of them was still thinking, even if she was as distracted by the attraction between them as he was. "What do you want?"

"Anything. I'm easy." Her eyes widened. "That wasn't innuendo."

His fight to contain a grin evaporated. Gods she was adorable. His fight to resist pulling her in for another kiss evaporated, too.

She melted against him, easy, without even a moment of hesitation, and met him halfway, the kiss an explosive burst of mutual passion. He sank into her, loving her soft moan and the way she rubbed up against him. Her taste, the scent of her, the softness of her curves against him. All of her imprinted on him. Until he couldn't remember what his life had been without her in it. He was pretty sure there'd been a lot of years there without Elle. Just…he couldn't remember what they'd felt like.

Two fucking days and she'd become his world. How very very strange.

He lifted his head reluctantly, though he did savor her quiet whimper. Knowing she was as happy to stand in a parking lot kissing as he was gave him an unholy amount of satisfaction. He brushed a finger over her cheek, then took a deliberate step away so they weren't touching. She swayed toward him before catching herself and straightening. The telling move made him want to growl in triumph.

"I'll wait till you're back in the room before I leave," he said, then had to clear his throat. "Text me when you have the door locked."

Her soft smile made his heart bound harder. His turn to take an involuntary step toward her.

She opened her mouth as if to say something, but then shook her head, and turned abruptly back toward the motel.

He watched until she'd walked up the stairs and disappeared behind the building. Then he watched his cellphone screen until he got her text. When he was sure she was safe, he drove to the first fast food drive thru he could find. His need to feed her surprised him as much as any other part of this experience. The need to ensure she ate, was safe and comfortable, as instinctive as knowing she was his Nam-tar.

After ordering enough food to feed his youngest sister—which was to say more than four humans could eat in one sitting—just so he had enough to ensure Elle was content, he started to rush back to the motel. But the reason they were doing this, aside from food, had him parking the car so he could take a few minutes to assess how he was feeling.

Eager to get back? Definitely. Heart-pounding panic that she wasn't right here next to him? Less than earlier that day. Worried monsters might be going after her while he was away? A little. Although, that was probably more a side effect of his job than their bond. The grinluk had seen a wolf jump through her and had assumed she was a Seven Families hunter. That put Elle on the monsters' radar, putting her in danger even if she hadn't been his Nam-tar. So worrying about the monsters going after her was reasonable.

He sat staring at the dashboard for a long few moments, trying to work out how he felt, if he wanted so desperately to get back to her because he just liked being with her or because he *had* to or he'd lose his mind.

In the end, he decided he just wanted to. There wasn't that panicked compulsion driving him. That overwhelming sense that if he didn't reach her soon, he'd go stark raving mad. His wolf wasn't clawing at his mind, driving him to hurry. They were both restless and wanting to get back to her. But it wasn't anything like the earlier sensation.

Ben let out a long breath. So. That seemed to have worked. At least from his end.

He pulled out his phone and texted her to check if she was doing okay. He might not have the physical imperative to get back to her before he lost his mind, but he was still desperate to hear from her.

That, he suspected, would never change.

CHAPTER TWENTY-FIVE

lle stared at the flatscreen TV on the wall across from her bed, watching a "feel good" news story about a charity event hosted by the billionaire Logan family. She thought they might be opening a new art museum somewhere, but she was only half listening to the broadcast. The rest of her attention was on tracking her feelings, checking for those telltale adrenaline-fueled bolts of panic from earlier.

And remembering the kiss.

What a kiss it had been. Several kisses actually. Her head had spun during, and she was restless and needy after, and none of that was going to help their current situation. Not that her body cared. Her body wanted Ben there so she could strip him naked and fuck him until morning. Her body wanted to see if he kissed her pussy as thoroughly as he kissed her mouth. Her body had all *kinds* of ideas about how they should spend this night in a motel room and how it didn't matter even a little bit that they'd only met yesterday.

Her body was a horny bitch who was not thinking clearly.

She threw herself backward on the bed and stared up at the ceiling, the background ramble of the newscaster a droning hum that barely penetrated her consciousness. How was she feeling besides horny? Well, she didn't seem to have the same panic bubbling over. She'd done her usual job of locking the room door and even locked the connecting door between her room and Ben's just in case. She'd hunted the room, bathroom, under the bed—which Ben had kindly reassembled before they'd gone down to the car—ensuring she was alone and no monsters were lurking nearby. Would Ben have thought her overcaution ridiculous or warranted?

Since his life's work was hunting monsters, she thought he might be one of the very few people in the world who appreciated her excessively cautious streak. Why did that make her feel less lonely? Had she been lonely before? She didn't think she had. Hadn't recognized being lonely anyway. She'd been busy with her work and content with the life she'd built for herself. She hadn't been on any dates in a few months, but she blamed work for that. And she hadn't made a lot of effort to hang out with her friends for a while. Again, though, she blamed work. She spent a lot of time on the road when tracking a missing person. That made regular visits with people difficult.

That would make life with Ben more difficult.

Wait. What?

The thought startled her so much she sat up and blinked at the TV. What did she mean "life with Ben?" When had she started thinking about them spending their lives together? Wasn't the point of finishing the ritual so she'd have the option, the choice, to stay or leave?

Had she already decided to stay?

Not consciously. She hadn't stopped and said, *You know what? I think I'll just stay with this man for the rest of my life and break his curse. He's nice. I like kissing him. He feeds me. Sure he hunts monsters on the side, but that's fine. This could really work.*

She hadn't once had that thought. Having any of those thoughts felt wildly premature. Thinking about how their two jobs would affect their relationship *was* wildly premature. Hell, they still weren't sure if the ritual had worked.

Except…

She wasn't panicking and desperate for him to return. In fact, after her epiphany, she was glad he wasn't in the room. She needed some space to consider her own thoughts, and Ben was a distraction to thinking. Also, he might be able to smell her surprise and that would lead to questions she wasn't ready to answer yet—and the fact that he could scent her emotions was another thing she'd have to consider at some point in the future.

But she definitely wasn't panicking about him being gone. She wasn't so desperate to have him close again she wanted to scream. She didn't feel like she was losing her mind because he wasn't next to her, wasn't being pulled apart by his absence.

That was...

Great! Her casually considering their life together was a little disturbing, but at least they could be apart without it driving her crazy. That was such a relief she collapsed back onto the bed again.

Only to pop right back up when her phone pinged with an incoming text message.

Another reason she was glad Ben wasn't in the room with her. The way she scrambled for the phone to check the message was undignified and embarrassing. Although, if he'd been in the room with her, her reason for scrambling for her phone wouldn't exist. She was only in such a hurry because she hoped the message was from him.

She smiled when his name popped up on her phone. (Sexy) Ben. She really should get his last name. Though she suspected he'd remain (Sexy) Ben even after she got it.

Ben: *How are you doing?*

Elle: *Fine. Watching TV. Not crawling out of my skin in panic.*

Ben: *Me neither.*

Elle: *Great. Then it worked. Right?*

Ben: *I think so ... I'm still in a hurry to get back to you.*

Her smile deepened. Elle: *Good. Then get back here.*

Ben: *On my way.*

Elle: *What food did you get me?*

The pause had her frowning at the phone. Was he on the road already? She didn't want him texting while he drove so she supposed she could wait for the answer. He'd be here soon.

Then her phone pinged again.

Ben: *Chicken and sides. I had to check. I forgot what I ordered.*
She chuckled.
Ben: *I was thinking about you.*
And that just made her melt.
Elle: *Hurry back.*
Ben: *Be there soon.*
She stared at his last message for a long moment before flicking off her phone and setting it gently on the bedside table. What a difference thirty hours could make in a person's life. Just two days ago, she'd been happily single—or at least hadn't really had romance on her mind because she'd been too focused on finding the professor. Now she was contemplating spending her life with a man she'd just met and getting all soft inside from a series of texts.

Realizing he'd be back soon, her heart started to thump hard with anticipation and that needy lust. She glanced down at her clothes, then jumped up to look at her hair in the mirror over the bathroom sink. She probably didn't have time for a full shower, blow dry, and make up thing. And besides, wow, would that be obvious. But she could at least change into clean clothes and wash her face. They'd had a day with a lot of noxious smells. Getting into something that didn't still carry that lingering smell under it felt rather important. And the fact that she hadn't even thought about it yet only proved how distracted she was.

She changed, washed with a surprisingly soft hand towel and the nice smelling hand soap, finger combed her hair. And tried to force a casual appearance when he knocked on the door between their rooms. She was still smiling widely when she unlocked the door.

"Smart to lock everything behind me," he said on his way through. Then stopped in his tracks and just stared at her.

His hands were full of bags of food—looked like enough to feed a small army—and the smell of chicken and biscuits made her stomach growl. But that look on his face had her hungry for a completely different type of sustenance. She did glance down, to make sure she hadn't forgotten something or didn't have something weird on her clothes. Nope. Just an ordinary blue t-shirt and tan cargo pants—the staples of her wardrobe when she was tracking someone. Not even particularly nice clothes either. Just ordinary. She'd combed her hair. But other than that, she looked like she had when he'd left.

She frowned up at him. "I'm a safety girl when it comes to door locks. Why are you looking at me like that? Do I have something on my face?" She touched her cheek.

He shook his head. Dropped the bags of food onto the floor. Then pulled her into his arms. She went willingly, eagerly even, but she was still frowning just before his mouth dropped to hers.

And whatever she'd been worried about left her mind at the first touch of his lips. There was a sort of restrained desperation to his kiss, his arms rock solid around her, his muscles tense, his hands fisted against her lower back. But his mouth was gentle on hers, his lips soft, the deepening kiss almost languid and rich. Like he had all the time in the world and just wanted to taste her like this for hours. The kiss was a luxury, a moment to be savored. So she savored it with him, returning the languid dance of his tongue with hers even as her heartbeat pounded and her knees weakened.

It seemed like ages before their kiss ended and yet seemed to be over too soon when he lifted his head. She was breathing hard, and the feel of his erection hard against her lower abdomen didn't settle her pulse at all.

"That was a nice way to say hi," she murmured.

"Hmm."

She grinned. "Best you can do for conversation at the moment?"

"Hmm."

That made her laugh. And when she did, he smiled, so she suspected he'd done that on purpose. "In that case, maybe we should eat. And celebrate the fact that the ritual worked. We can physically manage to be apart without tearing the world to pieces. That feels like a success."

"It does," he said, though he didn't immediately loosen his hold on her. "There are more implications…"

"Which we can discuss later. After food. Or even tomorrow. We have a long drive ahead of us and plenty of time to talk while we're traveling. We don't have to solve everything tonight."

"Practical. Pragmatic." He brushed his fingers over her temple and across her cheek. "Beautiful. En really knew what he was doing."

She felt her cheeks heating even though she wasn't sure why she was blushing. She couldn't remember the last time someone told her she was beautiful. Maybe that was why. Or maybe it was the direct, focused attention of his stunning dark-eyed gaze.

"Let's eat before I forget what my name is," she said.

That admission brought out his smile, but not the simple pleased, amused smile. This one was all wicked intent and satisfaction. The kind of smile that, quite literally, made her forget her name because all the blood left her head and dropped right to her pussy.

She blinked hard and tried to reorganize her thoughts—and rein in her libido—when he released her and leaned down for the food bags he'd dropped.

When he moved everything to the dresser under the TV, she let out a breath that fluttered the short hairs on her forehead. Wow. If he flashed her that smile too often, she was going to combust and then where would that leave them?

Probably tangled in the sheets, sweating, with the sounds of their orgasms echoing in the room.

She was the one who'd decided that should wait. And she'd had a very good reason. Something to do with only having met him yesterday. But with him so close and large and warm and giving her that smile, she was rethinking that decision. She was rethinking her entire life, actually.

He arranged the food on the dresser, then handed her a box into which he'd added several extra biscuits to the chicken tenders and potatoes with gravy already in the box. She blinked at the food and forced herself to concentrate. She did need to eat. She was hungry. Very hungry considering it hadn't been that long since her last meal.

Clearing her throat, she sat on the bed and said, "Did the ritual affect my appetite? Because I feel like I could eat a house right now."

"Probably," he said, his back to her as he added things to a box for his own meal. "I hadn't considered it before, but it makes sense. You have a little of my wolf in you. All the things you're capable of now will require more energy than you're used to needing. You'll have to eat more."

"Such a hardship," she said with a feigned sigh. In truth, she liked food. A lot. She wasn't a small woman because of that love of food. But also, thanks to her father's training, she always low-level worried about not having enough food one day. So when there was food around, she ate. The fact that she was going to need more now was going to take some adjustment.

She waited until they'd both eaten a little before she said, "This is permanent. Right? I mean, there's no way to reverse the ritual or for me to just…go back to normal suddenly? I've literally just changed my entire life tonight."

He winced and kept his gaze on his food. "I'm afraid so. There's no way to reverse what we did." He met her gaze. "Are you regretting it?"

"Not finishing the ritual. I couldn't have lived that other way. But… I'm going to need time to adjust to this. I mean, it's not every day a girl goes through a life changing ritual that makes her superhuman strong and extends her life. How long, by the way? How long will I live now?"

"Unless you're killed, you'll naturally live for several centuries now."

She dropped the spork she'd been using to eat her potatoes and gravy. "Centuries." She blinked. That was a very long time. She couldn't even conceive of that many years, her brain just refused to accept that she'd still be walking this planet even a hundred years from now, nonetheless several hundred years. "Yeah, that's one of the things that's going to take time to get used to."

He shrugged. "You have it now. The time."

She gave him a look for that horrible attempt at a joke, then returned to her food. But she didn't miss his mouth quirk at her glare. If he gave her that toe-curling smile again, she was going to throw potatoes at him. She needed to think and that smile wouldn't help.

Except… What was there left to think about? As he said. It was done. She was…this now. Whatever this was. No going back.

"How can I be killed?" she asked. Because while thinking might be unnecessary, knowing her new limits was most certainly important.

"The usual ways. Stabbed, shot, beheaded, immolated."

She shivered. "Beheaded?"

"Since that's how the monsters have to be killed, it's on my list of how things get dead. Sorry. But…most things don't survive beheading so." He shrugged.

She let out a sharp breath through her nose. "How about things like diseases?"

"You're immune to most human diseases now."

"Even colds? Flus?"

"Immune."

"That's cool." She stared down at her food. She hated being sick. The whole life-changing ritual might be worth it just for the no-sick-days and eat-all-you-want part of this. "Am I harder to kill, like you, or will getting shot in the chest pretty much end me?"

He didn't look up from his food when he said, "I'm afraid—and I mean that literally—you could die from getting shot in the chest. Since you can't turn to stone to give the body time to heal, something like a massive chest wound would be bad. You might be okay if you got to a hospital in time, and they'd be working on someone who appeared human." He swallowed and did finally look up at her. "But it would be better if you didn't get shot."

"Didn't much like seeing you shot either," she said, holding his gaze.

"I'll try to avoid it in the future."

"Thank you. Does it come up much?"

He shook his head. "Monsters don't use guns. They have enough weapons of their own, they don't need them. It's only during those times when they partner with humans that guns become an issue."

"How often do humans partner with monsters?" She was appalled by the thought that this was the kind of thing that happened all the time. Why?

"It's happened through the millennia," Ben said. "There are humans who seem to think if they partner with the creatures, *they* won't be destroyed when every other human is killed. It's a delusion. The monsters' divine goal is to wipe out humanity. All humanity. Even the ones who work with them. And monsters don't have qualms about that." He gave a slight head tilt of a shrug. "Well, there are some monsters who are more loyal to their allies than others. The grinluk—"

"I remember it." Quite clearly. It would haunt her nightmares for… well, probably centuries now since she had that much time.

"Grinluk would consider their human allies things they'd protect until there were no more humans left. That's one of the reasons humans and grinluk end up working together occasionally. They're very loyal. But in the end, a grinluk will destroy all its human allies, too. That's the monsters' imperative, as much a part of them as the duty to destroy monsters is a part of the Families. Given them by a god. And monsters will always choose destruction and chaos over life."

"Good to know." She nodded, staring at the now empty food box in her lap. "Good to know."

"Important to know."

"You think I'd join the monsters' side?"

"Not you. But…there might come a time when someone in your life does. Someone you thought you could trust." He glanced away, his brows creased, and a muscle in his jaw jumped.

"There's a story there," she murmured.

But she didn't ask for it. If he wanted to tell her, he would. And if he didn't, he wouldn't. Shouldn't. For all they'd been through, even the trust exercise that was the ritual wasn't enough to force confidences. She had things she didn't like to talk about. She respected other people's privacy as much as she insisted on her own.

"There is," he agreed. He glanced at her, his gaze speculative.

"You don't have to tell me," she assured him. "Only when, or even if, you want to."

"I think it might be important when we find the professor that you know. It's all part of the same…situation."

"But it's personal." She didn't have to ask. She could tell by his hesitance and the tension around his eyes. Without conscious thought, she reached out and smoothed the lines on his brow, pushing some of his hair back off his forehead. "When you're ready. Doesn't have to be tonight."

"I think I'd like to tell you tonight."

He stood and put his also-now-empty food box on the dresser, took hers and set it aside too. Then stood leaning against the dresser, blocking the TV, his arms crossed over his massive chest as he stared at her. The TV behind him, muted so there wasn't any sound now, sent flickers of colored light dancing across his face and added to the shadows in his eyes.

"My father was murdered," he said abruptly into the silence. "He was betrayed by one of my cousins, a member of our Wolf Family. And that betrayal got my father killed. Murdered. They tried for my mother and oldest brother, Eric, too. It was an effort to throw my Family into chaos so we wouldn't be able to uncover the conspiracy my cousin was a part of."

"Conspiracy with the monsters?"

He nodded. "And with a sided-Elemental."

"Which is what exactly?"

"Elementals are what they sound like. Entities of the elements. Water, fire, earth, air. They're mostly neutral in the workings of the rest of the natural world. They just are and don't side with anyone. They *are* the elements. They've existed since the planet was born and will exist in some form until its destroyed. At least some of them. Water is the most vulnerable to the Earth's early destruction, that period before the sun swallows the planet, and that's…a problem. Because at least one, maybe more, Water Elementals have sided with the monsters to destroy humanity. They blame humanity for rushing the destruction of the planet."

"That doesn't sound good."

"It's not. For a lot of reason. Not least because Elementals can't be killed."

"That sounds even worse. You can't fight them?"

"Oh, we can fight them, even though we'd rather not have to. While they can't be killed, they can be temporarily made…irrelevant. Scattered so they can't coalesce into something that can interact with us. That gives us time to sort out any issues a sided-Elemental might have stirred up. The amount of time depends on the weapon used to scatter them and how accurately it's used."

Because she was watching closely, she noticed when his body went more rigid and tight, like he was holding himself very carefully before saying the next part.

"I'm the one who makes those weapons in our Family. The smith who can create things with…extra abilities. Like the power to dissipate an Elemental."

"Wow." She blinked a few times. "So…you have blacksmith magic?"

His mouth quirked but he didn't smile. "Yes. That's it exactly. Comes along in the Families about once per generations."

"Do the monsters and the sided-Elementals and whatever know this about you?" Because that struck her as very dangerous.

"Might. After my cousin… We don't know exactly what the monsters know about us anymore. The Elemental we know for sure was involved has been taken out of the equation. For a while at least. But we don't know how many are involved. And we have no idea exactly what the monsters know now."

He sighed but the sigh didn't relax his tense shoulders. At least not in any way she could see. "Jason got tired of hunting monsters and waiting on his Nam-tar. He resented his duty and the gods who'd forced it on him—his words. Forced. He could have just simply chosen not to hunt and gone his own way. He didn't have to betray the Family. But he did. He wanted…more. He wanted out of the curse but without waiting for his Nam-tar. He doubted he'd ever receive that blessing and his anger and resentfulness pushed him to side with the enemy."

"Are you telling me we might have a run-in with your cousin when we find the professor?"

"No. He's dead. Eric killed him. Eric's duty to the Family, as the new head of our Family, was to administer justice for our father's murderer. That was the justice necessary. But…it meant our cousin died under his curse so his death was even more unpleasant that it might have been."

"One day you're going to have to tell me more about this curse, you know? I know you don't want to…what was it? Play on my sympathy and coerce me into staying with you. Since that doesn't work anyway, right?"

"It wouldn't work on the curse, no."

"That's fair. But I still need to know one day."

He nodded. "I'll tell you. One day. But not tonight. There's been too much already."

"Yeah there has," she said with a wide-eyed groan. How had it only been thirty hours? Felt like a month. And she'd had her world turned so upside down she wasn't even sure where to start to right herself in all this.

"You didn't react to me telling you my brother killed my cousin."

"Your cousin got your father murdered, and in your world, I doubt you can go to the cops for justice. So it makes sense to me. Not my place to judge your brother in a world that can't be judged by human standards."

Finally, some of that tension in his shoulders started to ease.

"I was worried," he admitted. "That you'd think our form of justice was…barbaric. Or that my brother was the murderer. He isn't. My cousin was."

"Family is complicated," she said with a shrug. And that shrug had been hard earned through years of therapy. She wanted to repay Ben's trust, with a truth of her own. She knew he wasn't looking for quid pro quo, but she also wanted them to be on even footing since so much else about this situation was unbalanced. "My father died in prison. But before that, he kidnapped me. When I was…seven. Took me into a compound in the woods and raised me there until I was eleven when he returned me to my mother."

Ben didn't move except for a faint nod. He didn't look away from her or show any other emotion. No pity. No disgust. Just quiet patience for her to finish her story. That patience made it possible for her to go into the details.

"He was a fanatic, my father. A prepper and a conspiracy theorist who thought the government was coming to murder him and everyone he loved. When he and my mother married, he thought she agreed with him that the government couldn't be trusted because she was, at the time, a devoutly religious woman. He saw someone who fit into his twisted worldview perfectly. Except she didn't. She didn't live in fear of the conspiracies that drove him. She wasn't an overt racist. She wasn't even a religious fanatic. In fact, she's an atheist now. She…lost her interest in religion over time. But even in the beginning, in a lot of ways, she was very open and accepting of others. All the things my father was not."

Elle pulled in a breath, let it out slowly, but she couldn't hold his gaze for this next part. "After I was born, he got worse. Worried I'd be kidnapped by the government and indoctrinated into some sort of…I don't know. Some way of thinking that wasn't his way of thinking. He thought my mother would let it happen. He kidnapped me to protect me from what he saw as a great evil."

That was the part that kept coming up in therapy. The part where her father wasn't *just* a horrible man who'd kidnapped her and told her her mother didn't love her enough to keep her safe. The part where he was also a father who'd very much loved her in his own twisted way.

"Why did he bring you back to your mother then?" Ben asked quietly.

"We spent three and a half years in the compound, where he taught me how to survive off the grid, how to build weapons from nothing, taught me about guns and how to fill my own ammunition, how to hunt and build a fire and fish… All the things he thought I'd need when the end of the world happened. He even taught me how to sow and grow crops. He was convinced he was helping me to survive the apocalypse that no one else believed was coming. Well, not no one. There were others in the compound with us. Mostly other men who believed what my father did. All planning for the end of the world. Storing weapons and food and drilling and… They thought they'd be the only ones left. The ones who would rebuild society."

She shivered. It had taken her a good two years in therapy before she'd been able to talk about this next part to anyone. Her mother knew, because her father had left a note when he'd dropped Elle off at her mother's house. But Elle hadn't been able to talk about it for years.

"I wasn't hurt in the end, because my father rescued me," she said, slowly, "but… One of the men… He wanted me for a wife. To make babies with. Immediately. And he wasn't prepared to wait for me to grow up."

Ben's low growl was his only response. Quiet, almost like he wasn't aware of it. And the sound made the hairs on her arm stand up because it was the sound of a deadly predator. Her reaction to that sound wasn't fear, though, as she might have expected. Especially given what she was telling him. No. Not fear of him. Instead, a warmth seeped through her. A softening.

"Because my father wouldn't agree to that arrangement, the man came and tried to take me from my father by force. My father killed him. Shot him."

"You saw?"

"Not…not the actual shooting. I was cowering in a corner, covering my head with my arms as the men fought. I was only eleven. I was scared. The man had come into my room in the middle of the night…" She swallowed. "Anyway, once my father killed him, he spent about an hour packing up the few things I had that were important to me. He wrote out a note. And that night, he drove me out of the compound. I didn't know where we were going and had learned not to question my father over the years I'd lived with him. We drove for two days. I was asleep when we pulled up in front of my mother's house. My childhood home. I barely remembered it, but…I remembered my mother."

She pulled in a stuttering breath. Let it out on a long exhale. "So… yeah, he returned me to her. With a note. And then he disappeared. I found out later he'd turned himself in to the very authorities he'd feared and told them about the compound and the men there. There was a sting. Lot of militia people arrested for various things. My father went to jail for murder. I saw him once after that. Then he was killed in jail. I don't know by who or why. No one bothered to find out, or if they did, they never told me." Her shrug this time covered a whole lot of emotion. "So, as you can see, I understand complicated families."

He nodded, his expression soft and understanding. No pity still. Not anger anymore either. Just…understanding.

"And so there we are."

"Complicated," Ben said with a nod.

A few moments passed as they stared at each other, as the understanding sunk in for both of them. Eventually, she thought she might tell him more of the details. How the time after she'd returned to her mother had been so difficult. How it had taken years to learn to trust her mother again, love her again. But, for now, this was enough. For now, this was good.

"Thank you for telling me," he said. "I'm honored by your trust."

She smiled a little at that. "Thank you for tell me about your family, too."

He dropped his hands to his sides, but his fists were still clenched against his thighs. "It's late and you've been through a lot today. I'm going to go next door so you can sleep. I would rather ask if I can stay here with you. But…today has been a lot. I want to give you some space and time." He shrugged. "And if you let me stay here with you, I don't think we'll sleep much."

Her nerves tingled and her thighs clenched. He was right. The last thing she'd want to do with Ben in bed was sleep. But she did need to sleep. It felt like she hadn't slept in days and she could feel her eyes drooping, her head bobbing, as the exhaustion swept through her. As much an emotional exhaustion as a physical one.

She stood on wobbly legs and walked with him to the door that joined their rooms.

"Do you feel comfortable leaving the door unlocked?" he asked when he faced her. "I'd like to be able to reach you quickly if you need help. But I'll understand completely if you'd feel better with the door locked."

Under different circumstances, she would. But with him… "No. I'll feel safer with it open. You?"

"I'll feel better that way, too."

"Good. Decided. Door open. Or at least unlocked."

He brushed the backs of his fingers gently down her cheek. The sensation woke all the nerves in her body and made her suck in a breath. Without really thinking about it, she leaned into him, rising up on her toes when he cupped her face in one large palm and kissed her. The kiss was a slow, luscious exploration that left Elle a puddle of hot, liquid lust. Ben wrapped an arm around her waist, securing her to his big, strong body so solidly it didn't matter that he'd made her knees weak and she could barely stand up. She didn't have to. He was strong enough to take her weight. She buried her fingers in his hair and clung to him, kissed him like he was everything, and felt herself falling much harder and deeper than she would have thought possible after such a short amount of time.

When he eased away, she let go of him reluctantly. She had to grip the doorframe to stay upright, and she couldn't even be mad at him for his smug smile. Not when he was standing there looking at her like that. She wanted to sink back against him, explore that erection she'd felt pressing against her stomach. She wanted to take his face in her hands and kiss him again. But she didn't.

She whispered, "Goodnight," and when he was in his own room, she gently closed the door halfway. Not fully. And not locked. But with the show of a barrier between them. More of a reminder to her that she needed sleep more than she needed sex right then.

Because her libido wanted to argue that point.

CHAPTER TWENTY-SIX

Elle slept like a rock and woke up the next morning feeling surprisingly refreshed. Given the day before, and *everything* that had happened in just one day, feeling good and well rested felt like a miracle.

The motel room was dim and quiet, only a little light leaking around the sides of the blackout curtains. She'd turned the TV off last night—something she rarely did when in a hotel room alone—and hadn't noticed the difference. Probably because she'd left the door between her room and Ben's cracked open and that was enough to reassure her she was safe and could sleep comfortably.

Though, now that she was well rested and awake, that half-open door posed a problem. There was no *real* barrier between her and Ben just then. She could walk into his room without trouble. And once there, if he was still in bed, it would be incredibly easy to crawl into that bed with him, slip under the covers, see if he slept in pajamas or naked. Do something about those states no matter which it was.

She pressed her legs together under her own blankets and tried to bring her mind back under control. Didn't work. Her gaze jumped to the half-open door. Temptation beckoned. Would he mind? From the way he'd kissed her yesterday, last night, from the remembered feel of his erection, she was pretty sure he wouldn't mind. Pretty sure. But not absolutely sure.

Still. It never hurt to ask.

She swallowed and considered the door as she cupped her breast through her t-shirt and pinched her nipple. What would his mouth feel like there? Did she want him to be rough or gentle? She tightened her fingers and twisted hard, pressing her lips together so she wouldn't moan out loud. Both. She'd want him rough and gentle. And she had a feeling he could manage that.

He was several centuries old. That meant he probably had a great deal of experience with sex and pleasure. That sounded…useful. She cupped her other breast and nibbled her bottom lip, still contemplating that half-open door.

Despite the building restlessness and need, a small part of her still hesitated to take that last step. To walk through that door and wake him up with her mouth on his and see where that took them. Maybe leave her clothes behind when she did. The thought was so so appealing. So so tempting. And she was pretty sure he'd welcome that kind of good morning.

But… But this wouldn't be an ordinary fuck. They were talking about a lifetime together. If she chose to stay. They were irrevocably linked now. Tightening that link too soon seemed like a bad idea.

Her body disagreed. A lot. She sighed and closed her eyes, dropping her head back onto her pillow. Really, she wasn't going to hold out long like this. She was just torturing herself for no real reason. She wanted to fuck him so bad she was wet just thinking about it.

A light knock on the door between their rooms startled a gasp from her. She hadn't heard any movement in his room, had just assumed he was still asleep. She scooted higher up in the bed, and said, "Ben?"

Why the hell was she asking if that was him? Who else would it be?

Well, given the last few days, she supposed it could be monsters. But she doubted they'd knock.

"Did I wake you?" he asked through the crack in the door.

The sound of his voice settled her sudden worry about monsters but did nothing to calm her raging lust. In fact, her body tingled everywhere, like his voice had been a caress along her already sensitive skin.

"I was awake. Is something wrong?" Her voice sounded breathy and husky. She cleared her throat.

He didn't open the door, continuing to speak through the small opening. Was that better or worse for her hormones? She couldn't see him, that seemed like a good thing for her ability to think. But the sound of his voice, with no other distractions, was stroking over her, sparking tremors of sensation.

"I was going to go get some breakfast," he said. Did his voice sound even deeper now? "Do you want anything?"

You. "I could really use some coffee." There was a little squeak in her voice that made her cheeks heat.

"You should eat, too."

Now she was sure his voice was deeper. And huskier. She clutched the blanket in an attempt to remain where she was, because all her more lusty instincts were urging her to go fling that door open and step into his arms. Was he dressed yet? Or only half dressed? The thought of him standing just the other side of that door without anything on left her dizzy, sent a surge of wetness between her thighs.

And all this with a few words, no visual, and a perfectly mundane conversation. She would combust if he started actually talking dirty to her right now.

She nearly said she was easy again, but that might be too on the nose considering how she was feeling. "Something with eggs would probably be good."

"Coffee and eggs. Got it. Anything else?"

You. You naked and in this bed with me. You with your mouth on me. "That should be good."

"Okay. I'll be back soon."

She listened intently as he left his room, his door closing solidly behind him. Then she collapsed back against the pillow and let out a loud groan. She wasn't going to resist this pull much longer. She'd be lucky to get through breakfast without jumping his bones. She was just too desperate for him.

A shower would help. Getting dressed would definitely be a good idea. Being half naked herself when he got back was not going to help matters at all.

She couldn't stand cold showers—her father had tried to get her used to cold baths as a kid and she'd never adjusted—so she kept the water scorching hot instead, hoping it would boil the lust out of her. Not quite how it worked. But the heat did feel very good so she luxuriated in it for just a little longer than she would have normally.

When she found her hand sliding down her body to her throbbing pussy, she gave in. If she had a quick orgasm, she'd be able to control herself better when he got back. Sliding her finger through her wetness, with the hot water pouring over her back, felt decadent and delicious. With thoughts of Ben, naked and hard and so big and strong, filling her head, she fingered her clit, hissing in a breath when the first stroke made her legs tremble.

She imagined Ben's fingers on her, Ben's mouth, Ben's cock filling her. She throbbed with just the thought of stroking his thick erection, of filling her mouth with him. But the thing that pushed her over the edge was an image of Ben between her thighs, looking up at her as he tongue fucked her pussy. The orgasm tore through her, sudden and hard, the sound of her gasping cry echoed in the small shower stall.

Taking in a shaky breath, she rested her forehead against the cool tiles as her body shivered and settled. As the hot water continued to slide over her back. Okay. Okay. That should help. She'd be able to be in the same room with him now. At least for a little while. Maybe.

They had a long drive ahead of them today. Important things they had to do. An innocent man to rescue and some monsters to face. She needed to focus on that. Not get distracted by plans to get Ben's mouth on her clit.

She climbed out of the shower and got dressed quickly, hoping routine would keep her head out of Ben's pants and focused on the job ahead. When she concentrated, she could pick up Professor Arron's trail, sense the direction they needed to go. North and west still. But not as far west as she'd feared. Her tracking sense was honing in on a specific place now, not just a vague direction. Oh, that was good. The kidnappers had probably stopped moving, settled into a new location. If they were in one place, she and Ben could reach them that much quicker.

Still, they had some ground to cover today. They didn't have time for a morning of fucking. Desperate as she still somehow was even after that shower orgasm. Nope. Coffee, breakfast, check out, then get on the road. No sex in the middle of all that.

A refrain she kept repeating to her hormones for the rest of the morning.

When Ben got back with breakfast, she nearly scorched her mouth drinking her hot coffee too fast to cover her reaction to actually seeing him. How had he gotten more handsome overnight? She'd *been* looking at him for two days. But as soon as he walked through the door adjoining their rooms, she found it impossible to stop staring at him.

He'd showered sometime that morning too, though she hadn't heard his shower when she'd woken up. And he'd shaved, which made her fingers twitch to touch him and test the difference between his scruff from last night and the smooth skin over his jaw now. He smelled like the hotel soap, which was nice, and like him, which was delicious. Even the smell of coffee wasn't enough to block out just how yummy he smelled. She did a sort of lean in and sniff when he passed her to set the bags of food down and then closed her eyes as her cheeks heated, hoping he hadn't noticed.

The coffee was better than she'd expected from a chain diner, and the eggs and toast hearty enough to see her through the morning. But still, what she really wanted was Ben. And all the food and coffee in the world didn't seem to change that equation.

"They've stopped moving," she said to get her mind focused on what they needed to do, not what she wanted to do on the bed she was using as a seat. He'd settled in the plastic chair still lodged against her room door, which she thought showed great wisdom on his part even if she was ready to go climb onto his lap and ride him like the world was ending.

"The professor?" Ben's attention was on the plastic tray in his lap, his breakfast a huge pile of omelet and toast and potatoes and bacon.

"I'm getting a precise location now, not just a direction. North and a little farther west. Once I look at a map, I should be able to pinpoint the exact place."

"Good. Easier to catch up to them if they've stopped moving."

He glanced up from his tray and Elle nearly melted. He had beautiful eyes. She blinked. "Exactly. And since I'm still able to track him, I'm hoping that means he's still alive."

"He will be. They still need him. Whatever those experiments are they're running, whatever those new monsters are, it's obvious the professor is the one responsible for making that happen. They won't want to lose him."

Talk of the monsters and the things they'd seen in the house and in the woods by the river helped cool her raging lust. Finally. She probably should have thought of that sooner.

They finished breakfast quickly, with her eating significantly more than she normally would, including the second breakfast of eggs and toast he'd brought her and a little bit of his second omelet and potatoes, which he'd offered almost eagerly, as if feeding her made him happy.

She flicked on the TV as he went to his room to get his bags, wanting to check the local news in case they'd missed a monster. She was waiting through another report on the billionaire Logan family's latest museum opening when Ben came back in.

"This is the second story on this museum opening in the last twenty-four hours," she said. "I just want to make sure there haven't been any more monster sightings."

Ben glanced at the TV and winced. "Yeah, we usually don't do that many stories at once. We're pretty controlled on what we allow the press to report on. But this museum is one of my mother's pet projects, so she must be doing more PR than usual."

"Wait…" She turned slowly to look at him. "Who is *we*?"

He frowned and gestured to the TV. "What do you mean?"

"You said *my mother*."

"Yes."

"Is she, like, the head of the PR firm or something?"

"She's Laksana Logan. She's the museum's primary financial backer. And on the board, I think. She's gotten back more into in person charitable work recently. Took her a while after my father died. I don't think her heart's been in these things much. But the museum is for young sculptors, so it's special to her. That's helping."

Elle blinked at him more. "Laksana Logan is your mother?"

He nodded. "What's wrong?"

"Ben Logan? You're Ben Logan? Logan is your last name?"

"Benjamin Logan. Yes." He frowned. "I didn't tell you my full name yet?"

She shook her head.

"You did a bonding ritual with me and didn't even know my last name?" he murmured almost to himself.

"I didn't know your first name when your wolf leapt through me the first time, making the ending of the bonding ritual necessary."

He flinched. "I thought I told you my last name at some point… So much has happened, I just didn't think…" He raised his brows. "I don't know yours either."

"Barker. Elle Barker. That's my mother's name." She shook her head. "Logan." She still couldn't quite make the puzzle pieces fit. "These Logans?" She gestured at the TV. "The billionaire philanthropist family of import-exporters?"

"Yeah," he said.

"So. You're a billionaire?" And she'd taken him into a *bait stop* for clothes. A billionaire. Wearing *bait shop* clothes. Her brain couldn't even make those two things fit together.

"The Family doesn't have to worry about money." He shrugged. "Gives us the resources we need to do our work and stay hidden. Keep the existence of monsters hidden." He glanced at her. "Does the money bother you?"

"Well." Billionaire. It was an amount of money and resources she could scarcely wrap her head around. "I would typically be one of the 'eat the rich' crowd."

His eyes darkened as he met her gaze. "What if it's 'the rich eat you' instead?"

"That depends. If that's innuendo, then that's okay." And didn't her body respond immediately to the idea. "But since you have a wolf that leaps out every so often, that could also be taken literally, and that's less okay."

His mouth ticked up at one corner. She couldn't tell if that was a smile or a wince.

"Innuendo," he said, his voice quiet, and deeper now.

"Then that's okay, then."

Her heartbeat started to pound again, and all those lusty feelings that had been plaguing her throughout the morning came roaring back with a vengeance at the look in his eyes. He raised a brow and the little tick at the corner of his mouth turned into an actual smile. A smile that looked distinctly…wolfish.

She narrowed her eyes and pointed a finger at him. "That's not an invitation. We have to get on the road. I'm not giving you permission to eat me." *Yet*. And the fact that she thought that "yet" was embarrassing.

His smile grew. "Did you just think 'yet'?"

"No." She winced. "Maybe."

His low chuckle danced along her skin, sending little electrical sparks down her spine and right to her pussy. She tried hard not to imagine in detail what it would be like having Ben eat her. An effort she failed at miserably. Especially since it was the very image that had sent her over the edge in her shower orgasm. Now that he'd mentioned it, it was all she could think about again.

The fact that *he* was thinking about it in that moment just made things worse. And that "yet" seemed a more significant disclaimer than it had been just a minute ago.

She scowled. "How did you know?"

He tapped his nose. "Excellent sense of smell, remember. And you smell…delicious right now."

Well. She wasn't sure which was worse, the blush making her face so hot, or the way her thighs just wobbled with the need to wrap herself around him. Both. Both things were bad.

But especially the fact that she so desperately wanted to wrap herself around him. Without delay. And they had a long drive ahead of them and a lot of things to do and survive before she could do that.

There was no *if* in her thoughts. It was only a matter of when. When she could get her legs wrapped around his head. When she could ride his tongue. When she finally gave in to the lust that was such a hot spike of want in her blood she could barely see straight.

She took a step toward him, without thinking, and then stopped herself. If she so much as brushed against him in that moment, they'd never get out of this motel room. And they had to get out of this motel room. They were already two days behind the professor and his kidnappers. Since the kidnappers had stopped moving, she and Ben had to take advantage of that. They didn't have an extra few hours to fuck.

And frankly, she didn't want to fuck him in a rush. She wanted to strip him and take her time exploring him. They just didn't have that kind of time.

She swallowed hard and took a deliberate step back, but her voice was rough and breathy when she said, "We'd better go."

Ben's eyes were so dark now, they were nearly black. His nostrils flared and she knew he could scent every little bit of her desire. Which probably wasn't helping their situation.

He didn't move as she threw her toiletries into her bag. Stood so still in fact she could almost think he'd turned to his stone statue. She'd have hunted the room for his wolf if he didn't murmur, "Ready?" with his back still to her as she zipped up her duffle bag.

She glanced one last time at the TV. Nothing that resembled a suspicious monster sighting, that she could see. "Ready." She tossed her bag up over her shoulder and proceeded him out of the room. But she walked on wobbly legs, knowing he was right behind her, practically feeling the heat of him along her spine.

This was going to be a very long day.

CHAPTER TWENTY-SEVEN

She was killing him. Slowly. Steadily. Killing him.

Ben took his turn at the wheel because focusing on the road kept him from thinking about just how much he wanted to get inside Elle. Her scent had been driving him slowly mad all morning. Even before he'd knocked on her door and asked about breakfast, her scent had carried from her room into his, weaving around him, invading his dreams. He woke hard and aching and reached for her before he realized she wasn't in the bed beside him.

Which hadn't left him in the best of moods. He'd left to get breakfast to clear his head and try to regain some of his control. The instant he was back in the room with her, though, all that effort went out the window. The only thing that kept him from tumbling her back onto the bed that morning was the equally strong desire to make sure she ate enough. To make sure she didn't suffer after being forced into the ritual. And if he were being honest with himself, he liked feeding her, making sure she was looked after. He wanted to have the right to look after her. For the rest of their lives.

But she still had to be the one to make that choice.

At least, he hoped she still had the choice.

And that uncertainty was the other thing that kept him from making a reality of all the lusty things he wanted to do to her. The lingering fear that he'd fucked up their future already. He didn't want to do anything that made that worse.

But not kissing her this morning, not rolling her onto her back and burying his cock deep inside her, had taken more restraint and will than he thought he had.

"We need to talk about something," he said. "Anything that's…not sexy. Or I'm going to crash the car."

The spike of desire in her scent did not help his state of mind.

She swallowed audibly and squeaked, "What?"

He glanced at her, but dragged his gaze back to the road as quickly as he'd looked away, because looking at her made things worse and he really would crash the car if he did that. "You've smelled like dessert all morning, and I'm having a hard time concentrating because of it. If I'm driving, I need to concentrate. If you're driving, I need to let you concentrate. All these things require we find a way to get all that delicious lust out of your scent—at least for now—so we need to talk about something that's…distracting."

His little speech left her quiet for a long moment. He didn't look at her again, but his hands flexed on the steering wheel. Her scent had an added note of surprise to it, and he'd swear she was nodding, but he'd have to look directly at her to be sure because the movement was subtle. He kept his gaze on the passing traffic—lot of big rigs this time of day, so he had to focus—and the trees bracketing the highway on either side. It wasn't a huge highway, only two lanes in each direction, which made concentrating around the big trucks even more important.

"Monsters," she finally said, though she still squeaked a little, and that deliciously spicy scent of her lust was still perfuming the air.

If he asked her what she was really thinking about, and she actually told him, he was pretty sure he'd drive the car into a tree.

"Monsters," he said. "Right. What about them?"

"Just…they're pretty gross and disgusting and will hopefully be… distracting. Let's talk about monsters. How about what we saw outside that town. The little things popping out of the dead monster's goo. That's new, right. That's pretty gross."

"New. Dangerous." When he'd gone out for breakfast and a run to the drugstore, he'd called Eric to see how the sweep of the house and the area around it had gone. No signs of living monsters, but they'd been able to dig more into the remains of the professor's lab and what had been inside all those boxes. "The black goo that was in the boxes at the house? My Family got some samples of that and sent them to my sister Judith. She's the resident biologist. She's going to work on analyzing what the stuff is and what it can do."

"You have a sister who's a biologist?"

"A few of us have work beyond just hunting and destroying monsters."

"Like how you're a blacksmith?"

"Mine is driven by a magic I was born with. I don't have much choice but don't mind that because I like metallurgy and working with weapons. Judith's choice to study biology and genetics was just something she wanted to do. And it's proven really helpful in our work. There's usually a few scientists in each Family that do this kind of study."

"You obviously know a lot about monsters. You keep…records?"

"Complete records on every named and known monster. Vulnerabilities and dangers and reproductive capabilities."

"Diet?"

"They all eat anything they can get, but are specifically designed to crave eating humans."

"Eew."

"We need to talk about something distracting and gross."

"That's working."

It was. Her scent was no longer quite so overwhelmingly filled with lust and that helped both of them. "Ne hates humans. He wants to see them destroyed."

"The Elemental you mentioned, the one that sided with the monsters, that one was a water element, right?"

"It was."

"So…does that mean every time it rains, we could be in danger?"

"Potentially, yes. But the one we know for sure that was working with my cousin has been dissipated. It'll be unable to coalesce into something that can endanger us for years."

"But there could be more? It's still possible every rainstorm and puddle could be deadly?"

He relented. "It's possible."

"Any other Elementals involved besides water?"

"Not that have made themselves known to us."

"How do you fight a Water Elemental?"

"I make special weapons. Fire daggers, and recently I've started making arrowheads with the same fire magic. Takes skill and my brand of magic to create them. I make weapons suited to dissipating all Elementals, but I've only ever kept a few on hand. Until a year and half ago, when the Water made itself known. Since then, I've made…a lot more. And we've been spreading them around to all our Family."

"Your bag full of weapons?"

"Includes some of everything I might need. Including four fire daggers and a quiver of fire arrows."

"Fire for Water, right. What else? How do they work?"

"Fire weapons need to be stabbed into a Water's head area to dissipate them for centuries. Anywhere else, they'll still dissipate but not for as long. Usually the length of a human lifetime, though, which is helpful for humans."

She huffed out a chuckle.

"Air requires a sort of suction dagger called an aefier. Strike it into an Air Elemental anywhere and it pulls at their base element, then blows it apart so the entity is dissipated. Again, the closer you get to the head, the longer they'll stay fragmented."

"Useful. Lot of needing to get at things heads in all this. Monsters killed by chopping off their heads. Elementals dissipated by stabbing them in the head."

He shrugged, then nodded.

"Useful to bear in mind in this world," she said dryly. "What about Fire and Earth Elementals?"

"Molten daggers for Earth will loosen their hold on coherence, basically melting them."

"You turn them into lava?"

"It sinks into the ground fast enough not to be dangerous," he said, almost defensively.

"Sure sure. Cause lava is good that way. What works on Fire? A water dagger?"

"Yup."

"That's…a little on the nose."

"Like a fire dagger wasn't? We've been making these weapons for millennia. They need names that translate and can carry through centuries of changing language. We try to keep it basic. Aefier is the only one that doesn't translate well so we just stick with that word."

He could swear her mouth twitched into a smile, but since he was trying not to look at her directly, he couldn't be sure.

"What does a water dagger do?"

"Same as the others, stabbed into a Fire, it'll turn them to smoke and dissipate them for a time dependent on where they were stabbed."

"Lot of stabbing going on here, too," she commented.

"I can work with guns and other kinds of weaponry, but my preferences are swords and daggers and arrowheads. It's where my magic leans. Most blacksmiths born to the Families are similar."

"Arrowheads? You said you had a quiver with you. Why not make all the weapons as arrows. So you don't have to get too close to an Elemental?"

"You'd have to be a good shot, though. Getting a solid hit on an Elemental is difficult at the best of times. Miss a shot, and you're not likely to get a second. Most of our hunters find swords and daggers easier. Though some have specialized in archery over the centuries so that's why we still make the arrowheads."

"I'm an excellent shot with a bow and arrow," she said, quietly, "but don't have a clue how to use a sword or dagger—in this context. I can clean a fish or skin a rabbit well enough. I even learned how to fletch. A friend of my father's taught me. My dad could do it, but not as well as his friend. So he made sure I learned from Deke. Deke was old and nice for a militia man. So we spent a lot of time fletching. I liked it better even than learning to reload ammunition. Felt more comfortable with the arrows than the guns."

The insight into her youth, and what had to have been a scary period of time, left him hungry for more. "Can you still use bow and arrow? Have you kept that up?"

"I like it, so yes." A quiet pause. Then, "I've kept up most of the skills my father had me learn. I'm not sure why."

The hesitance in her voice made him want to pull her close and comfort her, and he wasn't entirely certain why. But knowing she could defend herself, if it became necessary, was something of a relief. He wouldn't always be around to protect her, even if he wanted to. Her having skills with various weapons would help her survive his world. An unintended benefit to her difficult youth.

He flicked a glance at her. Then said, "Because of your relationship to me, you're more vulnerable to the monsters who understand what Nam-tar are. They could come after you to get to me."

"Well that sucks."

He couldn't agree more. "But now that we've done the ritual, you're less vulnerable. Stronger and can heal faster. And knowing you can use some of our weapons… That'll be useful in this world. Even though you shouldn't have to face monsters very often. That's my job, not yours."

She let out a long breath. "I prefer tracking."

She had so many skills that were useful in his world, thanks to her upbringing and her own innate talent. He wasn't sure he'd met a Nam-tar more suited to coming into their world. And yet, she didn't want to use those skills to hunt monsters. He couldn't blame her. She had only just learned all these things existed. Accepting a centuries-long duty to destroy Ne's creatures wasn't something that could happen overnight.

Besides that, though, Ben didn't want her to do anything she didn't want to do. If she wanted to sit around a large house doing nothing at all, he'd happily make that possible for her. He wanted her content, safe, and satisfied with her life more than he wanted anything else in the world.

Thinking about satisfying her led him back down the dangerous thought road, though, so he cleared his throat and said, "You're free to do whatever you like. If you stay—" and wow, did that "if" hurt to say, "—you'll be able to make all those decisions."

"Thank you," she said quietly. "I'm… It's important to me that I'm free to decide what I do and when I do it."

"Because of what happened to you as a child," he said. Didn't ask. The answer was obvious. "I won't ever try to take that away from you. I promise."

She nodded, and glanced out the window, falling silent for a few minutes.

While he didn't want to bring this up, he had to remind her, "That monster, the grinluk, will think you're a Family member with a weird ability to split your entities. The grinluk thought you were one of us and yet different. They'll see that as dangerous. It makes you more vulnerable when we catch up to them. Even without knowing you're my Nam-tar, the grinluk will want to destroy you. Or…capture and use you."

He caught her shiver from the corner of his eyes.

"Either way," he said, "it's important you know so you can be careful."

"Thanks for the warning."

After a moment, he said, quietly, "Well that was distracting."

A beat, and then she started to laugh. The sound made him smile. She had a great laugh. Bold and full and unrestrained.

They drove and talked for the next few hours. Her telling him more about her childhood, and how difficult it had been returning to her mother's house after everything. How she'd doubted her mother really wanted her, because of what her father had spent three years telling her. The therapy and time it had taken to unlearn some of those destructive lessons.

He told her about some of his past. His time in the military during the two world wars—the monsters came out in higher numbers during big conflicts so Families found ways to put themselves into the middle of combat zones when necessary. He told her about his brother Nick who specialized in hunting in warzones around the world. They talked about his other brothers and sisters. About the time since his father's murder.

They talked so much, he was surprised when he heard her stomach growl and realized they hadn't eaten in a while. He pulled off the highway at the first offramp that led to food.

"You heard my stomach?" she asked.

"You should have mentioned being hungry."

She stared at the side of his head for a moment. "You are always trying to feed me."

"I warned you after the ritual, you'd need more food." He shrugged, not so much as glancing at her while he navigated the side roads to the series of quick restaurants and a few decent sit-down places.

"You were doing that before the ritual." He caught her wince from the corner of his eye. "Or, well, before we finished the ritual."

He did glance at her then, but only briefly. "I like making sure you're taken care of. Does that bother you?"

"No. I'm not used to it. But...no. I'm not bothered. It's nice. I just find it funny that the same man who dives into killing monsters is also so sweet when he's not."

He felt his cheeks heating and scowled at the road. He was more than three hundred years old and he was blushing. Because his Nam-tar called him sweet. He was almost as embarrassed by his embarrassment as he was by her compliment.

She chuckled. "Let's go in somewhere. I need to stretch my legs."

They picked a diner with a range of food options. She ate steak and eggs. He had a burger and a pasta dinner. The waiter made no comment over the amount of food they finished, and Ben left him a good tip.

Back in the car, Elle took over the driving. "We'd planned to drive straight through yesterday. We should still do that."

He glanced at her as she made a show of adjusting mirrors and resetting the seat to suit her shorter legs.

"Since they've stopped moving, we can catch up to them faster." She still didn't look at him.

What she was saying out loud made lots of sense and was actually their original plan. But there was something in her voice, her scent, that made him think their plan wasn't really why she didn't want to stop for the night.

"You don't want to be in another motel room with me," he said.

Her turn to blush. The color swept up her neck and across her sharp cheekbones. Charming him.

"That's not precisely the problem," she said, her chin high as she navigated back to the highway. "We need to get to Professor Arron sooner rather than later. He's in danger."

"He is. And we do. But that's not why you don't want to stop."

"Actually," she said, with a groan, "the problem is I *do* want to be in another motel room with you. Desperately. And I'm afraid if we do stop, we'll miss our chance to rescue Professor Arron and prevent whatever it is the monsters are doing." She flicked him a brief glance before focusing on the traffic again. "I'm afraid, once I have you in bed, I won't want to leave that bed for days."

He held very still and breathed slowly, deeply, for a long moment, while he absorbed what she'd just admitted. While he let the waves of desire wash over him and his body tightened and his imagination filled with exactly what he would do with her the instant he got her into bed.

She was right. Once he got her there, he had no intention of leaving that bed for as long as he could keep her there. He wanted to lose himself in her. And if he did that, he *would* forget his duty. At least for a few days.

"I hate that you're right about this," he said quietly. "Because after that admission, all I want to do is get you somewhere quiet and alone and with a bed."

Her hands tightened on the steering wheel and her scent spiked with her lust. "Which is why we need to keep driving."

They should. They really should. But he found himself hunting for alternatives. Ways he could get her somewhere private. Ways he could indulge in her, fuck her until they both screamed, and not get so carried away they'd miss their chance to rescue Professor Arron. He had a job, a duty, and losing himself in his Nam-tar would derail all that. But that didn't stop him considering the quiet rest stops they passed, and the tree cover flashing by along parts of the highway with a depth that could definitely hide two people from view.

He was glad he wasn't the one driving just then. His imagination was filled with everything he wanted to do to her, with her, all the ways he intended on exploring her body. The way he'd drag his lips over her shoulder, down her arm, across her breasts. Stopping to suck first one nipple, until she was panting, then move to the next. The feel of her hands in his hair as he kissed his way lower, moving across her stomach. Would she be more sensitive around her waist or her across her hip bone? Would she suck in a breath when he kissed the inside of her thigh? How would she react when he grazed his teeth over her ass?

Shifting in his seat, he tried to rein in his imagination. Definitely good he wasn't driving because he was now so hard and hungry for her, he couldn't see straight. And gods, her scent was filling the car, filling his head, surrounding him in the dark heated velvet of her desire.

He was going to lose his mind this way.

And he couldn't even regret it.

CHAPTER TWENTY-EIGHT

Elle drove for hours in discomfort and so outrageously aware of Ben next to her, her skin constantly tingled. They tried to return to distracting conversation, but as the sun set and the interior of the car grew dark, the intimacy of their positions heightened. Her awareness of him grew. The sound of his jeans rasping against the seat as he changed positions. The sound of his breathing. The scent of him all hot male under the nice soap from their last motel.

If his hands moved, she was hyper aware of their movement. When he glanced at her, she felt his gaze like a touch. Every cell in her body seemed attuned to him, to his every movement. And the tension of wanting him and not allowing herself to indulge was going to kill her.

She kept trying to think of monster goo and a client's husband in danger. Those things helped for short periods of time. Kept her distracted enough she didn't crash the car.

But then Ben would drop his hand to his thigh and her attention would drop with the gesture. And then all she could think about was his thighs. And how they'd feel bracketed by her legs. What it might feel like to ride one of those thick thighs, rubbing his rough leg hair against her clit until she came. Then she'd get distracted by his hands. His large, roughened, competent hands. The fantasies then involved those hands on her, on her breasts, her ass, his blunt, rough fingers pushing into her wet pussy. Sucking one of his fingers as he fucked her.

She couldn't believe how desperate she was. She'd always found sex a bit hit or miss. Sometimes it was fun and she got off and enjoyed herself. Sometimes…not so much. She enjoyed sex well enough. But she'd never been so desperate to get a man inside her she thought she might scream.

Was this part of the Nam-tar thing? Would it always be like this? They could technically be apart now, and that was a relief, but would she spend the rest of her life desperate to get Ben naked and get him inside her?

There were worse ways to spend her life, she supposed.

He said she still—probably—had a choice to stay or go. A choice that determined if he remained cursed or not. Would her choice matter anymore, though? Would he still remain cursed even if she stayed because of the premature ritual? And if so…what exactly did that mean? What did the curse do to him?

She opened her mouth to ask again before she remembered why he'd specifically declined to give her details. He didn't want her manipulated by the truth. He was afraid she'd stay out of sympathy and not because she *chose* to.

With a glance at him from the corner of her eye, she realized that argument was moot. Because she was already leaning toward staying with him. She was already in deep enough she wasn't sure she could leave. She knew, with an instinct that surprised her, that she didn't *want* to leave him. Ever. She wanted him in her life from this point forward. In fact, she couldn't even imagine life without him now.

It was like, when he'd opened her eyes to the world of monsters, her life had changed so radically that there was no going back to the person or life she'd had before. No matter what. And if she had to live in *this* version of reality, she absolutely wanted that reality to contain Ben. In her life. With her as much as possible.

She'd told him things she hadn't discussed with anyone but her therapist. She'd laid bare her years with her father and even more upsetting, the years after, with her mother, when she'd had such a hard time readjusting the "real life" and that her mother actually loved her. She didn't discuss those things with strangers. She'd never discussed them with past lovers. She hadn't even talked about these things in a therapy session for years now because the feelings had been dealt with and worked through. Revisiting all those things with Ben...meant something.

Meant she wanted him to know her. The real her. Maybe to see if he'd run away once he learned the truth. But he hadn't. Not even close. And that had changed the equation between them again.

Feelings. She had feelings for him that went beyond this being an intense situation, beyond the lust and the whole Nam-tar thing. She wasn't prepared to label those feelings yet. Not quite ready for that part yet. But she could acknowledge the feelings were there.

And wasn't that just the oddest surprise.

The call of nature required a stop, so she pulled off at the first rest stop they came across. They parked a short walk away from the toilets in a parking lot surrounded by pines. There were two other cars in the lot when they got out. The area was really dark now, and the other cars had stopped under the lights illuminating the lot, but she'd parked in the shadows near the trees. She wasn't even sure why. The lights just looked too harsh to her.

By the time she came out, Ben was already waiting by the car. She scanned the lot on her way back to him. Empty now, with only the sounds of traffic from the highway just the other side of a copse of trees. It was actually surprisingly quietly given how close they were to the highway.

Given they were tracking monsters, she'd have thought she'd be worried about walking around in the dark at an empty rest stop. Even without the monsters, she'd probably have skipped the rest stop and gone to a twenty-four hour fast food place if she were traveling alone. But having Ben waiting for her, all big and strong and deadly dangerous, left her feeling surprisingly secure.

As she neared him, his gaze never wavered from her, and in the shadows where she'd parked, his eyes seemed to glimmer. He had his arms crossed over his big chest and was leaning against the side of the car. Looking large and intimidating and a little scary.

She shivered. But not from fear.

Stalking toward him, she watched his gaze scan down her body, rising slowly back up as she neared. She felt that look along her skin, leaving sparks in its wake. And despite the cold air biting her cheeks, heat coiled in her, through her, sending her pulse thumping rapidly.

He stared down at her without comment for a long moment, that reflected light in his eyes all focus and intent on her. The delicious smell of hot male and soap mixed with the pines surrounding them, made her breath in deeper to pull more of that scent in.

When he finally spoke, his voice was low and rough. "Ready?"

Was she?

Yeah. Yeah, she was.

She stepped into him, ran her hands up his chest to his big broad shoulders. He didn't uncross his arms but his nostrils flared and a muscle in his jaw flexed. She pressed up against his folded arms, going up on her toes so her breasts rested just above his arms, then she brought her hands up around his neck, threading her fingers into his hair. She felt his breathing speed and deepen.

Her gaze on his, she pulled his head down to her. He didn't resist, didn't take his gaze off hers, but he didn't move to hold her either.

Curious what he'd do next, and needing to taste him more than she needed her next meal, she brushed her lips over his, once, twice, gently. Then she sank in, angling her head to deepen the kiss.

And he came undone.

His arms coiled around her, hard and fast, flattening her against his chest. He swept his tongue into her mouth, tasting her, so desperate he was almost harsh. She loved it. Answered in kind. She couldn't get close enough, couldn't feel enough of him pressed against her, but she tried, rubbing against him to ease the need for more contact. His hands spread along her back, then started to explore. One dropped to her ass, squeezing with a restrained intensity that left her breathless. His other slid over her hip, dragged up her spine, cupped the back of her head.

His fingers burrowed through her hair, his fist flexing in a grip that made her moan.

She was so desperate for him after the day, after this morning, she was near mindless with the want. It occurred to her, in some dim part of her brain, that they'd be warmer in the car, but she couldn't get the words out. And anyway, the heat that pumped off his big body was doing a remarkably good job of warming her up. That and the desperate need racing through her blood. She nearly crawled up him in an attempt to get closer, hooking one leg around his thigh.

With a suddenness that made her gasp, he grabbed her thighs and lifted her off the ground. She wrapped her legs around his waist as he turned so her back was to the car and leaned her gently against it. He slid one hand under her ass to hold her up and set his other hand against the car roof so he wasn't actually pressing her hard into the rough metal. And she sank deeper into the kiss. She buried both hands in his hair again, holding him in place. His groan and her moan mingled in the chilled air, until those sounds were her whole world.

The hard ridge of his erection nestled between her thighs, rubbing against her through her cargo pants, driving her more and more crazy with every grind and thrust of his hips. She wanted him. Desperately. She'd never wanted anyone like this before in her life.

Car in a rest stop would have to do, because there was no way she'd be able to go the rest of the night without fucking him. Her brain was chanting *now, now, now* in a steady litany as she ground down against his hard cock and nearly came just from the rub of her clit against the seam in her pants.

But she wanted his hands on her naked skin. His mouth on her. And she wanted to explore him without the barrier of clothes getting in her way.

She reached down and fumbled at the car's back door, nowhere near close enough to reach the handle. But he understood without her having to pull her mouth from his long enough to speak. His hold on her secure, he stepped away from the car, taking all her weight easily, and opened the back door. He crawled in, still with her clinging to him, her legs and arms tight around him, as if she could melt into him by sheer force of her lust.

Once they were sprawled on the back seat, he lifted away from her enough to close the door, and then he sank into their kiss again. The car wasn't nearly large enough or long enough to accommodate his size. The backseat not exactly huge. But he didn't seem to pay any attention. He settled one leg on the ground and the other folded on the seat and he devoured her mouth even as they pushed and pulled at each other's clothes.

The interior of the car heated rapidly, warming enough that by the time Elle got her flannel and t-shirt off, she was comfortable, no chill or cold to interfere with her pleasure. She grabbed fistfuls of his shirt along his back and dragged the material up until they had to stop kissing so she could get it over his head. Once off, her hands went right to his chest, exploring. She dragged her near non-existent nails over his skin along his ribs, and he shuddered, grinding his hips down harder into hers. And wow, the feel of his cock, hard and thick and so ready for her. She didn't think she could wait to get their pants off, but she wanted him inside her so badly, she forced herself to slow down, just a little.

Before she could demand he get his jeans off, though, his moved his mouth from hers to her neck, nuzzling the area between her shoulder and throat. She moaned and everything in her melted. Then his mouth moved across her chest, to her breasts. He tugged her bra down under her breast, not actually taking it off, and then sucked her nipple into his mouth. The heat and suction had her arching up under him, her whole body a livewire of sensation and need.

Without even thinking about it, she ground up against the ridge of his cock, grinding, sure she couldn't wait to get the rest of their clothes off anymore. He buried his face against her neck again, groaning deeply as he pressed down into her. Then he lifted off her, just enough for his glittering gaze to sweep over her in the dark.

"Too many clothes still," he muttered.

"Yes. Too many. Off." She barely recognized her own voice. Had she ever sounded that breathless and desperate? Not that she remembered.

She untangled her legs from around his waist as he sat up, her hands going to the button of her cargo pants. He watched her as she wiggled her pants and underwear off at the same time, pushing them down as far as she was able in the confined space, with him kneeling on the far side of the seat. Fortunately, he helped and dragged her clothes down the rest of her legs, where they got caught on her boots. His hungry gaze still raking her body, he removed her boots with quick movements and then got the rest of her clothing off in a rush. Then he just knelt there, staring at her. His hands fisted against his thighs.

"Beautiful," he murmured.

"You're not naked yet," she answered.

His lips lifted in that wicked grin that made her forget her own name, and then he removed his jeans without any more delay.

Once he was naked, she sat up so she could grip his cock in her hand, test the length, the thickness, the silky smooth skin over hardness. He hissed at her touch, dropping his head back, his eyes closing.

Without him looking at her, she let herself soak in the rest of his body as well, even as she stroked his cocked, slowly, steady, a firm hard grip. He was magnificent. Large, muscled, the now familiar hair over is chest. No sign of the wound he'd received that first day. She had tried, even when he was shirtless, not to stare too long, because she didn't have the permission. She had the permission now. And she took advantage, letting her free hand roam over the place where he'd been shot, feeling the smooth skin over rippling muscles, the rougher texture of his chest hair. Then she let that hand slide down his abdomen and cross one of those magnificent muscles over his hip. She'd never been with a man who had that muscle in real life. She'd only seen that muscle on sculptures.

And the realization that he occasionally turned to stone and looked like a sculpture just fascinated her more. Were some of those stone statues she'd seen in pictures and museums…real living people inside?

The idea was weirdly distracting, so she set it aside for now. Because in that moment, all she wanted to do was explore Ben.

She moved her hand over his thick thigh, across more rough hair, and danced her fingers over his tight fist where it still rested against his lap. When she looked up, he was staring down at her, his eyes dark, his jaw tight. She smiled and gripped his cock harder on her next stroke and he rewarded her with a low growl that made her shiver.

He leaned forward and captured her mouth with his, swooping down so fast she gasped. And before she knew what he was doing, he'd moved her hand from his cock and eased her back against the seat cushion again. She wrapped her arms and legs around him again, bumping up against his erection in a wordless invitation.

"First," he said against her mouth, "I need to taste you. I've needed to taste you so badly." He kissed down across her body, pausing at her tits to suck each nipple deeply before sliding his lips down over her belly as she scooted a little farther up and back to make room for him to settle between her legs.

She sucked in a breath when he hovered over her curls, his breath fanning hotly against her. She was wet and desperate and panting as she watched him. "I imagined this this morning," she whispered, hoarsely. "In the shower. You like this, looking up at me. You licking me."

"Were you touching yourself when you pictured me here?"

She nodded. "This is the image that sent me over. That made me come."

His eyes fairly glittered as he stared at her, a slight smile curving his mouth. "I'm delighted to bring that fantasy to life for you."

"Yes." She dropped her head back against the door when he licked her slick folds. Her hips bucked up against his mouth. And then he sank in, licking into her.

He toyed with her clit, sucking and licking her until she was writhing, panting, clawing at the seat cushions as her orgasm built and her body tightened and everything in her gasped and reached and tumbled. She cried out when she came, the orgasm hitting her hard, lasting longer than usual as he continued to lick her, pressing his tongue to her clit, drawing out every ounce of sensation.

When he licked her folds again, she was too sensitive and the feeling zinged through her almost like pain. Her hips jerked up and she had to grab his hair and ease him away. "Need a minute," she murmured, dragging him, unresisting, back up so she could kiss him. His body was so hot against hers he was like a furnace, but in the best possible way. She was too limp to warp her legs around him just yet, but she did wrap her arms around his neck, holding all that heat close to her.

He lifted his head with some reluctance, still dropping kisses over her cheeks, across her neck, as he murmured, "I need to get into the trunk. Really quick. I'll be right back."

She barely had time to frown, no time at all to ask a question, before he was gone and back. Moving so fast, he was already closing the back door as she felt the car bounce under the trunk slamming shut. She giggled at the speed and the delayed reactions.

"What was that for?"

He held up a box of condoms. "In my bag. I hadn't exactly planned on ravishing you at a rest stop."

"Would have put them in the glove compartment otherwise?" she asked with a cheeky grin.

His chuckle lit up her nerves again, like a caress all its own. "I'm not the only one who's been thinking about this, am I?"

She shook her head as he slipped on a condom. "Shower and my own fingers were nothing to reality," she murmured.

He leaned over her, his gaze sweeping over her face. "The reality is…everything," he murmured. "Not exactly where I wanted our first time together to be, but…"

"It's perfect. You're perfect. Shut up and fuck me." She wrapped her legs around him again, angling her hips for him.

He slid into her slowly, the friction drawing out his entrance and making her moan. But when he settled, seated fully in her, filling her so full, she felt home. Like this was always the way her life had been, having this magnificent man inside her. He rocked against her once and the sensation rippled through her, just that to start the building tension again. Another thrust and she gasped. Hard, but slow and steady, he drove into her. Holding her head in one hand so she wasn't bouncing against the car door, his other hand braced on the car seat as he looked down at her, watching her. Her every gasp and moan made him drive in harder, but he kept up the slow pace, the steady rhythm, pushing her until she was desperate once more.

She gripped his shoulders and looked down, watching their bodies come together, watching his cock slide in and out of her. When she looked up he was watching as well. He growled in a way that felt like possession, and she ground up against him to claim him too. All hers, she thought. All hers. She was his. Somewhere in all this, that had become an indisputable fact. She couldn't imagine him out of her life anymore. And yet he'd been a part of her life for such a short time. None of that mattered, though, because she knew, in her soul, this was what she wanted, what they'd been made for.

The building tension coiling inside her hit a tipping point, moved beyond her ability to slow it down. She tried to savor him longer, but then he sped up, changed his rhythm, fucking her harder and faster and all her attempts at control shattered. And so did she.

And then so did he. She felt him come apart, in her arms, in his thrusts, in the growl that filled the small car interior. But she missed the sight of it because her eyes were closed as her own orgasm ripped and rippled through her.

Next time, she promised herself. Next time she'd watch him come.

He gathered her close and shifted a little so they were laying on their sides, facing each other, his back to the seat and her securely held in his big warm arms, their legs tangled together.

For several moments, they stared at each other, quiet but for their settling breaths. Her cooling sweat left her back a little cold, but her front was toasty warm against the furnace of his heat.

"I know we have to get back on the road," she murmured, "but I could fall asleep like this."

"Rather we did that in a proper bed," he said, brushing his fingers gently across her cheek, around her neck, toying with the short strands of her hair near her nap.

"Can't afford to stop long enough for a proper bed." She smiled. "Yet."

"That might just be the best and worst word in the English language," he said, kissing her hard and deep when she chuckled. But when he eased back from the kiss, his expression was serious again. "I'm sorry I couldn't give you a bed this time. I'm sorry I couldn't wait for that."

She snorted and shook her head. "Don't. This was perfect. I couldn't have waited either. If you hadn't noticed, I was pretty desperate for you."

Really, she wasn't sure she'd have been able to drive another mile without losing her mind wanting him. Even now, the want, the need was still there, banked but not extinguished, ready to explode into flames again.

Was this the Nam-tar thing? The rite? Or just…Ben? And would it always be like this?

For the first time since discovering the reality of his world, what she was to him, what her attraction to him might mean for her life, she actually welcomed the bond. Welcomed the thought of all those years ahead of them. All that time to explore and learn each other. All those moments like this, secure in his arms…

If she got to spend the next few centuries with Ben, just like this, she'd considered herself a very lucky woman.

CHAPTER TWENTY-NINE

After a full night and another day of driving, Elle's tracking skills brought them to a multi-story box of a building not more than a mile from the Canadian border, in another isolated area surrounded by pines and maples. This building looked new, though, like it had just been finished in the last few months, with a clean, light tan exterior and no windows anywhere.

No windows meant no light leaking out. And no idea if anyone was inside.

She and Ben had left the car a few miles back, parked at a short pull-off just off the narrow two-lane road that climbed into the area. The evening had closed in around them as she turned off the ignition. Long shadows stretched across the darkening road, the sun setting behind the trees as Ben opened the car trunk. And finally showed her all the weapons in his weapons bag.

An impressive array that would have pleased her father—a fact that left her conflicted over how she felt about the number of swords and daggers inside the bag. But since they were going in to extract Professor Arron from the midst of a lot of humans and possibly a lot of monsters, she decided being prepared far outweighed any conflicting emotions she had from her childhood.

Watching Ben gear up wasn't as disturbing as she'd have suspected either. Not given what they were about to face. He strapped on various knives and daggers, slipping them into his boot, belted on scabbards for some of the smaller weapons. And he pulled out the sword he'd taken from the guard that first night and used one of his own scabbards to drop the sword over his head to lay along his spine.

At her raised brow, he said, "It's a good sword."

He offered her her choice of weaponry. But as she'd already told him, the daggers and swords weren't within her skillset. She'd probably have to bring them into her skillset if she was going to live in a world full of monsters, but for the moment, her preferences were her two smaller hand guns, including the plastic one from the backseat, her shotgun, and the recurve bow and quiver of arrows Ben had brought.

He nodded in approval as she slipped the quiver over her head. "Every arrow in there is a fire arrow, in case there's another Water Elemental involved. Don't hesitate to use them."

"Will they work on the other monsters? Like normal arrows?"

"They'll seriously wound and burn any other monster you hit them with. They won't take a head. That's the drawback. But they'll slow a monster down more than an ordinary arrow would."

She angled the bow over her head so the bowstring lay across her chest. She'd already tucked her two handguns into the side pockets of her cargo pants—she didn't have a holster for them as she never carried them around. Then she lifted up the shotgun. "I know this won't remove a head either, but the shots are heavy. They'll slow a monster down, too?"

"Yes. But…" He took hold of her shoulders and brought her as close as their various weaponry would allow. "Don't engage the monsters if you can avoid it. I'll take care of them. You get the professor. Get him out. Get him back to the car. That's the job. Your job. Mine is the monsters. Okay."

"Not sure the monsters will give me a choice, but I'm in no hurry to face them so I'm good with this plan."

After they had what Ben deemed a sufficient array of weaponry, they hiked up to the building in the woods. Elle's nerves tingled as they approached, confirming they were in the right area. She could practically feel herself being pulled toward the building, knowing the professor was in there somewhere.

There was a dirt road that led up to the building, a road that looked half-finished, like it might be paved eventually, and that added to the sense that the building and everything here was new. No cars were parked outside, though, and no evidence of tire tracks in the dirt road. That might have worried her if her tracking sense hadn't honed in on the place so thoroughly. The building was large enough to have parking inside, on the lower level, and still have plenty of room for labs and offices on the second and third floors. At least, she assumed the building was split into three stories, but without windows, she realized, she couldn't be sure. Just a giant block. Could have any configuration.

"So," she whispered to Ben, who was standing very close to her shoulder, "this is definitely the place, but I'm not seeing a way inside."

They'd circled the building from the cover of the woods, and there didn't appear to be any way in, at least not at ground level. No garage doors, no people doors, no obvious openings of any kind. Like the architect and builders and forgotten all about the part where people had to get inside somehow.

"There's got to be something," he murmured, "since they had to get the professor in. But it might not be at ground level."

"Can that tentacle monster fly?" That was a horrifying thought.

"No. But it can climb well. Scaling the side of a building wouldn't be difficult for it, and doing that while carrying a human wouldn't push its abilities either."

"There was more than just Professor Arron, though. All the human guards?"

He shrugged without taking his attention off the building. "Grinluk can carry more than one human. Bastards are extremely strong."

"Oh good. That's what we need right now."

"We'll have to search closer to the building to find the entrance. But they likely have cameras or a lookout or something. We're not going to have much time to get close before being discovered." He glanced at her. "You're stronger now, and faster, but you can't move at the speeds I can. Would you be willing to wait here while I scouted at my top speed?"

For some reason, she thought of him rushing from the backseat of her car to get condoms, the sound and bounce of the trunk slamming shut happening just as he got back into the car. The man moved like lightning when he wanted to.

But thinking about that moment distracted her from what they had to do, so she jerked her focus back to the moment and the building they had to get into. "I'll keep an eye out for anyone patrolling in the woods." She looked at him, held his gaze. "Don't go in without me. Don't try to do this on your own."

"I am used to working alone."

His attempt at sounding reassuring did nothing to ease her worry. Especially when he pulled the sword from the scabbard across is back. That looked suspiciously like he was preparing to fight. While leaving her in the woods. No. That wasn't happening.

"Tough. This is my job, too. I agreed to let you handle the monsters. But I have to go in to get Professor Arron out." She lifted her shotgun and pulled the quiver strap that lay across her chest. "I won't be helpless. We've done this together from the start. We're not changing that now."

A muscle in his jaw jumped, and she thought for a moment he'd argue with her. Unlike when they'd tracked the monster through that small town, he didn't look relieved to have her with him. He looked a lot more worried, the crease between his eyebrows deep as he stared down at her.

But he nodded. "I'll be back in a minute, whether I find an entrance or not."

Before she could respond, he flashed away, moving so fast, she didn't actually see him go. Only felt the brush of air after he'd passed. She blinked and scowled at the trees. He could have at least given her a warning.

She hunted the immediate area again, looking for footprints or tell-tale signs of someone walking the perimeter. She'd barely made it a few yards before Ben was back at her side.

She let out a breath, relieved for more reasons than she wanted to get into at that moment. "Find anything?"

"Small hidden door on the opposite side of the building. Motion detectors near the wall—I had to move outside their range to search."

"We won't be able to go in without them knowing. Unlike the house."

"Unless we go through the roof, but I didn't search up there yet."

She blinked. Glanced at the three-story building. Looked back at Ben with raised brows. "The roof?"

"I can leap us up there. But it might still be sensor protected. And the doors, up there as well as down here, are going to be hard to get through. Locks designed to keep monsters as well as humans inside."

"I can pick a lock if it doesn't have biometrics. Does it have biometrics?"

Ben's turn to blink. Well, that was a nice change of pace. Especially after the revelation that he could leap up to the roof of a three story building while carrying her. She was still processing that. Three stories? That was really high. Lock picking was nothing to that.

"I'm not sure why you being able to pick a lock surprises me," he said, almost as if in answer to her thoughts. "You made yourself a plastic gun and knew how to rig an explosion in a gas generator. Of course you can pick locks."

She shrugged. "My father wasn't the one responsible for that skill, though. I learned that on my own later. When I started tracking for a living. Useful skill when trying to rescue someone."

"It really is. Do you have lockpicking tools with you?"

She gestured to one of her thigh pockets and her ever presence multi-purpose knife. "Got a few picks in the knife that I can use for most ordinary locks. Codes and card swipes and biosensors are a lot harder, though. I won't be able to do those on the fly. Which kind of locks did the doors have?"

He was still giving her a look, but said, "I didn't look that closely. I was just going to kick it in."

She chuckled despite herself. "Brut. That's not a very subtle entrance."

"The motion sensors are going to take this out of our hands, anyway. We'll have to save your lock picking skills for another time."

"Making that much noise to get inside isn't going to make this easy." She glanced back at the building, at the roof. Her gaze narrowed. "You can really leap all the way up there?"

"I can. It's a bit of a stretch, but possible. Some monsters are pretty large and we have to be able to cut off their heads, so…the ability to jump high comes with the job."

She wondered if she could jump higher than she was used to now. "What would happen if you set off motion detectors up there?"

"Make a hell of a noise inside, I imagine. Send all the monsters and humans with guns up to the roof—except for the ones that would hurry to remove the professor from the building or put him into a more secure section."

She nodded. "Would they still hear the motion detectors around the ground level?" She met his gaze, her lips pursed. "Or would they be too distracted to notice a second break in?"

He lifted his head, and his brows snapped down. And for a few beats she was certain he'd argue against her plan. She wasn't particularly happy about the plan herself since it involved splitting up and she'd just made a point of ensuring they'd do this together. But technically, this was "doing this together" because they would be working together to the same end. Not him just running in blind and leaving her behind.

To her surprise, he didn't argue against her plan. "They might have enough people to still notice the second break in," he said. "But given the number they had at the house, given what we've found during previous attempts to retrieve one of their scientists, I doubt they have many more, if any more, than they did previously. For all the building is huge, they keep personnel numbers down. Either they just don't have that many humans working with them that they trust, or they're doing it on purpose to minimize leaks and mistakes."

"Makes sense." She hoped. If there were only the same number of humans with weapons as had been at the house—five at a minimum, but probably not more than seven had been there based on the number of cars—they could divide and conquer that number to get the professor out.

The hitch was the monsters. How many? What kind? Would there be more of that goo with half formed monsters ready to attack. She shivered at the thought.

At Ben's sharp look, she said, "Just remembering the black goo with monster parts. They'll have that here, boxes with that stuff in it, won't they?"

"Maybe. Hard to say. But possible." He sighed. "Probable."

She tried not to let doubt creep in. She wasn't sure how she'd face Sherry Arron if she failed and the professor died. So Elle just wouldn't fail. Black goo be damned.

"Anything I should know before we split up and make this happen?" she asked. The fact that she hadn't had to actually say the plan out loud, that he'd figured out her idea without her needing to outline it, left her feeling…soft. Settled. Like they were a team already. And that shored up her wobbly confidence.

"The grinluk will be in there. I'll try to keep it occupied. If it comes after you, run. Avoid it. There might be more than one grinluk, too. As well as other monsters."

She forced herself not to shiver again. The memory of that first monster, of the horrible sound of its voice speaking actual words, haunted her. Running away from something like that was not going to be difficult.

"The humans will have guns, too," Ben warned.

"I'm not worried about the humans." And she wasn't. She could shoot them. Shooting the grinluk, even repeatedly in the face, wouldn't kill it. She just hoped her new speed meant she could outrun it. She glanced upward. There were no clouds in in the dark sky, just stars winking down at them, oblivious to the troubles of mere mortals. No clouds meant no rain. Probably. But she patted the quiver strap again. "And I have some of these in case an Elemental shows up."

Ben closed his eyes briefly. "If there's an Elemental, we're fucked, so run away. No matter what. Run away. Better yet, don't let the Elemental see you or know about you."

She nodded. She was already running high on adrenaline, but the thought of facing something like an Elemental pushed that rush of fear and focus a little higher.

"Remember," Ben said, facing her fully, "if you have to use the arrows, hitting an Elemental in the head will dissipate it for a very long time. Longer than either of our lifetimes. But hitting it anywhere else will at least dissipate it long enough for us to escape."

"Got it. Aim for the head. Be happy with anywhere else at all."

He handed her one of the fire daggers he'd brought as well, despite her protest that she couldn't use it. "Just in case," he said. "Just…in case."

She glanced down at the weapon. At first blush it looked like a pretty ordinary dagger. It was beautifully made of course. Ben's craftsmanship was impressive. About seven inches long, two-sided blade honed to extremely sharp edges. The hilt was simple, wrapped in soft black leather, with a small t-shaped hand guard, and a silver pommel etched with a stylized flame. As Ben handed her the dagger, faint bluish light danced along the blade briefly, illuminating a series of archaic symbols along its length, then faded away so the symbols were no longer visible, even when she turned the blade to catch what light the half moon and stars provided. The arrows hadn't done that. But then, she hadn't had time to study the arrowheads.

"Careful with it. Don't cut yourself."

She glanced up. "What happens if I use this on a human?"

"They'll burn."

"Ah!" She held the thing out from her, carefully keeping the blade angled away from her body.

"Not immolate," he reassured. "They'll get a burn around the stab wound. But the magic is designed for Water Elementals, not humans. No dissipating for humans."

"Okay." She happily took the small scabbard he handed her for the blade and tucked the sharp edges of the knife away. Then she slid the whole thing into the thigh pocket of her cargo pants next to the smallest of her guns, leaving the pocket's flap tucked behind the dagger so she could grab the weapon easier. "We'd better get moving." She gave Ben a long look. "Be careful."

Without a word, he pulled her close and kissed her, hard and quick, but with a lot of feeling she didn't have time to analyze.

When he released her, he brushed his knuckles along her cheek. "Give me two minutes to get to the roof and cause a distraction. Then go in. And if anything goes wrong, run back to the car. I'll find you. Just get out of here."

She nodded, even though, honestly, if something went wrong, she wasn't sure she'd live long enough to run away. "Don't get killed," she said. "We still have unresolved issues I'd like to resolve."

A tick at the side of his mouth that looked suspiciously like a smile. He kissed her hard again, leaving her breathless.

Then flashed away in that movement that was too fast for her to see.

CHAPTER THIRTY

Elle crept around the house to the side of the building where Ben had said the door was. Looking from the trees, she couldn't see it herself. But once she started across the small expanse of open, grassy ground toward the structure, she spotted it. The faint rectangular outline against the rest of the three-story box's unbroken stonework.

She crouched low as she jogged to the door. Despite the darkness and only a half moon for light, she was able to see decently. Which meant the other humans could probably see too. She had no idea if the grinluk could see in the dark but since that would be just her luck, she assumed she was visible, even in the shadows beside the building. Those shadows were deeper on this side. No security lights popped on when she neared the door. The motion detectors weren't apparently set to scare intruders off, just alert those inside to someone creeping around outside.

She scanned her surroundings as she knelt down next to the door, then turned to study the lock. There wasn't a fancy locking panel or biometrics to get thru. Not even a code panel. There was a flat metal panel to one side of the door, which after some study looked to be a place holder for something. She could be wrong, the panel could have a purpose, but she'd swear this building's security wasn't finished yet.

There probably was meant to be some sort of coded lock installed at some point. It just hadn't been yet. That made her life a bit easier.

The flat, mostly featureless door did have a key-lock—a pickable one—but no doorknob, peephole or handle. She glanced at the panel again. Maybe a camera rather than a placeholder for a more complicated lock?

Too late to worry about that now. She'd set off motion detectors getting next to the building anyway. If the entire place hadn't raced up to the roof to confront Ben's more obvious attack, there'd be someone…or something waiting on the other side of this door.

She pulled out her multi-purpose knife and slid out the set of picks that slotted into the top of the knife's casing. The picks were her custom addition to the tool, after she'd swapped out weak metal tweezers, because, as her father had taught her a little too well, you never knew what you might need.

Noise from overhead finally disturbed the quiet night. Shouting. The sound of gunfire. Fuck. Okay. Ben's distraction was in full swing.

Elle fisted her hand when it started to shake, relaxed it and let out a long breath at the same time. Concentrate. This took focus and a steady hand and her panicking over Ben being in danger wasn't going to get her part of the job done.

The irony of worrying about a man who regularly fought monsters confronting some humans with guns was not lost on her. But he *had* just been shot a couple of days ago. And if he got shot again, he'd have to let his wolf leap from his body. And that would leave his stone human form vulnerable.

And none of this thinking was helping!

She focused on the lock and slowing her breathing. When she was sure her hands were steady, she inserted the picks and made quick work of the lock. It wasn't a complicated one. She'd practice on a lot worse. Given some of the other security, the simple lock seemed weird. But again, maybe the place wasn't finished?

Or maybe having monsters roaming around inside was enough of a deterrent, no one thought they needed anything more sophisticated.

Once the lock was open, the door swung outward enough for her to slide her fingers into a small gap and push it the rest of the way open. No door handle needed. She stood to one side as she eased the door wide, waiting for the rush of an attack or gunfire. She stayed low to the ground as she peeked around the edge of the door frame, quickly, testing.

When no shots ricocheted over her head, she risked a longer look. It was dark inside. Almost too dark. But there was just enough illumination from dim blue emergency lights lining the floor near the walls that she could see the corridor was clear. No monsters waiting and ready to jump on her. No visible tentacles.

She shivered and for some reason looked up at the corridor ceiling, then sagged against the wall when she didn't spot anything there. That would have been creepy as fuck.

Once she was certain nothing would jump at her the minute she got inside, she slipped through the doorway and into the darker shadows against the corridor wall. The door behind her swung shut, but not fully. Without the lock engaged, it hung open about an inch. She left it that way. Someone patrolling would notice, but she didn't want to lock her escape route behind her and then not be able to get out of the building fast. She'd just have to hope no one else came along and locked the door.

From the distant shouting and continued gunfire overhead, she had to assume Ben was keeping everyone else occupied. There weren't any sounds inside that she could hear, though she was straining the edge of her abilities to catch even the tiniest of noise. She crept forward along the windowless, doorless expanse of white walls and white linoleum floors. The sterility of that left her edgy and uncomfortable. The place felt sort of like a hospital.

But it didn't smell like one. In fact, it didn't smell like anything at all. Which was really surprising. With monsters and humans here, she'd have assumed she'd smell...something. Not even cleaning solution or bleach, though. Nothing at all.

Weird.

When she reached the end of the corridor, it branched off in two directions into the building. She scanned both, moving one direction a few yards, looking for a door, then the other, hunting for a clue for which way to go. Letting her tracking sense pick up the appropriate path.

A skittering noise from farther down one corridor made her gut clench. Ben had warned her there'd be monsters in here. Her brain pulled up the image of those little monsters jumping out of the burning goo, only to get caught in the fire. What happened when there was no fire to stop all those tiny monsters from escaping?

The thought made her muscles tight and sent a wave of nausea through her. Her every primitive instinct screamed to run away, get as far from this building as possible. There were fucking *monsters* in here. Real ones. The kind in horror movies and novels that skittered around and jumped out of nowhere and ate the humans stupid enough to just be standing there in the middle of a dark corridor.

Which she was doing. Just standing there. Frozen after hearing that skittering sound.

She tightened her jaw, grinding her teeth together to hold in the squealing scream clawing to get out. Screaming would only draw attention. Last thing she wanted was attention from the monsters. She slid her multi-purpose knife back into her thigh pocket and took a two-handed grip on her shotgun.

With a deep breath, she followed the skittering sound. Cussing up a storm in her head as she went.

This was just the kind of dumb ass thing that got people killed in movies. Walking *toward* the strange noise instead of running away. She couldn't believe she was walking *toward* a probable monster. Unfortunately, her tracking instincts insisted that was the direction she had to go.

The corridor bent into another and then another, a kind of maze that she realized mimicked the stacks of wooden crates in the house in the woods. Those crates had been filled with black goo and monsters and that filled her imagination with the unlikely possibility that the walls were filled with black goo and monsters.

She readjusted her grip on her shotgun, keeping the muzzle pointed toward the ground in front of her, her finger alongside the trigger, near to but not on it. She was so jumpy she was likely to shoot her foot off if she wasn't careful.

Another skittering sound ahead and a high-pitched chittering. She jumped and locked her teeth together to hold in another scream trying to escape. Walking *towards* the monsters? She couldn't believe she was doing this.

A flash of movement ahead of her, too fast for her to see more than a shadow. A steady stream of *fuck, fuck, fuck, fuck* ran through her head as she raised her shotgun just a little and continued to creep forward. She kept her back to the corridor wall now, sliding along it, scanning the corridor behind her as well as in front, hoping she'd see the attack before it happened.

More skittering, like a thousand sharp needles moving over the linoleum floor. She shivered.

And then she heard a grunt. A very human sounding grunt. A muted curse. And… Was that a hiss?

She moved faster, as fast as she dared, toward another bend in the maze, her ears hurting she was straining so hard to hear what was happening ahead of her.

Rounding the corner with her gun half raised, her heart pounding in her throat, she skidded to a halt and blinked at the scene before her.

"Professor Arron?"

CHAPTER THIRTY-ONE

The older man stood in the middle of the corridor, over… something, a sword in one hand, panting, sweat coating his dark skin. Blood dripped from the sword, but the thing, whatever it had been, lay in a heap, and there was a smaller heap rolled up against the wall.

Elle didn't look too closely at the dead monster, or the creature's head. There were some images she just didn't need in her memory. The sewage and decay stench of the dead monster, the first thing she'd smelled since entering the box building, was enough to make her gag without having to see the creature in detail. She got the impression of lots of spindly legs and a hard shell of a body, though. Which was more than she wanted to know. She did note that the creature wasn't spilling black goo and that gave her room to breathe around her fear and disgust.

But she kept most of her attention on the man she was here to save.

Gabe Arron startled and blinked, looking up at her. His glasses reflected faint light from an open door at his back, so she couldn't see his eyes, but his mouth opened in a silent gasp. The room through the open door showed a series of tables and lab equipment like there'd been in the house.

Elle took a single step toward the man, her free hand raised in a calming gesture. "I'm Elle Barker. Your wife, Sherry, sent me to find you. We have to get you out of here. I have a friend. He's keeping the others occupied. Let's go." She reached toward him, flicking her fingers, motioning him to follow.

"My wife? My wife sent you?"

"Hurry, Professor. I'll explain when we're safe."

He stumbled around the body of the dead monster, his breathing rapid. "My wife sent you? She…she sent you?"

"Yes." Elle, shoulders to the corridor wall again, crept back the direction she'd come. She'd memorized the turns, but given the lack of features, doors, or even smells beyond the stench of the dead monster behind them, she had to hope she could get them out without getting lost.

At the second turn, Professor Arron tugged her arm. "There's a closer exit this way." His voice shook as he pointed the sword down a corridor in the opposite direction Elle had come. There was still blood dripping off the tip of the sword, forming dark pools in the mostly dark corridor. The blue emergency lights recessed into the floor near the walls made the blood look black.

Which unfortunately made Elle think of the black goo.

"I know there aren't any monsters this way, though," she murmured, nodding the direction she was heading.

"Can't know that," he said. "They're everywhere. You got lucky missing them."

"Friend distracting everyone, remember."

"Your friend is probably dead already." Professor Arron didn't look at her when he said, "These things are voracious. They kill everything."

"Got that part already. And we're going to talk more about your part in all this. But now we have to get out. And I know the direction I came."

"Trust me. This will be quicker."

"I only saw one door from the outside. That's this way." She gestured toward her corridor again. She was sure the professor knew the exits. But she was reluctant to try a route she didn't know for sure led outside.

"There are two more doors that can only be accessed from inside. They aren't visible from the outside at all. This one is closer." He was already moving in the direction he wanted to go, tugging her arm once more before letting go and hurrying down the unfamiliar-to-her route.

Fuck. "Professor. Wait." She jogged after him, everything in her screaming that this was the exact moment the monsters jumped out and ate them. This was the decision that fucked them.

Fortunately for Elle, this wasn't a horror movie. Even if it was filled with horror movie monsters. They reached a door in one more turn. Significantly closer than the exit she'd been heading toward.

Though, at first, she couldn't quite believe the door led outside. This *felt* like they were still somewhere in the middle of the maze of the building. And that door looked like the one that had led into the professor's lab. There was a doorknob and a key lock. And next to the key lock, another of those metal panels that looked like it was a placeholder. She was starting to think maybe that wasn't a placeholder, after all, but a feature.

She gestured to it. "What?"

The professor glanced at it briefly as he patted his pockets with his free hand. He wore dress slacks and a button-down shirt, but no white lab coat like he'd had on the last time she'd seen him. He found and pulled out a set of keys from his pants pocket.

"My guard dropped these when he rushed off suddenly," Arron muttered. "Knew I had to take my chance." His hands trembling, he slid the key into the lock. "The panel is a sensor for detecting monsters. Ensures none escape."

"Why was there one on the outside of the door I came through?"

"Don't want unauthorized monsters getting in either, do we?"

"We need to talk about this."

The door lock finally gave and they both let out a breath. He stared at her as he turned the handle slowly. When the door opened, his shoulders relaxed.

"Let me go first." She lifted her shotgun just enough he could see it.

"That's no good against monsters. Have to take their heads." He swallowed hard as he shoved the set of keys back into his pants pocket and sort of gestured with his sword.

"Got that part. But the gun is good for humans."

She eased them both to one side of the doorway, scanning the corridor behind them as she did. So far, Ben seemed to be keeping everyone occupied. Now they just had to get out and reach the car before someone noticed Arron was gone. She tried not to think about how Ben was doing and if he needed help. She had to trust he had his part under control. Just as he was trusting her to get the professor out.

Pushing the door open a few inches, she did a quick scan of the area, looking out through the crack. The open ground to the tree line was wider from this side of the building. They'd be exposed longer. That made her gut tight. But no help for it.

When she was sure there weren't any monsters or guards immediately in their way, she pushed the door open and swung out, letting the professor follow as she kept most of her attention on the surroundings. She didn't have to worry. Arron stuck to her back, jogging with her as they rushed to the tree cover.

From behind them, near the roof, she heard a shout. She glanced back in time to see one of the humans aiming a gun at them. Fuck.

"Run!"

She paused, letting Arron rush past her into the woods, and took aim with her shotgun. Firing before the guard did. Her weapon was nowhere near capable of shooting someone that far away. But apparently, the guard didn't realize that, because he ducked back down behind the low roof wall.

That was all the distraction she needed. She spun and raced into the trees, just behind the professor. Then she moved ahead of Arron to lead the way.

"Don't stop," she shouted.

They dodged through the trees, barreling toward the car. Their exit had put them closer to the car so they didn't have to do as much circling through the woods. She realized as she ran, she wasn't nearly as winded as she'd have normally been. Only realized she was running so easily when she glanced back and notice Arron was wheezing and struggling to keep up.

There was a lot of noise behind them now. Shouts. Curses. Sounds she didn't want to think about too closely.

Where was Ben?

She shut off that thought quickly. She couldn't afford to get distracted by worry for him yet. She stopped and the professor doubled over his knees, panting hard. Shit, he wasn't going to make it to the car at this rate.

She adjusted the bow and quiver over her back. Then motioned at the professor. "This will sound weird. Don't argue. I'm going to carry you. We'll get there faster."

"You can't…"

"I said don't argue." She took a step closer. "Is the blood on that sword dangerous? If I touch it, will it burn or anything?"

"The aghrises don't have acid blood. It's just gross, not dangerous."

Something about Professor Gabe Arron calling blood gross struck her as strange given what he'd been doing. "Hold onto it. We might still need it. But carefully." Then she turned and gestured to her back. He awkwardly climbed up, piggyback style, the position shoving the quiver and bow farther to one side. She wrapped her free arm under one of his legs, keeping her shotgun in her free hand, having to rely on him to keep his other leg up around her hips and out of the way.

Her newfound strength from the ritual with Ben served her well. The professor didn't feel much heavier than the bow and quiver.

She blinked. Yeah, she was going to have to get used to this. Arron wasn't a tiny man. A little taller than her and comfortably thick around the middle. Her old body would have been strained and certainly couldn't have run with him like this.

"What are you?" he asked.

"Mostly? Human." The mostly part was pretty important, though.

She spun and started hurrying through the trees, moving as fast as she dared while carrying a man holding a sword over uneven ground in the middle of the night. She might be strong enough to do this more easily, but she didn't trust her footing to have caught up to her strength.

Her night vision was definitely better, though. The darkness under the trees should have been nearly impossible to navigate without a flashlight or even a penlight. But she was able to see as if there was a full moon pouring light over an open clearing. She hadn't noticed her heightened sight earlier in the night with Ben, because she was relying on his better eyesight to guide her through the trees. It only just occurred to her she hadn't actually needed much help from him. She'd been able to see fine.

More things to think about later. She rushed around a fallen tree, as more shouts sounded behind her. She was nearly to the car. Nearly there. And once she had the professor safely inside, she'd have to consider if she went back for Ben or drove away as he'd told her to do.

She nearly stumbled at the thought of driving away from him. Everything in her rebelled at the idea.

She skidded out of the trees to the side of the dirt road about a hundred yards away from the car. With the open road all that lay between her and escape, she ran forward, and was shocked to reach the car so fast she nearly passed it.

She stopped abruptly, and grunted when Arron's arm around her neck tightened so he wouldn't fall. She set him back onto his feet, hoping her shock didn't show on her face. "Get in." She turned to study the woods, scanning their surroundings as Arron slid into the passenger seat.

Things approached in the woods, branches breaking and ground cover crunching under fast moving boots. She raised the shotgun, two rounds left and a few shells in her pocket. The two guns in her thigh pockets were loaded. But she'd only had room for one extra magazine each. The bow string across her chest reminded her she had more options than her guns. But the gun would be faster.

"Get in!" Arron shouted back through the closed door. "We have to get out of here."

They did. They really did. The running was getting closer. They'd lose their chance if she didn't hurry. And yet...

Ben.

Fuck!

Swallowing hard, she skimmed around the car to the driver's side, a steady stream of cursing running through her mind as she threw the door open.

Then screamed when something heavy landed on the roof.

She looked up into the face of a horror with fathomless black eyes, gray tentacles…

And a lot of very sharp teeth.

CHAPTER THIRTY-TWO

Elle scrambled backward without thinking. Couldn't think as she looked into the face of the monster she'd seen on that first day. The monster in the house. Gray. Huge when seen outside the confines of the house. Those black black eyes. Scale-covered tentacles. Skeletal face. So many teeth. And…oh god. The eyes on the tips of the tentacles. Those swung toward her, all of them looking at her as the monster's smile widened.

Her brain broke in that moment. She was certain it did. How could anything like that exist? How could this be real life?

It didn't matter that she'd seen it before. It didn't matter that she'd seen the other monsters, the black goo with body parts in it, the monster whose inside was all black goo that went on to create more monsters. There was something primally terrifying about this creature standing on top of her car.

The smile. The knowledge. It was aware of her fear. It *liked* her fear. It knew what it was doing.

Those sharp teeth gnashed together, making a noise that scraped across Elle's nerves. Another scream crawled up her throat. In the deep recesses of her mind, a memory she rarely looked at rose of a man standing over her bed in the middle of the night, when she was only eleven years old. Staring down at her. Smiling.

The grinluk had the same smile.

The part of her that had taken in all the therapy lessons over the years knew her imagination was conflating her current horror with a past horror. Her lizard brain was screaming to run away because the monsters were here and combining all the monsters she'd known in her life into one convenient mold.

"You're the one," the creature whispered. And the fact that it spoke sent her brain scrambling into a corner to hide as it whimpered. "Will you let your wolf out to play?"

A tentacle in her peripheral vision drew closer.

She heard someone else shouting. Professor Arron? But she couldn't look away from the monster's smile. Couldn't stop the terror overwhelming her, freezing her in place. A tentacle reached toward her, slowly, as the smile grew. She watched the tentacle approach from the side of her eye. But she couldn't look away from that smile. All those teeth. That *knowledge*.

A scream. Not hers. Not of horror. A scream of…anger?

And then a sword swung down across the tentacle.

Elle finally blinked and stumbled back a step as blood sprayed out across the dirt road. The creature reared back, screaming itself, a high, piercing screech.

Finally, able to look away, she turned to see Professor Arron, sword in hand, standing over the fallen tentacle.

She opened her mouth to thank him, to say something. But then the monster swung back toward them, tentacles waving. Too fast. Too fast. It would kill Arron.

Instinct and action finally kicked in. Elle moved, wrapping her arms around the professor and dragging him out of harm's way— moving faster than she'd ever moved and lifting him off the ground on accident as she did.

They blinked at each other when she stopped, suddenly a hundred yards away from the car and the grinluk.

She kept forgetting. Kept forgetting she was stronger now. Faster.

Not like Ben. But she wasn't as vulnerable as she'd been the first time she saw this monster. And she wasn't a child anymore.

"Thanks," she said to Arron.

"Thank you."

They faced the grinluk.

It had risen above the car, its legs and taloned, gorilla-like feet dangling beneath it as it balanced on thicker tentacles. The sharp black talons scraped across the car's roof, leaving gouges.

Elle saw Arron raise his sword, gripping it with two hands. And she remembered the shotgun in her own hand. She hadn't dropped it, which amazed her, and was still clenching the barrel. Only two shots left before she'd have to reload. But those two shots could give her time. Time to reload if she needed to. Time to pull out one of her other, smaller guns—though she didn't want to be close enough to the grinluk for those weapons.

But she also had the bow and arrows.

Arrows designed for an Elemental. But they'd still do the job of an ordinary arrow with a monster, wouldn't they? Might even burn it the way Ben said the arrows would burn a human.

She raised her shotgun and without a word or comment, fired the last two shots into the monster's face. The accuracy at this distance wasn't great, but the buckshot still barreled into the monster, making it rear up and back, swiping with tentacles like it would bat the shot pellets away.

Before she could think, even a little, she dropped the shotgun to the dirt road, pulled the bow over hear head and nocked an arrow against the string. She'd trained using both recurve and compound bows when she was a kid, and the compound bow in particular had been incredibly hard to pull because she wasn't strong enough, even with the low-tension settings. As she'd grown, so had her strength and her ability to use either bow easier, but the pull on a compound bow was still hard.

The perfectly balanced and crafted recurve bow that Ben had given her was a different animal to all the ones she'd used before, though. And she was a lot stronger now than she'd been even a week ago.

She set the bow into position, sited on the monster's face as she pulled the string back to its full extension. Let out a breath. Released the string.

The first arrow flew so far past the grinluk she gasped. Shit. And oops.

She nocked another arrow, this time adjusting her pull to compensate for her strength, and readjusted her aim. This arrow flew true, slamming into the monster's already damaged face.

Its tentacles slashed at the air as it reared back, seeming to grow even larger. One tentacle snapped the arrow out, leaving behind a bleeding mess and the distinct sound of a sizzle.

She couldn't remove its head this way. She'd need to be closer. With the sword. But she couldn't use the sword, which meant getting closer to the monster would just get her killed.

"How good are you with that?" she asked Arron, nodding down to the sword he still clenched in both hands. She fired a third arrow. This time she aimed at one of the thicker tentacles holding the grinluk off the ground.

The arrow slammed into the tentacle and pinned it to the dirt road. The monster screamed through its damaged face—a sound that would haunt her nightmares—and, using other tentacles, tried to pull the thick one free.

"Not great," Arron said. "I did fencing as an undergrad. Thirty years ago. This is not the same."

No it was not. But he'd at least held that kind of weapon before, or a version of it.

"Still more experience than I've had." She nocked and fired another arrow, attempting to pin a second tentacle. Tendrils of smoke rose from the spots on the grinluk she'd hit. As if the arrows were burning it. Good. Okay. That was good.

"We have to remove its head," Arron said. "I'm not good enough with the sword to do that."

What they needed to do was run. That's what Ben had said. Run. But… How far could she get them on foot? The grinluk hovered over the car. They couldn't reach it. And if they ran, there might be more of the monsters in the woods.

Even as that thought occurred to her, she heard something crashing through the trees. Fuck. They were in deep enough trouble with the grinluk.

The monster kept trying to remove the arrows Elle fired into it, thrashing and screeching, its skin burning. And as it thrashed, it thumped and smashed the car. Her poor car was starting to look like it had been dropped into one of those scrap metal compactors.

If she survived, she'd be grateful she got the good insurance, but still... How did you tell your insurance company that your car got smashed by monster?

More crashing in the trees. "We have to get out of here," Arron said, already backing away, further down the road. "We have to run."

She knew that, but where? Blindly running down an empty dirt road in a part of northern Michigan infrequently visited by other humans in the dead of night? They'd last an extra few minutes. Maybe.

Still, she backed away from the grinluk with Arron, firing two more arrows in rapid succession as she went.

A primal scream from the woods, froze her in her tracks again. A sound so deep and angry she wasn't sure she'd heard anything like it before.

A monster tore out of the trees, so fast she barely had time to recognize lots of legs and a round mouth full of teeth. She scrambled backward half a step, her brain all instinct and no thought.

Then something huge landed between her and the monster.

The flash of metal in the moonlight. A squeal cut off abruptly.

And the huge person turned to face her.

CHAPTER THIRTY-THREE

Elle nearly sobbed as she stepped into Ben's arms. He was covered in blood, his face harsh and hard in the darkness. And she didn't care. He was here. He was alive.

The relief was so profound she wobbled as she clung to him. His one-armed grip around her waist was so tight, though, she didn't have to worry about falling. She allowed herself the comfort of his warmth and strength for exactly two seconds. But they didn't stay that way for long.

There were still monsters.

She stepped back as quickly as she stepped into him, moved so she could see the grinluk, nocked and fired another arrow. Then finally said, "Glad you're alive. What do we do now?"

If she hadn't known better, she'd swear his lips twitched in a smile. But he turned to face the grinluk before she could be sure.

"Keep it distracted," he growled. And his voice really was a growl. Like the wolf that lived in him was about to break out. "I'll get its head."

Elle fired another arrow. Into the creature's face again.

Its head was a mess now, between the buckshot and the magic-tipped arrows hitting it. She was pretty sure its eyes were useless. But it had a whole bunch more eyes on the tips of its tentacles to compensate. So she focused another two arrows on trying to pin tentacles as Ben stalked toward the creature.

He was a huge man, and yet the creature still rose easily six feet over his head. The monster's tentacles thrashed at the air, whipping out, forced Ben to leap away.

She tried not to let her worry distract her. He'd been doing this for centuries. He could kill the monster.

Something the monster must have realized, too.

It scrambled at its pinned limbs with its hands and gorilla feet and other tentacles. Jerking at the arrows sticking it to the dirt. Thrashing at Ben almost as an afterthought as it scrambled to free itself.

Elle fired again.

"Is the shotgun empty?" Arron asked next to her, gesturing to the dropped weapon.

"More shots in my pocket. Other side." She fired another arrow. She was down to maybe ten more. Couldn't afford to waste them. "You know how to reload and shoot a shotgun?" she asked.

"Not as well as I know how to fence," he said, digging in her thigh pocket for the handful of loose shots she had there.

"Don't shoot your foot off."

Arron snorted. "You've got a second gun in here. Will it work?"

She fired another arrow, up over the top of Ben and into the grinluk. "Not very well or accurately from this distance. But take it out, anyway." The more weapons they had to use against the creature, the better.

Ben leapt up into the air, straight up and too high for a human to have jumped, landing in the middle of a wrath of flailing tentacles. She swallowed a scream as she watched him slice through those limbs, taking out one of the big ones the monster had been standing on, then jumping away so fast he blurred.

The moment Ben was out of the way, she fired another arrow and Arron fired the shotgun. He didn't have her aim, but most of the buckshot hit the grinluk and not the dirt. And those hits were further distraction for the monster.

They both stopped firing. Ben jumped high into the air again. The creature screamed, lashed out. Ben swung his sword.

And the creature's head fell.

The sound, the sight of that severing sent two totally conflicting emotions rushing through her system, so hard and fast, she had to lower the bow as her knees wobbled.

She'd seen things killed, killed animals for food, seen a man killed by her father… Watching the grinluk's head drop away from its body and roll along the dirt road ranked right at the top of her list for one of the most disturbing and disgusting things she'd ever seen.

And it filled her with such profound relief her muscles went slack. She nearly dropped the bow now dangling from her fingers and had to tighten her grip.

She and Arron both scanned their surroundings, hunting for other monsters. Nothing—not human or monster—came charging out of the trees.

Elle let her relief sink in a little deeper.

Ben stood a few yards from the dead monster, his head down. Some of the tentacles continued to wave futilely around, but other than that, the monster was still.

When Ben didn't turn to face them, she hurried to him, worried he'd been injured again. "Ben," she called. And when she was near enough that he could hear her without Arron overhearing them, she said more quietly, "Are you hurt? Do you need to do the stone statue thing?"

He finally turned to her. He looked feral, his eyes glowing in the moonlight, his hair a mess, covered in blood, his jaw tight. He was breathing hard, though she wasn't sure if that was from the fight or something else. Because she was suddenly breathing hard and it wasn't from the fight.

"Are you hurt?" he asked, his voice so guttural she barely recognized it.

"No," she said even as she scanned him for injuries. "Is any of that blood yours?"

"My injuries are healing or healed."

She nodded. Then she dropped the bow at the same time he dropped the sword. She walked into his arms, again, wrapping herself around him, and dove in for a kiss that felt like life itself. He lifted her up onto her toes as he kissed her, held her with arms so big and strong she felt engulfed in his strength. And yet a tremor ran through his entire body, even as he deepened his kiss, even as his arms flexed and brought her even tighter against him. She trembled, too. And it was all relief this time.

She leaned back enough to cup his face between her palms. "You sure you're okay? Not hurt?"

"Not anything that won't heal quickly. You? This isn't how I wanted to test your ability to heal."

She snort-laughed, but it sounded more choked than amused so she stopped. "Me neither. But I'm not hurt. The others? The humans? Anymore monsters?"

"I took care of them. Two of the human guards got away. The living monsters were killed—not many here. Yet."

Yet. That had such an ominous ring to it. A sharp contrast to the way they'd been using that word just yesterday. "Do you have to destroy the building again?"

He shook his head. "My Family will want to look through it, see what they can uncover." He glanced behind her and she followed his gaze. Professor Arron stood a few yards away, his arms limp at his side, staring at the smashed car. He still held her shotgun in one hand, but he didn't seem aware of it.

"Are you okay, professor?" Elle called.

"Don't suppose you have a second car around here somewhere?" He didn't look at them and his voice was dull, almost emotionless. Elle wasn't sure if that was exhaustion, resignation, or something else.

"The car." Elle sighed. "How I'm going to explain this to the insurance company?"

"I'll take care of it," Ben said, matter-of-factly.

After learning who he was, she realized he probably could. Billionaires could do things normal people couldn't, right? They could "take care of" things and those things got sorted out without too much fuss. Handy.

"Don't suppose you have an idea how we'll get back to a main road or…anywhere?" she asked. "I'm not sure the professor is up for a long walk." The last she murmured for Ben's ears only. He hadn't loosened his hold or let her back onto her feet yet. And she found herself relying so much on his strength to hold her upright, she wasn't actually sure she'd be up for a long walk either.

"That's taken care of, too," he said, before nuzzling his face against her neck.

The hug left her breathless again. She threaded her fingers through his hair, and tightened her arms, hugging him back. Her relief at knowing he was alive was profound. Between that relief and his hug, she almost missed the distant *whomp whomp whomp* sound approaching. When the noise sank in, she straightened, looking behind Ben into the distance.

It was too dark to see much more than a headlamp which scanned over the ground, but the sound was unmistakable.

"Do monsters fly helicopters?" she asked.

"That will be our ride," Ben said.

She blinked at him. "When did you…?"

"Sent a text with the location earlier. Before we went in."

She wanted to ask about him calling in backup, what it meant, what he'd been thinking that he'd done that, but the sound of the approaching helicopter made a quiet conversation impossible.

By the time the chopper set down, Ben had wrenched open the destroyed car's trunk and they'd gotten the rest of their gear out. Professor Arron looked between them and the chopper, still holding her shotgun—which she took gently from him because his gaze was glassy and he didn't appear very steady.

"Help?" he asked, nodding to the chopper and straightening his glasses.

"Friends," she assured.

"Family," Ben said.

From the passenger side of the helicopter, a woman jumped out, running low under the still whirling blades, and then straightening as she jogged up to them. She was a smallish woman, slim, with dark hair and eyes, pale skin, dressed in jeans and a t-shirt. With two swords strapped along her thighs like she was some kind of sword gunslinger. The dual swords made Elle blink.

"Hey, Ben," the woman said with a grin. "What sort of fun have you been up to?"

"Andrea Logan, this is Elle Barker. Elle, my youngest sister, Rea." Ben's voice was still gravely and low as he made the introductions.

Rea swung her grin to Elle and pumped Elle's hand in a firm shake that nearly knocked Elle off her feet. "Looking forward to getting to know you. I have all the good gossip on Ben. We'll talk."

Ben's groan made Elle smile, though she was too wiped out now for the effort to hold.

Rea's grin dropped too as she faced her brother again. "What happened?"

Ben gave her a brief run down. "The building is still intact. A lot of what they've been doing is there." He glanced at Arron, who was staring at Rea. "And I think he'll be willing to talk with us."

Arron startled. "Talk? With you? Who are you?" His shoulders shook and then he said, "Wait, Logan? Are you...? Are you one of *those* Logans? The ones the grinluk talked about?"

"Probably," Rea answered. "And I think we have a lot to talk about, Professor Arron. If you're willing."

"Willing. Ashamed. But willing."

"We need to get him back to his family," Elle murmured to Ben. "Sooner rather than later. They've been worried about him for a year."

"Mansion first to clean up and get our questions answered," Ben said. "Then we'll fly him directly home. Or we can bring his family to the mansion for the reunion. They'll be safe there."

"Mansion?"

Rea grinned. "Our home in New York. You'll love it." She patted Ben on the arm, hard enough he winced. Which Elle found interesting. Then the young woman walked into the woods.

"Where's she going?" Elle asked.

"To scout the house and ensure it and the area are clear of monsters."

"Alone?"

Ben didn't get a chance to answer her question before the second person in the chopper leaned out the door. Between the darkness and the lights on the front of the helicopter, Elle couldn't see the person at all. But their shout was clear enough. "Are you coming?"

"Who's that?" Elle asked, leaning in to Ben.

"One of my brothers," Ben said. "Richard. And he's impatient." Ben ushered her and the professor toward the helicopter, carrying most of the luggage in one hand and his sword in the other.

"Wait." Elle glanced back toward the woods where Rea had disappeared. "We're not leaving your sister here, right?"

"She'll be fine," he said. "She can get home on her own. That's why she's here."

"What?"

"Long story." He looked at her then glanced at the professor briefly and she got the hint. Something they weren't going to talk about in front of him. Got it.

Though the minute they were alone…

Except, as she stared at him while he tossed their luggage into the back of the helicopter and then gently helped the professor inside, she realized when she got him alone, the very first thing she wanted to do was not talk about any of this. The very first thing she wanted when she got Ben alone again was to wrap herself around that big body and get him inside her fast.

Maybe it was their bond or maybe it was the adrenaline of the night, or maybe it was just a joy at being alive. Whatever it was, she didn't really care.

So long as she got Ben alone. Soon.

CHAPTER THIRTY-FOUR

The flight took them a few hours, and to Elle's surprise, she fell asleep. It was her first time in a helicopter, and the experience was a little terrifying—hard not to feel like this kind of machine should *not* be able to stay in the air. The ground seemed a really long way down and there wasn't nearly enough metal around her. But her exhaustion and emotional overwhelm were stronger than her fear.

She woke as they were landing, the surroundings so dark she couldn't make out anything about their location. Her stomach dropped and a spike of adrenaline shot through her blood as the helicopter descended, the *whomp whomp whomp* of the blades above blocking most other sound. When the helicopter set down gently, she let out a breath and glanced over at Professor Arron. He looked as nervous about helicopter landings as she'd been. He gave her a hesitant smile, that she returned in an attempt to reassure them both.

Given what he'd been through, Gabe Arron was handling all this with a lot of grace. She hoped she could get him back to Sherry and his kids soon. But at least they were somewhere safe now.

At least, she hoped they were safe.

They climbed carefully out of the helicopter as the blades slowly stopped spinning. Ben gathered all the gear again, and they all followed the pilot brother—Richard, right?—across an expanse of tarmac that turned out to be on top of a building. A single steel door leading inside opened before they reached it. From her place trailing behind Ben and his brother, keeping Professor Arron at her side, she didn't at first see who'd opened the door. Then an older man in a very formal-looking black and gray butler's suit stepped out.

"It's good to have you all back," the man said. "Eric is in the front library when you're ready. I've prepared rooms for our two guests."

As Elle and Professor Arron reached the door, the older man said, "You're very welcome. I'm Gregory. If you need anything, please let me know."

"Elle Barker," she introduced herself, blinking at the man. She was still half asleep. "This is Professor Gabe Arron."

Gregory gave them both a stiff nod and then led everyone down a set of concrete stairs into what turned out to be a mansion.

Elle gaped as they stepped into a long, elegant corridor. White and cream walls with polished hardwood floors and fancy crown molding. Might have passed for a fancy hotel corridor but for the statuary art tucked into wall insets, the impressive paintings hanging between those insets, and the row of crystal chandeliers illuminating the hallway.

Could still be a very fancy hotel, she supposed. But Ben had said they were going to the family home. This was someone's actual house. She scanned the place, a little dumbfounded. People lived here? Actually *lived* in a place like this? *Ben* lived in a place like this?

She knew the Logan's were loaded, billionaires and all that, but she supposed she hadn't stopped to think about what that meant in the real world. In his life when he wasn't hunting monsters. It meant his family had mansions and butlers and landing pads for helicopters on the roofs of their *houses*, and a life that was so far removed from her existence it was shocking.

And she was supposed to be meant for Ben? Old gods had determined she was his destiny? Her? When he lived in the middle of all this?

If they hadn't already performed a ritual that wouldn't have been possible with anyone but his Nam-tar, she'd be convinced he'd gotten something wrong.

As if he sensed the spike in her worry, he fell back from his position beside his brother to join her. "You okay?" he asked, leaning in close to speak in her ear.

"Keep forgetting your loaded and I'm a little overwhelmed by all this. Including the helicopter pad on top of your house."

He shrugged. "It's useful. That's all. You'll get used to it."

That almost made her trip. Get used to all this? She was supposed to…be part of this?

And she'd thought a lifetime of knowing monsters existed was going to be weird.

The butler, Gregory, led them through twists and turns with corridors ever more impressive, until they reached a huge foyer with marble floors, columns bracketing a giant oak door, and a grand, curved staircase leading down to the lower levels. She glanced up to see an arched roof with an elaborate painting on it, which reminded her of pictures she'd seen of the Sistine Chapel. Except this picture seemed to be filled with wolves running around different settings—in woods, deserts, even city streets. But she wasn't given much time to study the mural. They went down the first set of split stairs to the second-floor landing, where Gregory took all the gear from Richard and Ben, carrying everything remarkably easily, and disappeared down a side corridor.

Richard turned to face her, Ben, and the professor, and it was the first time Elle got a good look at the pilot. He wasn't nearly as tall as Ben, but was still above average height, broad shouldered and handsome. His buzz cut hair and the solid green fatigues gave him a military baring that was what her father and his friends had always aspired to without ever quite reaching. The familial resemblance with Ben was obvious, but Richard's short hair was a few shades darker, he had blue eyes instead of brown, and his features were more angular.

"I'll go check on Rea," he said to Ben, turning toward the corridor opposite the one Gregory had disappeared down. Before leaving, though, he gave Elle a small smile. "Really nice to meet you, Elle." His gaze darted to Ben, briefly, then he moved on.

Leaving Elle to wonder just how much Ben's family knew about her.

With their escort gone, Ben led the way down the huge central staircase to the first floor. Elle was afraid to touch the elaborate carved wood handrails since she was still dirty from the monster fight and had dried blood on her shirt from hugging Ben. Who was also still covered in blood. He didn't seem too aware of his state. But Elle was growing more and more conscious of the fact that she'd been meeting members of Ben's family while covered in blood and stinking of sweat and monsters.

The fact that she, the professor, and Ben all kind of stank didn't really help her growing self-consciousness. She'd been so eager to just get away from the monsters and get Gabe Arron somewhere safe, she hadn't thought about much else. Now she was uncomfortably aware of the fact that she'd met a butler, an actual, honest-to-god butler, while caked in blood and sweat. And was being led to meet Ben's older brother, the man in charge of the Logan family, while she was a stinky mess.

Nice. Helpful. That would set the right impression that she belonged here.

They stepped into a room off the main foyer that was the sort of library Elle had always wanted as a teenager when she'd discovered public libraries. Big fireplace, bookshelf-lined walls, a mix of comfortable furniture, like the couch, with more formal pieces, like a delicate looking settee. Floor to ceiling velvet curtains blocking out the night—or early morning? Elle realized she had no idea what time of day it was.

She stopped in her tracks when she spotted the man standing in the room.

He wasn't as tall as Ben, but he was tall enough and broad enough to take up space. He was scary handsome—he and Ben had that in common—and the family resemblance in the dark eyes was obvious. Where Ben's hair was a lighter brown, almost blond, the new man's hair was such a dark brown it was nearly black. His skin was pale, but not an unhealthy pale, and he was dressed in black dress slacks and a button-down black shirt. He stood near the fireplace, his hands folded behind him, looking extremely intimidating and serious. A man not to be messed with.

Elle unconsciously took a step closer to Ben. His warm hand at the small of her back reassured her.

The man took one look at her and Ben and said, "Been through some things tonight."

Ben snorted. "We left Rea to look through the building and secure it. No more of the black goo monsters." He nodded at Gabe. "This is the geneticist. Professor Gabe Arron. Professor Arron, this is my brother, Eric Logan." To Eric, he added, "The professor is going to need rest before talking."

Gabe's gaze jumped between Ben and Eric. "I'm not sure who any of you are, or what's going on, but I need to see my wife. I need to call her. Tell her I'm okay." He frowned. "I am okay now, right?"

"You're safe here, professor," Eric said, his tone gentler than Elle would have given him credit for. "But we have a lot of questions for you. You've been making new monsters. And we have to know everything about that work."

Arron swallowed visibly. "They threatened my family if I didn't do the work. They threatened to kill my kids. My wife. In…in horrible ways. I had to do what they asked. You understand that, right? I *had* to do what they asked."

"His wife hired me to get him out," Elle added. "He wasn't there voluntarily."

Eric's dark gaze turned on her and without thought, she leaned closer to Ben. Ben wrapped his arm around her waist and held her tight against his side.

"I understand," Eric said. "Which is why he's a guest here and not a prisoner. But we do need to know everything he's done and everything he's learned while being held by the monsters."

That the Logan's could kidnap someone and bring them here as a prisoner was a possibility not lost on her in Eric's speech. Had he meant to point that out, or was he really trying to reassure her and Gabe?

"Who are you?" Gabe asked, raising a hand when Eric opened his mouth. "I know you're the Logan family. The grinluk talked about you. And I've seen at least one of you kill multiple monsters." He flicked a glance at Ben. "But… Who *are* you all?"

"We hunt monsters," Eric said simply. "It's our duty to destroy them and protect humans from them. And we will do whatever is necessary to do that."

Gabe held Eric's gaze for a long, silent moment, which Elle found pretty fucking brave, and then nodded. "I have questions of my own," he said, adjusting his glasses. "After a year of this, I have as many questions as I have answers."

"We'll try to tell you what we can," Eric said. "So long as you're willing to talk to us."

"The monsters are terrifying," Gabe said. "They'll sweep over the world and destroy everything in their wake if left to continue. So yes, I'm willing to talk if your aim is to stop them."

With that, the tension in the room seemed to ease, though Elle couldn't say why she felt that. Eric's imposing presence didn't change. Ben didn't loosen his hold on her. No one even moved. But the unseen tension dripped away until the meeting felt a lot less potentially volatile.

Eric let his gaze move over everyone. "Gregory has rooms for you all. Mrs. Patterson will have food up to you by the time you've finished cleaning up. We can talk tomorrow." His gaze danced between Ben and Elle, and a very faint smile changed his expression completely. "I think we have a lot to talk about."

Ben didn't respond to that, but Elle didn't miss the goading in the comment. She glanced up at Ben. He looked stoic and relaxed and wasn't rising at all to his brother's baited comment. But his hand did flex against her waist.

Gregory reappeared, stepping just inside the library doorway. "If you all will follow me, I'll show you to your rooms."

They were in a corridor on the second floor, when Gregory, his back to them, said, "I've taken the liberty of placing Ms. Barker in the room next to Benjamin's. I hope that will suit, Ms. Barker?"

Elle felt her cheeks heating, but she said, "That will be fine." Honestly, she only felt safe in the middle of all this with Ben beside her. She wouldn't have wanted to be in a room too far away from him.

Gregory showed Gabe to a nice, comfortable room, pointing out the bathroom door and showing him the closet filled with clothes he would be able to use while he was there. Elle left the professor reluctantly, promising she'd make sure he got to call his wife soon. Gregory stepped in to offer the Gabe use of the house line, and promised to return shortly to make the phone call possible.

Then Gregory led her and Ben down another corridor which curved away from the first, moving into a different part of the house. This hallway was decorated with colorful glass bulbs lining the walls and shelves covered in plants with little wood and stone statues poking out from the leaves. It was a charming and startling contrast to the more elegant décor in the rest of the house.

"Rea's tastes," Ben said against her ear.

That said a lot about the younger woman. Elle just wasn't quite sure what yet.

Gregory stopped again and pushed open a door, seemingly at random. "This is your room, Ms. Barker. These rooms were last used by Ms. Judith, so they've been unoccupied for a while, but I've taken the liberty of placing some clothing in the closet that should fit you. You can use anything that suits. If you need anything else, just let me know."

"My room's there," Ben said, pointing to a door a little farther down the hall.

Elle nodded, but didn't immediately step inside the room she'd been given, and after a single beat, Gregory gave a slight head nod and walked away. Leaving Elle and Ben alone.

When there was no one to overhear, Ben said, "Are you really okay? You weren't hurt?"

"No. I'm physically fine. I'm just…overwhelmed. And tired. And I really need a shower."

"But?"

That he'd heard the *but* in her sentence made her smile. "But I'm… reluctant to be alone." Part of her thought she needed time alone, to process everything that had happened. To really settle herself and get some perspective. But a much larger part of her just didn't want to be by herself. Didn't want to think. Didn't want to sleep alone.

Ben brushed his knuckles down the side of her cheek. "I don't want to be away from you either. It's not the weird reaction we had the other day, I just…don't want to be away from you."

"We have a lot to discuss."

"We do."

"I'm happy to delay those conversations until tomorrow."

He smiled. "Me too."

Elle took Ben's hands and walked backward into the room, pulling Ben with her. Everything else going on around them was almost too much for her to process. But the one thing she knew, the one solid thing she could hold on to, was that Ben made her feel safe and she didn't want to be anywhere else but with him.

She wasn't sure that would change. She had no idea what their future held. But for tonight, for just the rest of tonight, she'd hold him.

And worry about the future tomorrow.

CHAPTER THIRTY-FIVE

Ben had never been so scared in his life as he'd been tonight. First, leaving Elle's side to distract the monsters while she got the professor out. Then knowing the grinluk and one other monster had escaped him and were on their way to her. And then the fucking aghris had slowed him down, preventing him from reaching Elle before the grinluk did.

Coming out of the trees, seeing her still alive but firing arrows at the grinluk, seeing the aghris that had gone underground to escape him coming for her while she still had a grinluk to worry about... Those moments were the most horrifying of his life. Maybe even more horrifying than that moment when he'd jumped in front of a bullet to save her. He never wanted to feel that way again. Never wanted her to be in that position again.

But gods was she magnificent. Standing there firing *arrows* into a grinluk, pinning it, holding it at bay. That was a sight he'd never get over either. That was the one he wanted to hold on to.

That was the sight that went with him into her room and drove all thoughts of the rest of the night and their future and curses and everything else out of his head. He brought her into his arms the minute they were over the threshold, kicking the door shut behind him, spinning to pin her against the door as he devoured her mouth. She melted into him, her tongue tangling with his the moment he dove in between her parted lips. The feel of her against the length of him was so perfect, so exactly right. Knowing she was meant for him was nothing to *feeling* how perfect they fit together.

He was a mess. The stench of dead monsters and blood still covered him. She was covered in sweat and blood. And none of that mattered. Nothing but getting inside her. Now. This minute. She tore at his shirt, pushing it up and tugging at it at the same time. Her hands running over his back and shoulders, her short nails raking him, her kiss as rough as his. He lifted away to tear off his shirt. She whipped her own off before he'd reached for her again. Her bra next, without waiting for him, and then she was climbing him, wrapping her legs around his hips, flattening her breasts against his chest.

And gods it was the best thing he'd ever felt. He braced one hand under her ass, the other wrapped around her waist, and scraped his mouth across hers, over her jaw, down her throat. She rocked against him, her sex riding his hard cock through the barrier of their pants. The sensation too good. Too much. He wanted to be inside her.

"Drop your legs," he muttered as he worked his mouth back up to hers.

The minute she unwound around him, still clinging tight to his neck, he reached for her zipper. He pushed down her pants and underwear at the same time, everything getting caught on her boots. When she couldn't toe out of her tightly laced shoes, she growled and said, "Rip the pants."

Gods, yes. He knelt and tore the material, freeing her legs, and because he was already on his knees, he pushed her back against the wall, lifted one leg over his shoulder, and licked into her already wet pussy. The taste of her exploded on his tongue and her strangled cry filled him with a greedy need. He devoured her, licking, sucking, tonguing her until she writhed against the wall, until she tightened around his tongue. Until she came into his mouth, shouting his name.

He rose, kissing his way up her abdomen, pausing to suck at her nipples, biting gently to make her shiver. Her entire body trembled against his. He dove into her mouth again as he lowered his zipper and pushed his pants aside to free his painfully hard cock. Gods he wanted to be inside her this instant. But first…

"Can you stand here for two seconds?" he said against her mouth before kissing her again, which prevented her answer.

She still managed a nod around their kiss, her hands buried in his hair, holding him to her. He sank into that kiss a moment longer, then released her in a rush, and zipped next door for the supply of condoms he'd picked up yesterday. Just yesterday? Time seemed to have warped with Elle so that only a few days felt like a lifetime.

He was back to her before the air around her had a chance to cool, pulling her close again, tasting her groan as he dove in for another desperate kiss. He somehow managed to get the condom on with shaking hands, and then he was lifting her again, or she was wrapping around him again, positioning herself above his straining cock, sliding down onto him as he thrust up. The feel of her sheathing him, taking him all, the friction and tight cling of her around his cock was his everything. Nothing else and no one else would hold him like this.

She groaned, long and low as he drove fully into her, her head back against the wall, her eyes closed, her lips parted. He drank in the sight of her, this beautiful, glorious woman who'd become his life, filling himself with her just like this. Then he buried his face against her neck to drag in her scent, to fill himself with that, too. Until remaining still was no longer an option. He pulled out to nearly his tip, then thrust up into her again, making her groan. Loved that sound. Loved the way her nails dug into his shoulders. He thrust up again. Hard enough to make her tits bounce, to draw a gasp from her. And again. And again. Growling against her skin when she panted and whimpered and begged.

He fucked her hard, fast, because his body demanded it, because she demanded it. Her every moan and gasp imprinted on him. He wanted more. He wanted all of her like this. Every moment of her life, his… Because he was so thoroughly hers.

She came suddenly, tightening, her legs cinching around his hips, her back arching against the wall. He kept one arm around her waist and braced his other against the wall as he rode the wave of her orgasm, clenched his teeth to hold on to his own for a breath longer so he could savor the way her muscles spasmed around him. Then he banged into her twice more and his orgasm crashed through him with a violence that left him blinking back spots.

"Fucking hell," she murmured into his hair as she clung to his neck.

He chuckled, still using the wall to brace himself because now he was trembling. He nuzzled her neck, and the words slipped out before he thought about them. "I love you."

She went very still for a split second, then her fingers dug into his hair and she hugged him tight, so tight it felt like she wanted to meld them together. The spike of emotion in her scent, of something sweet and promising, settled into his bones. He'd take that. He'd hold that as his hope.

Because if his confession of love didn't send her running away, maybe the truth about his curse wouldn't either.

* * *

BEN WOKE WITH DAWN CRAWLING THROUGH A BREAK IN THE THICK curtains, just starting to shed light into the room. The warmth of Elle in his arms, her back to his front, her scent surrounding him, left him so overwhelmed and content he could hardly believe such a feeling existed. How had he not known about this before? How had he gone more than three hundred years without this?

The last thing he wanted to do was leave the cocoon of warmth and satisfaction. What he really wanted to do was ease Elle awake with his mouth and hands, until she was writhing beneath him, panting and sweaty and crying out his name. What he wanted was to spend time actually seducing her, wooing her, convincing her they could be good together outside the hunt and the terror of facing monsters.

But he had to talk to Eric, like it or not. He needed some answers. And he needed to make a confession.

He found Eric in the kitchen, drinking coffee and staring through the large French doors at the manicured backyard. The kitchen was quiet, even Mrs. Patterson absent.

"Rea back yet?" he asked, going to the machine for a cup of coffee himself.

"About an hour ago. She says Judith is going to need to go through the place. If the geneticist will tell us what he was doing, that'll save some time. But Rea found things…"

"That black goo?"

He nodded. "That's going to…complicate our lives."

"It is. All the Families. If any of the other scientists are using it to make monsters, we have an impending disaster on our hands."

"We absolutely do," Eric said, still staring out the window as Ben settled onto the long wooden table in the middle of the room that the family used for casual meals. "I have a call with the other Family heads this afternoon. I wanted to question Professor Arron first."

Ben nodded, and not for the first time thanked his lucky stars for his birth order and metallurgy skills. He'd never be put in charge of the entire Logan Family, never have to carry the responsibility Eric did. And he was grateful for that.

Eric finally faced him. "So… You're Nam-tar doing okay after…everything?"

"She's sleeping. It'll probably take time for her to be okay again. But she's not injured. And she seems to be holding up to all this pretty well." He shrugged. "She got thrown in to the deep end that first night." He frowned down at his mug, considered the black liquid rather than face his brother's frown. "I have something I need to ask you."

"You're probably better off asking Mom if it has to do with your Nam-tar. I'm no expert."

"You have one now."

Ben glanced up in time to see Eric actually smiling softly. "No thanks to my own efforts. I nearly fucked up the whole thing. Took some groveling to fix my mistake."

He'd have liked to have seen Eric grovel. "I might have fucked things up, too."

He told Eric everything then, about that first night, his wolf leaping through Elle on accident, the way they'd been unable to be apart until after finishing the process, testing Elle's strength and speed, everything.

When he was done, Eric sat cradling his mug, staring at a spot in the middle distance, a frown creasing his brow. "That's…complicated."

Ben snorted and raised his mug in a mock solute. "Understatement." He picked at a whorl in the wooden table. "Have I fucked up?" he murmured. "Ruined any chance of my curse being broken?"

Eric was quiet for a long time. Then, "What if you have? What would that mean for you and Elle?"

"Nothing, I guess," he said. "I'd still want her to stay." He loved Elle. He wanted her no matter what happened with his curse. He couldn't imagine his life without her anymore.

Eric nodded. "Mom told me something I hadn't realized, when I was worrying about…everything."

The fact that Eric worried about aspects of his relationship with his Nam-tar was a little more reassuring than Ben would have thought. At least he wasn't the only one.

"She said," Eric continued, "that the process of *staying* is ongoing. It isn't one choice forever and always. The choice is made by both of us, every day, through all the years, to stay. To continue together. Once that choice is made, over and over, the rest doesn't really matter."

"I don't want to die like Jason did," Ben said quietly, "But… honestly, I don't care as much about breaking the curse anymore. I just want Elle to be happy."

Eric smiled. "Felt the same way. Though…I tried to push Katie away for her own sake. Wouldn't recommend that. Just backfires on you."

Ben chuckled. He could almost imagine trying to push Elle away for her own sake, for her own safety. But that would be taking the choice to stay or leave away from her, too. He'd already done enough damage in that respect, taking her through the ritual too soon. He wouldn't force any other choices on her. Where they went now, that was up to her.

But he intended to make sure she knew where he stood, that he wanted her to stay. That he hadn't just been speaking from the aftereffects of a mind-blowing orgasm when he'd said he loved her. He did. And he wanted to spend his life with her. Once she knew that, the choice to stay or leave would be hers. Curse or not, he wanted her to choose him because she wanted *him*. And everything else was just noise.

"I need to spend some time in the forge this morning," he said, setting his coffee mug aside. "We had to use the fire arrows on the grinluk. I need to make more."

Before he'd even stood, Mrs. Patterson came bustling into the kitchen, her gray hair pulled up tight in a bun. "I'll get you some food before you go," she said, her back to them as she started throwing together a to-go bag for him of cheeses and cold cuts and bread.

The fact that Mrs. Patterson had probably been listening in on their conversation, waiting for the moment she could come in and get him food, made him smile.

"Where's Elle?" Eric asked.

"Still sleeping. Been a tough few days. I didn't want to wake her."

"You want her to find you in the forge after she's up, or you want to meet her in here?"

He considered that for a long moment, taking the offered bag of food from Mrs. Patterson with a thanks. "Show her to the forge, if you don't mind." He had a feeling his Elle would like that space. And suddenly he was excited to show her that part of his life.

He made his way down into the basement room devoted to his smithy work feeling lighter than he had in days. Not because Eric had come up with any helpful revelations about whether or not the curse could still be broken. But because Ben finally realized it didn't matter. If Elle stayed, if there was hope she might one day love him in return, then he'd count himself a lucky man.

The rest didn't really matter anymore.

CHAPTER THIRTY-SIX

Elle woke late in the morning, sun streaming in past partially opened curtains, creeping across polished hardwood floors she'd barely noticed last night. There was a lot about the room she'd barely noticed last night because she'd spent most of the night overwhelmed by Ben.

First fucking against the wall because she couldn't wait to have him inside her. And fucking again in the shower because once wasn't nearly enough. Afterward, eating a meal so large she was a little surprised she had that kind of room in her body. Then sleep sweeping her under so fast, she didn't remember getting into bed. She was pretty sure she hadn't and Ben had carried her there.

And in the background of all that, his beautiful words. *I love you.*

Impossible. Amazing. Too soon. Perfect. Just right.

And now…

Now, as the sunshine streamed into this borrowed room, she realized she had a choice to make. Accept that love. Allow herself to admit to her own.

Or leave.

He'd insisted, over and over, that she had the choice. That it was her decision and he wasn't allowed to manipulate her into staying. She wondered if confessions of love counted as manipulation to an old god? She assumed not. Lot of people ran away from those kinds of confessions. She probably would have run from those words from anyone else. She had before. She didn't trust love all that much. It made people do strange, sometimes horrible things.

Yet that nagging worry that Ben's love would drive him to do something horrible, maybe even something horrible to her... She searched for it. Searched for the worry. The fear.

Not there. Not with him.

Was that the Nam-tar bond or was that Ben? Or her? Her therapist would call this growth either way.

She rolled over in the massive bed, luxuriating in her naked skin rubbing against the soft cotton sheets, savoring the weight of the heavy duvet. She'd known the instant she woke that Ben wasn't in the room. She still had his masculine scent mixed with the soap from the shower surrounding her, though. A scent so much better than the one they'd started the night with. She pressed her face into his pillow.

In the middle of the night—or more likely early morning—she'd woken to feel the weight of him behind her, and the heaviness of his arm across her waist, holding her securely to him. His big body wrapped around hers felt so secure and comfortable, she'd drifted right back to sleep.

It was only just now occurring to her that last night was the first night they'd shared a bed. How strange. Because having him beside her, and waking to his scent on the pillow next to her, all felt so perfectly...normal. Right. Like she was used to all this already.

That had to be the Nam-tar stuff.

She shoved off the blankets finally and made her way to the massive bathroom. The temperature in the room was surprisingly comfortable, the hardwood floors covered in thick rugs that cushioned her bare feet. Everything felt soft and luxurious in this room with its pale walls and solid wooden furniture and not much else. Even without the hominess of knickknacks or clutter, the space still felt welcoming. Maybe that was because she'd spent an enormously pleasurable night here.

As she showered again, because the hot water felt glorious, she started to worry, though. Worry about how Ben was feeling this morning. Worry that he'd confessed to loving her and she hadn't said the words out loud yet. She wanted to make that final decision, the one to stay, first. She wasn't entirely sure why. Just that announcing her feelings before confirming she'd stay felt cruel. And making that decision lightly, because she was overwhelmed and in love, also felt wrong. Logic. She had to be reasonable and in her right mind when she decided.

Though, how she thought she could be logical or in her right mind about Ben, she had no idea.

She was toweling off and hunting in the large walk-in closet for a full set of clothes when it occurred to her she still didn't know what his curse did to him. What he might face if she didn't stay. Did she need to know what that was before making her choice? He'd claimed it might be too manipulative on his part to tell her. And she believed him. But that meant whatever it was was bad.

Just how bad, though?

When she finally felt ready to leave the room, she realized that she had no idea where to go. She'd had an impression of massiveness last night—the place was huge, large enough for a helicopter to land on the roof! There'd definitely been a lot of surrounding wealth, too. She was going to feel like an interloper wandering through this place without a tour guide. But she wanted to check on Gabe and make sure he'd gotten the chance to call his wife. She wanted to make sure arrangements had been made for him to be reunited safely with his family.

And she wanted to see Ben.

None of that would happen with her hiding in her room. So she opened the door and studied the corridor outside. She had a vague memory of the direction they'd come last night so she headed back that way, wondering if she could find Gabe's room and if he'd be there. But before she reached the first turn, Eric Logan rounded a corner, walking right toward her.

The instinctive urge to backpedal and walk away from him

surprised her. As did the spike of adrenaline. The man was intimidating as hell, and she wasn't sure if he was doing that on purpose or if that was just him. She thought of Ben, easily half a foot or more taller than his brother and all solid blacksmith muscle, and how she wasn't even a little scared of him. Strange that Eric sparked that response when Ben didn't.

Eric approached her slowly and smiled when she did stop in her tracks and glance around, looking for an escape route.

"Sorry to startle you," he said. "I was sent to ensure you didn't get lost."

"You were sent?" That didn't sound right.

He shrugged. "I had to flip a coin with Gregory for it."

He said this last like a grudging admission and the whole idea was so ridiculous she huffed out a laugh. The laugh settled her enough she didn't feel quite so ready to run away from him. "I probably would have gotten lost, so I appreciate the escort. But I imagine you have better things to do." She glanced around again. "Where's Ben?" She sort of assumed if someone was going to give her the grand tour it would be him—he was the only reason she was here.

"Ben's in his workshop. I'll show you where that is, by way of the kitchen so Mrs. Patterson can feed you." He raised a hand as if she might object to breakfast. "Mrs. Patterson insists, and I don't dare argue with her."

The thought of someone intimidating enough to cow Eric Logan sparked her curiosity. So she fell into step beside him.

The kitchen was a big bright room, with shiny appliances, huge windows, and large French doors looking out onto a gorgeously landscaped, and absolutely massive, backyard. A long wooden table bracketed by wooden benches and chairs took up the center of the room. The huge, fancy coffee machine on the marble counter drew Elle's attention. She could do with some coffee this morning.

An older woman with a pleasantly plump figure and a tight bun of steel gray hair bustled about in front of an industrial sized stove. And the smell of bacon and eggs filled the big, airy space.

"You don't eat meat, I'll leave the bacon off your plate," the woman said, her back to them. "I don't cross contaminate, so I've used different utensils for eggs as for bacon."

Elle found herself smiling. "I eat meat. Bacon sounds good."

"Fair enough. Have a seat. You'll want to eat fast. Rea will be back soon and there won't be much left in her wake."

Eric gestured to the table and Elle sat reluctantly. Being around all these people without Ben to have her back was more than a little nerve-wracking. Though now she kind of got why Eric might not want to gainsay Mrs. Patterson. She had that way about her. Ruled-with-an-iron-fist kind of woman. Elle liked that. But was also not ashamed to admit she was cowed by it, too.

Mrs. Patterson gestured to the coffee machine, her back still to them. "Get our guest coffee. I've got my hands full here."

Eric did as ordered without so much as a scowl. And that was fascinating enough Elle forgot some of her own discomfort.

"Black, milk, sugar?" he asked as he poured.

"Black is good." Milk and sugar in coffee meant she was relaxed and savoring. She was not relaxed now and wasn't sure she could savor.

Eric frowned at her as he set the cup down in front of her. "Did you sleep well?"

"Yes." Once she'd slept.

"I'm glad. Ben would want you to be comfortable here. Though he doesn't come here very often these days. He lives in Philadelphia."

Was that said to make her feel better? Because it kind of did.

"Most of the family lives in other places," he said, taking the seat across from her as Mrs. Patterson set a plate heaped with food down in front of her. "We're scattered to better deal with monster outbreaks."

"Fair enough."

"We're about to have a big one."

"The black goo? Have you talked to Professor Arron?" Which reminded her. "Has he called his wife? Does she know he's okay now?" Then with a sideways look at her host. "Is he okay now?"

"He's been well fed and went back to sleep. He called his wife last night. I've arranged to have her and his kids brought here for the reunion. There's still a lot I want to discuss with him and this house is safer for everyone anyway. At least until we make sure the monsters won't try to retrieve him."

She shivered at the thought. "Thank you for bringing his family here. His wife was desperate when she came to me. No one else would help her."

Eric nodded, sipping at his coffee. She realized about five bites into her gorgeous meal that he wasn't eating. At her raised brows, he said, "I've eaten already."

Must be later in the morning than she'd realized. But the sleep had done her good. She hadn't had enough in the last few days. The food did her good, too. She hadn't really thought about how hungry she was until the first forkful of fluffy scrambled eggs hit her tongue. She inhaled the meal. And the second plate Mrs. Patterson wordlessly put in front of her. The fact that she could eat so much now, seemed to *need* this much food, was going to take some getting used to. Her grocery bills were going to be outrageous.

One of the many consequences of the ritual she hadn't really thought about.

Had Ben told his brother about that yet? Did any of them know? Or did they just assume she ate this much normally? Did they even notice?

She really wanted to see Ben again. After the second plate of food and two cups of coffee, she assured both Mrs. Patterson and Eric she was full, standing to make her point.

Eric's gaze narrowed slightly but he didn't do more than thank Mrs. Patterson before leading Elle from the kitchen. Elle also thanked the cook for the two excellent meals she'd been fed, then followed Eric, eager to reach Ben.

On the way, she did say, "I thought you'd interrogate me more about what happened. I kind of thought that's why you insisted on feeding me first."

"That was Mrs. Patterson insisting," Eric said. "I was being honest about that. And she wouldn't have allowed me to interrogate you in the kitchen while you were eating anyway." He glanced at her briefly before focusing ahead again. "I do have questions. About what you saw at both the house and the larger lab. About the monsters and the black…goo. And I have a lot of questions about the monster made up of the black substance that then produced more monsters.”

“Professor Arron will have better answers for you on all of that. I can only tell you what I saw.”

“Small monsters being created by the black substance when it came into contact with fire?”

“Yes. Or they would have come out without the fire. They burned up in the flames, so I’m not sure that triggered anything. But again, ask the professor.”

“He didn’t know about the additional monsters spontaneously arising from the black substance. He calls it ankorge. That wasn’t something he worked on. The ankorge was created by another scientist or scientists. He worked primarily on using it to build brand new monsters.”

“Sounds bad.”

“It’s not good.”

Eric paused. Elle looked around the corridor. There weren’t any doors here. Just plain, if nicely painted, white walls with a few paintings hanging on them and a few insets with more stone statuary.

Eric noticed her looking at one of the statues. “Have Ben take you through the atrium when you have time. It’s been recently renovated. It’s quite lovely. And there are a lot of our mother’s statues in there.”

“Camouflage?” she asked, facing Eric again.

He smiled. It wasn’t a big smile, but it was more than she’d seen from him so far. “Exactly.” He pressed a seemingly random point on the wall, opening a hidden panel. Inside was a code lock as well as biometric scanners. He used both retinal and palm prints after entering a number code before another disguised panel opened, this one a door.

“Good security,” she said.

“We need it.”

She imagined they did.

He gestured her through the door and she proceeded him into a comfortably lit corridor that felt a lot homier than the rest of the house. The scuffed wooden floor had a long maroon runner down the length of a long hallway. The walls were covered in less museum quality art and the overhead lights were ordinary recessed lighting rather than the chandeliers in other parts of the house.

This area looked like the kind of place people lived. Elle's shoulders almost immediately relaxed, and she only then realized how tense she'd been in the grandeur of the rest of the mansion.

She hoped Ben preferred living this way than he did the elegant mansion outside, because she wasn't sure she'd ever get used to those kinds of surroundings.

Eric led her along the corridor, which moved in an arc and led them past a movie theater and an actual diner, before turning down another hallway that led to a thick metal door. He knocked on the door once, then pushed the heavy metal open and a wash of heat blew over her.

"There's a swimming pool down here, too," Eric said. "If you need to cool off after being in the forge, Ben can show you." He gave her a considering look, his dark eyes narrowed. Then, "Good luck." And he walked away.

Leaving her at the entrance to a fiery hell.

Okay, it wasn't that bad. Once she'd adjusted to the heat pumping out of the room, she realized it had been the contrast to the cooler corridor that had really made the place feel so hot.

After taking a deep, fortifying breath, she stepped cautiously over the threshold.

CHAPTER THIRTY-SEVEN

The forge, as Eric had called it, was lit by several huge fires and bright overhead lights. There were wracks of metal, several huge anvils, and a lot of clanging as she stepped into the room. Overhead extractor fans hummed quietly, pulling up the heat and smoke from the fires.

A huge tub sizzled as something hot hit the cooler water inside, filling the center of the room with steam.

And from that steam, Elle watched Ben emerge.

He was a sight to behold. Over a fitted long-sleeved shirt and cargo pants, he wore a heavy leather apron and protective fire-proof gloves. Sweat dripped down his face, damped his hair, and had his shirt clinging to his thick muscles. His eyes were intent on her as he walked out of the stream, and she lost her breath. He was as glorious as an old god himself.

She wasn't sure how long she just stood there and stared, but by the time she could think again, he was standing in front of her, removing his protective gloves. He was so damned tall, she had her head thrown back, not sure whether she was more off balance from the angle or the sheer sexiness of the man in front of her.

"Didn't meant to interrupt your work," she said, though she sounded breathy and anything but sorry to be here.

"Good interruption," he said, his voice deep and rumbly.

Her nerves danced, her skin itched to touch him, and it took a lot of willpower not to immediately plaster herself to him. But she was trying to do reason and logic. She couldn't remember why. She couldn't remember her name. She just knew there was a reason she couldn't push him against the nearest wall and fuck him right this minute.

His gaze dropped to her mouth and his eyes darkened. She swore he let loose a very faint growl.

Why wasn't she supposed to push him against the wall again? There *was* a reason. Damned if she could remember.

Without meaning to, she took a step closer, until they were almost touching, barely any space between them. "Have you been down here long?" she murmured, her hands rising without her permission to his shoulders, then up around his neck. He was slick with sweat and his skin was hot, the muscles hard from work.

"A few hours, I think. Not sure. No clock. Did you sleep good?" All this while he snaked his arms around her, finally pulling her tight against him. The rub of the leather apron against her t-shirt felt surprisingly sexy.

"Very good. Once I slept." She smiled. "That bed was amazing."

"You're amazing."

Well. A compliment she was neither expecting nor knew how to deal with except to blush. "You're making more of the fire daggers and arrowheads?"

He nodded, but his attention seemed to have honed in on her mouth again.

"Can I watch you work or is that private?"

"You can watch me work. I won't let anyone else. It's intense when I need to use the more magical element, and having other people in the room is irritating. But not with you. I like having you close."

Her heart did more dancing around in her chest, like they were actually dancing and not just standing perfectly still wrapped in a sweaty embrace that was seconds away from dissolving into a kiss and more.

"Your brother said there's a pool down here? Is that true? A real pool or just a lap pool?"

"Real full-sized pool."

"You all are very rich."

"Family has money. Bothers you, though."

A statement, but she also heard the hesitance and question. "Not… exactly. It's just overwhelming. Eric said you don't live here. You live in Philadelphia?"

"Where I have my big forge."

She blinked and looked around. "Bigger than this?"

"A lot. It's my main work space. So I suppose it's my main home. But when I'm not at the forge, I travel a lot. For work."

"Hunting monsters," she said.

His arms flexed around her, almost like he thought she might push away from him and he didn't want to let her go. But since she didn't want to let go of him either, she snuggled closer. Her gesture seemed to reassure him enough to relax his grip a fraction.

"I need to tell you something," he said. "The…last part of the curse."

"Actually, you don't." He frowned and opened his mouth, but she squeezed him and went on before he could argue. "I mean it. You don't. It's bad right? Without breaking the curse, your death will be horrible."

He nodded.

"I don't need the details, then. Especially because the only way we'll know your curse is broken or not is if you die. And since I don't want you to die…I'd rather not be haunted by the details."

"If you stay," he said quietly, "it's not knowledge you'll be able to avoid forever. It'll come up. Among the Family if nothing else."

The hesitance and wariness when he said *if you stay* made her chest tight. "I'll deal with that when it happens. But… I've been thinking about the curse. How we've been worried about not being able to break it because of rushing the ritual." She frowned. "But… But the only way to be sure the curse is broken is for you to die, right? I mean, you'll never know for sure unless you're on the verge of death. And I know your job is dangerous enough that you might have to deal with that moment more often and sooner than I'd like to think about. So, yeah, we'll know eventually, I suppose. But right now… Right now, it's still a choice I have. I feel like I *could* leave if I wanted to, even with this tie between us."

A muscle in his jaw flexed and his expression closed up. "You want to leave. I understand. My world is a lot. I'd like to—"

"Hush," she snapped, so sharply he did. "I don't want to leave. Your world *is* a lot. The wealth almost as much of an adjustment as the monsters. But I'm adaptable. I'll get used to it. And we'll have some logistics to deal with since my home and business is in Detroit. But I'm not wedded to the place even though that's where I grew up. I like Philly. I could live there. Or we could find somewhere neutral. Not this house," she added before he could suggest it.

But he was blinking down at her with such surprise, looking like someone had hit him in the face with a 2x4, that she wasn't sure he could speak anyway.

She leaned away from him, to better study his face, and his arms tightened reflexively again, keeping her from getting too far.

"What I'm saying, since you look like you're having trouble processing this, is that I'm staying. If you'll have me. There're things to work out. And with so many years ahead of us, well, I imagine there will be times we have to make this decision again. And again. I'm no expert. My first experience of relationships was not a good example. But my mom did a lot better in her second marriage. And she says it takes effort. Constant communication. A repeated decision to continue with each other and not cut and run when things get hard. So I think… I think if we do that, communicate and continue to make the choice to stay with each other… I think that'll work. I hope it'll break your curse, too. I mean, we'll be making the decision, the choice throughout our lives, right? So, one of those decisions will work. And in the meantime… Just don't die."

She made a little face at that last sentence and shook her head. She had no idea if anything she'd just said made any sense at all. But her instincts told her she was on to something. And that was all she needed.

Ben blinked at her a few times before saying in a voice gruff and scratchy, "Eric said my mother said something similar. That it wasn't one decision but repeated choices throughout life to stay with each other. And that making that choice was the important part."

"Your mother sounds quite smart." She ducked her head when she said, "I hope I'll get to meet her one day." When she glanced up from under her lashes, he was smiling, a slow, sexy smile that made her stomach dance and her thighs clench.

"You're staying. You're going to stay. With me."

"Well. Who else?" She huffed out a laugh.

"Are you sure? Are you sure you're sure?"

"I love you, Ben. I'm sure. I don't want to be anywhere else but with you."

He sucked in a ragged breath, almost like he'd forgotten to breathe until that moment. Then he very gently set his forehead to hers. "I love you, Elle," he murmured. "I will always choose you. No matter how long we live, I will choose you."

She cupped his face in her hands, her eyes closed briefly before she nudged his head up so she could meet his gaze. "I will always choose you, too."

His kiss was gentle. That brush of lips that felt almost reverent. A blessing in a moment of intense poignancy.

He set his forehead to hers again when he said, "I still want to… court you, though."

She grinned. "Court me? How?"

"Take you on a date, or dates. Wine and dine you. Feed you meals that don't come from a fast food restaurant. All the ways I would have pursued you if the monsters hadn't interfered."

Her stomach did a happy flip. "What do you have in mind for a first date?"

"Dinner and a movie? There's a theater just down the hall."

"I noticed." She laughed. "So long as the movie is a comedy, I'm game."

"Fancy dinner or not?"

"First date? Not. Then we can get fancy. I wouldn't mind seeing you dressed up in a suit."

His chuckle rumbled through her, making her heart hammer and her world fill with warmth and love. She kissed him again, another slow brush of lips. But slowly the kiss deepened, languidly rolling into something more, until the heat of the forge was nothing to the heat building in her. She wrapped around him, the desire mixing with her joy until she thought she might just burst. The love and the relief and the need to get him naked all left her light-headed and giddy.

"So," she said as he trailed his lips down her throat, "about that pool…"

He chuckled again, a sound she could…*would* spend the rest of her life loving. Just like she'd spend the rest of her life loving him.

"Not too far away," he said as he found her mouth again. "Think we can make it there?"

"Eventually," she said as she dove into another deep kiss.

Eventually. Because now they had all the time in the world.

THANK YOU

Thank you for reading FATED IN STONE, the third book in the Seven Families: Wolf series. I hope you enjoyed the story!

This was an interesting book to write, because it started from a single idea that I thought would be the opening scene, or close to the opening scene—a scene with one of the Logan siblings having their wolf jump *through* a human on accident, before learning that human was their Nam-tar. This entire series has been percolating in my head for many years now, and in all that time, a vague image of that scene remained the basis for this book.

Until I started writing.

When I discovered that I couldn't start the book at that scene and needed to build up to it. By the time I got there—in Chapter Four!—a lot of interesting things had happened that I didn't expect, including Ben *knowing* Elle was his Nam-tar before his wolf had to leap, and that he was injured and had to leap because he was rescuing her! Originally, I'd just had some fuzzy idea of him being shot during the fight with the humans working with the monsters and her finding him already wounded. But him getting shot saving her was so much more interesting and fun to write.

All of these epiphanies sent the book down a road I hadn't

anticipated. But it was a fun journey. And by the time I got to the end, I couldn't image the book turning out any other way. Those moments in writing are the kind of thing this particular author lives for. I hope you enjoyed the journey as a reader as much as I did as a writer.

For more of my paranormal romance, don't miss my Tiger Shifters Series, starting with the first book, ONCE UPON A TIGER, which is currently available for free. To keep up to date on my upcoming releases and news, please consider joining my newsletter. All new subscribers get two free stories—one very sexy short story from the Tiger Shifters series, and one novella from my urban fantasy Cary Redmond series.

You can also get updates by visiting my website, following me at BookBub, or following my author page at your favorite vendor.

Thanks again for reading!

~Kat

BOOKS BY KAT SIMONS

The Seven Families Series

Wolf Family

Darkness in Stone

Redemption in Stone

Fated in Stone

Tiger Shifters Series

* Once Upon a Tiger * Along Came a Tiger * Here There Be Tigers * Her Tiger To Take * To Tempt a Tiger * Down Will Come Tiger * To Catch a Tiger * What a Tiger Wants * Taming Her Tiger

Tiger Shifters Series Vol 1 (Books 1 - 3)

Tiger Shifters Series Vol 2 (Books 4 - 6)

Romancing the Leopard: A Tiger Shifters-Cary Redmond Crossover Novel

The Cary Redmond Series

* The Trouble Black Cats and Demons * The Trouble with Ghouls and Serial Killers * The Trouble with Leopard Queens and Shifter Wars * The Trouble with Baby Gods and Vampires * The Trouble with Magic and Faery Curses * The Trouble with Wizards and Old Enemies * The Trouble with Death and Demon Gods

The Cary Redmond Series Box Set Books 1-3

Cary Redmond Short Stories

* When Cary Met Jaxer * When Cary Met Pickles * When Cary Met Marianne * When Cary Met Lucy * When Cary Met Angie * Cary and Deacon (Try to) Go on a Date * Date Night Take Two * Third Date's the Charm * Cary vs the Goblin King * Dinner with the Joneses * Cary and the Cursed Jack-O'-Lantern * Cary and the Demon Witch * Cary Goes to Hawaii * Cary Holidays * Cary and Dragons and Goblins * Cary's Galentine's Day * Cary at the Haunt and Howl * Cary's Leprechaun Troubles *

When Cary Met the Good Guys (Collection 1)

Dates, Dinners, and Other Disasters (Collection 2)

Witches and Weavers and Ghosts, Oh Boy (Collection 3)

A Very Cary Holiday (Collection 4)

Demon Witch Series

* Howling Dreadful * Moonlit Strange
* Bone Lantern Witch * Spiderweb Witch

Joan of Kerry Series

Joan of Kerry: Joan and the Abhartach

Joan and the Leprechaun

Joan and the Kraken

Haunts and Howls Collections

Haunts and Howls and Guardian Spells

Haunts and Howls Where Demons Dwell

*Tombstone Wizard * The Unshattered Sword * Destiny Through the Cats Eyes * Going Out of Business: Everything's for Sale

ABOUT THE AUTHOR

Kat Simons earned her Ph.D. in animal behavior, working with animals as diverse as dolphins and deer. She brought her experience and knowledge of biology to her paranormal romance and urban fantasy fiction, where she delights in taking nature and turning it on its ear. She writes urban fantasy, contemporary fantasy, and paranormal romance in series which combine action adventure, the otherworldly, and a frequent dose of sexy romance.

The novel Darkness in Stone launches the newest paranormal romance series for Kat, following the exploits and loves of the Seven Families of monster hunters. The first trilogy follows the Wolf Family, as our heroes and heroines struggle to win their fated mates while fending off deadly monsters bent on destroying the world.

The latest book in her bestselling romantic urban fantasy series about Protector Cary Redmond, The Trouble with Death and Demon Gods, is also out now. As are the newest stories in the romantic urban fantasy Demon Witch series, including the first "meet cute" for Angie and her demon hunter boyfriend Sebastian in the novella *Howling Dreadful*.

For something a little different, Kat also publishes fantasy, science fiction, and the occasional hockey romance under the name Isabo Kelly (https://www.isabokelly.com).

After traveling the world, living in places like Hawaii, Germany, and Ireland, Kat now lives in New York City with her family and a library's worth of books.

For more on Kat and her future books

Website: https://www.katsimons.com
Newsletter: https://bit.ly/KatSimonsNewsletter

Kat Simons Bookstore
https://tanddpublishingbookstore.com/

Social Media
Facebook Page: https://www.facebook.com/KatSimonsAuthor
BookBub: https://www.bookbub.com/authors/kat-simons
Instagram: https://www.instagram.com/isabokelly/
Twitter: https://twitter.com/IsaboKelly

KAT'S NEWSLETTER

Don't miss the latest Kat Simons

news, updates, excerpts, cover reveals, and more!

All new subscribers get two free stories.

* * *

Mate Run

A Tiger Shifters Paranormal Romance short story

and

When Cary Met Ariel

A Cary Redmond Urban Fantasy novella

* * *

Join Now!

https://bit.ly/KatSimonsNewsletter